D1229629

# SCIENCE FICTION AND FANTASY

## Short Stories

# SCIENCE FICTION AND FANTASY

## *Short Stories*

This edition published in 2018 by Arcturus Publishing Limited
26/27 Bickels Yard, 151–153 Bermondsey Street,
London SE1 3HA



ISBN: 978-1-78828-408-0
AD006166US

Printed in China

# Contents

# Introduction

Science fiction and fantasy writers today are best known for their sprawling epics. Yet many of the masters of the genre honed their craft writing short stories. With the birth of the pulp magazine in the early 20th century, writers like H. G. Wells, Robert E. Howard and John York Cabot (the alias of David Wright O'Brien) found an outlet for their imaginative fiction in magazines like the *Argosy*, *Amazing Stories* and *Weird Tales*. As well as those known for their mastery of the genre, classic writers like Nathaniel Hawthorne used the medium of the short story to explore their imaginations in ways they could not in their more realistic novels.

In the tales collected in this volume, the heroes explore magical realms, fight terrifying enemies, encounter alien races and use their ingenuity to devise fascinating solutions to the problems they meet along the way. Many of the writers used invented technologies and magical settings to explore the problems of the day. The first half of the 20th century, when most of these stories were written, was a period of profound change. Dictatorships rose up across central Europe, communism bloomed in Russia and the two world wars upset the established world order. Francis Flagg's 'Dancer in the Crystal' is one of a raft of apocalyptic stories that explores a world where electricity has suddenly stopped working. In other tales, such as H. G. Wells' 'Under the Knife', writers turned to the unpredictable workings of the mind, exploring the psychological stresses that unusual situations could put on their characters.

Despite their serious undertones, these writers never forgot that the primary purpose of fiction is to entertain. The daring adventures of Robert E. Howard's Conan the Barbarian remain incredibly exciting and atmospheric. The exuberance of space travel and the joy of discovering Mars, written when such ideas seemed ludicrous, can hardly be matched by modern writers.

These stories are as diverse as you could hope for. Their settings range from the Hyborian Age of Conan to the frozen wastes of Antarctica to the moon. Robots, spaceships, polar bears, wizards and witches populate the tales in this collection. They are united by their immense imagination. Each tale is an adventure into an unknown world – one that will not be easy to forget.

# Under the Knife

by H. G. Wells

"What if I die under it?" The thought recurred again and again, as I walked home from Haddon's. It was a purely personal question. I was spared the deep anxieties of a married man, and I knew there were few of my intimate friends but would find my death troublesome chiefly on account of their duty of regret. I was surprised indeed, and perhaps a little humiliated, as I turned the matter over, to think how few could possibly exceed the conventional requirement. Things came before me stripped of glamour, in a clear dry light, during that walk from Haddon's house over Primrose Hill. There were the friends of my youth: I perceived now that our affection was a tradition, which we foregathered rather laboriously to maintain. There were the rivals and helpers of my later career: I suppose I had been cold-blooded or undemonstrative—one perhaps implies the other. It may be that even the capacity for friendship is a question of physique. There had been a time in my own life when I had grieved bitterly enough at the loss of a friend; but as I walked home that afternoon the emotional side of my imagination was dormant. I could not pity myself, nor feel sorry for my friends, nor conceive of them as grieving for me.

I was interested in this deadness of my emotional nature–no doubt a concomitant of my stagnating physiology; and my thoughts wandered off along the line it suggested. Once before, in my hot youth, I had suffered a sudden loss of blood, and had been within an ace of death.

I remembered now that my affections as well as my passions had drained out of me, leaving scarce anything but a tranquil resignation, a dreg of self-pity. It had been weeks before the old ambitions and tendernesses and all the complex moral interplay of a man had re-asserted themselves. It occurred to me that the real meaning of this numbness might be a gradual slipping away from the pleasure–pain guidance of the animal man. It has been proven, I take it, as thoroughly as anything can be proven in this world, that the higher emotions, the moral feelings, even the subtle unselfishness of love, are evolved from the elemental desires and fears of the simple animal: they are the harness in which man's mental freedom goes. And it may be that as death overshadows us, as our possibility of acting diminishes, this complex growth of balanced impulse, propensity and aversion, whose interplay inspires our acts, goes with it. Leaving what?

I was suddenly brought back to reality by an imminent collision with the butcher-boy's tray. I found that I was crossing the bridge over the Regent's Park Canal, which runs parallel with that in the Zoological Gardens. The boy in blue had been looking over his shoulder at a black barge advancing slowly, towed by a gaunt white horse. In the Gardens a nurse was leading three happy little children over the bridge. The trees were bright green; the spring hopefulness was still unstained by the dusts of summer; the sky in the water was bright and clear, but broken by long waves, by quivering bands of black, as the barge drove through. The breeze was stirring; but it did not stir me as the spring breeze used to do.

Was this dulness of feeling in itself an anticipation? It was curious that I could reason and follow out a network of suggestion as clearly as ever: so, at least, it seemed to me. It was calmness rather than dulness that was coming upon me. Was there any ground for the relief in the presentiment of death? Did a man near to death begin instinctively to withdraw himself from the meshes of matter and sense, even before the cold hand was laid upon his? I felt strangely isolated—isolated without regret—from the life and existence about me. The children playing in the sun and gathering strength and experience for the business of life, the park-keeper gossiping with a nursemaid, the nursing mother, the young couple intent upon each other as they passed me, the trees by the wayside spreading new pleading leaves to the sunlight, the stir in their branches—I had been part of it all, but I had nearly done with it now.

Some way down the Broad Walk I perceived that I was tired, and that my feet were heavy. It was hot that afternoon, and I turned aside and sat down on one of the green chairs that line the way. In a minute I had dozed into a dream, and the tide of my thoughts washed up a vision of the resurrection. I was still sitting in the chair, but I thought myself actually dead, withered, tattered, dried, one eye (I saw) pecked out by birds. "Awake!" cried a voice; and incontinently the dust of the path and the mould under the grass became insurgent. I had never before thought of Regent's Park as a cemetery, but now, through the trees, stretching as far as eye could see, I beheld a flat plain of writhing graves and heeling tombstones. There seemed to be some trouble: the rising dead appeared to stifle as they struggled upward, they bled in their struggles, the red flesh was torn away from the white bones. "Awake!" cried a voice; but I determined I would not rise to such horrors. "Awake!" They would not let me alone. "Wake up!" said an angry voice. A cockney angel! The man who sells the tickets was shaking me, demanding my penny.

I paid my penny, pocketed my ticket, yawned, stretched my legs, and, feeling now rather less torpid, got up and walked on towards Langham Place. I speedily lost myself again in a shifting maze of thoughts about death. Going across Marylebone Road into that crescent at the end of Langham Place, I had the narrowest escape from the shaft of a cab, and went on my way with a palpitating heart and a bruised shoulder. It struck me that it would have been curious if my meditations on my death on the morrow had led to my death that day.

But I will not weary you with more of my experiences that day and the next. I knew more and more certainly that I should die under the operation; at times I think I was inclined to pose to myself. The doctors were coming at eleven, and I did not get up. It seemed scarce worth while to trouble about washing and dressing, and though I read my newspapers and the letters that came by the first post, I did not find them very interesting. There was a friendly note from Addison, my old school-friend, calling my attention to two discrepancies and a printer's error in my new book, with one from Langridge venting some vexation over Minton. The rest were business communications. I breakfasted in bed. The glow of pain at my side seemed more massive. I knew it was pain, and yet, if you can understand, I did not find it very painful. I had been awake and hot and thirsty in the night, but in the morning bed felt comfortable. In the night-time I had lain thinking of things that were past; in the morning I dozed over the question of immortality. Haddon came, punctual to the minute, with a neat black bag; and Mowbray soon followed. Their arrival stirred me up a little. I began to take a more personal interest in the proceedings. Haddon moved the little octagonal table close to the bedside, and, with his broad back to me, began taking things out of his bag. I heard the light click of steel upon steel. My imagination, I found, was not altogether stagnant. "Will you hurt me much?" I said in an off-hand tone.

"Not a bit," Haddon answered over his shoulder. "We shall chloroform you. Your heart's as sound as a bell." And as he spoke, I had a whiff of the pungent sweetness of the anaesthetic.

They stretched me out, with a convenient exposure of my side, and, almost before I realized what was happening, the chloroform was being administered. It stings the nostrils, and there is a suffocating sensation at first. I knew I should die—that this was the end of consciousness for me. And suddenly I felt that I was not prepared for death: I had a vague sense of a duty overlooked—I knew not what. What was it I had not done? I could think of nothing more to do, nothing desirable left in life; and yet I had the strangest disinclination to death. And the physical sensation was painfully oppressive. Of course the doctors did not know they were going to kill me. Possibly I struggled. Then I fell motionless, and a great silence, a monstrous silence, and an impenetrable blackness came upon me.

There must have been an interval of absolute unconsciousness, seconds or minutes. Then with a chilly, unemotional clearness, I perceived that I was not yet dead. I was still in my body; but all the multitudinous sensations that come sweeping from it to make up the background of consciousness had gone, leaving me free of it all. No, not free of it all; for as yet something still held me to the poor stark flesh upon the bed—held me, yet not so closely that I did not feel myself external to it, independent of it, straining away from it. I do not think I saw, I do not think I heard; but I perceived all that was going on, and it was as if I both heard and saw. Haddon was bending over me, Mowbray behind me; the scalpel—it was a large scalpel—was cutting my flesh at the side under the flying ribs. It was interesting to see myself cut like cheese, without a pang, without even a qualm. The interest was much of a quality with that one might feel in a game of chess between strangers. Haddon's face was firm and his hand steady; but I was surprised to perceive (*how* I know not) that he was feeling the gravest doubt as to his own wisdom in the conduct of the operation.

Mowbray's thoughts, too, I could see. He was thinking that Haddon's manner showed too much of the specialist. New suggestions came up like bubbles through a stream of frothing meditation, and burst one after another in the little bright spot of his consciousness. He could not help noticing and admiring Haddon's swift dexterity, in spite of his envious quality and his disposition to detract. I saw my liver exposed. I was puzzled at my own condition. I did not feel that I was dead, but I was different in some way from my living self. The grey depression, that had weighed on me for a year or more and coloured all my thoughts, was gone. I perceived and thought without any emotional tint at all. I wondered if everyone perceived things in this way under chloroform, and forgot it again when he came out of it. It would be inconvenient to look into some heads, and not forget.

Although I did not think that I was dead, I still perceived quite clearly that I was soon to die. This brought me back to the consideration of Haddon's proceedings. I looked into his mind, and saw that he was afraid of cutting a branch of the portal vein. My attention was distracted from details by the curious changes going on in his mind. His consciousness was like the quivering little spot of light which is thrown by the mirror of a galvanometer. His thoughts ran under it like a stream, some through the focus bright and distinct, some shadowy in the half-light of the edge. Just now the little glow was steady; but the least movement on Mowbray's part, the slightest sound from outside, even a faint difference in the slow movement of the living flesh he was cutting, set the light-spot shivering and spinning. A new sense-impression came rushing up through the flow of thoughts; and lo! The light-spot jerked away towards it, swifter than a frightened fish. It was wonderful to think that upon that unstable, fitful thing depended all the complex motions of the man; that for the next five minutes, therefore, my life hung upon its movements. And he was growing more and more nervous in his work. It was as if a little picture of a cut vein grew brighter, and struggled to oust from his brain another picture of a cut falling short of the mark. He was afraid: his dread of cutting too little was battling with his dread of cutting too far.

Then, suddenly, like an escape of water from under a lock-gate, a great uprush of horrible realization set all his thoughts swirling, and simultaneously I perceived that the vein was cut. He started back with a hoarse exclamation, and I saw the brown-purple blood gather in a swift bead, and run trickling. He was horrified. He pitched the red-stained scalpel on to the octagonal table; and instantly both doctors flung themselves upon me, making hasty and ill-conceived efforts to remedy the disaster. "Ice!" said Mowbray, gasping. But I knew that I was killed, though my body still clung to me.

I will not describe their belated endeavours to save me, though I perceived every detail. My perceptions were sharper and swifter than they had ever been in life; my thoughts rushed through my mind with incredible swiftness, but with perfect definition. I can only compare their crowded clarity to the effects of a reasonable dose of opium. In a moment it would all be over, and I should be free. I knew I was immortal, but what would happen I did not know. Should I drift off presently, like a puff of smoke from a gun, in some kind of half-material body, an attenuated version of my material self? Should I find myself suddenly among the innumerable hosts of the dead, and know the world about me for the phantasmagoria it had always seemed? Should I drift to some spiritualistic *séance*, and there make foolish, incomprehensible attempts to affect a purblind medium? It was a state of unemotional curiosity, of colourless expectation. And then I realized a growing stress upon me, a feeling as though some huge human magnet was drawing me upward out of my body. The stress grew and grew. I seemed an atom for which monstrous forces were fighting. For one brief, terrible moment sensation came back to me. That feeling of falling headlong which comes in nightmares, that feeling a thousand times intensified, that and a black horror swept across my thoughts in a torrent. Then the two doctors, the naked body with its cut side, the little room, swept away from under me and vanished, as a speck of foam vanishes down an eddy.

I was in mid-air. Far below was the West End of London, receding rapidly,—for I seemed to be flying swiftly upward,—and as it receded, passing westward like a panorama. I could see, through the faint haze of smoke, the innumerable roofs chimney-set, the narrow roadways, stippled with people and conveyances, the little specks of squares, and the church steeples like thorns sticking out of the fabric. But it spun away as the earth rotated on its axis, and in a few seconds (as it seemed) I was over the scattered clumps of town about Ealing, the little Thames a thread of blue to the south, and the Chiltern Hills and the North Downs coming up like the rim of a basin, far away and faint with haze. Up I rushed. And at first I had not the faintest conception what this headlong rush upward could mean.

Every moment the circle of scenery beneath me grew wider and wider, and the details of town and field, of hill and valley, got more and more hazy and pale and indistinct, a luminous grey was mingled more and more with the blue of the hills and the green of the open meadows; and a little patch of cloud, low and far to the west, shone ever more dazzlingly white. Above, as the veil of atmosphere between myself and outer space grew thinner, the sky, which had been a fair springtime blue at first, grew deeper and richer in colour, passing steadily through the intervening shades, until presently it was as dark as the blue sky of midnight, and presently as black as the blackness of a frosty starlight, and at last as black as no blackness I had ever beheld. And first one star, and then many, and at last an innumerable host broke out upon the sky: more stars than anyone has ever seen from the face of the earth. For the blueness of the sky in the light of the sun and stars sifted and spread abroad blindingly: there is diffused light even in the darkest skies of winter, and we do not see the stars by day only because of the dazzling irradiation of the sun. But now I saw things—I know not how; assuredly with no mortal eyes—and that defect of bedazzlement blinded me no longer. The sun was incredibly strange and wonderful. The body of it was a disc of blinding white light: not yellowish, as it seems to those who live upon the earth, but livid white, all streaked with scarlet streaks and rimmed about with a fringe of writhing tongues of red fire. And shooting half-way across the heavens from either side of it and brighter than the Milky Way, were two pinions of silver white, making it look more like those winged globes I have seen in Egyptian sculpture than anything else I can remember upon earth. These I knew for the solar corona, though I had never seen anything of it but a picture during the days of my earthly life.

When my attention came back to the earth again, I saw that it had fallen very far away from me. Field and town were long since indistinguishable, and all the varied hues of the country were merging into a uniform bright grey, broken only by the brilliant white of the clouds that lay scattered in flocculent masses over Ireland and the west of England. For now I could see the outlines of the north of France and Ireland, and all this Island of Britain, save where Scotland passed over the horizon to the north, or where the coast was blurred or obliterated by cloud. The sea was a dull grey, and darker than the land; and the whole panorama was rotating slowly towards the east.

All this had happened so swiftly that until I was some thousand miles or so from the earth I had no thought for myself. But now I perceived I had neither hands nor feet, neither parts nor organs, and that I felt neither alarm nor pain. All about me I perceived that the vacancy (for I had already left the air behind) was cold beyond the imagination of man; but it troubled me not. The sun's rays shot through the void, powerless to light or heat until they should strike on matter in their course. I saw things with a serene self-forgetfulness, even as if I were God. And down below there, rushing away from me,—countless miles in a second,—where a little dark spot on the grey marked the position of London, two doctors were struggling to restore life to the poor hacked and outworn shell I had abandoned. I felt then such release, such serenity as I can compare to no mortal delight I have ever known.

It was only after I had perceived all these things that the meaning of that headlong rush of the earth grew into comprehension. Yet it was so simple, so obvious, that I was amazed at my never anticipating the thing that was happening to me. I had suddenly been cut adrift from matter: all that was material of me was there upon earth, whirling away through space, held to the earth by gravitation, partaking of the earth-inertia, moving in its wreath of epicycles round the sun, and with the sun and the planets on their vast march through space. But the immaterial has no inertia, feels nothing of the pull of matter for matter: where it parts from its garment of flesh, there it remains (so far as space concerns it any longer) immovable in space. *I* was not leaving the earth: the earth was leaving *me*, and not only the earth but the whole solar system was streaming past. And about me in space, invisible to me, scattered in the wake of the earth upon its journey, there must be an innumerable multitude of souls, stripped like myself of the material, stripped like myself of the passions of the individual and the generous emotions of the gregarious brute, naked intelligences, things of new-born wonder and thought, marvelling at the strange release that had suddenly come on them!

As I receded faster and faster from the strange white sun in the black heavens, and from the broad and shining earth upon which my being had begun, I seemed to grow in some incredible manner vast: vast as regards this world I had left, vast as regards the moments and periods of a human life. Very soon I saw the full circle of the earth, slightly gibbous, like the moon when she nears her full, but very large; and the silvery shape of America was now in the noonday blaze wherein (as it seemed) little England had been basking but a few minutes ago. At first the earth was large, and shone in the heavens, filling a great part of them; but every moment she grew smaller and more distant. As she shrank, the broad moon in its third quarter crept into view over the rim of her disc. I looked for the constellations. Only that part of Aries directly behind the sun and the Lion, which the earth covered, were hidden. I recognized the tortuous, tattered band of the Milky Way with Vega very bright between sun and earth; and Sirius and Orion shone splendid against the unfathomable blackness in the opposite quarter of the heavens. The Pole Star was overhead, and the Great Bear hung over the circle of the earth. And away beneath and beyond the shining corona of the sun were strange groupings of stars I had never seen in my life—notably a dagger-shaped group that I knew for the Southern Cross. All these were no larger than when they had shone on earth, but the little stars that one scarce sees shone now against the setting of black vacancy as brightly as the first-magnitudes had done, while the larger worlds were points of indescribable glory and colour. Aldebaran was a spot of blood-red fire, and Sirius condensed to one point the light of innumerable sapphires. And they shone steadily: they did not scintillate, they were calmly glorious. My impressions had an adamantine hardness and brightness: there was no blurring softness, no atmosphere, nothing but infinite darkness set with the myriads of these acute and brilliant points and specks of light. Presently, when I looked again, the little earth seemed no bigger than the sun, and it dwindled and turned as I looked, until in a second's space (as it seemed to me), it was halved; and so it went on swiftly dwindling. Far away in the opposite direction, a little pinkish pin's head of light, shining steadily, was the planet Mars. I swam motionless in vacancy, and, without a trace of terror or astonishment, watched the speck of cosmic dust we call the world fall away from me.

Presently it dawned upon me that my sense of duration had changed; that my mind was moving not faster but infinitely slower, that between each separate impression there was a period of many days. The moon spun once round the earth as I noted this; and I perceived clearly the motion of Mars in his orbit. Moreover, it appeared as if the time between thought and thought grew steadily greater, until at last a thousand years was but a moment in my perception.

At first the constellations had shone motionless against the black background of infinite space; but presently it seemed as though the group of stars about Hercules and the Scorpion was contracting, while Orion and Aldebaran and their neighbours were scattering apart. Flashing suddenly out of the darkness there came a flying multitude of particles of rock, glittering like dust-specks in a sunbeam, and encompassed in a faintly luminous cloud. They swirled all about me, and vanished again in a twinkling far behind. And then I saw that a bright spot of light, that shone a little to one side of my path, was growing very rapidly larger, and perceived that it was the planet Saturn rushing towards me. Larger and larger it grew, swallowing up the heavens behind it, and hiding every moment a fresh multitude, of stars. I perceived its flattened, whirling body, its disc-like belt, and seven of its little satellites. It grew and grew, till it towered enormous; and then I plunged amid a streaming multitude of clashing stones and dancing dust-particles and gas-eddies, and saw for a moment the mighty triple belt like three concentric arches of moonlight above me, its shadow black on the boiling tumult below. These things happened in one-tenth of the time it takes to tell them. The planet went by like a flash of lightning; for a few seconds it blotted out the sun, and there and then became a mere black, dwindling, winged patch against the light. The earth, the mother mote of my being, I could no longer see.

So with a stately swiftness, in the profoundest silence, the solar system fell from me as it had been a garment, until the sun was a mere star amid the multitude of stars, with its eddy of planet-specks lost in the confused glittering of the remoter light. I was no longer a denizen of the solar system: I had come to the outer Universe, I seemed to grasp and comprehend the whole world of matter. Ever more swiftly the stars closed in about the spot where Antares and Vega had vanished in a phosphorescent haze, until that part of the sky had the semblance of a whirling mass of nebulae, and ever before me yawned vaster gaps of vacant blackness, and the stars shone fewer and fewer. It seemed as if I moved towards a point between

Orion's belt and sword; and the void about that region opened vaster and vaster every second, an incredible gulf of nothingness into which I was falling. Faster and ever faster the universe rushed by, a hurry of whirling motes at last, speeding silently into the void. Stars glowing brighter and brighter, with their circling planets catching the light in a ghostly fashion as I neared them, shone out and vanished again into inexistence; faint comets, clusters of meteorites, winking specks of matter, eddying light-points, whizzed past, some perhaps a hundred millions of miles or so from me at most, few nearer, travelling with unimaginable rapidity, shooting constellations, momentary darts of fire, through that black, enormous night. More than anything else it was like a dusty draught, sunbeam-lit. Broader and wider and deeper grew the starless space, the vacant Beyond, into which I was being drawn. At last a quarter of the heavens was black and blank, and the whole headlong rush of stellar universe closed in behind me like a veil of light that is gathered together. It drove away from me like a monstrous jack-o'-lantern driven by the wind. I had come out into the wilderness of space. Ever the vacant blackness grew broader, until the hosts of the stars seemed only like a swarm of fiery specks hurrying away from me, inconceivably remote, and the darkness, the nothingness and emptiness, was about me on every side. Soon the little universe of matter, the cage of points in which I had begun to be, was dwindling, now to a whirling disc of luminous glittering, and now to one minute disc of hazy light. In a little while it would shrink to a point, and at last would vanish altogether.

Suddenly feeling came back to me—feeling in the shape of overwhelming terror; such a dread of those dark vastitudes as no words can describe, a passionate resurgence of sympathy and social desire. Were there other souls, invisible to me as I to them, about me in the blackness? Or was I indeed, even as I felt, alone? Had I passed out of being into something that was neither being nor not-being? The covering of the body, the covering of matter, had been torn from me, and the hallucinations of companionship and security. Everything was black and silent. I had ceased to be. I was nothing. There was nothing, save only that infinitesimal dot of light that dwindled in the gulf. I strained myself to hear and see, and for a while there was naught but infinite silence, intolerable darkness, horror, and despair.

Then I saw that about the spot of light into which the whole world of matter had shrunk there was a faint glow. And in a band on either side of that the darkness was not absolute. I watched it for ages, as it seemed to me, and through the long waiting the haze grew imperceptibly more distinct. And then about the band appeared an irregular cloud of the faintest, palest brown. I felt a passionate impatience; but the things grew brighter so slowly that they scarce seemed to change. What was unfolding itself? What was this strange reddish dawn in the interminable night of space?

The cloud's shape was grotesque. It seemed to be looped along its lower side into four projecting masses, and, above, it ended in a straight line. What phantom was it? I felt assured I had seen that figure before; but I could not think what, nor where, nor when it was. Then the realization rushed upon me. *It was a clenched Hand.* I was alone in space, alone with this huge, shadowy Hand, upon which the whole Universe of Matter lay like an unconsidered speck of dust. It seemed as though I watched it through vast periods of time. On the forefinger glittered a ring; and the universe from which I had come was but a spot of light upon the ring's curvature. And the thing that the hand gripped had the likeness of a black rod. Through a long eternity I watched this Hand, with the ring and the rod, marvelling and fearing and waiting helplessly on what might follow. It seemed as though nothing could follow: that I should watch for ever, seeing only the Hand and the thing it held, and understanding nothing of its import. Was the whole universe but a refracting speck upon some greater Being? Were our worlds but the atoms of another universe, and those again of another, and so on through an endless progression? And what was I? Was I indeed immaterial? A vague persuasion of a body gathering about me came into my suspense. The abysmal darkness about the Hand filled with impalpable suggestions, with uncertain, fluctuating shapes.

Then, suddenly, came a sound, like the sound of a tolling bell: faint, as if infinitely far; muffled, as though heard through thick swathings of darkness: a deep, vibrating resonance, with vast gulfs of silence between each stroke. And the Hand appeared to tighten on the rod. And I saw far above the Hand, towards the apex of the darkness, a circle of dim phosphorescence, a ghostly sphere whence these sounds came throbbing; and at the last stroke the Hand vanished, for the hour had come, and I heard a noise of many waters. But the black rod remained as a great band across the sky. And then a voice, which seemed to run to the uttermost parts of space, spoke, saying, "There will be no more pain."

At that an almost intolerable gladness and radiance rushed in upon me, and I saw the circle shining white and bright, and the rod black and shining, and many things else distinct and clear. And the circle was the face of the clock, and the rod the rail of my bed. Haddon was standing at the foot, against the rail, with a small pair of scissors on his fingers; and the hands of my clock on the mantel over his shoulder were clasped together over the hour of twelve. Mowbray was washing something in a basin at the octagonal table, and at my side I felt a subdued feeling that could scarce be spoken of as pain.

The operation had not killed me. And I perceived, suddenly, that the dull melancholy of half a year was lifted from my mind.

# The Door in the Wall

by H. G. Wells

## I

One confidential evening, not three months ago, Lionel Wallace told me this story of the Door in the Wall. And at the time I thought that so far as he was concerned it was a true story.

He told it me with such a direct simplicity of conviction that I could not do otherwise than believe in him. But in the morning, in my own flat, I woke to a different atmosphere, and as I lay in bed and recalled the things he had told me, stripped of the glamour of his earnest slow voice, denuded of the focussed shaded table light, the shadowy atmosphere that wrapped about him and the pleasant bright things, the dessert and glasses and napery of the dinner we had shared, making them for the time a bright little world quite cut off from every-day realities, I saw it all as frankly incredible. "He was mystifying!" I said, and then: "How well he did it! . . . It isn't quite the thing I should have expected him, of all people, to do well."

Afterwards, as I sat up in bed and sipped my morning tea, I found myself trying to account for the flavour of reality that perplexed me in his impossible reminiscences, by supposing they did in some way suggest, present, convey—I hardly know which word to use—experiences it was otherwise impossible to tell.

Well, I don't resort to that explanation now. I have got over my intervening doubts. I believe now, as I believed at the moment of telling, that Wallace did to the very best of his ability strip the truth of his secret for me. But whether he himself saw, or only thought he saw, whether he himself was the possessor of an inestimable privilege, or the victim of a fantastic dream, I cannot pretend to guess. Even the facts of his death, which ended my doubts forever, throw no light on that. That much the reader must judge for himself.

I forget now what chance comment or criticism of mine moved so reticent a man to confide in me. He was, I think, defending himself against an imputation of slackness and unreliability I had made in relation to a great public movement in which he had disappointed me. But he plunged suddenly. "I have" he said, "a preoccupation—"

"I know," he went on, after a pause that he devoted to the study of his cigar ash, "I have been negligent. The fact is—it isn't a case of ghosts or apparitions—but—it's an odd thing to tell of, Redmond—I am haunted. I am haunted by something—that rather takes the light out of things, that fills me with longings. . . . "

He paused, checked by that English shyness that so often overcomes us when we would speak of moving or grave or beautiful things. "You were at Saint Athelstan's all through," he said, and for a moment that seemed to me quite irrelevant. "Well"—and he paused. Then very haltingly at first, but afterwards more easily, he began to tell of the thing that was hidden in his life, the haunting memory of a beauty and a happiness that filled his heart with insatiable longings that made all the interests and spectacle of worldly life seem dull and tedious and vain to him.

Now that I have the clue to it, the thing seems written visibly in his face. I have a photograph in which that look of detachment has been caught and intensified. It reminds me of what a woman once said of him—a woman who had loved him greatly. "Suddenly," she said, "the interest goes out of him. He forgets you. He doesn't care a rap for you—under his very nose. . . . "

Yet the interest was not always out of him, and when he was

holding his attention to a thing Wallace could contrive to be an extremely successful man. His career, indeed, is set with successes. He left me behind him long ago; he soared up over my head, and cut a figure in the world that I couldn't cut—anyhow. He was still a year short of forty, and they say now that he would have been in office and very probably in the new Cabinet if he had lived. At school he always beat me without effort—as it were by nature. We were at school together at Saint Athelstan's College in West Kensington for almost all our school time. He came into the school as my co-equal, but he left far above me, in a blaze of scholarships and brilliant performance. Yet I think I made a fair average running. And it was at school I heard first of the Door in the Wall—that I was to hear of a second time only a month before his death.

To him at least the Door in the Wall was a real door leading through a real wall to immortal realities. Of that I am now quite assured.

And it came into his life early, when he was a little fellow between five and six. I remember how, as he sat making his confession to me with a slow gravity, he reasoned and reckoned the date of it. "There was," he said, "a crimson Virginia creeper in it—all one bright uniform crimson in a clear amber sunshine against a white wall. That came into the impression somehow, though I don't clearly remember how, and there were horse-chestnut leaves upon the clean pavement outside the green door. They were blotched yellow and green, you know, not brown nor dirty, so that they must have been new fallen. I take it that means October. I look out for horse-chestnut leaves every year, and I ought to know.

"If I'm right in that, I was about five years and four months old."

He was, he said, rather a precocious little boy—he learned to talk at an abnormally early age, and he was so sane and "old-fashioned," as people say, that he was permitted an amount of initiative that most children scarcely attain by seven or eight. His mother died when he was born, and he was under the less vigilant and authoritative care of a nursery governess. His father was a stern, preoccupied lawyer, who gave him little attention, and expected great things of him. For all his brightness he found life a little grey and dull I think. And one day he wandered.

He could not recall the particular neglect that enabled him to get away, nor the course he took among the West Kensington roads. All that had faded among the incurable blurs of memory. But the white wall and the green door stood out quite distinctly.

As his memory of that remote childish experience ran, he did at the very first sight of that door experience a peculiar emotion, an attraction, a desire to get to the door and open it and walk in.

And at the same time he had the clearest conviction that either it was unwise or it was wrong of him—he could not tell which—to yield to this attraction. He insisted upon it as a curious thing that he knew from the very beginning—unless memory has played him the queerest trick—that the door was unfastened, and that he could go in as he chose.

I seem to see the figure of that little boy, drawn and repelled. And it was very clear in his mind, too, though why it should be so was never explained, that his father would be very angry if he went through that door.

Wallace described all these moments of hesitation to me with the utmost particularity. He went right past the door, and then, with his hands in his pockets, and making an infantile attempt to whistle, strolled right along beyond the end of the wall. There he recalls a number of mean, dirty shops, and particularly that of a plumber and decorator, with a dusty disorder of earthenware pipes, sheet lead ball taps, pattern books of wall paper, and tins of enamel. He stood pretending to examine these things, and coveting, passionately desiring the green door.

Then, he said, he had a gust of emotion. He made a run for it, lest hesitation should grip him again, he went plump with outstretched hand through the green door and let it slam behind him. And so, in a trice, he came into the garden that has haunted all his life.

It was very difficult for Wallace to give me his full sense of that garden into which he came.

There was something in the very air of it that exhilarated, that gave one a sense of lightness and good happening and well being; there was something in the sight of it that made all its colour clean and perfect and subtly luminous. In the instant of coming into it one was exquisitely glad—as only in rare moments and when one is young and joyful one can be glad in this world. And everything was beautiful there. . . .

Wallace mused before he went on telling me. "You see," he said, with the doubtful inflection of a man who pauses at incredible things, "there were two great panthers there . . . Yes, spotted panthers. And I was not afraid. There was a long wide path with marble-edged flower borders on either side, and these two huge velvety beasts were playing there with a ball. One looked up and came towards me, a little curious as it seemed. It came right up to me, rubbed its soft round ear very gently against the small hand I held out and purred. It was, I tell you, an enchanted garden. I know. And the size? Oh! It stretched far and wide, this way and that. I believe there were hills far away. Heaven knows where West Kensington had suddenly got to. And somehow it was just like coming home.

"You know, in the very moment the door swung to behind me, I forgot the road with its fallen chestnut leaves, its cabs and tradesmen's carts, I forgot the sort of gravitational pull back to the discipline and obedience of home, I forgot all hesitations and fear, forgot discretion, forgot all the intimate realities of this life. I became in a moment a very glad and wonder-happy little boy—in another world. It was a world with a different quality, a warmer, more penetrating and mellower light, with a faint clear gladness in its air, and wisps of sun-touched cloud in the blueness of its sky. And before me ran this long wide path, invitingly, with weedless beds on either side, rich with untended flowers, and these two great panthers. I put my little hands fearlessly on their soft fur, and caressed their round ears and the sensitive corners under their ears, and played with them, and it was as though they welcomed me home. There was a keen sense of home-coming in my mind, and when presently a tall, fair girl appeared in the pathway and came to meet me, smiling, and said 'Well?' to me, and lifted me, and kissed me, and put me down, and led me by the hand, there was no amazement, but only an impression of delightful rightness, of being reminded of happy things that had in some strange way been overlooked. There were broad steps, I remember, that came into view between spikes of delphinium, and up these we went to a great avenue between very old and shady dark trees. All down this avenue, you know, between the red chapped stems, were marble seats of honour and statuary, and very tame and friendly white doves. . . .

"And along this avenue my girl-friend led me, looking down—I recall the pleasant lines, the finely-modelled chin of her sweet kind face—asking me questions in a soft, agreeable voice, and telling me things, pleasant things I know, though what they were I was never able to recall . . . And presently a little Capuchin monkey, very clean, with a fur of ruddy brown and kindly hazel eyes, came down a tree to us and ran beside me, looking up at me and grinning, and presently leapt to my shoulder. So we went on our way in great happiness. . . . "

He paused.

"Go on," I said.

"I remember little things. We passed an old man musing among laurels, I remember, and a place gay with paroquets, and came through a broad shaded colonnade to a spacious cool palace, full of pleasant fountains, full of beautiful things, full of the quality and promise of heart's desire. And there were many things and many people, some that still seem to stand out clearly and some that are a little vague, but all these people were beautiful and kind. In some way—I don't know how—it was conveyed to me that they all were kind to me, glad to have me there, and filling me with gladness by their gestures, by the touch of their hands, by the welcome and love in their eyes. Yes—"

He mused for awhile. "Playmates I found there. That was very much to me, because I was a lonely little boy. They played delightful games in a grass-covered court where there was a sun-dial set about with flowers. And as one played one loved. . . .

"But—it's odd—there's a gap in my memory. I don't remember the games we played. I never remembered. Afterwards, as a child, I spent long hours trying, even with tears, to recall the form of that happiness. I wanted to play it all over again—in my nursery—by myself. No! All I remember is the happiness and two dear playfellows who were most with me. . . . Then presently came a sombre dark woman, with a grave, pale face and dreamy eyes, a sombre woman wearing a soft long robe of pale purple, who carried a book and beckoned and took me aside with her into a gallery above a hall—though my playmates were loth to have me go, and ceased their game and stood watching as I was carried away. 'Come back to us!' they cried. 'Come back to us soon!' I looked up at her face, but she heeded them not at all. Her face was very gentle and grave. She took me to a seat in the gallery, and I stood beside her, ready to look at her book as she opened it upon her knee. The pages fell open. She pointed, and I looked, marvelling, for in the living pages of that book I saw myself; it was a story about myself, and in it were all the things that had happened to me since ever I was born. . . .

"It was wonderful to me, because the pages of that book were not pictures, you understand, but realities."

Wallace paused gravely—looked at me doubtfully.

"Go on," I said. "I understand."

"They were realities—yes, they must have been; people moved and things came and went in them; my dear mother, whom I had near forgotten; then my father, stern and upright, the servants, the nursery, all the familiar things of home. Then the front door and the busy streets, with traffic to and fro: I looked and marvelled, and looked half doubtfully again into the woman's face and turned the pages over, skipping this and that, to see more of this book, and more, and so at last I came to myself hovering and hesitating outside the green door in the long white wall, and felt again the conflict and the fear.

"'And next?' I cried, and would have turned on, but the cool hand of the grave woman delayed me.

"'Next?' I insisted, and struggled gently with her hand, pulling up her fingers with all my childish strength, and as she yielded and the page came over she bent down upon me like a shadow and kissed my brow.

"But the page did not show the enchanted garden, nor the panthers, nor the girl who had led me by the hand, nor the playfellows who had been so loth to let me go. It showed a long grey street in West Kensington, on that chill hour of afternoon before the lamps are lit, and I was there, a wretched little figure, weeping aloud, for all that I could do to restrain myself, and I was weeping because I could not return to my dear play-fellows who had called after me, 'Come back to us! Come back to us soon!' I was there. This was no page in a book, but harsh reality; that enchanted place and the restraining hand of the grave mother at whose knee I stood had gone—whither have they gone?"

He halted again, and remained for a time, staring into the fire.

"Oh! The wretchedness of that return!" he murmured.

"Well?" I said after a minute or so.

"Poor little wretch I was—brought back to this grey world again! As I realized the fullness of what had happened to me, I gave way to quite ungovernable grief. And the shame and humiliation of that public weeping and my disgraceful homecoming remain with me still. I see again the benevolent-looking old gentleman in gold spectacles who stopped and spoke to me—prodding me first with his umbrella. 'Poor little chap,' said he; 'and are you lost then?'—and me a London boy of five and more! And he must needs bring in a kindly young policeman and make a crowd of me, and so march me home. Sobbing, conspicuous and frightened, I came from the enchanted garden to the steps of my father's house.

"That is as well as I can remember my vision of that garden—the garden that haunts me still. Of course, I can convey nothing of that indescribable quality of translucent unreality, that difference from the common things of experience that hung about it all; but that—that is what happened. If it was a dream, I am sure it was a day-time and altogether extraordinary dream. . . . H'm!—naturally there followed a terrible questioning, by my aunt, my father, the nurse, the governess—everyone. . . .

"I tried to tell them, and my father gave me my first thrashing for telling lies. When afterwards I tried to tell my aunt, she punished me again for my wicked persistence. Then, as I said, everyone was forbidden to listen to me, to hear a word about it. Even my fairy tale books were taken away from me for a time—because I was 'too imaginative.' Eh? Yes, they did that! My father belonged to the old school. . . . And my story was driven back upon myself. I whispered it to my pillow—my pillow that was often damp and salt to my whispering lips with childish tears. And I added always to my official and less fervent prayers this one heartfelt request: 'Please God I may dream of the garden. Oh! Take me back to my garden! Take me back to my garden!'

"I dreamt often of the garden. I may have added to it, I may have changed it; I do not know. . . . All this you understand is an attempt to reconstruct from fragmentary memories a very early experience. Between that and the other consecutive memories of my boyhood there is a gulf. A time came when it seemed impossible I should ever speak of that wonder glimpse again."

I asked an obvious question.

"No," he said. "I don't remember that I ever attempted to find my way back to the garden in those early years. This seems odd to me now, but I think that very probably a closer watch was kept on my movements after this misadventure to prevent my going astray. No, it wasn't until you knew me that I tried for the garden again. And I believe there was a period—incredible as it seems now—when I forgot the garden altogether—when I was about eight or nine it may have been. Do you remember me as a kid at Saint Athelstan's?"

"Rather!"

"I didn't show any signs did I in those days of having a secret dream?"

## II

He looked up with a sudden smile.

"Did you ever play North-West Passage with me? . . . No, of course you didn't come my way!"

"It was the sort of game," he went on, "that every imaginative child plays all day. The idea was the discovery of a North-West Passage to school. The way to school was plain enough; the game consisted in finding some way that wasn't plain, starting off ten minutes early in some almost hopeless direction, and working one's way round through unaccustomed streets to my goal. And one day I got entangled among some rather low-class streets on the other side of Campden Hill, and I began to think that for once the game would be against me and that I should get to school late. I tried rather desperately a street that seemed a cul de sac, and found a passage at the end. I hurried through that with renewed hope. 'I shall do it yet,' I said, and passed a row of frowsy little shops that were inexplicably familiar to me, and behold! There was my long white wall and the green door that led to the enchanted garden!

"The thing whacked upon me suddenly. Then, after all, that garden, that wonderful garden, wasn't a dream!". . . .

He paused.

"I suppose my second experience with the green door marks the world of difference there is between the busy life of a schoolboy and the infinite leisure of a child. Anyhow, this second time I didn't for a moment think of going in straight away. You see . . . For one thing my mind was full of the idea of getting to school in time—set on not breaking my record for punctuality. I must surely have felt *some* little desire at least to try the door—yes, I must have felt that. . . . But I seem to remember the attraction of the door mainly as another obstacle to my overmastering determination to get to school. I was immediately interested by this discovery I had made, of course—I went on with my mind full of it—but I went on. It didn't check me. I ran past tugging out my watch, found I had ten minutes still to spare, and then I was going downhill into familiar surroundings. I got to school, breathless, it is true, and wet with perspiration, but in time. I can remember hanging up my coat and hat . . . Went right by it and left it behind me. Odd, eh?"

He looked at me thoughtfully. "Of course, I didn't know then that it wouldn't always be there. School boys have limited imaginations. I suppose I thought it was an awfully jolly thing to have it there, to know my way back to it, but there was the school tugging at me. I expect I was a good deal distraught and inattentive that morning, recalling what I could of the beautiful strange people I should presently see again. Oddly enough I had no doubt in my mind that they would be glad to see me . . . Yes, I must have thought of the garden that morning just as a jolly sort of place to which one might resort in the interludes of a strenuous scholastic career.

"I didn't go that day at all. The next day was a half holiday, and that may have weighed with me. Perhaps, too, my state of inattention brought down impositions upon me and docked the margin of

time necessary for the detour. I don't know. What I do know is that in the meantime the enchanted garden was so much upon my mind that I could not keep it to myself.

"I told—What was his name?—a ferrety-looking youngster we used to call Squiff."

"Young Hopkins," said I.

"Hopkins it was. I did not like telling him, I had a feeling that in some way it was against the rules to tell him, but I did. He was walking part of the way home with me; he was talkative, and if we had not talked about the enchanted garden we should have talked of something else, and it was intolerable to me to think about any other subject. So I blabbed.

"Well, he told my secret. The next day in the play interval I found myself surrounded by half a dozen bigger boys, half teasing and wholly curious to hear more of the enchanted garden. There was that big Fawcett—you remember him?—and Carnaby and Morley Reynolds. You weren't there by any chance? No, I think I should have remembered if you were. . . .

"A boy is a creature of odd feelings. I was, I really believe, in spite of my secret self-disgust, a little flattered to have the attention of these big fellows. I remember particularly a moment of pleasure caused by the praise of Crawshaw—you remember Crawshaw major, the son of Crawshaw the composer?—who said it was the best lie he had ever heard. But at the same time there was a really painful undertow of shame at telling what I felt was indeed a sacred secret. That beast Fawcett made a joke about the girl in green—"

Wallace's voice sank with the keen memory of that shame. "I pretended not to hear," he said. "Well, then Carnaby suddenly called me a young liar and disputed with me when I said the thing was true. I said I knew where to find the green door, could lead them all there in ten minutes. Carnaby became outrageously virtuous, and said I'd have to—and bear out my words or suffer. Did you ever have

Carnaby twist your arm? Then perhaps you'll understand how it went with me. I swore my story was true. There was nobody in the school then to save a chap from Carnaby though Crawshaw put in a word or so. Carnaby had got his game. I grew excited and red-eared, and a little frightened, I behaved altogether like a silly little chap, and the outcome of it all was that instead of starting alone for my enchanted garden, I led the way presently—cheeks flushed, ears hot, eyes smarting, and my soul one burning misery and shame—for a party of six mocking, curious and threatening school-fellows.

"We never found the white wall and the green door . . . "

"You mean?—"

"I mean I couldn't find it. I would have found it if I could.

"And afterwards when I could go alone I couldn't find it. I never found it. I seem now to have been always looking for it through my schoolboy days, but I've never come upon it again."

"Did the fellows—make it disagreeable?"

"Beastly. . . . Carnaby held a council over me for wanton lying. I remember how I sneaked home and upstairs to hide the marks of my blubbering. But when I cried myself to sleep at last it wasn't for Carnaby, but for the garden, for the beautiful afternoon I had hoped for, for the sweet friendly women and the waiting playfellows and the game I had hoped to learn again, that beautiful forgotten game. . . .

"I believed firmly that if I had not told— . . . I had bad times after that—crying at night and woolgathering by day. For two terms I slackened and had bad reports. Do you remember? Of course you would! It was *you*—your beating me in mathematics that brought me back to the grind again."

## III

For a time my friend stared silently into the red heart of the fire. Then he said: "I never saw it again until I was seventeen.

"It leapt upon me for the third time—as I was driving to Paddington on my way to Oxford and a scholarship. I had just one momentary glimpse. I was leaning over the apron of my hansom smoking a cigarette, and no doubt thinking myself no end of a man of the world, and suddenly there was the door, the wall, the dear sense of unforgettable and still attainable things.

"We clattered by—I too taken by surprise to stop my cab until we were well past and round a corner. Then I had a queer moment, a double and divergent movement of my will: I tapped the little door in the roof of the cab, and brought my arm down to pull out my watch. 'Yes, sir!' said the cabman, smartly. 'Er—well—it's nothing,' I cried. '*My* mistake! We haven't much time! Go on!' and he went on . . .

"I got my scholarship. And the night after I was told of that I sat over my fire in my little upper room, my study, in my father's house, with his praise—his rare praise—and his sound counsels ringing in my ears, and I smoked my favourite pipe—the formidable bulldog of adolescence—and thought of that door in the long white wall. 'If I had stopped,' I thought, 'I should have missed my scholarship, I should have missed Oxford—muddled all the fine career before me! I begin to see things better!' I fell musing deeply, but I did not doubt then this career of mine was a thing that merited sacrifice.

"Those dear friends and that clear atmosphere seemed very sweet to me, very fine, but remote. My grip was fixing now upon the world. I saw another door opening—the door of my career."

He stared again into the fire. Its red lights picked out a stubborn strength in his face for just one flickering moment, and then it vanished again.

"Well", he said and sighed, "I have served that career. I have done—much work, much hard work. But I have dreamt of the enchanted garden a thousand dreams, and seen its door, or at least glimpsed its door, four times since then. Yes—four times. For a while this world was so bright and interesting, seemed so full of meaning and opportunity that the half-effaced charm of the garden was by comparison gentle and remote. Who wants to pat panthers on the way to dinner with pretty women and distinguished men? I came down to London from Oxford, a man of bold promise that I have done something to redeem. Something—and yet there have been disappointments. . . .

"Twice I have been in love—I will not dwell on that—but once, as I went to someone who, I know, doubted whether I dared to come, I took a short cut at a venture through an unfrequented road near Earl's Court, and so happened on a white wall and a familiar green door. 'Odd!' said I to myself, 'but I thought this place was on Campden Hill. It's the place I never could find somehow—like counting Stonehenge—the place of that queer day dream of mine.' And I went by it intent upon my purpose. It had no appeal to me that afternoon.

"I had just a moment's impulse to try the door, three steps aside were needed at the most—though I was sure enough in my heart that it would open to me—and then I thought that doing so might delay me on the way to that appointment in which I thought my honour was involved. Afterwards I was sorry for my punctuality—I might at least have peeped in I thought, and waved a hand to those panthers, but I knew enough by this time not to seek again belatedly that which is not found by seeking. Yes, that time made me very sorry. . . .

"Years of hard work after that and never a sight of the door. It's only recently it has come back to me. With it there has come a sense as though some thin tarnish had spread itself over my world. I began to think of it as a sorrowful and bitter thing that I should never see that door again. Perhaps I was suffering a little from overwork—perhaps it was what I've heard spoken of as the feeling of forty. I don't know. But certainly the keen brightness that makes effort easy has gone out of things recently, and that just at a time with all these new political developments—when I ought to be working. Odd, isn't it? But I do begin to find life toilsome, its rewards, as I come near them, cheap. I began a little while ago to want the garden quite badly. Yes—and I've seen it three times."

"The garden?"

"No—the door! And I haven't gone in!"

He leaned over the table to me, with an enormous sorrow in his voice as he spoke. "Thrice I have had my chance—*thrice*! If ever that door offers itself to me again, I swore, I will go in out of this dust and heat, out of this dry glitter of vanity, out of these toilsome futilities. I will go and never return. This time I will stay. . . . I swore it and when the time came—*I didn't go*.

"Three times in one year have I passed that door and failed to enter. Three times in the last year.

"The first time was on the night of the snatch division on the Tenants' Redemption Bill, on which the Government was saved by a majority of three. You remember? No one on our side—perhaps very few on the opposite side—expected the end that night. Then the debate collapsed like eggshells. I and Hotchkiss were dining with his cousin at Brentford, we were both unpaired, and we were called up by telephone, and set off at once in his cousin's motor. We got in barely in time, and on the way we passed my wall and door—livid in the moonlight, blotched with hot yellow as the glare of our lamps lit it, but unmistakable. 'My God!' cried I. 'What?' said Hotchkiss. 'Nothing!' I answered, and the moment passed.

"'I've made a great sacrifice,' I told the whip as I got in. 'They all have,' he said, and hurried by.

"I do not see how I could have done otherwise then. And the next occasion was as I rushed to my father's bedside to bid that stern old man farewell. Then, too, the claims of life were imperative. But the third time was different; it happened a week ago. It fills me with hot remorse to recall it. I was with Gurker and

Ralphs—it's no secret now you know that I've had my talk with Gurker. We had been dining at Frobisher's, and the talk had become intimate between us. The question of my place in the reconstructed ministry lay always just over the boundary of the discussion. Yes—yes. That's all settled. It needn't be talked about yet, but there's no reason to keep a secret from you. . . . Yes—thanks! Thanks! But let me tell you my story.

"Then, on that night things were very much in the air. My position was a very delicate one. I was keenly anxious to get some definite word from Gurker, but was hampered by Ralphs' presence. I was using the best power of my brain to keep that light and careless talk not too obviously directed to the point that concerns me. I had to. Ralphs' behaviour since has more than justified my caution. . . . Ralphs, I knew, would leave us beyond the Kensington High Street, and then I could surprise Gurker by a sudden frankness. One has sometimes to resort to these little devices. . . . And then it was that in the margin of my field of vision I became aware once more of the white wall, the green door before us down the road.

"We passed it talking. I passed it. I can still see the shadow of Gurker's marked profile, his opera hat tilted forward over his prominent nose, the many folds of his neck wrap going before my shadow and Ralphs' as we sauntered past.

"I passed within twenty inches of the door. 'If I say good-night to them, and go in,' I asked myself, 'what will happen?' And I was all a-tingle for that word with Gurker.

"I could not answer that question in the tangle of my other problems. 'They will think me mad,' I thought. 'And suppose I vanish now!—Amazing disappearance of a prominent politician!' That weighed with me. A thousand inconceivably petty worldlinesses weighed with me in that crisis."

Then he turned on me with a sorrowful smile, and, speaking slowly; "Here I am!" he said.

"Here I am!" he repeated, "and my chance has gone from me. Three times in one year the door has been offered me—the door that goes into peace, into delight, into a beauty beyond dreaming, a kindness no man on earth can know. And I have rejected it, Redmond, and it has gone—"

"How do you know?"

"I know. I know. I am left now to work it out, to stick to the tasks that held me so strongly when my moments came. You say, I have success—this vulgar, tawdry, irksome, envied thing. I have it." He had a walnut in his big hand. "If that was my success," he said, and crushed it, and held it out for me to see.

"Let me tell you something, Redmond. This loss is destroying me. For two months, for ten weeks nearly now, I have done no work at all, except the most necessary and urgent duties. My soul is full of inappeasable regrets. At nights—when it is less likely I shall be recognized—I go out. I wander. Yes. I wonder what people would think of that if they knew. A Cabinet Minister, the responsible head of that most vital of all departments, wandering alone—grieving—sometimes near audibly lamenting—for a door, for a garden!"

## IV

I can see now his rather pallid face, and the unfamiliar sombre fire that had come into his eyes. I see him very vividly tonight. I sit recalling his words, his tones, and last evening's Westminster Gazette still lies on my sofa, containing the notice of his death. At lunch today the club was busy with him and the strange riddle of his fate.

They found his body very early yesterday morning in a deep excavation near East Kensington Station. It is one of two shafts that have been made in connection with an extension of the railway southward. It is protected from the intrusion of the public by a hoarding upon the high road, in which a small doorway has been cut for the convenience of some of the workmen who live in that direction. The doorway was left unfastened through a misunderstanding between two gangers, and through it he made his way. . . .

My mind is darkened with questions and riddles.

It would seem he walked all the way from the House that night—he has frequently walked home during the past Session—and so it is I figure his dark form coming along the late and empty streets, wrapped up, intent. And then did the pale electric lights near the station cheat the rough planking into a semblance of white? Did that fatal unfastened door awaken some memory?

Was there, after all, ever any green door in the wall at all?

I do not know. I have told his story as he told it to me. There are times when I believe that Wallace was no more than the victim of the coincidence between a rare but not unprecedented type of hallucination and a careless trap, but that indeed is not my profoundest belief. You may think me superstitious if you will, and foolish; but, indeed, I am more than half convinced that he had in truth, an abnormal gift, and a sense, something—I know not what—that in the guise of wall and door offered him an outlet, a secret and peculiar passage of escape into another and altogether more beautiful world. At any rate, you will say, it betrayed him in the end. But did it betray him? There you touch the inmost mystery of these dreamers, these men of vision and the imagination.

We see our world fair and common, the hoarding and the pit. By our daylight standard he walked out of security into darkness, danger and death. But did he see like that?

# Polaris of the Snows

by Charles B. Stilson

## I. POLARIS OF THE SNOWS

"North! North! To the north, Polaris. Tell the world—ah, tell them—boy—The north! The north! You must go, Polaris!"

Throwing the covers from his low couch, the old man arose and stood, a giant, tottering figure. Higher and higher he towered. He tossed his arms high, his features became convulsed; his eyes glazed. In his throat the rising tide of dissolution choked his voice to a hoarse rattle. He swayed.

With a last desperate rallying of his failing powers he extended his right arm and pointed to the north. Then he fell, as a tree falls, quivered, and was still.

His companion bent over the pallet, and with light, sure fingers closed his eyes. In all the world he knew, Polaris never had seen a human being die. In all the world he now was utterly alone!

He sat down at the foot of the cot, and for many minutes gazed steadily at the wall with fixed, unseeing eyes. A sputtering little lamp, which stood on a table in the center of the room, flickered and went out. The flames of the fireplace played strange tricks in the strange room. In their uncertain glare, the features of the dead man seemed to writhe uncannily.

Garments and hangings of the skins of beasts stirred in the wavering shadows, as though the ghosts of their one-time tenants were struggling to reassert their dominion. At the one door and the lone window the wind whispered, fretted, and shrieked. Snow as fine and hard as the sands of the sea rasped across the panes. Somewhere without a dog howled—the long, throaty ululation of the wolf breed. Another joined in, and another, until a full score of canine voices wailed a weird requiem.

Unheeding, the living man sat as still as the dead.

Once, twice, thrice, a little clock struck a halting, uncertain stroke. When the fourth hour was passed it rattled crazily and stopped. The fire died away to embers; the embers paled to ashes. As though they were aware that something had gone awry, the dogs never ceased their baying. The wind rose higher and higher, and assailed the house with repeated shocks. Pale-gray and changeless day that lay across a sea of snows peered furtively through the windows.

At length the watcher relaxed his silent vigil. He arose, cast off his coat of white furs, stepped to the wall of the room opposite to the door, and shoved back a heavy wooden panel. A dark aperture was disclosed. He disappeared and came forth presently, carrying several large chunks of what appeared to be crumbling black rock.

He threw them on the dying fire, where they snapped briskly, caught fire, and flamed brightly. They were coal.

From a platform above the fireplace he dragged down a portion of the skinned carcass of a walrus. With the long, heavy-bladed knife from his belt he cut it into strips. Laden with the meat, he opened the door and went out into the dim day.

The house was set against the side of a cliff of solid, black, coal. A compact stockade of great boulders enclosed the front of the dwelling. From the back of the building, along the base of the cliff, ran a low shed of timber slabs, from which sounded the howling and worrying of the dogs.

As Polaris entered the stockade the clamor was redoubled. The rude plank at the front of the shed, which was its door, was shaken repeatedly as heavy bodies were hurled against it.

Kicking an accumulation of loose snow away from the door, the man took from its racks the bar which made it fast and let it drop forward. A reek of steam floated from its opening. A shaggy head was thrust forth, followed immediately by a great, gray body, which shot out as if propelled from a catapult.

Catching in its jaws the strip of flesh which the man dangled in front of the doorway, the brute dashed across the stockade and crouched against the wall, tearing at the meat. Dog after dog piled pell-mell through the doorway, until at least twenty-five grizzled animals were distributed about the enclosure, bolting their meal of walrus-flesh.

For a few moments the man sat on the roof of the shed and watched the animals. Although the raw flesh stiffened in the frigid air before even the jaws of the dogs could devour it and the wind cut like the lash of a whip, the man, coatless and with head and arms bared, seemed to mind neither the cold nor the blast.

He had not the ruggedness of figure or the great height of the man who lay dead within the house. He was of considerably more than medium height, but so broad of shoulder and deep of chest that he seemed short. Every line of his compact figure bespoke unusual strength—the wiry, swift strength of an animal.

His arms, white and shapely, rippled with muscles at the least movement of his fingers. His hands were small, but powerfully shaped. His neck was straight and not long. The thews spread from it to his wide shoulders like those of a splendid athlete. The ears were set close above the angle of a firm jaw, and were nearly hidden in a mass of tawny, yellow hair, as fine as a woman's, which swept over his shoulders.

Above a square chin were full lips and a thin, aquiline nose. Deep, brown eyes, fringed with black lashes, made a marked contrast with the fairness of his complexion and his yellow hair and brows. He was not more than twenty-four years old.

Presently he re-entered the house. The dogs flocked after him to the door, whining and rubbing against his legs, but he allowed none of them to enter with him. He stood before the dead man and, for the first time in many hours, he spoke:

"For this day, my father, you have waited many years. I shall not delay. I will not fail you."

From a skin sack he filled the small lamp with oil and lighted its wick with a splinter of blazing coal. He set it where its feeble light shone on the face of the dead. Lifting the corpse, he composed its limbs and wrapped it in the great white pelt of a polar bear, tying it with many thongs. Before he hid from view the quiet features he stood back with folded arms and bowed head.

"I think he would have wished this," he whispered, and he sang softly that grand old hymn which has sped so many Christian soldiers from their battlefield. "Nearer, My God, to Thee," he sang in a subdued, melodious baritone. From a shelf of books which hung on the wall he reached a leather-covered volume. "It was his religion," he muttered: "It may be mine," and he read from the book: "*I am the resurrection and the life, whoso believeth in Me, even though he died—*" and on through the sonorous burial service.

He dropped the book within the folds of the bearskin, covered the dead face, and made fast the robe. Although the body was of great weight, he shouldered it without apparent effort, took the lamp in one hand, and passed through the panel in the wall.

Within the bowels of the cliff a large cavern had been hollowed in the coal. In a far corner a gray boulder had been hewn into the shape of a tombstone. On its face were carved side by side two words: "Anne" and "Stephen." At the foot of the stone were a mound and an open grave. He laid the body in the grave and covered it with earth and loose coal.

Again he paused, while the lamplight shone on the tomb.

"May you rest in peace, O Anne, my mother, and Stephen, my father. I never knew you, my mother, and, my father, I knew not who you were nor who I am. I go to carry your message."

He rolled boulders onto the two mounds. The opening to the cave he walled up with other boulders, piling a heap of them and of large pieces of coal until it filled the low arch of the entrance.

In the cabin he made preparations for a journey.

One by one he threw on the fire books and other articles within the room, until little was left but skins and garments of fur and an assortment of barbaric weapons of the chase.

Last he dragged from under the cot a long, oaken chest.

Failing to find its key, he tore the lid from it with his strong hands.

Some articles of feminine wearing apparel which were within it he handled reverently, and at the same time curiously; for they were of cloth. Wonderingly he ran his fingers over silk and fine laces. Those he also burned.

From the bottom of the chest he took a short, brown rifle and a brace of heavy revolvers of a pattern and caliber famous in the annals of the plainsmen. With them were belt and holsters.

He counted the cartridges in the belt. Forty there were, and in the chambers of the revolvers and the magazine of the rifle, eighteen more. Fifty-eight shots with which to meet the perils that lay between himself and that world of men to the north—if, indeed, the passing years had not spoiled the ammunition.

He divested himself of his clothing, bathed with melted snow-water, and dressed himself anew in white furs. An omelet of eggs of wild birds and a cutlet of walrus-flesh sufficed to stay his hunger, and he was ready to face the unknown.

In the stockade was a strongly built sledge. Polaris packed it with quantities of meat both fresh and dried, of which there was a large store in the cabin. What he did not pack on the sledge he threw to the eager dogs.

He laid his harness out on the snow, cracked his long whip, and called up his team. "Octavius, Nero, Julius." Three powerful brutes bounded to him and took their places in the string. "Juno, Hector, Pallas." Three more grizzled snow-runners sprang into line. "Marcus." The great, gray leader trotted sedately to the place at the head of the team. A seven-dog team it was, all of them bearing the names before which Rome and Greece had bowed.

Polaris added to the burden of the sledge the brown rifle, several spears, carved from oaken beams and tipped with steel, and a sealskin filled with boiled snow-water. On his last trip into the cabin he took from a drawer in the table a small, flat packet, sewn in membranous parchment.

"This is to tell the world my father's message and to tell who I am," he said, and hid it in an inner pocket of his vest of furs. He buckled on the revolver-belt, took whip and staff from the fireside, and drove his dog-team out of the stockade onto the prairie of snow, closing the gate on the howling chorus left behind.

He proceeded several hundred yards, then tethered his dogs with a word of admonition, and retraced his steps.

In the stockade he did a strange and terrible thing. Long used to seeing him depart from his team, the dogs had scattered and were mumbling their bones in various corners. "If I leave these behind me, they will perish miserably, or they will break out and follow, and I may not take them with me," he muttered.

From dog to dog he passed. To each he spoke a word of farewell. Each he caressed with a pat on the head. Each he killed with a single grip of his muscular hands, gripping them at the nape of the neck, where the bones parted in his powerful fingers. Silently and swiftly he proceeded until only one dog remained alive, old Paulus, the patriarch of the pack.

He bent over the animal, which raised its dim eyes to his and licked at his hands.

"Paulus, dear old friend that I have grown up with; farewell, Paulus," he said. He pressed his face against the noble head of the dog. When he raised it tears were coursing down his cheeks. Then Paulus's spirit sped.

Two by two he dragged the bodies into the cabin.

"Of old a great general in that far world of men burned his ships that he might not turn back. I will not turn back," he murmured. With a splinter of blazing coal he fired the house and the dog-shed. He tore the gate of the stockade from its hinges and cast it into the ruins. With his great strength he toppled over the capping-stones of the wall, and left it a ruin also.

## II. THE FIRST WOMAN

Probably in all the world there was not the equal of the team of dogs which Polaris had selected for his journey. Their ancestors in the long ago had been the fierce, gray timberwolves of the north. Carefully cross-bred, the strains in their blood were of the wolf, the great Dane, and the mastiff; but the wolf strain held dominant. They had the loyalty of the mastiff, the strength of the great Dane, and the tireless sinews of the wolf. From the environment of their rearing they were well furred and inured to the cold and hardships of the Antarctic. They would travel far.

Polaris did not ride on the sledge. He ran with the dogs, as swift and tireless as they. A wonderful example of the adaptability to conditions of the human race, his upbringing had given him the strength and endurance of an animal. He had never seen the dog that he could not run down.

He, too, would travel fast and far.

In the nature of the land through which they journeyed on their first dash to the northward, there were few obstacles to quick progress. It was a prairie of snow, wind-swept, and stretching like a desert as far as eye could discern. Occasionally were upcroppings of coal cliffs similar to the one where had been Polaris's home. On the first drive they made a good fifty miles.

Need of sleep, more than fatigue, warned both man and beasts of camping-time. Polaris, who seemed to have a definite point in view, urged on the dogs for an hour longer than was usual on an ordinary trip, and they came to the border of the immense snow-plain.

To the northeast lay a ridge of what appeared to be snow-covered hills. Beyond the edge of the white prairie was a forest of ice. Millions of jagged monoliths stood and lay, jammed closely together, in every conceivable shape and angle.

At some time a giant ice-flow had crashed down upon the land. It had fretted and torn at the shore, had heaved itself up, with its myriad gleaming tusks bared for destruction. Then nature had laid upon it a calm, white hand, and had frozen it quiet and still and changeless.

Away to the east a path was open, which skirted the field of broken ice and led in toward the base of the hills.

Polaris did not take that path. He turned west, following the line of the ice-belt. Presently he found what he sought. A narrow lane led into the heart of the iceberg.

At the end of it, caught in the jaws of two giant bergs, hung fast, as it had hung for years, the sorry wreck of a stout ship. Scarred and rent by the grinding of its prison-ice, and weather-beaten by the rasping of wind-driven snow in a land where the snow never melts, still on the square stern of the vessel could be read the dimming letters which spelled "Yedda."

Polaris unharnessed the pack, and man and dogs crept on board the hulk. It was but a timber shell. Much of the decking had been cut away, and everything movable had been taken from it for the building of the cabin and the shed, now in black ruins fifty miles to the south.

In an angle of the ice-wall, a few yards from the ship, Polaris pitched his camp and built a fire with timbers from the wreck. He struck his flame with a rudely fashioned tinder-box, catching the spark in fine scrapings of wood and nursing it with his breath. He fed the dogs and toasted meat for his own meal at the fire. With a large robe from the sledge he bedded the team snugly beside the fire.

With his own parka of furs he clambered aboard the ship, found a bunk in the forecastle, and curled up for the night.

Several hours later hideous clamor broke his dreamless slumber. He started from the bunk and leaped from the ship's side into the ice-lane. Every dog of the pack was bristling and snarling with rage. Mixed with their uproar was a deeper, hoarser note of anger that came from the throat of no dog—a note which the man knew well.

The team was bunched a few feet ahead of the fire as Polaris came over the rail of the ship. Almost shoulder to shoulder the seven crouched, every head pointed up the path. They were quivering from head to tail with anger, and seemed to be about to charge.

Whipping the dogs back, the son of the snows ran forward to meet the danger alone. He could afford to lose no dogs. He had forgotten the guns, but he bore weapons with which he was better acquainted.

With a long-hafted spear in his hand and the knife loosened in his belt he bounded up the pathway and stood, wary but unafraid, fronting an immense white bear.

He was not a moment too soon. The huge animal had set himself for the charge, and in another instant would have hurled its enormous weight down on the dogs. The beast hesitated, confronted by this new enemy, and sat back on its haunches to consider.

Knowing his foe aforetime, Polaris took that opportunity to deliver his own charge. He bounded forward and drove his tough spear with all his strength into the white chest below the throat. Balanced as it was on its haunches, the shock of the man's onset upset the bear, and it rolled backward, a jet of blood spurting over its shaggy coat and beyond, dyeing the snow.

Like a flash the man followed his advantage. Before the brute could turn or recover Polaris reached its back and drove his long-bladed knife under the left shoulder. Twice he struck deep, and sprang aside. The battle was finished.

The beast made a last mighty effort to rear erect, tearing at the spear-shaft, and went down under an avalanche of snarling, ferocious dogs. For the team could refrain from conflict no longer, and charged like a flying wedge to worry the dying foe.

Replenishing his store of meat with strips from the newly slain bear, Polaris allowed the pack to make a famous meal on the carcass. When they were ready to take the trail again, he fired the ship with a blazing brand, and they trotted forth along the snow-path to the east with the skeleton of the stout old *Yedda* roaring and flaming behind them.

For days Polaris pressed northward. To his right extended the range of the white hills. To the left was the seemingly endless ice-field that looked like the angry billows of a storm-tossed sea which had been arrested at the height of tempest, its white-capped, upthrown waves paralyzed cold and dead.

Down the shore-line, where his path lay, a fierce wind blew continuously and with increasing rigor. He was puzzled to find that instead of becoming warmer as he progressed to the north and away from the pole, the air was more frigid than it had been in his homeland. Hardy as he was, there were times when the furious blasts chilled him to the bone and when his magnificent dogs flinched and whimpered.

Still he pushed on. The sledge grew lighter as the provisions were consumed, and there were few marches that did not cover forty miles. Polaris slept with the dogs, huddled in robes. The very food they ate they must warm with the heat of their bodies before it could be devoured. There was no vestige of anything to make fuel for a camp-fire.

He had covered some hundreds of miles when he found the contour of the country was changing. The chain of the hills swung sharply away to the east, and the path broadened, fanwise, east and west. An undulating plain of snow and ice-caps, rent by many fissures, lay ahead.

This was the most difficult traveling of all.

In the middle of their second march across the plain, the man noticed that his gray snow-coursers were uneasy. They threw their snouts up to the wind and growled angrily, scenting some unseen danger. Although he had seen nothing larger than a fox since he entered the plain, bear signs had been frequent, and Polaris welcomed a hunt to replenish his larder.

He halted the team and outspanned the dogs so they would be unhampered by the sledge in case of attack. Bidding them remain behind, he went to reconnoiter.

He clambered to the summit of a snow-covered ice-crest and gazed ahead. A great joy welled into his heart, a thanksgiving so keen that it brought a mist to the eyes.

He had found man!

Not a quarter of a mile ahead of him, standing in the lee of a low ridge, were two figures unmistakably human. At the instant he saw them the wind brought to his nostrils, sensitive as those of an animal, a strange scent that set his pulses bounding. He *smelled* man and man's fire! A thin spiral of smoke was curling over the back of the ridge. He hurried forward.

Hidden by the undulations of slopes and drifts he approached within a few feet of them without being discovered. On the point of crying aloud to them he stopped, paralyzed, and crouched behind a drift. For these men to whom his heart called madly—the first of his own kind but one whom he had ever seen—were tearing at each other's throats like maddened beasts in an effort to take life!

Like a man in a dream, Polaris heard their voices raised in curses. They struggled fiercely but weakly. They were on the brink of one of the deep fissures, or crevasses, which seamed this strange, forgotten land. Each was striving to push the other into the chasm.

Then one who seemed the stronger wrenched himself free and struck the other in the face. The stricken man staggered, threw his arms above his head, toppled, and crashed down the precipice.

Polaris's first introduction to the civilization which he sought was murder! For those were civilized white men who had fought. They wore garments of cloth. Revolvers hung from their belts. Their speech, of which he had heard little but cursing, was civilized English.

Pale to the lips, the son of the wilderness leaped over the snow-drift and strode toward the survivor. In the teachings of his father, murder was the greatest of all crimes; its punishment was swift death. This man who stood on the brink of the chasm which had swallowed his companion had been the aggressor in the fight. He had struck first. He had killed. In the heart of Polaris arose a terrible sense of outraged justice. This waif of the eternal snows became the law.

The stranger turned and saw him. He started violently, paled, and then an angry flush mounted to his temples and an angry glint came into his eyes. His crime had been witnessed, and by a strange white man.

His hand flew to his hip, and he swung a heavy revolver up and fired, speeding the bullet with a curse. He missed and would have fired again, but his hour had struck. With the precision of an automaton Polaris snatched one of his own pistols from the holster. He raised it above the level of his shoulder, and fired on the drop.

Not for nothing had he spent long hours practicing with his father's guns, sighting and pulling the trigger countless times, although they were empty. The man in front of him staggered, dropped his pistol, and reeled dizzily. A stream of blood gushed from his lips. He choked, clawed at the air, and pitched backward.

The chasm which had received his victim, received the murderer also.

Polaris heard a shrill scream to his right, and turned swiftly on his heel, automatically swinging up his revolver to meet a new peril.

Another being stood on the brow of the ridge—stood with clasped hands and horror-stricken eyes. Clad almost the same as the others, there was yet a subtle difference which garments could not disguise.

Polaris leaned forward with his whole soul in his eyes. His hand fell to his side. He had made his second discovery. He had discovered woman!

## III. POLARIS MAKES A PROMISE

Both stood transfixed for a long moment—the man with the wonder that followed his anger, the woman with horror. Polaris drew a deep breath and stepped a hesitating pace forward.

The woman threw out her hands in a gesture of loathing.

"Murderer!" she said in a low, deep voice, choked with grief. "Oh, my brother; my poor brother!" She threw herself on the snow, sobbing terribly.

Rooted to the spot by her repelling gesture, Polaris watched her. So one of the men had been her brother. Which one? His naturally clear mind began to reassert itself.

"Lady," he called softly. He did not attempt to go nearer to her.

She raised her face from her arms, crept to her knees, and stared at him stonily. "Well, murderer, finish your work," she said. "I am ready. Ah, what had he—what had they done that you should take their lives?"

"Listen to me, lady," said Polaris quietly. "You saw me—kill. Was that man your brother?"

The girl did not answer, but continued to gaze at him with horror-stricken eyes. Her mouth quivered pitifully.

"If that man was your brother, then I killed him, and with reason," pursued Polaris calmly. "If he was not, then of your brother's death, at least, I am guiltless. I did but punish his slayer."

"His *slayer*! What are you saying?" gasped the girl.

Polaris snapped open the breech of his revolver and emptied its cartridges into his hand. He took the other revolver from its holster and emptied it also. He laid the cartridge in his hand and extended it.

"See," he said, "there are twelve cartridges, but only one empty shell. Only two shots were fired—one by the man whom I killed, the other by me." He saw that he had her attention, and repeated his question: "Was that man your brother?"

"No," she answered.

"Then, you see, I could not have *shot* your brother," said Polaris. His face grew stern with the memory of the scene he had witnessed. "They quarreled, your brother and the other man. I came behind the drift yonder and saw them. I might have stopped them—but, lady, they were the first men I had ever seen, save only one. I was bound by surprise. The other man was stronger. He struck your brother into the crevasse. He would have shot me, but my mind returned to me, and with anger at that which I saw, and I killed him.

"In proof, lady, see—the snow between me and the spot yonder where they stood is untracked. I have been no nearer."

Wonderingly the girl followed with her eyes and the direction of his pointing finger. She comprehended.

"I—I believe you have told me the truth," she faltered. "They *had* quarreled. But—but—you said they were the first men you had ever seen. How—what—"

Polaris crossed the intervening slope and stood at her side.

"That is a long tale, lady," he said simply. "You are in distress. I would help you. Let us go to your camp. Come."

The girl raised her eyes to his, and they gazed long at one another. Polaris saw a slender figure of nearly his own height. She was clad in heavy woolen garments. A hooded cap framed the long oval of her face.

The eyes that looked into his were steady and gray. Long eyes they were, delicately turned at the corners. Her nose was straight and high, its end tilted ever so slightly. Full, crimson lips and a firm little chin peeped over the collar of her jacket. A wisp of chestnut hair swept her high brow and added its tale to a face that would have been accounted beautiful in any land.

In the eyes of Polaris she was divinity.

The girl saw a young giant in the flower of his manhood. Clad in splendid white furs of fox and bear, with a necklace of teeth of the polar bear for adornment, he resembled those magnificent barbarians of the Northland's ancient sagas.

His yellow hair had grown long, and fell about his shoulders under his fox-skin cap. The clean-cut lines of his face scarce were shaded by its growth of red-gold beard and mustache. Except for the guns at his belt he might have been a young chief of vikings. His countenance was at once eager, thoughtful, and determined.

Barbaric and strange as he seemed, the girl found in his face that which she might trust. She removed a mitten and extended a small, white hand to him. Falling on one knee in the snow, Polaris kissed it, with the grace of a knight of old doing homage to his lady fair.

The girl flashed him another wondering glance from her long, gray eyes that set all his senses tingling. Side by side they passed over the ridge.

Disaster had overtaken the camp which lay on the other side. Camp it was by courtesy only—a miserable shelter of blankets and robes, propped with pieces of broken sledge, a few utensils, the partially devoured carcass of a small seal, and a tiny fire, kindled from fragments of the sledge. In the snow some distance from the fire lay the stiffened bodies of several sledge dogs, sinister evidence of the hopelessness of the campers' position.

Polaris turned questioningly to the girl.

"We were lost in the storm," she said. "We left the ship, meaning to be gone only a few hours, and then were lost in the blinding snow. That was three days ago. How many miles we wandered I do not know. The dogs became crazed and turned upon us. The men shot them. Oh, there seems so little hope in this terrible land!" She shuddered. "But you—where did you come from?"

"Do not lose heart, lady," replied Polaris. "Always, in every land, there is hope. There must be. I have lived here all my life. I have come up from the far south. I know but one path—the path to the north, to the world of men. Now I will fetch my sledge up, and then we shall talk and decide. We will find your ship. I, Polaris, promise you that."

He turned from her to the fire, and cast on its dying embers more fragments of the splintered sledge. His eyes shone. He muttered to himself: "A ship, a ship! Ah, but my father's God is good to his son!"

He set off across the snow slopes to bring up the pack.

## IV. HURLED SOUTH AGAIN

When his strong form had bounded from her view, the girl turned to the little hut and shut herself within. She cast herself on a heap of blankets, and gave way to her bereavement and terror.

Her brother's corpse was scarcely cold at the bottom of the abyss. She was lost in the trackless wastes—alone, save for this bizarre stranger who had come out of the snows, this man of strange saying, who seemed a demigod of the wilderness.

Could she trust him? She must. She recalled him kneeling in the snow, and the courtierlike grace with which he kissed her hand. A hot flush mounted to her eyes. She dried her tears.

She heard him return to the camp, and heard the barking of the dogs. Once he passed near the hut, but he did not intrude, and she remained within.

Womanlike, she set about the rearrangement of her hair and clothing. When she had finished she crept to the doorway and peeped out. Again her blushes burned her cheeks. She saw the son of the snows crouched above the camp-fire, surrounded by a group of monstrous dogs. He had rubbed his face with oil. A bright blade glittered in his hand. Polaris was *shaving*!

Presently she went out. The young man sprang to his feet, cracking his long whip to restrain the dogs, which would have sprung upon the stranger. They huddled away, their teeth bared, staring at her with glowing eyes. Polaris seized one of them by the scruff of the neck, lifted it bodily from the snow, and swung it in front of the girl.

"Talk to him, lady," he said; "you must be friends. This is Julius."

The girl bent over and fearlessly stroked the brute's head.

"Julius, good dog," she said. At her touch the dog quivered and its hackles rose. Under the caress of her hand it quieted gradually. The bristling hair relaxed, and Julius's tail swung slowly to and fro in an overture of amity. When Polaris loosed him, he sniffed in friendly fashion at the girl's hands, and pushed his great head forward for more caresses.

Then Marcus, the grim leader of the pack, stalked majestically forward for his introduction.

"Ah, you have won Marcus!" cried Polaris. "And Marcus won is a friend indeed. None of them would harm you now." Soon she had learned the name and had the confidence of every dog of the pack, to the great delight of their master.

Among the effects in the camp was a small oil-stove, which Polaris greeted with brightened eyes. "One like that we had, but it was worn out long ago," he said. He lighted the stove and began the preparation of a meal.

She found that he had cleared the camp and put all in order. He had dragged the carcasses of the dead dogs to the other side of the slope and piled them there. His stock of meat was low, and his own dogs would have no qualms if it came to making their own meals of these strangers of their own kind.

The girl produced from the remnants of the camp stores a few handfuls of coffee and an urn. Polaris watched in wonderment as she brewed it over the tiny stove and his nose twitched in reception of its delicious aroma. They drank the steaming beverage, piping hot, from tin cups. In the stinging air of the snowlands even the keenest grief must give way to the pangs of hunger. The girl ate heartily of a meal that in a more moderate climate she would have considered fit only for beasts.

When their supper was completed they sat huddled in their furs at the edge of the fire. Around them were crouched the dogs, watching with eager eyes for any scraps which might fall to their share.

"Now tell me who you are, and how you came here," questioned the girl.

"Lady, my name is Polaris, and I think that I am an American gentleman," he said, and a trace of pride crept into the words of the answer. "I came here from a cabin and a ship that lie burned many leagues to the southward. All my life I have lived there, with but one companion, my father, who now is dead, and who sends me to the north with a message to that world of men that lies beyond the snows, and from which he long was absent."

"A ship—a cabin—" The girl bent toward him in amazement. "And burned? And you have lived—have grown up in this land of snow and ice and bitter cold, where but few things can exist—I don't understand!"

"My father has told me much, but not all. It is all in his message which I have not seen," Polaris answered. "But that which I tell you is truth. He was a seeker after new things. He came here to seek that which no other man had found. He came in a ship with my mother and others. All were dead before I came to knowledge. He had built a cabin from the ruins of the ship, and he lived there until he died."

"And you say that you are an American gentleman?"

"That he told me, lady, although I do not know my name or his, except that he was Stephen, and he called me Polaris."

"And did he never try to get to the north?" asked the girl.

"No. Many years ago, when I was a boy, he fell and was hurt. After that he could do but little. He could not travel."

"And you?"

"I learned to seek food in the wilderness, lady; to battle with its beasts, to wrest that which would sustain our lives from the snows and the wastes."

Much more of his life and of his father he told her under her wondering questioning—a tale most incredible to her ears, but, as he said, the truth. Finally he finished.

"Now, lady, what of you?" he asked. "How came you here, and from where?"

"My name is Rose—"

"Ah, that is the name of a flower," said Polaris. "You were well named."

He did not look at her as he spoke. His eyes were turned to the snow slopes and were very wistful. "I have never seen a flower," he continued slowly, "but my father said that of all created things they were the fairest."

"I have another name," said the girl. "It is Rose—Rose Emer."

"And why did you come here, Rose Emer?" asked Polaris.

"Like your father, I—we were seekers after new things, my brother and I. Both our father and mother died, and left my brother John and myself ridiculously rich. We had to use our money, so we traveled. We have been over most of the world. Then a man—an American gentleman—a very brave man, organized an expedition to come to the south to discover the south pole. My brother and I knew him. We were very much interested in his adventure. We helped him with it. Then John insisted that he would come with the expedition, and—oh, they didn't wish me to come, but I never had been left behind—I came, too."

"And that brave man who came to seek the pole, where is he now?"

"Perhaps he is dead—out there," said the girl, with a catch in her voice. She pointed to the south. "He left the ship and went on, days ago. He was to establish two camps with supplies. He carried an airship with him. He was to make his last dash for the pole through the air from the farther camp. His men were to wait for him until—until they were sure that he would not come back."

"An airship!" Polaris bent forward with sparkling eyes. "So there *are* airships, then! Ah, this man must be brave! How is he called?"

"James Scoland is the name—Captain Scoland."

"He went on whence I came? Did he go by that way?" Polaris pointed where the white tops of the mountain range which he skirted pierced the sky.

"No. He took a course to the east of the mountains, where other explorers of years before had been before him."

"Yes, I have seen maps. Can you tell me where, or nearly where, we are now?" he asked the girl.

"This is Victoria Land," she answered. "We left the ship in a long bay, extending in from Ross Sea, near where the 160th meridian joins the 80th parallel. We are somewhere within three days' journey from the ship."

"And so near to open water?"

She nodded.

Rose Emer slept in the little shelter, with the grim Marcus curled on a robe beside her pallet. Crouched among the dogs in the camp, Polaris slept little. For hours he sat huddled, with his chin on his hands, pondering what the girl had told him. Another man was on his way to the pole—a very brave man—and he might reach it. And then—Polaris must be very wary when he met that man who had won so great a prize.

"Ah, my father," he sighed, "learning is mine through patience. History of the world and of its wars and triumphs and failures, I know. Of its tongues you have taught me, even those of the Roman and the Greek, long since passed away; but how little do I know of the ways of men—and of women! I shall be very careful, my father."

Quite beyond any power of his to control, an antagonism was growing within him for that man whom he had not seen; antagonism that was not all due to the magnitude of the prize which the man might be winning, or might be dying for. Indeed, had he been able to analyze it, that was the least part of it.

When they broke camp for their start they found that the perverse wind, which had rested while they slept, had risen when they would journey, and hissed bitterly across the bleak steppes of snow. Polaris made a place on the sledge for the girl, and urged the pack into the teeth of the gale. All day long they battled ahead in it, bearing left to the west, where was more level pathway, than among the snow dunes.

In an ever increasing blast they came in sight of open water. They halted on a far-stretching field, much broken by huge masses, so snow-covered that it was not possible to know whether they were of rock or ice. Not a quarter of a mile beyond them, the edge of the field was fretted by wind-lashed waves, which extended away to the horizon rim, dotted with tossing icebergs of great height.

Polaris pitched camp in the shelter of a towering cliff, and they made themselves what comfort they could in the stinging cold.

They had slept several hours when the slumbers of Polaris were pierced by a woman's screams, the frenzied howling of the dogs, and the thundering reverberations of grinding and crashing ice cliffs. A dash of spray splashed across his face.

He sprang to his feet in the midst of the leaping pack; as he did so he felt the field beneath him sway and pitch like a hammock. For the first time since he started for the north the Antarctic sun was shining brightly—shining cold and clear on a great disaster!

For they had pitched their camp on an ice floe. Whipped on by the gale, the sea had risen under it, heaved it up and broken it. On a section of the floe several acres in extent their little camp lay, at the very brink of a gash in the ice-field which had cut them off from the land over which they had come.

The water was raging like a millrace through the widening rift between them and the shore. Caught in a swift current and urged by the furious wind, the broken-up floe was drifting, faster and faster—*back to the south*!

## V. BATTLE ON THE FLOE

Helpless, Polaris stood at the brink of the rift, swirling water and tossing ice throwing the spray about him in clouds. Here was opposition against which his naked strength was useless. As if they realized that they were being parted from the firm land, the dogs grouped at the edge of the floe and sent their dismal howls across the raging swirl, only to be drowned by the din of the crashing icebergs.

Turning, Polaris saw Rose Emer. She stood at the doorway of the tent of skins, staring across the wind-swept channel with a blank despair looking from her eyes.

"Ah, all is lost, now!" she gasped.

Then the great spirit of the man rose into spoken words. "No, lady," he called, his voice rising clearly above the shrieking and thundering pandemonium. "We yet have our lives."

As he spoke there was a rending sound at his feet. The dogs sprang back in terror and huddled against the face of the ice cliff. Torn away by the impact of some weightier body beneath, nearly half of the ledge where they stood was split from the main body of the floe, and plunged, heaving and crackling into the current.

Polaris saved himself by a mighty spring. Right in the path of the gash lay the sledge, and it hung balanced at the edge of the ice floe. Down it swung, and would have slipped over, but Polaris saw it going.

He clutched at the ends of the leathern dog-harness as they glided from him across the ice, and, with a tug, into which he put all the power of his splendid muscles, he retrieved the sledge. Hardly had he dragged it to safety when, with another roar of sundered ice, their foothold gaped again and left them but a scanty shelf at the foot of the beetling berg.

"Here we may not stay, lady," said Polaris. He swept the tent and its robes into his arms and piled them on the sledge. Without waiting to harness the dogs, he grasped the leather bands and alone pulled the load along the ledge and around a shoulder of the cliff.

At the other side of the cliff a ridge extended between the berg which they skirted and another towering mountain of ice of similar formation. Beyond the twin bergs lay the level plane of the floe, its edges continually frayed by the attack of the waves and the onset of floating ice.

Along the incline of the ridge were several hollows partially filled with drift snow. Knowing that on the ice cape, in such a tempest, they must soon perish miserably, Polaris made camp in one of these depressions where the deep snow tempered the chill of its foundation.

In the clutch of the churning waters the floe turned slowly like an immense wheel as it drifted in the current. Its course was away from the shore to the southwest, and it gathered speed and momentum with every passing second. The cove from whence it had been torn was already a mere notch in the faraway shore line.

Around them was a scene of wild and compelling beauty. Leagues and leagues of on-rushing water hurled its white-crested squadrons against the precipitous sides of the flotilla of icebergs, tore at the edges of the drifting floes, and threw itself in huge waves across the more level planes, inundating them repeatedly. Clouds of lacelike spray hung in the air after each attack, and cascading torrents returned to the waves.

Above it all the Antarctic sun shone gloriously, splintering its golden spears on the myriad pinnacles, minarets, battlements, and crags of towering masses of crystal that reflected back into the quivering air all the colors of the spectrum. Thinner crests blazed flame-red in the rays. Other points glittered coldly blue. From a thousand lesser scintillating spires the shifting play of the colors, from vermilion to purple, from green to gold, in the lavish magnificence of nature's magic, was torture to the eye that beheld.

On the spine of the ridge stood Polaris, leaning on his long spear and gazing with heightened color and gleaming eyes on those fairy symbols of old mother nature. To the girl who watched him he seemed to complete the picture. In his superb trappings of furs, and surrounded by his shaggy servants, he was at one with his weird and terrible surroundings. She admired—and shuddered.

Presently, when he came down from the ridge, she asked him, with a brave smile, "What, sir, will be the next move?"

"That is in the hands of the great God, if such a one there be," he said. "Whatever it may be, it shall find us ready. Somewhere we must come to shore. When we do—on to the north and the ship, be it half a world away."

"But for food and warmth? We must have those, if we are to go in the flesh."

"Already they are provided for," he replied quickly. He was peering sharply over her shoulder toward the mass of the other berg. With his words the clustered pack set up an angry snarling and baying. She followed his glance and paled.

Lumbering forth from a narrow pass at the extremity of the ridge was a gigantic polar bear. His little eyes glittered wickedly, hungrily, and his long, red tongue crept out and licked his slavering chops. As he came on, with ungainly, padding gait, his head swung ponderously to and fro.

Scarcely had he cleared the pass of his immense bulk when another twitching white muzzle was protruded, and a second beast, in size nearly equal to the first, set foot on the ridge and ambled on to the attack.

Reckless at least of this peril, the dogs would have leaped forward to close with the invaders but their master intervened. The stinging, cracking lash in his hand drove them from the foe. Their overlord, man, elected to make the battle alone.

In two springs he reached the sledge, tore the rifle from its coverings, and was at the side of the girl. He thrust the weapon into her hands.

"Back, lady; back to the sledge!" he cried. "Unless I call, shoot not. If you do shoot, aim for the throat when they rear, and leave the rest to me and the dogs. Many times have I met these enemies, and I know well how to deal with them."

With another crack of the whip over the heads of the snarling pack, he left her and bounded forward, spear in hand and long knife bared.

Awkward of pace and unhurried, the snow kings came on to their feast. In a thought the man chose his ground. Between him and the bears the ridge narrowed so that for a few feet there was footway for but one of the monsters at once.

Polaris ran to where that narrow path began and threw himself on his face on the ice.

At that ruse the foremost bear hesitated. He reared and brushed his muzzle with his formidable crescent-clawed paw. Polaris might have shot then and ended at once the hardest part of his battle. But the man held to a stubborn pride in his own weapons. Both of the beasts he would slay, if he might, as he always had slain. His guns were reserved for dire extremity.

The bear settled to all fours again, and reached out a cautious paw and felt along the path, its claws gouging seams in the ice. Assured that the footing would hold, it crept out on the narrow way, nearer and nearer to the motionless man. Scarce a yard from him it squatted. The steam of its breath beat toward him.

It raised one armed paw to strike. The girl cried out in terror and raised the rifle. The man moved, and she hesitated.

Down came the terrible paw, its curved claws projected and compressed for the blow. It struck only the adamantine ice of the pathway, splintering it. With the down stroke timed to the second, the man had leaped up and forward.

As though set on a steel spring, he vaulted into the air, above the clashing talons and gnashing jaws, and landed light and sure on the back of his ponderous adversary. To pass an arm under the bear's throat, to clip its back with the grip of his legs was the work of a heartbeat's time for Polaris.

With a stifled howl of rage the bear rose to its haunches, and the man rose with it. He gave it no time to turn or settle. Exerting his muscles of steel, he tugged the huge head back. He swung clear from the body of his foe. His feet touched the path and held it. He shot one knee into the back of the bear.

The spear he had dropped when he sprang, but his long knife gleamed in his hand, and he stabbed, once, twice, sending the blade home under the brute's shoulder. He released his grip; spurned the yielding body with his foot, and the huge hulk rolled from the path down the slope, crimsoning the snow with its blood.

Polaris bounded across the narrow ledge and regained his spear. He smiled as there arose from the foot of the slope a hideous clamor that told him that the pack had charged in, as usual, not to be restrained at sight of the kill. He waved his hand to the girl, who stood, statue-like, beside the sledge.

Doubly enraged at its inability to participate in the battle which had been the death of its mate, the smaller bear waited no longer when the path was clear, but rushed madly with lowered head. Strong as he was, the man knew that he could not hope to stay or turn that avalanche of flesh and sinew. As it reached him he sprang aside where the path broadened, lashing out with his keen-edged spear.

His aim was true. Just over one of the small eyes the point of the spear bit deep, and blood followed it. With tigerish agility the man leaped over the beast, striking down as he did so.

The bear reared on its hindquarters and whimpered, brushing at its eyes with its forepaws. Its head gashed so that the flowing blood blinded it, it was beaten. Before it stood its master. Bending back until his body arched like a drawn bow, Polaris poised his spear and thrust home at the broad chest.

A death howl that was echoed back from the crashing cliffs was answer to his stroke. The bear settled forward and sprawled in the snow.

Polaris set his foot on the body of the fallen monster and gazed down at the girl with smiling face.

"Here, lady, are food and warmth for many days," he called.

# The Artist of the Beautiful

by Nathaniel Hawthorne

An elderly man, with his pretty daughter on his arm, was passing along the street, and emerged from the gloom of the cloudy evening into the light that fell across the pavement from the window of a small shop. It was a projecting window; and on the inside were suspended a variety of watches, pinchbeck, silver, and one or two of gold, all with their faces turned from the streets, as if churlishly disinclined to inform the wayfarers what o'clock it was. Seated within the shop, sidelong to the window with his pale face bent earnestly over some delicate piece of mechanism on which was thrown the concentrated lustre of a shade lamp, appeared a young man.

"What can Owen Warland be about?" muttered old Peter Hovenden, himself a retired watchmaker, and the former master of this same young man whose occupation he was now wondering at. "What can the fellow be about? These six months past I have never come by his shop without seeing him just as steadily at work as now. It would be a flight beyond his usual foolery to seek for the perpetual motion; and yet I know enough of my old business to be certain that what he is now so busy with is no part of the machinery of a watch."

"Perhaps, father," said Annie, without showing much interest in the question, "Owen is inventing a new kind of timekeeper. I am sure he has ingenuity enough."

"Poh, child! He has not the sort of ingenuity to invent anything better than a Dutch toy," answered her father, who had formerly been put to much vexation by Owen Warland's irregular genius. "A plague on such ingenuity! All the effect that ever I knew of it was to spoil the accuracy of some of the best watches in my shop. He would turn the sun out of its orbit and derange the whole course of time, if, as I said before, his ingenuity could grasp anything bigger than a child's toy!"

"Hush, father! He hears you!" whispered Annie, pressing the old man's arm. "His ears are as delicate as his feelings; and you know how easily disturbed they are. Do let us move on."

So Peter Hovenden and his daughter Annie plodded on without further conversation, until in a by-street of the town they found themselves passing the open door of a blacksmith's shop. Within was seen the forge, now blazing up and illuminating the high and dusky roof, and now confining its lustre to a narrow precinct of the coal-strewn floor, according as the breath of the bellows was puffed forth or again inhaled into its vast leathern lungs. In the intervals of brightness it was easy to distinguish objects in remote corners of the shop and the horseshoes that hung upon the wall; in the momentary gloom the fire seemed to be glimmering amidst the vagueness of unenclosed space. Moving about in this red glare and alternate dusk was the figure of the blacksmith, well worthy to be viewed in so picturesque an aspect of light and shade, where the bright blaze struggled with the black night, as if each would have snatched his comely strength from the other. Anon he drew a white-hot bar of iron from the coals, laid it on the anvil, uplifted his arm of might, and was soon enveloped in the myriads of sparks which the strokes of his hammer scattered into the surrounding gloom.

"Now, that is a pleasant sight," said the old watchmaker. "I know what it is to work in gold; but give me the worker in iron after all is said and done. He spends his labor upon a reality. What say you, daughter Annie?"

"Pray don't speak so loud, father," whispered Annie, "Robert Danforth will hear you."

"And what if he should hear me?" said Peter Hovenden. "I say again, it is a good and a wholesome thing to depend upon main strength and reality, and to earn one's bread with the bare and brawny arm of a blacksmith. A watchmaker gets his brain puzzled by his wheels within a wheel, or loses his health or the nicety of his eyesight, as was my case, and finds himself at middle age, or a little after, past labor at his own trade and fit for nothing else, yet too poor to live at his ease. So I say once again, give me main strength for my money. And then, how it takes the nonsense out of a man! Did you ever hear of a blacksmith being such a fool as Owen Warland yonder?"

"Well said, uncle Hovenden!" shouted Robert Danforth from the forge, in a full, deep, merry voice, that made the roof re-echo. "And what says Miss Annie to that doctrine? She, I suppose, will think it a genteeler business to tinker up a lady's watch than to forge a horseshoe or make a gridiron."

Annie drew her father onward without giving him time for reply.

But we must return to Owen Warland's shop, and spend more meditation upon his history and character than either Peter Hovenden, or probably his daughter Annie, or Owen's old school-fellow, Robert Danforth, would have thought due to so slight a subject. From the time that his little fingers could grasp a penknife, Owen had been remarkable for a delicate ingenuity, which sometimes produced pretty shapes in wood, principally figures of flowers and birds, and sometimes seemed to aim at the hidden mysteries of mechanism. But it was always for purposes of grace, and never with any mockery of the useful. He did not, like the crowd of school-boy artisans, construct little windmills on the angle of a barn or watermills across the neighboring brook. Those who discovered such peculiarity in the boy as to think it worth their while to observe him closely, sometimes saw reason to suppose that he was attempting to imitate the beautiful movements of Nature as exemplified in the flight of birds or the activity of little animals. It seemed, in fact, a new development of the love of the beautiful, such as might have made him a poet, a painter, or a sculptor, and which was as completely refined from all utilitarian coarseness as it could have been in either of the fine arts. He looked with singular distaste at the stiff and regular processes of ordinary machinery. Being once carried to see a steam-engine, in the expectation that his intuitive comprehension of mechanical principles would be gratified, he turned pale and grew sick, as if something monstrous and unnatural had been presented to him. This horror was partly owing to the size and terrible energy of the iron laborer; for the character of Owen's mind was microscopic, and tended naturally to the minute, in accordance with his diminutive frame and the marvellous smallness and delicate power of his fingers. Not that his sense of beauty was thereby diminished into a sense of prettiness. The beautiful idea has no relation to size, and may be as perfectly developed in a space too minute for any but microscopic investigation as within the ample verge that is measured by the arc of the rainbow. But, at all events, this characteristic minuteness in his objects and accomplishments made the world even more incapable than it might otherwise have been of appreciating Owen Warland's genius. The boy's relatives saw nothing better to be done—as perhaps there was not–than to bind him apprentice to a watchmaker, hoping that his strange ingenuity might thus be regulated and put to utilitarian purposes.

Peter Hovenden's opinion of his apprentice has already been expressed. He could make nothing of the lad. Owen's apprehension of the professional mysteries, it is true, was inconceivably quick; but he altogether forgot or despised the grand object of a watchmaker's business, and cared no more for the measurement of time than if it had been merged into eternity. So long, however, as he remained under his old master's care, Owen's lack of sturdiness made it possible, by strict injunctions and sharp oversight, to restrain his creative eccentricity within bounds; but when his apprenticeship was served out, and he had taken the little shop which Peter Hovenden's failing eyesight compelled him to relinquish, then did people recognize how unfit a person was Owen Warland to lead old blind Father Time along his daily course. One of his most rational projects was to connect a musical operation with the machinery of his watches, so that all the harsh dissonances of life might be rendered tuneful, and each flitting moment fall into the abyss of the past in golden drops of harmony. If a family clock was intrusted to him for repair,—one of those tall, ancient clocks that have grown nearly allied to human nature by measuring out the lifetime of many generations,—he would take upon himself to arrange a dance or funeral procession of figures across its venerable face, representing twelve mirthful or melancholy hours. Several freaks of this kind quite destroyed the young watchmaker's credit with that steady and matter-of-fact class of people who hold the opinion that time is not to be trifled with, whether considered as the medium of advancement and prosperity in this world or preparation for the next. His custom rapidly diminished—a misfortune, however, that was probably reckoned among his better accidents by Owen Warland, who was becoming more and more absorbed in a secret occupation which drew all his science and manual dexterity into itself, and likewise gave full employment to the characteristic tendencies of his genius. This pursuit had already consumed many months.

After the old watchmaker and his pretty daughter had gazed at him out of the obscurity of the street, Owen Warland was seized with a fluttering of the nerves, which made his hand tremble too violently to proceed with such delicate labor as he was now engaged upon.

"It was Annie herself!" murmured he. "I should have known it, by this throbbing of my heart, before I heard her father's voice. Ah, how it throbs! I shall scarcely be able to work again on this exquisite mechanism tonight. Annie! Dearest Annie! Thou shouldst give firmness to my heart and hand, and not shake them thus; for if I strive to put the very spirit of beauty into form and give it motion, it is for thy sake alone. O throbbing heart, be quiet! If my labor be thus thwarted, there will come vague and unsatisfied dreams which will leave me spiritless tomorrow."

As he was endeavoring to settle himself again to his task, the shop door opened and gave admittance to no other than the stalwart figure which Peter Hovenden had paused to admire, as seen amid the light and shadow of the blacksmith's shop. Robert Danforth had brought a little anvil of his own manufacture, and peculiarly constructed, which the young artist had recently bespoken. Owen examined the article and pronounced it fashioned according to his wish.

"Why, yes," said Robert Danforth, his strong voice filling the shop as with the sound of a bass viol, "I consider myself equal to anything in the way of my own trade; though I should have made but a poor figure at yours with such a fist as this," added he, laughing, as he laid his vast hand beside the delicate one of Owen. "But what then? I put more main strength into one blow of my sledge hammer than all that you have expended since you were a 'prentice. Is not that the truth?"

"Very probably," answered the low and slender voice of Owen. "Strength is an earthly monster. I make no pretensions to it. My force, whatever there may be of it, is altogether spiritual."

"Well, but, Owen, what are you about?" asked his old schoolfellow, still in such a hearty volume of tone that it made the artist shrink, especially as the question related to a subject so sacred as the absorbing dream of his imagination. "Folks do say that you are trying to discover the perpetual motion."

"The perpetual motion? Nonsense!" replied Owen Warland, with a movement of disgust; for he was full of little petulances. "It can never be discovered. It is a dream that may delude men whose brains are mystified with matter, but not me. Besides, if such a discovery were possible, it would not be worth my while to make it only to have the secret turned to such purposes as are now effected by steam and water power. I am not ambitious to be honored with the paternity of a new kind of cotton machine."

"That would be droll enough!" cried the blacksmith, breaking out into such an uproar of laughter that Owen himself and the bell glasses on his work-board quivered in unison. "No, no, Owen! No child of yours will have iron joints and sinews. Well, I won't hinder you any more. Good night, Owen, and success, and if you need any assistance, so far as a downright blow of hammer upon anvil will answer the purpose, I'm your man."

And with another laugh the man of main strength left the shop.

"How strange it is," whispered Owen Warland to himself, leaning his head upon his hand, "that all my musings, my purposes, my passion for the beautiful, my consciousness of power to create it,—a finer, more ethereal power, of which this earthly giant can have no conception,—all, all, look so vain and idle whenever my path is crossed by Robert Danforth! He would drive me mad were I to meet him often. His hard, brute force darkens and confuses the spiritual element within me; but I, too, will be strong in my own way. I will not yield to him."

He took from beneath a glass a piece of minute machinery, which he set in the condensed light of his lamp, and, looking intently at it through a magnifying glass, proceeded to operate with a delicate instrument of steel. In an instant, however, he fell back in his chair and clasped his hands, with a look of horror on his face that made its small features as impressive as those of a giant would have been.

"Heaven! What have I done?" exclaimed he. "The vapor, the influence of that brute force,—it has bewildered me and obscured my perception. I have made the very stroke—the fatal stroke—that I have dreaded from the first. It is all over—the toil of months, the object of my life. I am ruined!"

And there he sat, in strange despair, until his lamp flickered in the socket and left the Artist of the Beautiful in darkness.

Thus it is that ideas, which grow up within the imagination and appear so lovely to it and of a value beyond whatever men call valuable, are exposed to be shattered and annihilated by contact with the practical. It is requisite for the ideal artist to possess a force of character that seems hardly compatible with its delicacy; he must keep his faith in himself while the incredulous world assails him with its utter disbelief; he must stand up against mankind and be his own sole disciple, both as respects his genius and the objects to which it is directed.

For a time Owen Warland succumbed to this severe but inevitable test. He spent a few sluggish weeks with his head so continually resting in his hands that the towns-people had scarcely an opportunity to see his countenance. When at last it was again uplifted to the light of day, a cold, dull, nameless change was perceptible upon it. In the opinion of Peter Hovenden, however, and that order of sagacious understandings who think that life should be regulated, like clockwork, with leaden weights, the alteration was entirely for the better. Owen now, indeed, applied himself to business with dogged industry. It was marvellous to witness the obtuse gravity with which he would inspect the wheels of a great old silver watch thereby delighting the owner, in whose fob it had been worn till he deemed it a portion of his own life, and was accordingly jealous of its treatment. In consequence of the good report thus acquired, Owen Warland was invited by the proper authorities to regulate the clock in the church steeple. He succeeded so admirably in this matter of public interest that the merchants gruffly acknowledged his merits on 'Change'; the nurse whispered his praises as she gave the potion in the sick-chamber; the lover blessed him at the hour of appointed interview; and the town in general thanked Owen for the punctuality of dinner time. In a word, the heavy weight upon his spirits kept everything in order, not merely within his own system, but wheresoever the iron accents of the church clock were audible. It was a circumstance, though minute, yet characteristic of his present state, that, when employed to engrave names or initials on silver spoons, he now wrote the requisite letters in the plainest possible style, omitting a variety of fanciful flourishes that had heretofore distinguished his work in this kind.

One day, during the era of this happy transformation, old Peter Hovenden came to visit his former apprentice.

"Well, Owen," said he, "I am glad to hear such good accounts of you from all quarters, and especially from the town clock yonder, which speaks in your commendation every hour of the twenty-four. Only get rid altogether of your nonsensical trash about the beautiful, which I nor nobody else, nor yourself to boot, could ever understand,—only free yourself of that, and your success in life is as sure as daylight. Why, if you go on in this way, I should even venture to let you doctor this precious old watch of mine; though, except my daughter Annie, I have nothing else so valuable in the world."

"I should hardly dare touch it, sir," replied Owen, in a depressed tone; for he was weighed down by his old master's presence.

"In time," said the latter,—"In time, you will be capable of it."

The old watchmaker, with the freedom naturally consequent on his former authority, went on inspecting the work which Owen had in hand at the moment, together with other matters that were in progress. The artist, meanwhile, could scarcely lift his head. There was nothing so antipodal to his nature as this man's cold, unimaginative sagacity, by contact with which everything was converted into a dream except the densest matter of the physical world. Owen groaned in spirit and prayed fervently to be delivered from him.

"But what is this?" cried Peter Hovenden abruptly, taking up a dusty bell glass, beneath which appeared a mechanical something, as delicate and minute as the system of a butterfly's anatomy. "What have we here? Owen! Owen! There is witchcraft in these little chains, and wheels, and paddles. See! With one pinch of my finger and thumb I am going to deliver you from all future peril."

"For Heaven's sake," screamed Owen Warland, springing up with wonderful energy, "as you would not drive me mad, do not touch it! The slightest pressure of your finger would ruin me forever."

"Aha, young man! And is it so?" said the old watchmaker, looking at him with just enough penetration to torture Owen's soul with the bitterness of worldly criticism. "Well, take your own course; but I warn you again that in this small piece of mechanism lives your evil spirit. Shall I exorcise him?"

"You are my evil spirit," answered Owen, much excited,—"you and the hard, coarse world! The leaden thoughts and the despondency that you fling upon me are my clogs, else I should long ago have achieved the task that I was created for."

Peter Hovenden shook his head, with the mixture of contempt and indignation which mankind, of whom he was partly a representative, deem themselves entitled to feel towards all simpletons who seek other prizes than the dusty one along the highway. He then took his leave, with an uplifted finger and a sneer upon his face that haunted the artist's dreams for many a night afterwards. At the time of his old master's visit, Owen was probably on the point of taking up the relinquished task; but, by this sinister event, he was thrown back into the state whence he had been slowly emerging.

But the innate tendency of his soul had only been accumulating fresh vigor during its apparent sluggishness. As the summer advanced he almost totally relinquished his business, and permitted Father

Time, so far as the old gentleman was represented by the clocks and watches under his control, to stray at random through human life, making infinite confusion among the train of bewildered hours. He wasted the sunshine, as people said, in wandering through the woods and fields and along the banks of streams. There, like a child, he found amusement in chasing butterflies or watching the motions of water insects. There was something truly mysterious in the intentness with which he contemplated these living playthings as they sported on the breeze or examined the structure of an imperial insect whom he had imprisoned. The chase of butterflies was an apt emblem of the ideal pursuit in which he had spent so many golden hours; but would the beautiful idea ever be yielded to his hand like the butterfly that symbolized it? Sweet, doubtless, were these days, and congenial to the artist's soul. They were full of bright conceptions, which gleamed through his intellectual world as the butterflies gleamed through the outward atmosphere, and were real to him, for the instant, without the toil, and perplexity, and many disappointments of attempting to make them visible to the sensual eye. Alas that the artist, whether in poetry, or whatever other material, may not content himself with the inward enjoyment of the beautiful, but must chase the flitting mystery beyond the verge of his ethereal domain, and crush its frail being in seizing it with a material grasp. Owen Warland felt the impulse to give external reality to his ideas as irresistibly as any of the poets or painters who have arrayed the world in a dimmer and fainter beauty, imperfectly copied from the richness of their visions.

The night was now his time for the slow progress of re-creating the one idea to which all his intellectual activity referred itself. Always at the approach of dusk he stole into the town, locked himself within his shop, and wrought with patient delicacy of touch for many hours. Sometimes he was startled by the rap of the watchman, who, when all the world should be asleep, had caught the gleam of lamplight through the crevices of Owen Warland's shutters. Daylight, to the morbid sensibility of his mind, seemed to have an intrusiveness that interfered with his pursuits. On cloudy and inclement days, therefore, he sat with his head upon his hands, muffling, as it were, his sensitive brain in a mist of indefinite musings, for it was a relief to escape from the sharp distinctness with which he was compelled to shape out his thoughts during his nightly toil.

From one of these fits of torpor he was aroused by the entrance of Annie Hovenden, who came into the shop with the freedom of a customer, and also with something of the familiarity of a childish friend. She had worn a hole through her silver thimble, and wanted Owen to repair it.

"But I don't know whether you will condescend to such a task," said she, laughing, "now that you are so taken up with the notion of putting spirit into machinery."

"Where did you get that idea, Annie?" said Owen, starting in surprise.

"Oh, out of my own head," answered she, "and from something that I heard you say, long ago, when you were but a boy and I a little child. But come, will you mend this poor thimble of mine?"

"Anything for your sake, Annie," said Owen Warland,—"anything, even were it to work at Robert Danforth's forge."

"And that would be a pretty sight!" retorted Annie, glancing with imperceptible slightness at the artist's small and slender frame. "Well; here is the thimble."

"But that is a strange idea of yours," said Owen, "about the spiritualization of matter."

And then the thought stole into his mind that this young girl possessed the gift to comprehend him better than all the world besides. And what a help and strength would it be to him in his lonely toil if he could gain the sympathy of the only being whom he loved! To persons whose pursuits are insulated from the common business of life—who are either in advance of mankind or apart from it—there often comes a sensation of moral cold that makes the spirit shiver as if it had reached the frozen solitudes around the pole. What the prophet, the poet, the reformer, the criminal, or any other man with human yearnings, but separated from the multitude by a peculiar lot, might feel, poor Owen felt.

"Annie," cried he, growing pale as death at the thought, "how gladly would I tell you the secret of my pursuit! You, methinks, would estimate it rightly. You, I know, would hear it with a reverence that I must not expect from the harsh, material world."

"Would I not? To be sure I would!" replied Annie Hovenden, lightly laughing. "Come; explain to me quickly what is the meaning of this little whirligig, so delicately wrought that it might be a plaything for Queen Mab. See! I will put it in motion."

"Hold!" exclaimed Owen, "hold!"

Annie had but given the slightest possible touch, with the point of a needle, to the same minute portion of complicated machinery which has been more than once mentioned, when the artist seized her by the wrist with a force that made her scream aloud. She was affrighted at the convulsion of intense rage and anguish that writhed across his features. The next instant he let his head sink upon his hands.

"Go, Annie," murmured he; "I have deceived myself, and must suffer for it. I yearned for sympathy, and thought, and fancied, and dreamed that you might give it me; but you lack the talisman, Annie, that should admit you into my secrets. That touch has undone the toil of months and the thought of a lifetime! It was not your fault, Annie; but you have ruined me!"

Poor Owen Warland! He had indeed erred, yet pardonably; for if any human spirit could have sufficiently reverenced the processes so sacred in his eyes, it must have been a woman's. Even Annie Hovenden, possibly might not have disappointed him had she been enlightened by the deep intelligence of love.

The artist spent the ensuing winter in a way that satisfied any persons who had hitherto retained a hopeful opinion of him that he was, in truth, irrevocably doomed to unutility as regarded the world, and to an evil destiny on his own part. The decease of a relative had put him in possession of a small inheritance. Thus freed from the necessity of toil, and having lost the steadfast influence of a great purpose,—great, at least, to him,—he abandoned himself to habits from which it might have been supposed the mere delicacy of his organization would have availed to secure him. But when the ethereal portion of a man of genius is obscured the earthly part assumes an influence the more uncontrollable, because the character is now thrown off the balance to which Providence had so nicely adjusted it, and which, in coarser natures, is adjusted by some other method. Owen Warland made proof of whatever show of bliss may be found in riot. He looked at the world through the golden medium of wine, and contemplated the visions that bubble up so gayly around the brim of the glass, and that people the air with shapes of pleasant madness, which so soon grow ghostly and forlorn. Even when this dismal and inevitable change had taken place, the young man might still have continued to quaff the cup of enchantments, though its vapor did but shroud life in gloom and fill the gloom with spectres that mocked at him. There was a certain irksomeness of spirit, which, being real, and the deepest sensation of which the artist was now conscious, was more intolerable than any fantastic miseries and horrors that the abuse of wine could summon up. In the latter case he could remember, even out of the midst of his trouble, that all was but a delusion; in the former, the heavy anguish was his actual life.

From this perilous state he was redeemed by an incident which more than one person witnessed, but of which the shrewdest could not explain or conjecture the operation on Owen Warland's mind. It was very simple. On a warm afternoon of spring, as the artist sat

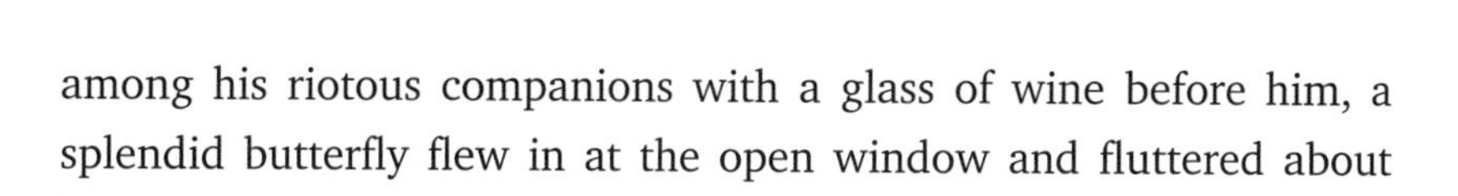


among his riotous companions with a glass of wine before him, a splendid butterfly flew in at the open window and fluttered about his head.

"Ah," exclaimed Owen, who had drank freely, "are you alive again, child of the sun and playmate of the summer breeze, after your dismal winter's nap? Then it is time for me to be at work!"

And, leaving his unemptied glass upon the table, he departed and was never known to sip another drop of wine.

And now, again, he resumed his wanderings in the woods and fields. It might be fancied that the bright butterfly, which had come so spirit-like into the window as Owen sat with the rude revellers, was indeed a spirit commissioned to recall him to the pure, ideal life that had so etheralized him among men. It might be fancied that he went forth to seek this spirit in its sunny haunts; for still, as in the summer time gone by, he was seen to steal gently up wherever a butterfly had alighted, and lose himself in contemplation of it. When it took flight his eyes followed the winged vision, as if its airy track would show the path to heaven. But what could be the purpose of the unseasonable toil, which was again resumed, as the watchman knew by the lines of lamplight through the crevices of Owen Warland's shutters? The towns-people had one comprehensive explanation of all these singularities. Owen Warland had gone mad! How universally efficacious–how satisfactory, too, and soothing to the injured sensibility of narrowness and dulness–is this easy method of accounting for whatever lies beyond the world's most ordinary scope! From St. Paul's days down to our poor little Artist of the Beautiful, the same talisman had been applied to the elucidation of all mysteries in the words or deeds of men who spoke or acted too wisely or too well. In Owen Warland's case the judgment of his towns-people may have been correct. Perhaps he was mad. The lack of sympathy–that contrast between himself and his neighbors which took away the restraint of example–was enough to make him so. Or possibly he had caught just so much of ethereal radiance as served to bewilder him, in an earthly sense, by its intermixture with the common daylight.

One evening, when the artist had returned from a customary ramble and had just thrown the lustre of his lamp on the delicate piece of work so often interrupted, but still taken up again, as if his fate were embodied in its mechanism, he was surprised by the entrance of old Peter Hovenden. Owen never met this man without a shrinking of the heart. Of all the world he was most terrible, by reason of a keen understanding which saw so distinctly what it did see, and disbelieved so uncompromisingly in what it could not see. On this occasion the old watchmaker had merely a gracious word or two to say.

"Owen, my lad," said he, "we must see you at my house tomorrow night."

The artist began to mutter some excuse.

"Oh, but it must be so," quoth Peter Hovenden, "for the sake of the days when you were one of the household. What, my boy! Don't you know that my daughter Annie is engaged to Robert Danforth? We are making an entertainment, in our humble way, to celebrate the event."

That little monosyllable was all he uttered; its tone seemed cold and unconcerned to an ear like Peter Hovenden's; and yet there was in it the stifled outcry of the poor artist's heart, which he compressed within him like a man holding down an evil spirit. One slight outbreak. However, imperceptible to the old watchmaker, he allowed himself. Raising the instrument with which he was about to begin his work, he let it fall upon the little system of machinery that had, anew, cost him months of thought and toil. It was shattered by the stroke!

Owen Warland's story would have been no tolerable representation of the troubled life of those who strive to create the beautiful, if, amid all other thwarting influences, love had not interposed to steal the cunning from his hand. Outwardly he had been no ardent or enterprising lover; the career of his passion had confined its tumults and vicissitudes so entirely within the artist's imagination that Annie herself had scarcely more than a woman's intuitive perception of it; but, in Owen's view, it covered the whole field of his life. Forgetful of the time when she had shown herself incapable of any deep response, he had persisted in connecting all his dreams of artistical success with Annie's image; she was the visible shape in which the spiritual power that he worshipped, and on whose altar he hoped to lay a not unworthy offering, was made manifest to him. Of course he had deceived himself; there were no such attributes in Annie Hovenden as his imagination had endowed her with. She, in the aspect which she wore to his inward vision, was as much a creature of his own as the mysterious piece of mechanism would be were it ever realized. Had he become convinced of his mistake through the medium of successful love,—had he won Annie to his bosom, and there beheld her fade from angel into ordinary woman,—the disappointment might have driven him back, with concentrated energy, upon his sole remaining object. On the other hand, had he found Annie what he fancied, his lot would have been so rich in beauty that out of its mere redundancy he might have wrought the beautiful into many a worthier type than he had toiled for; but the guise in which his sorrow came to him, the sense that the angel of his life had been snatched away and given to a rude man of earth and iron, who could neither need nor appreciate her ministrations,—this was the very perversity of fate that makes human existence appear too absurd and contradictory to be the scene of one other hope or one other fear. There was nothing left for Owen Warland but to sit down like a man that had been stunned.

He went through a fit of illness. After his recovery his small and slender frame assumed an obtuser garniture of flesh than it had ever before worn. His thin cheeks became round; his delicate little hand, so spiritually fashioned to achieve fairy task-work, grew plumper than the hand of a thriving infant. His aspect had a childishness such as might have induced a stranger to pat him on the head–pausing, however, in the act, to wonder what manner of child was here. It was as if the spirit had gone out of him, leaving the body to flourish in a sort of vegetable existence. Not that Owen Warland was idiotic. He could talk, and not irrationally. Somewhat of a babbler, indeed, did people begin to think him; for he was apt to discourse at wearisome length of marvels of mechanism that he had read about in books, but which he had learned to consider as absolutely fabulous. Among them he enumerated the Man of Brass, constructed by Albertus Magnus, and the Brazen Head of Friar Bacon; and, coming down to later times, the automata of a little coach and horses, which it was pretended had been manufactured for the Dauphin of France; together with an insect that buzzed about the ear like a living fly, and yet was but a contrivance of minute steel springs. There was a story, too, of a duck that waddled, and quacked, and ate; though, had any honest citizen purchased it for dinner, he would have found himself cheated with the mere mechanical apparition of a duck.

"But all these accounts," said Owen Warland, "I am now satisfied are mere impositions."

Then, in a mysterious way, he would confess that he once thought differently. In his idle and dreamy days he had considered it possible, in a certain sense, to spiritualize machinery, and to combine with the new species of life and motion thus produced a beauty that should attain to the ideal which Nature has proposed to herself in all her creatures, but has never taken pains to realize. He seemed, however, to retain no very distinct perception either of the process of achieving this object or of the design itself.

"I have thrown it all aside now," he would say. "It was a dream such as young men are always mystifying themselves with. Now

that I have acquired a little common sense, it makes me laugh to think of it."

Poor, poor and fallen Owen Warland! These were the symptoms that he had ceased to be an inhabitant of the better sphere that lies unseen around us. He had lost his faith in the invisible, and now prided himself, as such unfortunates invariably do, in the wisdom which rejected much that even his eye could see, and trusted confidently in nothing but what his hand could touch. This is the calamity of men whose spiritual part dies out of them and leaves the grosser understanding to assimilate them more and more to the things of which alone it can take cognizance; but in Owen Warland the spirit was not dead nor passed away; it only slept.

How it awoke again is not recorded. Perhaps the torpid slumber was broken by a convulsive pain. Perhaps, as in a former instance, the butterfly came and hovered about his head and reinspired him,—as indeed this creature of the sunshine had always a mysterious mission for the artist,—reinspired him with the former purpose of his life. Whether it were pain or happiness that thrilled through his veins, his first impulse was to thank Heaven for rendering him again the being of thought, imagination, and keenest sensibility that he had long ceased to be.

"Now for my task," said he. "Never did I feel such strength for it as now."

Yet, strong as he felt himself, he was incited to toil the more diligently by an anxiety lest death should surprise him in the midst of his labors. This anxiety, perhaps, is common to all men who set their hearts upon anything so high, in their own view of it, that life becomes of importance only as conditional to its accomplishment. So long as we love life for itself, we seldom dread the losing it. When we desire life for the attainment of an object, we recognize the frailty of its texture. But, side by side with this sense of insecurity, there is a vital faith in our invulnerability to the shaft of death while engaged in any task that seems assigned by Providence as our proper thing to do, and which the world would have cause to mourn for should we leave it unaccomplished. Can the philosopher, big with the inspiration of an idea that is to reform mankind, believe that he is to be beckoned from this sensible existence at the very instant when he is mustering his breath to speak the word of light? Should he perish so, the weary ages may pass away—the world's, whose life sand may fall, drop by drop—before another intellect is prepared to develop the truth that might have been uttered then. But history affords many an example where the most precious spirit, at any particular epoch manifested in human shape, has gone hence untimely, without space allowed him, so far as mortal judgment could discern, to perform his mission on the earth. The prophet dies, and the man of torpid heart and sluggish brain lives on. The poet leaves his song half sung, or finishes it, beyond the scope of mortal ears, in a celestial choir. The painter—as Allston did—leaves half his conception on the canvas to sadden us with its imperfect beauty, and goes to picture forth the whole, if it be no irreverence to say so, in the hues of heaven. But rather such incomplete designs of this life will be perfected nowhere. This so frequent abortion of man's dearest projects must be taken as a proof that the deeds of earth, however etherealized by piety or genius, are without value, except as exercises and manifestations of the spirit. In heaven, all ordinary thought is higher and more melodious than Milton's song. Then, would he add another verse to any strain that he had left unfinished here?

But to return to Owen Warland. It was his fortune, good or ill, to achieve the purpose of his life. Pass we over a long space of intense thought, yearning effort, minute toil, and wasting anxiety, succeeded by an instant of solitary triumph: let all this be imagined; and then behold the artist, on a winter evening, seeking admittance to Robert Danforth's fireside circle. There he found the man of iron, with his massive substance thoroughly warmed and attempered by domestic influences. And there was Annie, too, now transformed into a matron, with much of her husband's plain and sturdy nature, but imbued, as Owen Warland still believed, with a finer grace, that might enable her to be the interpreter between strength and beauty. It happened, likewise, that old Peter Hovenden was a guest this evening at his daughter's fireside, and it was his well-remembered expression of keen, cold criticism that first encountered the artist's glance.

"My old friend Owen!" cried Robert Danforth, starting up, and compressing the artist's delicate fingers within a hand that was accustomed to gripe bars of iron. "This is kind and neighborly to come to us at last. I was afraid your perpetual motion had bewitched you out of the remembrance of old times."

"We are glad to see you," said Annie, while a blush reddened her matronly cheek. "It was not like a friend to stay from us so long."

"Well, Owen," inquired the old watchmaker, as his first greeting, "how comes on the beautiful? Have you created it at last?"

The artist did not immediately reply, being startled by the apparition of a young child of strength that was tumbling about on the carpet,—a little personage who had come mysteriously out of the infinite, but with something so sturdy and real in his composition that he seemed moulded out of the densest substance which earth could supply. This hopeful infant crawled towards the newcomer, and setting himself on end, as Robert Danforth expressed the posture, stared at Owen with a look of such sagacious observation that the mother could not help exchanging a proud glance with her husband. But the artist was disturbed by the child's look, as imagining a resemblance between it and Peter Hovenden's habitual expression. He could have fancied that the old watchmaker was compressed into this baby shape, and looking out of those baby eyes, and repeating, as he now did, the malicious question: "The beautiful,

Owen! How comes on the beautiful? Have you succeeded in creating the beautiful?"

"I have succeeded," replied the artist, with a momentary light of triumph in his eyes and a smile of sunshine, yet steeped in such depth of thought that it was almost sadness. "Yes, my friends, it is the truth. I have succeeded."

"Indeed!" cried Annie, a look of maiden mirthfulness peeping out of her face again. "And is it lawful, now, to inquire what the secret is?"

"Surely; it is to disclose it that I have come," answered Owen Warland. "You shall know, and see, and touch, and possess the secret! For, Annie,—if by that name I may still address the friend of my boyish years,—Annie, it is for your bridal gift that I have wrought this spiritualized mechanism, this harmony of motion, this mystery of beauty. It comes late, indeed; but it is as we go onward in life, when objects begin to lose their freshness of hue and our souls their delicacy of perception, that the spirit of beauty is most needed. If,—forgive me, Annie,—if you know how to value this gift, it can never come too late."

He produced, as he spoke, what seemed a jewel box. It was carved richly out of ebony by his own hand, and inlaid with a fanciful tracery of pearl, representing a boy in pursuit of a butterfly, which, elsewhere, had become a winged spirit, and was flying heavenward; while the boy, or youth, had found such efficacy in his strong desire that he ascended from earth to cloud, and from cloud to celestial atmosphere, to win the beautiful. This case of ebony the artist opened, and bade Annie place her fingers on its edge. She did so, but almost screamed as a butterfly fluttered forth, and, alighting on her finger's tip, sat waving the ample magnificence of its purple and gold-speckled wings, as if in prelude to a flight. It is impossible to express by words the glory, the splendor, the delicate gorgeousness which were softened into the beauty of this object. Nature's ideal butterfly was here realized in all its perfection; not in the pattern of such faded insects as flit among earthly flowers, but of those which hover across the meads of paradise for child-angels and the spirits of departed infants to disport themselves with. The rich down was visible upon its wings; the lustre of its eyes seemed instinct with spirit. The firelight glimmered around this wonder–the candles gleamed upon it; but it glistened apparently by its own radiance, and illuminated the finger and outstretched hand on which it rested with a white gleam like that of precious stones. In its perfect beauty, the consideration of size was entirely lost. Had its wings overreached the firmament, the mind could not have been more filled or satisfied.

"Beautiful! Beautiful!" exclaimed Annie. "Is it alive? Is it alive?"

"Alive? To be sure it is," answered her husband. "Do you suppose any mortal has skill enough to make a butterfly, or would put himself to the trouble of making one, when any child may catch a score of them in a summer's afternoon? Alive? Certainly! But this pretty box is undoubtedly of our friend Owen's manufacture; and really it does him credit."

At this moment the butterfly waved its wings anew, with a motion so absolutely lifelike that Annie was startled, and even awestricken; for, in spite of her husband's opinion, she could not satisfy herself whether it was indeed a living creature or a piece of wondrous mechanism.

"Is it alive?" she repeated, more earnestly than before.

"Judge for yourself," said Owen Warland, who stood gazing in her face with fixed attention.

The butterfly now flung itself upon the air, fluttered round Annie's head, and soared into a distant region of the parlor, still making itself perceptible to sight by the starry gleam in which the motion of its wings enveloped it. The infant on the floor followed its course with his sagacious little eyes. After flying about the room, it returned in a spiral curve and settled again on Annie's finger.

"But is it alive?" exclaimed she again; and the finger on which the gorgeous mystery had alighted was so tremulous that the butterfly was forced to balance himself with his wings. "Tell me if it be alive, or whether you created it."

"Wherefore ask who created it, so it be beautiful?" replied Owen Warland. "Alive? Yes, Annie; it may well be said to possess life, for it has absorbed my own being into itself; and in the secret of that butterfly, and in its beauty,—which is not merely outward, but deep as its whole system,—is represented the intellect, the imagination, the sensibility, the soul of an Artist of the Beautiful! Yes; I created it. But"–and here his countenance somewhat changed—"this butterfly is not now to me what it was when I beheld it afar off in the daydreams of my youth."

"Be it what it may, it is a pretty plaything," said the blacksmith, grinning with childlike delight. "I wonder whether it would condescend to alight on such a great clumsy finger as mine? Hold it hither, Annie."

By the artist's direction, Annie touched her finger's tip to that of her husband; and, after a momentary delay, the butterfly fluttered from one to the other. It preluded a second flight by a similar, yet not precisely the same, waving of wings as in the first experiment; then, ascending from the blacksmith's stalwart finger, it rose in a gradually enlarging curve to the ceiling, made one wide sweep around the room, and returned with an undulating movement to the point whence it had started.

"Well, that does beat all nature!" cried Robert Danforth, bestowing the heartiest praise that he could find expression for; and, indeed, had he paused there, a man of finer words and nicer perception could not easily have said more. "That goes beyond me, I confess. But what then? There is more real use in one downright blow of my sledge hammer than in the whole five years' labor that our friend Owen has wasted on this butterfly."

Here the child clapped his hands and made a great babble of indistinct utterance, apparently demanding that the butterfly should be given him for a plaything.

Owen Warland, meanwhile, glanced sidelong at Annie, to discover whether she sympathized in her husband's estimate of the comparative value of the beautiful and the practical. There was, amid all her kindness towards himself, amid all the wonder and admiration with which she contemplated the marvellous work of his hands and incarnation of his idea, a secret scorn—too secret, perhaps, for her own consciousness, and perceptible only to such intuitive discernment as that of the artist. But Owen, in the latter stages of his pursuit, had risen out of the region in which such a discovery might have been torture. He knew that the world, and Annie as the representative of the world, whatever praise might be bestowed, could never say the fitting word nor feel the fitting sentiment which should be the perfect recompense of an artist who, symbolizing a lofty moral by a material trifle,—converting what was earthly to spiritual gold,—had won the beautiful into his handiwork. Not at this latest moment was he to learn that the reward of all high performance must be sought within itself, or sought in vain. There was, however, a view of the matter which Annie and her husband, and even Peter Hovenden, might fully have understood, and which would have satisfied them that the toil of years had here been worthily bestowed. Owen Warland might have told them that this butterfly, this plaything, this bridal gift of a poor watchmaker to a blacksmith's wife, was, in truth, a gem of art that a monarch would have purchased with honors and abundant wealth, and have treasured it among the jewels of his kingdom as the most unique and wondrous of them all. But the artist smiled and kept the secret to himself.

"Father," said Annie, thinking that a word of praise from the old watchmaker might gratify his former apprentice, "do come and admire this pretty butterfly."

"Let us see," said Peter Hovenden, rising from his chair, with a sneer upon his face that always made people doubt, as he himself did, in everything but a material existence. "Here is my finger for it to alight upon. I shall understand it better when once I have touched it."

But, to the increased astonishment of Annie, when the tip of her father's finger was pressed against that of her husband, on which the butterfly still rested, the insect drooped its wings and seemed on the point of falling to the floor. Even the bright spots of gold upon its wings and body, unless her eyes deceived her, grew dim, and the glowing purple took a dusky hue, and the starry lustre that gleamed around the blacksmith's hand became faint and vanished.

"It is dying! It is dying!" cried Annie, in alarm.

"It has been delicately wrought," said the artist, calmly. "As I told you, it has imbibed a spiritual essence–call it magnetism, or what you will. In an atmosphere of doubt and mockery its exquisite susceptibility suffers torture, as does the soul of him who instilled his own life into it. It has already lost its beauty; in a few moments more its mechanism would be irreparably injured."

"Take away your hand, father!" entreated Annie, turning pale. "Here is my child; let it rest on his innocent hand. There, perhaps, its life will revive and its colors grow brighter than ever."

Her father, with an acrid smile, withdrew his finger. The butterfly then appeared to recover the power of voluntary motion, while its hues assumed much of their original lustre, and the gleam of star-light, which was its most ethereal attribute, again formed a halo round about it. At first, when transferred from Robert Danforth's hand to the small finger of the child, this radiance grew so powerful that it positively threw the little fellow's shadow back against the wall. He, meanwhile, extended his plump hand as he had seen his father and mother do, and watched the waving of the insect's wings with infantine delight. Nevertheless, there was a certain odd expression of sagacity that made Owen Warland feel as if here were old Pete Hovenden, partially, and but partially, redeemed from his hard scepticism into childish faith.

"How wise the little monkey looks!" whispered Robert Danforth to his wife.

"I never saw such a look on a child's face," answered Annie, admiring her own infant, and with good reason, far more than the artistic butterfly. "The darling knows more of the mystery than we do."

As if the butterfly, like the artist, were conscious of something not entirely congenial in the child's nature, it alternately sparkled and grew dim. At length it arose from the small hand of the infant with an airy motion that seemed to bear it upward without an effort, as if the ethereal instincts with which its master's spirit had endowed it impelled this fair vision involuntarily to a higher sphere. Had there been no obstruction, it might have soared into the sky and grown immortal. But its lustre gleamed upon the ceiling; the exquisite texture of its wings brushed against that earthly medium; and a sparkle or two, as of stardust, floated downward and lay glimmering on the carpet. Then the butterfly came fluttering down, and, instead of returning to the infant, was apparently attracted towards the artist's hand.

"Not so! Not so!" murmured Owen Warland, as if his handiwork could have understood him. "Thou has gone forth out of thy master's heart. There is no return for thee."

With a wavering movement, and emitting a tremulous radiance, the butterfly struggled, as it were, towards the infant, and was about to alight upon his finger; but while it still hovered in the air, the little child of strength, with his grandsire's sharp and shrewd expression in his face, made a snatch at the marvellous insect and compressed it in his hand. Annie screamed. Old Peter Hovenden burst into a cold and scornful laugh. The blacksmith, by main force, unclosed the infant's hand, and found within the palm a small heap of glittering fragments, whence the mystery of beauty had fled forever. And as for Owen Warland, he looked placidly at what seemed the ruin of his life's labor, and which was yet no ruin. He had caught a far other butterfly than this. When the artist rose high enough to achieve the beautiful, the symbol by which he made it perceptible to mortal senses became of little value in his eyes while his spirit possessed itself in the enjoyment of the reality.

# The Darwinian Schooner

by W. L. Alden

"You're quite right, sir!" said the mate. "As you say, a man can't follow the sea for twenty or thirty years without meeting with a good many things that he can't explain, and that no living landsman will believe if you waste your time telling him about them. Once I came across a schooner that was manned by monkeys. There wasn't a soul aboard her except monkeys, from the captain down to the Jemmy Ducks, and those monkeys had fitted out that there schooner and gone a piratin' in her. What's the good of my telling that to any man ashore? I don't believe there's a man, except he's a sailorman, who would believe it if I took my Bible oath of it. And yet I saw that schooner with my own identical eyes, and what's more, I was aboard of her in company of those monkeys for eight mortal days, so I know what I'm talking about."

"It happened about ten years ago, or may be twelve—I don't keep any private log-book, and I can't always remember when—just when —anything did happen. However, I was second mate at the time of a brig—the *Jane G. Mather*—bound from London to Ryo Jenneero with a general cargo. The captain's name was Simmons – 'Old Bill Simmons' we used to call him, seeing as he has a younger brother, Jim Simmons, in the Mediterranean trade. He wasn't a bad sort, and the brig was a middling comfortable craft, barring that she was so overrun with rats that you couldn't turn in at night without battening down your blankets over your face to keep them from trimming your nose down to what was their idea of a ship-shape nose. We were strong-handed, having eighteen men all told before the mast, besides two mates and a bosen.

"We made a good run as far as the Line, and then we had baffling light winds and calms for the next three weeks. We were in about five degrees south, and Cape Saint Roque beating five hundred miles west, when we sighted this schooner that I'm telling you about. I came on deck that morning at eight o'clock, and the first thing I saw was a schooner under full sail about a mile windward of us, there being at the time a light breeze from the south, and not much more than enough to keep steerage way on the brig. The schooner was acting in a very curious sort of way. Her sheets were hauled flat aft, and every little while she'd come up in the wind and shake for a minute, and then she'd pay off on the other tack. Sometimes she'd lie close to the wind, and then again she'd fall off till she had the wind nearly on her quarter."

"'Either she's lost her rudder, or all hands have gone to breakfast and left her to shift for herself,' said I to the mate, after looking at the schooner for a little while."

"'She's deserted, that's what she is,' said the mate. 'We sighted her at daybreak this morning, and I've been watching her pretty close. There ain't a soul aboard her, according to my idea. Well! I'll turn in now, and I expect she'll run into us before eight bells if he don't keep a sharp lookout.'"

"About two hours later the captain came on deck, and I could see that he took a good deal of interest in the schooner. The breeze had died out by this time, and there wasn't hardly breath enough to fill the schooner's sails. She lay not half a mile from us, and we could hear her booms creak as she rolled with the swell that was setting in from the eastward. It was clear enough that she wasn't deserted, for we could see a lot of niggers, as we supposed, moving about her decks, though there was nobody at the wheel. All at once the old man says, 'Mr. Samuels! We'll board that schooner and see what is the matter with her. Take the port quarter boat and four men, and find out what she means by yawing all over the South Atlantic. Tell the captain that this ain't no Ratcliff Highway, nor no Playhouse Square, and a decent schooner ain't no right to be staggering drunk at this time of day.'"

"Old Bill was always fond of his joke. Once he towed the cook overboard for fifteen minutes, because he put too much salt in the grub. You see he thought the man would get enough salt in his system while he was soaking astern of us to make him remember to use less of it in his cooking. But it didn't seem to do no good, and it pretty nearly drowned the cook."

"Well, I sung out for the men to clear away the boat, and then we pulled over to the schooner. When we came close to her I saw that she hadn't any name on her stern nor anywhere else, and that what we had taken to be niggers were nothing less than big monkeys—baboons was their correct rating, I believe. Nobody had the manner to heave us a line, but we had no trouble in boarding the schooner. The monkeys were crowded together, watching us over the rail, but keeping as grave and quiet as a lot of man-of-war's men. On the quarter deck, all alone by himself, was an old white-haired monkey, that we took to be the captain, as he afterwards proved to be. He was sitting on the skylight, and was a great sight too dignified to be seen watching us."

"We made the boat fast and all hands of us climbed aboard the schooner. The monkeys fell back quite respectfully as we came aboard, and I could see that they were a pretty dispirited-looking lot. The deck was all in a litter, and there was nobody at the wheel or at the look-out. At first I didn't understand that the schooner was manned entirely by monkeys, so I went straight into the cabin to see if there were any signs of white men, or even niggers aboard her. The cabin was as neglected as the deck, and there wasn't a soul below. So I came on deck again, and after telling one of the men to have a look in the fokesell, to see if there was anybody there, I went up to the old white-haired monkey and says,—"

"'We came aboard to see if you wanted anything. If so be as you are the captain of this schooner, perhaps you'll tell me if you need a navigator, or a carpenter, or anything of the sort?'"

"The monkey didn't say a word, but he bowed as polite as if he was a Frenchman. Meanwhile the other monkeys had gathered in a circle around us, and were whining in a mournful sort of way. Just then the men who had searched the fokesell came up and said that there wasn't a soul aboard of her except the monkeys, and that they were half dead of thirst. There were a couple of full water casks on deck, beside one that was empty. When the monkeys saw that I was going to knock the bung out of a cask they went wild with joy, and even the old white-haired chap condescended to follow me, though he didn't chatter, and didn't show any especial interest in having the cask breached. You should have seen those monkeys go for that water! The poor beasts must have been days without a drop, and not one of them had sense enough to knock the bung out, though they knew the casks were full of water. There were provisions enough aboard the schooner, for I had seen a bread barge more than half full of good pilot bread in the cabin, and I knew that there must be plenty more where that came from."

"'I'm thinking, sir,' said one of the men to me, 'that this hyer'll be a salvage case.'"

"'Right you are,' said I—'that is, if the captain takes that view of it. We'll go back to the brig and report now, and if it be so that he wants this schooner to be carried into Ryo, there won't be much difficulty about doing it. You see the man—'Liverpool Dick' was his name—had been in two or three ships with me, and was as good a man as they make. So I could talk a little freer with him than a second mate can generally talk with the men."

"When I told old Bill Simmons that the schooner was deserted except for monkeys, and that she was in first-rate condition, provided he wanted to carry her into port, he said that if I wanted to take six hands and navigate her into Ryo I could do so."

"'Enough said,' said I. 'I'll get my sextant and dunnage and be aboard the schooner before a breeze comes up. I suppose you won't mind letting me have Liverpool Dick? He'll make a good enough mate for me.'"

"'Certainly,' says Old Bill. 'You'll probably beat us into Ryo, and we'll pick you up there. However, you'll have just to shove the schooner along, for if we do get there first I can't wait for you, and I'll have to ship another second-mate and half a dozen men. You know what owners are yourself. They can take a moderate-sized lie alongside sometimes, but it's a mighty hard job to get 'em to histe it in.'"

"It didn't take me very long to get back aboard the schooner. I had Liverpool Dick with me, and three middling good men, and three Rainecks that Old Bill was glad to get rid of. We all turned to and cleaned the decks up, and the breeze gradually freshened from the eastward, we slipped on our course and by night we had clean dropped the *Jane G. Mather*. Dick and I chose watches. I gave him three men, and I took two, and the odd man was put in the caboose and told to cook, though he swore he had never cooked so much as an egg since he was born. We managed to get some sort of supper about six o'clock, and the first watch on deck falling to Dick, I turned in feeling pretty comfortable."

"The monkeys hadn't said a word since we took charge of her. They saw what we meant as soon as we came on board, and they turned out on the fokesell and left it to the men of their own accord, which showed that they knew the difference between sailors and monkeys. The old white-haired chap that was in command of them bunked by himself in the lee of the caboose, and the rest of them curled up under the weather rail about amidships, and were as quiet as you could wish. They all came aft at eight bells, so the mate told me, as much as to say that they were waiting for orders; but, getting none, they went to sleep again by the time I came on deck."

"The next day, the breeze holding fair, and there being nothing to do except to let her go along comfortable, I overhauled the whole schooner, searching for her papers, and not finding them. Dick and I talked about it, and I made up my mind that she has been carrying a cargo of monkeys – for she had little else in her except ballast—and that her people had got panic-struck about something and had deserted her. I found one or two things curious though. She had a big rifled gun lying down on the ballast, and about fifty breech-loading rifles stowed away here and there, where nobody would be likely to see them. Then she had two boats, and it didn't seem likely that a schooner of her size would carry more than two. If so, how did her people get away from her without a boat? I couldn't understand it, and no more could Dick."

"The monkeys behaved well for the first two days. They were always on hand for their grub, which we served out to them regular; and they never grumbled—at least, not so far as we could understand. The old monkey captain would now and then come and walk the quarter deck with me, never venturing any remarks, but just meaning, as I supposed, to show that there was no hard feeling. But the third day, Dick comes to me and says, 'It's my opinion, sir, that there's mischief brewing among them chaps.'"

"'Why so?' says I."

"'Well,' says he, 'they have been doing a lot of talking on the quiet among themselves, and the old man's got something on his mind, for he's altogether too bloomin' sweet-tempered this morning. He's laid into two or three of his people with a rope's end, and then he's been walking the deck with me, and bowing and grinning as much as to say that he considers me as much his superior as if I was a

post-captain in the royal navy. I advise you to keep your weather eye liftin' while you're on deck tonight.'"

"'Why, what do you suppose they mean to do?' I asked."

"'What are they here for? Tell me that,' says Dick. 'This schooner wasn't never deserted with no crew. She sailed out of port with nobody but these 'ere monkeys aboard. That's my explanation of the thing.'"

"'Where were they bound to?' asks I. 'And what did they go to sea for?'"

"'They were going a-pirating, that's what they were doing,' says Dick. 'That's why she ain't got no name; that's why there ain't no papers of no kind aboard her; that's why she's in ballast; that's why she's got that big gun aboard, and all them rifles; that's why she's so strong-handed. Why, what do you think the old man dropped last night while he was a-calking in the lee of the caboose. He dropped this hyer knife, sir; and when a monkey takes to carrying a knife like that he means business, and you can just lay your last mag on that.'"

"It was a long clasp knife, with a sharp blade, made for stabbing and for nothing else. I didn't like the look of the thing; but I told Dick that his notion about the schooner having sailed with nobody aboard her but monkeys was rubbish. 'You saw for yourself,' said I, 'that they couldn't sail the schooner.'"

"'I saw that they didn't want to sail her for some reason or other,' says he. 'As to their not being able for to sail her, I have my doubts. Early this morning the man on the look-out went to sleep, and one of those monkeys, maybe the old man himself, went forrard and trimmed in the head sheets. The wind hand hauled round till, as you see now, it is pretty near abeam of us.'"

"'If they knew that much,' said I, 'we'll turn 'em all to, and make 'em do the rest of the work on this voyage.'"

"'Well, you'll see, sir,' said Dick, 'there's something in the wind, and we'll know what it is before long. I'm going to speak pretty plainly to the old man – that is, if you don't have no objection.'"

"'None in the world,' says I. 'You might ask him where his papers are, and perhaps he'll tell you.'"

"The next day Dick told me that he had had a long conversation with the monkey captain, and told him we had our suspicions of him."

"'It stands to reason,' said Dick to the monkey captain, 'that you don't like to have the command took away from you; but it was done for your own good. You're a passenger now, and all you've got to do is to conduct yourself as such. There's been altogether too much chin going on among the lot of you lately, and you'd better put a stopper on it just where you are. You needn't hope to catch us napping, and if you try any mutinous games you're bound to get the worst of it. Do you savey that now?'"

"The monkey grinned and bowed, swearing, as you might say, that he never had no intentions of no kind; and then he went forrard and took it out in cussin' his own people, as was quite right and natural."

"That very night, some time in the middle watch, I woke up, being in my bunk, and, being a very light sleeper, I heard someone moving in the cabin; and thinking that one of the men might be trying to steal one of my rum bottles – for there was a dozen of heavenly rum in the pantry – I slipped out and had a look. The lamp was burning, and there was the monkey captain stealing out of the cabin with a big chart, that I had marked her position on, under his arm. I sung out to him, and he dropped the chart, and took to smiling and ducking as respectful as you please."

"'I won't have none of this,' I said to him. 'You go forrard where you belong, and the next time I catch you here into irons you go.'"

"He didn't say anything, but he looked pretty mad, and slunk away without doing any more bowing."

"I told Dick of the affair when I relieved him at eight bells, and asked him what he made of it."

"'It's plain enough,' said he. 'Those fellows mean to seize this hyer schooner, and the old man wanted to know just what our position is. Have you got a pistol with you, sir?'"

"I told him I hadn't."

"'Then,' said he, 'my advice is that you load half a dozen of them rifles, and keep 'em where we can lay our hands to 'em if they're wanted. Those chaps mean bloody mutiny, and they'll begin before very long.'"

"I didn't much like the look of the thing myself. What did that monkey want with the chart? I told myself that, being a natural thief like all his sort, he just stole the first thing that came to hand when he got into the cabin; but why did he steal a chart when there was a bottle of rum standing in the rack on the table, with the cork already drawn?"

"When a monkey carries a big, bloody-minded knife, and comes into the cabin at night to steal a chart, there is something wrong; and I began to be half of Dick's opinion that there was a mutiny brewing."

"However, the next twenty-four hours the monkeys were as quiet as could be. The monkey captain was full of his smirks and bows, and didn't seem to remember anything about his having been caught in the cabin the night before. He brought me and Dick a box of cigars that he had found somewhere – and good cigars they were too! – and his general idea seemed to be to make us believe that he was our best friend, and was ready to do anything to please us. The other monkeys kept watching him, and when they caught me or Dick or any of the men looking at them they'd grin as affable as a boarding-house keeper that comes down aboard an incoming ship a-looking for boarders."

"Another queer thing happened that morning. When we hove the log, the monkey captain came aft and watched us, and tailed onto the log line to help haul it in, as though he was anxious for a chance to show his goodwill."

"'He's got our position yesterday from the chart,' says Dick, 'and now he's going to depend on dead reckoning till he can get another chance at the chart. I wish I knew as much about navigation as he does. I'd get a second mate's certificate and get out of the fokesell the next time I get to London.'"

"Now it did seem impossible that a monkey could know navigation, but it did look as if this particular monkey knew what charts and log lines are for. The man at the wheel told me that he's seen the monkey looking into the binnacle to see what course she was steering more than half a dozen times, and it was the opinion among the men that he was the devil himself. However, nobody could help noticing that when the monkey-captain's back was turned the rest of the monkeys kept up a low conversation among themselves, and it was easy to see that they had something on their minds."

"'I'd give a good deal to understand the lingo of them chaps,' says Dick to me. 'It's my belief that they know they're nearing the Brazil coast, and that they mean to take possession of the schooner by the time we sight land. I wish I had a pistol with me; though I don't doubt they're intelligent enough to understand what a belaying pin says when it hits 'em over the head.'"

"We were about two days' sail from Ryo, according to my calculation – that is, of course, if the wind held – and I was coming around to Dick's opinion that the monkeys had some sort of traverse that they calculated to work, though I couldn't chime in with his notion that they had fitted out the schooner and meant to go on a piratical cruise. After thinking the thing over more than a hundred times I came to the conclusion that the schooner had been on the west coast of Africa for slaves. That was why she was in ballast, and why there wasn't any name on her stern, nor any papers of any sort to be found aboard of her. I said so to Dick, but he wouldn't agree with me."

"'That's all very well as far as it goes,' says he, 'but it don't account for her being manned by nobody except monkeys. How did they get possession of her? That's what I'd like you to tell me.'"

"'Suppose she was lying in the river, waiting to take her cargo of slaves aboard, and suppose all hands got blazing drunk, and suppose the shippers sent aboard a cargo of monkeys instead of niggers. How does that strike you?' said I."

"'What's become of the crew?' asked Dick."

"'Why when they got sober and saw the monkeys they thought they had the horrors, and they all tumbled ashore to get more rum, or perhaps to get a little quiet sleep in the barracoon.'"

"'And the monkeys, seeing their chance, got up the anchor and made sail on her and carried her clear across the Atlantic! Seems to me, sir, that your story is about as tough as mine, and has got too many twists and turns in it. No, sir, I stick to my first opinion. This schooner was fitted out by monkeys, and no men never had anything to do with her, except perhaps to build her. Well, I'll go below now, and if you should want me on the deck in a hurry just knock on the deck over my bunk. I shall turn in all standing, and I'll answer your call about as quick as you can make it.'"

"I had no occasion to sing out for the mate during that watch, for the monkeys were quiet as lambs, and slept all curled up together, every man Jack of them taking a turn with his tail around the neck of the next one. It was an unseamanlike way of proceeding, for if there had been a sudden call of 'All hands!' it would have taken those monkeys ten minutes to cast themselves loose. But I suppose they got their ideas of seamanship from the Brazilians, and what could you expect of them?"

* * *

"The next day was Wednesday. I remembered it because it's my lucky day, though at one time it didn't look as if there was much luck about the day on that particular occasion. I noticed that every now and then one of the monkeys would lay aloft, for all the world as if he was looking out for land; and if you'd believe it, sir, one of them finally saw land, and reported it to the monkey-captain before any one of us white men saw it. I saw the fellow come down from the cross-trees and go up to the old man and say something, and then, after getting his orders, he went and told the rest of his people, and every one of them went forrard and began looking for the land, and chattering as if they were amazing glad that the voyage was almost over."

"The wind dropped about noon, and we were pretty near becalmed for the next twenty-four hours. I was getting anxious for fear the *Jane G. Mather* would reach Ryo before we did, in which case, as the captain had said, he wouldn't be able to wait for us, and I would lose a mighty good berth as a second-mate. At twelve o'clock I turned in, telling Dick to knock on the deck in case he should want me; and, remembering what he has said the night before about turning in all standing, I thought I would do the same, not knowing but what the calm might be followed, as it often is in those latitudes, by a sudden squall that might be more than the schooner wanted."

"I was sound asleep, and dreaming that I had come into a big fortune and had bought a big farm, stocked with elephants and codfish, somewhere down in Devon, and was going to raise cigars ready made, when Dick hammered on the deck with his boot heel, and woke me in a hurry. There was a tremendous row going on over my head, and my first idea was that we were going to be run down by one of those big French liners that are for ever running into other people along the South American coast; but before I could get on deck I heard Dick cursing and the monkeys snarling, and knew that he was having a fight with them. So I caught up a couple of rifles, which was about all I could carry, and was on deck inside of five seconds. The first thing I saw was that there was nobody at the wheel, and that Dick was backed up against the weather rail and fighting with all hands of the monkeys. They were jumping on him with their naked hands and feet, and trying to tear him limb from limb, and he was laying into them with a belaying pin as if he was mate of an old-time Black Ball packet breaking in a crew of packet rats. So far as I could judge the fight was a pretty equal thing, and Dick was keeping his end pretty well up. He had laid out half a dozen of the monkeys, but for all that they were full of pluck, and their captain, who kept a little on the outskirts of the shindy, kept encouraging them, and keeping them up to their work."

"I didn't wait many seconds before I got to work. I put a bullet through the monkey captain first of all. Then I fired promiscuous like into the middle of the muss; and then, using the rifle as a handspike, I let them see I didn't intend to allow no nonsense aboard of my schooner. They didn't stop to argue. Some of them went overboard; some went aloft; some laid out on the jib-boom; and the rest tried to hide wherever they could. In less than a minute the decks were cleared, and things were quiet again."

"It seems that the monkeys had made a sudden attack on Dick when he was least expecting them, and for a little while it looked as if he might lose the number of his mess."

"'You see, sir,' he said, 'it's just as I told you. Them devils tried to seize the schooner; and I will say this for 'em, that they did it in a way that showed a good deal of savey.'"

"'Are you hurt?' I asked; for I could see there was blood on his face.

"'Only a bite or two, and a few scratches. Nothing of any account,' he replied. 'You see, they didn't have any arms. If they'd had knives like the one the old man dropped, it would have been all day with me. They'd have cut me into fine slices before you could have got on deck.'"

"'Where are all the men?' I asked. 'Where's the man at the wheel?'"

"'He's gone overboard, sir,' said Dick, 'with his throat tore open. One watch of them monkeys attended to him while the other watch was trying to do the same for me. The rest of the men is hiding in the fokesell, according to my idea, and I'll just take a handspike and go have a talk with 'em.'"

"I went along with him, and we found that the hatch had been clapped on and made fast, so that not a man in the fokesell could get on deck. All the men were below, including the man who had been on the look-out, and who had jumped down to rouse the rest of the men when he saw what the monkeys were up to. The men were mighty glad to be released, for there wasn't any air coming into the fokesell except where the hatch was off, and the night was a middling hot one. In about an hour more they would all have been suffocated, which is probably what the monkeys were expecting."

"Of course it was all hands on deck for the rest of that night, for we didn't know what new game the monkeys might try; but we heard nothing of them until daylight. About eight bells in the morning watch we got a slant from the eastward, and before noon we were in the harbour of Ryo."

"The monkeys kept out of sight, so far as they could, until we were close in with the shore, when they all went overboard; and when they reached the land they bolted for the woods. Dick was not in favour of letting them go, but said they ought to be put in irons and tried for mutiny and murder, but I told him that it would save a lot of trouble for us to be well rid of them before handing the schooner over to the consul. I went with the men aft, and told them that the least said about the monkeys the sooner we'd get our salvage money; and they all swore they wouldn't say a blessed word about it. No more they did. We told the consul that we picked up the schooner derelict, without a soul aboard of her; and he took our depositions, and did the usual thing in such cases, which, as you know with being told, was to keep us waiting for our money for the best part of a year, and then pay us about a tenth of what we ought to have had, saying that the rest had been used up for expenses. Oh! I don't blame him. It wasn't his fault; but that's what always happens when one of these 'ere Admiralty courts gets its lines made fast to a salvage case."

"Nobody ever found out who that schooner belonged to, or where she has sailed from, or what her name was, or anything about her."

"What is your opinion, sir? I've given you the straight facts. There was a schooner manned by monkeys, and nobody else. How did it happen? That's what I never found out, and what nobody ever will find out, in my opinion. I don't expect you to believe the yarn, though it's the gospel truth. I never found but one man who believed it, and it turned out that he was a lunatic at the time, though he was generally supposed to be only what they call a philosopher."

# A Visit to the Moon

by George Griffith

## INTRODUCTORY NOTE

The adventures of Rollo Lenox Smeaton Aubrey, Earl of Redgrave, and his bride Lilla Zaidie, daughter of the late Professor Hartley Rennick, Demonstrator in Physical Science in the Smith-Oliver University in New York, were first made possible by that distinguished scientist's now famous separation of the Forces of Nature into their positive and negative elements. Starting from the axiom that everything in Nature has its opposite, he not only divided the Universal Force of Gravitation into its elements of attraction and repulsion, but also constructed a machine which enabled him to develop either or both of these elements at will. From this triumph of mechanical genius it was but a step to the magnificent conception which was subsequently realized by Lord Redgrave in the Astronef. Lord Redgrave had met Professor Rennick, about a year before his lamented death, when he was on a holiday excursion in the Canadian Rockies with his daughter. The young millionaire nobleman was equally fascinated by the daring theories of the Professor, and by the mental and physical charms of Miss Zaidie. And thus the chance acquaintance resulted in a partnership, in which the Professor was to find the knowledge and Lord Redgrave the capital for translating the theory of the "R. Force" (Repulsive or Antigravitational Force) into practice, and constructing a vessel which would be capable, not only of rising from the earth, but of passing the limits of the terrestrial atmosphere, and navigating with precision and safety the limitless ocean of Space.

Unhappily, before the Astronef, or star-navigator, was completed at the works which Lord Redgrave had built for her construction on his estate at Smeaton, in Yorkshire, her inventor succumbed to pulmonary complications following an attack of influenza. This left Lord Redgrave the sole possessor of the secret of the "R. Force." A year after the Professor's death he completed the Astronef, and took her across the Atlantic by rising into Space until the attraction of the earth was so far weakened that in a couple of hours' time he was able to descend in the vicinity of New York. On this trial trip he was accompanied by Andrew Murgatroyd, an old engineer who had superintended the building of the Astronef. This man's family had been attached to his Lordship's for generations and for this reason he was selected as engineer and steersman of the Navigator of the Stars.

The excitement which was caused, not only in America but over the whole civilized world, by the arrival of the Astronef from the distant regions of space to which she had soared; the marriage of her creator to the daughter of her inventor in the main saloon while she hung motionless in a cloudless sky a mile above the Empire City; their return to earth; the wedding banquet; and their departure to the moon, which they had selected as the first stopping-place on their bridal trip—these are now matters of common knowledge. The present series of narratives begins as the earth sinks away from under them, and their Honeymoon in Space has actually begun.

WHEN the Astronef rose from the ground to commence her marvellous voyage through the hitherto untraversed realms of Space, Lord Redgrave and his bride were standing at the forward-end of a raised deck which ran along about two-thirds of the length of the cylindrical body of the vessel. The walls of this compartment, which was about fifty feet long by twenty broad, were formed of thick, but perfectly transparent, toughened glass, over which, in cases of necessity, curtains of ribbed steel could be drawn from the floor, which was of teak and slightly convex. A light steel rail ran round it and two stairways ran up from the other deck of the vessel to two hatches, one fore and one aft, destined to be hermetically closed when the Astronef had soared beyond breathable atmosphere and was crossing the airless, heatless wastes of interplanetary space.

Lord and Lady Redgrave and Andrew Murgatroyd were the only members of the crew of the Star-navigator. No more were needed, for on board this marvellous craft nearly everything was done by machinery; warming, lighting, cooking, distillation and re-distillation of water, constant and automatic purification of the air, everything, in fact, but the regulation of the mysterious "R. Force" could be done with a minimum of human attention. This, however, had to be minutely and carefully regulated, and her commander usually performed this duty himself.

The developing engines were in the lowest part of the vessel amidships. Their minimum power just sufficed to make the Astronef a little lighter than her own bulk of air, so that when she visited a planet possessing an atmosphere sufficiently dense, the two propellers at her stern would be capable of driving her through the air at the rate of about a hundred miles an hour. The maximum power would have sufficed to hurl the vessel beyond the limits of the earth's atmosphere in a few minutes.

When they had risen to the height of about a mile above New

York, her ladyship, who had been gazing in silent wonder and admiration at the strange and marvellous scene, pointed suddenly towards the East and said: "Look, there's the moon! Just fancy—our first stopping-place! Well, it doesn't look so very far off at present."

Redgrave turned and saw the pale yellow crescent of the new moon just rising above the eastern edge of the Atlantic Ocean.

"It almost looks as if we could steer straight to it right over the water, only, of course, it wouldn't wait there for us," she went on.

"Oh, it'll be there when we want it, never fear," laughed his lordship, "and, after all, it's only a mere matter of about two hundred and forty thousand miles away, and what's that in a trip that will cover hundreds of millions? It will just be a sort of jumping-off place into Space for us."

"Still I shouldn't like to miss seeing it," she said. "I want to know what there is on that other side which nobody has ever seen yet, and settle that question about air and water. Won't it just be heavenly to be able to come back and tell them all about it at home? But fancy me talking stuff like this when we are going, perhaps, to solve some of the hidden mysteries of Creation and, maybe, to look upon things that human eyes were never meant to see," she went on, with a sudden change in her voice.

He felt a little shiver in the arm that was resting upon his, and his hand went down and caught hers.

"Well, we shall see a good many marvels, and, perhaps, miracles, before we come back, but I hardly think we shall see anything that is forbidden. Still, there's one thing we shall do, I hope. We shall solve once and for all the great problem of the worlds–whether they are inhabited or not. By the way," he went on, "I may remind your ladyship that you are just now drawing the last breaths of earthly air which you will taste for some time, in fact until we get back! You may as well take your last look at earth as earth, for the next time you see it, it will be a planet."

She went to the rail and looked over into the enormous void beneath, for all this time the Astronef had been mounting towards the zenith. She could see, by the growing moonlight, vast, vague shapes of land and sea. The myriad lights of New York and Brooklyn were mingled in a tiny patch of dimly luminous haze. The air about her had suddenly grown bitterly cold, and she saw that the stars and planets were shining with a brilliancy she had never seen before. Her husband came to her side, and, laying his arm across her shoulder, said:

"Well, have you said goodbye to your native world? It is a hit solemn, isn't it, saying goodbye to a world that you have been born on; which contains everything that has made up your life, everything that is dear to you?"

"Not quite everything!" she said, looking up at him. "At least, I don't think so."

He immediately made the only reply which was appropriate under the circumstances; and then he said, drawing her towards the staircase: "Well, for the present this is our world; a world travelling among worlds, and as I have been able to bring the most delightful of the Daughters of Terra with me, I, at any rate, am perfectly happy. Now, I think it's getting on to supper time, so if your ladyship will go to your household duties, I'll have a look at my engines and make everything snug for the voyage."

The first thing he did when he got on to the main deck, was to hermetically close the two companion-ways; then he went and carefully inspected the apparatus for purifying the air and supplying it with fresh oxygen from the tanks in which it was stored in liquid form. Lastly he descended into the lower hold of the ship and turned on the energy of repulsion to its full extent, at the same time stopping the engines which had been working the propellers.

It was now no longer necessary or even possible to steer the Astronef. She was directed solely by the repulsive force which would carry her with ever-increasing swiftness, as the attraction of the earth became diminished, towards that neutral point some two hundred thousand miles away, at which the attraction of the earth is exactly balanced by the moon. Her momentum would carry her past this point, and then the "R. Force" would be gradually brought into play in order to avert the unpleasant consequences of a fall of some forty odd thousand miles.

Andrew Murgatroyd, relieved from his duties in the wheelhouse, made a careful inspection of the auxiliary machinery, which was under his special charge, and then retired to his quarters forward to prepare his own evening meal. Meanwhile her ladyship, with the help of the ingenious contrivances with which the kitchen of the Astronef was stocked, and with the use of which she had already made herself quite familiar, had prepared a dainty little *souper à deux*. Her husband opened a bottle of the finest champagne that the cellars of New York could supply, to drink at once to the prosperity of the voyage, and the health of his beautiful fellow-voyager.

When supper was over and the coffee made he carried the apparatus up the stairs on to the glass-domed upper deck. Then he came back and said: "You'd better wrap yourself up as warmly as you can, dear, for it's a good deal chillier up there than it is here."

When she reached the deck and took her first glance about her, Zaidie seemed suddenly to lapse into a state of somnambulism. The whole heavens above and around were strewn with thick clusters of stars which she had never seen before. The stars she remembered seeing from the earth were only little pinpoints in the darkness compared with the myriads of blazing orbs which were now shooting their rays across the silent void of Space. So many millions of new ones had come into view that she looked in vain for the familiar constellations. She saw only vast clusters of living gems of all colours crowding the heavens on every side of her. She walked slowly round the deck, looking to right and left and above, incapable for the moment either of thought or speech, but only of dumb wonder, mingled with a dim sense of overwhelming awe. Presently she craned her neck backwards and looked straight up to the zenith. A huge silver crescent, supporting, as it were, a dim, greenish coloured body in its arms stretched overhead across nearly a sixth of the heavens.

Her husband came to her side, took her in his arms, lifted her as if she had been a little child, so feeble had the earth's attraction now become, and laid her in a long, low deck-chair, so that she could look at it without inconvenience. The splendid crescent grew swiftly larger and more distinct, and as she lay there in a trance of wonder and admiration she saw point after point of dazzlingly white light flash out on to the dark portions, and then begin to send out rays as though they were gigantic volcanoes in full eruption, and were pouring torrents of living fire from their blazing craters.

"Sunrise on the moon!" said Redgrave, who had stretched himself on another chair beside her. "A glorious sight, isn't it? But nothing to what we shall see tomorrow morning–only there doesn't happen to be any morning just about here."

"Yes," she said dreamily, "glorious, isn't it? That and all the stars–but I can't think of anything yet, Lenox! It's all too mighty and too marvellous. It doesn't seem as though human eyes were meant to look upon things like this. But where's the earth? We must be able to see that still."

"Not from here," he said, "because it's underneath us. Come below, and you shall see Mother Earth as you have never seen her yet."

They went down into the lower part of the vessel, and to the after-end behind the engine-room. Redgrave switched on a couple of electric lights, and then pulled a lever attached to one of the side-walls. A part of the flooring, about 6ft. square, slid noiselessly away; then he pulled another lever on the opposite side and a similar piece disappeared, leaving a large space covered only by absolutely transparent glass. He switched off the lights again and led her to the edge of it, and said:

"There is your native world, dear; that is the earth!"

Wonderful as the moon had seemed, the gorgeous spectacle, which lay seemingly at her feet, was infinitely more magnificent. A vast disc of silver grey, streaked and dotted with lines and points of dazzling light, and more than half covered with vast, glittering, greyish-green expanses, seemed to form, as it were the floor of the great gulf of space beneath them. They were not yet too far away to make out the general features of the continents and oceans, and fortunately the hemisphere presented to them happened to be singularly free from clouds.

Zaidie stood gazing for nearly an hour at this marvellous vision of the home-world which she had left so far behind her before she could tear herself away and allow her husband to shut the slides again. The greatly diminished weight of her body almost entirely destroyed the fatigue of standing. In fact, at present on board the Astronef it was almost as easy to stand as it was to lie down.

There was of course very little sleep for any of the travellers on this first night of their adventurous voyage, but towards the sixth hour after leaving the earth her ladyship, overcome as much by the emotions which had been awakened within her as by physical fatigue, went to bed, after making her husband promise that he would wake her in good time to see the descent upon the moon. Two hours later she was awake and drinking the coffee which Redgrave had prepared for her. Then she went on to the upper deck.

To her astonishment she found on one hand, day more brilliant than she had ever seen it before, and on the other hand, darkness blacker than the blackest earthly night. On the right hand was an intensely brilliant orb, about half as large again as the full moon seen from earth, shining with inconceivable brightness out of a sky black as midnight and thronged with stars. It was the sun, the sun shining in the midst of airless space.

The tiny atmosphere enclosed in the glass-domed space was lighted brilliantly, but it was not perceptibly warmer, though Redgrave warned her ladyship not to touch anything upon which the sun's rays fell directly as she would find it uncomfortably hot. On the other side was the same black immensity of space which she had seen the night before, an ocean of darkness clustered with islands of light. High above in the zenith floated the great silver-grey disc of earth, a good deal smaller now, and there was another object beneath which was at present of far more interest to her. Looking down to the left she saw a vast semi-luminous area in which not a star was to be seen. It was the earth-lit portion of the long familiar and yet mysterious orb which was to be their resting-place for the next few hours.

"The sun hasn't risen over there yet," said Redgrave, as she was peering down into the void. "It's earth-light still. Now look at the other side."

She crossed the deck and saw the strangest scene she had yet beheld. Apparently only a few miles below her was a huge crescent-shaped plain arching away for hundreds of miles on either side. The outer edge had a ragged look, and little excrescences, which soon took the shape of flat-topped mountains projected from it and stood out bright and sharp against the black void beneath, out of which the stars shone up, as it seemed, sharp and bright above the edge of the disc.

The plain itself was a scene of the most awful and utter desolation that even the sombre fancy of a Dante could imagine. Huge mountain walls, towering to immense heights and enclosing great circular and oval plains, one side of them blazing with intolerable light, and the other side black with impenetrable obscurity; enormous valleys reaching down from brilliant day into rayless night—perhaps down into the empty bowels of the dead world itself; vast, grey-white plains lying round the mountains, crossed by little ridges and by long, black lines which could only be immense fissures with perpendicular sides—but all hard grey-white and black, all intolerable brightness or repulsive darkness; not a sign of life anywhere, no shady forests, no green fields, no broad, glittering oceans; only a ghastly wilderness of dead mountains and dead plains.

"What an awful place!" said Zaidie, in a slowly spoken whisper. "Surely we can't land there. How far are we from it?"

"About fifteen hundred miles," replied Redgrave, who was sweeping the scene below him with one of the two powerful telescopes which stood on the deck. "No, it doesn't look very cheerful, does it; but it's a marvellous sight for all that, and one that a good many people on earth would give their ears to see from here. I'm letting her drop pretty fast, and we shall probably land in a couple of hours or so. Meanwhile, you may as well get out your moon atlas and your Jules Verne and Flammarion, and study your lunography. I'm going to turn the power a bit astern so that we shall go down obliquely and see more of the lighted disc. We started at new moon so that you should have a look at the full earth, and also so that we could get round to the invisible side while it is lighted up."

They both went below, he to deflect the repulsive force so that one set of engines should give them a somewhat oblique direction, while the other, acting directly on the surface of the moon, simply retarded their fall; and she to get her maps and the ever-fascinating works of Jules Verne and Flammarion. When they got back, the Astronef had changed her apparent position, and, instead of falling directly on to the moon, was descending towards it in a slanting direction. The result of this was that the sunlit crescent rapidly grew in breadth, whilst peak after peak and range after range rose up swiftly out of the black gulf beyond. The sun climbed quickly up through the star-strewn, mid-day heavens, and the full earth sank more swiftly still behind them.

Another hour of silent, entranced wonder and admiration followed, and then Lenox remarked to Zaidie: "Don't you think it's about time we were beginning to think of breakfast, dear, or do you think you can wait till we land?"

"Breakfast on the moon!" she exclaimed. "That would be just too lovely for words! Of course we'll wait."

"Very well," he said, "you see that big, black ring nearly below us, that, as I suppose you know, is the celebrated Mount Tycho. I'll try and find a convenient spot on the top of the ring to drop on, and then you will be able to survey the scenery from seventeen or eighteen thousand feet above the plains."

About two hours later a slight jarring tremor ran through the frame of the vessel, and the first stage of the voyage was ended. After a passage of less than twelve hours the Astronef had crossed a gulf of nearly two hundred and fifty thousand miles and rested quietly on the untrodden surface of the lunar world.

"We certainly shan't find any atmosphere here," said Redgrave, when they had finished breakfast, "although we may in the deeper parts, so if your ladyship would like a walk we'd better go and put on our breathing dresses."

These were not unlike diving dresses, save that they were much lighter. The helmets were smaller, and made of aluminium covered with asbestos. A sort of knapsack fitted on to the back, and below this was a cylinder of liquefied air which, when passed through the expanding apparatus, would furnish pure air for a practically indefinite period, as the respired air passed into another portion of the upper chamber, where it was forced through a chemical solution which deprived it of its poisonous gases and made it fit to breathe again.

The pressure of air inside the helmet automatically regulated the supply, which was not permitted to circulate into the dress, as the absence of air-pressure on the moon would cause it to instantly expand and probably tear the material, which was a cloth woven chiefly of asbestos fibre. The two helmets could be connected for talking purposes by a light wire communicating with a little telephonic apparatus inside the helmet.

They passed out of the Astronef through an air-tight chamber in the wall of her lowest compartment, Murgatroyd closing the first door behind them. Redgrave opened the next one and dropped a short ladder on to the grey, loose, sand-strewn rock of the little plain on which they had stopped. Then he stood aside and motioned for Zaidie to go down first.

She understood him, and, taking his hand, descended the four easy steps. And so hers was the first human foot which, in all the ages since its creation, had rested on the surface of the World that Had Been. Redgrave followed her with a little spring which landed him gently beside her, then he took both her hands and pressed them hard in his. He would have kissed her if he could; but that of course was out of the question.

Then he connected the telephone wire, and hand in hand they crossed the little plateau towards the edge of the tremendous gulf, fifty-four miles across, and nearly twenty thousand feet deep. In the middle of it rose a conical mountain about five thousand feet high, the summit of which was just beginning to catch the solar rays. Half of the vast plain was already brilliantly illuminated, but round the central cone was a vast semi-circle of shadow impenetrable in its blackness.

"Day and night in this same valley, actually side by side!" said Zaidie. Then she stopped, and pointed down into the brightly lit distance, and went on hurriedly: "Look, Lenox, look at the foot of the mountain there! Doesn't that seem like the ruins of a city?"

"It does," he said, "and there's no reason why it shouldn't be. I've always thought that, as the air and water disappeared from the upper parts of the moon, the inhabitants, whoever they were, must have been driven down into the deeper parts. Shall we go down and see?"

"But how?" she said. He pointed towards the Astronef. She nodded her helmeted head, and they went back to the vessel. A few minutes later the Astronef had risen from her resting-place with a spring which rapidly carried her over half of the vast crater, and then she began to drop slowly into the depths. She grounded as gently as before, and presently they were standing on the lunar surface about a mile from the central cone. This time, however, Redgrave had taken the precaution to bring a magazine rifle and a couple of revolvers with him in case any strange monsters, relics of the vanished fauna of the moon, might still be taking refuge in these mysterious depths. Zaidie, although like a good many American girls, she could shoot excellently well, carried no weapon more offensive than a whole-plate camera and a tripod, which here, of course, only weighed a sixth of their earthly weight.

The first thing that Redgrave did when they stepped out on to the sandy surface of the plain was to stoop down and strike a wax match; there was a tiny glimmer of light which was immediately extinguished.

"No air here," he said, "so we shall find no living beings—at any rate, none like ourselves."

They found the walking exceedingly easy although their boots were purposely weighted in order to counteract to some extent the great difference in gravity. A few minutes' sharp walking brought them to the outskirts of the city. It had no walls, and in fact exhibited no signs of preparations for defence. Its streets were broad and well-paved; and the houses, built of great blocks of grey stone joined together with white cement, looked as fresh and unworn as though they had only been built a few months, whereas they had probably stood for hundreds of thousands of years. They were flat roofed, all of one storey and practically of one type.

There were very few public buildings, and absolutely no attempt at ornamentation was visible. Round some of the houses were spaces which might once have been gardens. In the midst of the city, which appeared to cover an area of about four square miles, was an enor-

mous square paved with flag stones, which were covered to the depth of a couple of inches with a light grey dust, and, as they walked across it, this remained perfectly still save for the disturbance caused by their footsteps. There was no air to support it, otherwise it might have risen in clouds about them.

From the centre of this square rose a huge Pyramid nearly a thousand feet in height, the sole building in the great, silent city which appeared to have been raised as a monument, or, possibly, a temple by the hands of its vanished inhabitants. As they approached this they saw a curious white fringe lying round the steps by which it was approached. When they got nearer they found that this fringe was composed of millions of white-bleached bones and skulls, shaped very much like those of terrestrial men except that the ribs were out of all proportion to the rest of the bones.

They stopped awe-stricken before this strange spectacle. Redgrave stooped down and took hold of one of the bones, a huge thigh bone. It broke in two as he tried to lift it, and the piece which remained in his hand crumbled instantly to white powder.

"Whoever they were," said Redgrave, "they were giants. When air and water failed above they came down here by some means and built this city. You see what enormous chests they must have had. That would be Nature's last struggle to enable them to breathe the diminishing atmosphere. These, of course, will be the last descendants of the fittest to breathe it; this was their temple, I suppose, and here they came to die—I wonder how many thousand years ago—perishing of heat, and cold, and hunger, and thirst, the last tragedy of a race, which, after all, must have been something like our own."

"It is just too awful for words," said Zaidie. "Shall we go into the temple? That seems one of the entrances up there, only I don't like walking over all those bones."

Her voice sounded very strange over the wire which connected their helmets.

"I don't suppose they'll mind if we do," replied Redgrave, "only we mustn't go far in. It may be full of cross passages and mazes, and we might never get out. Our lamps won't be much use in there, you know, for there's no air. They'll just be points of light, and we shan't see anything but them. It's very aggravating, but I'm afraid there's no help for it. Come along!"

They ascended the steps, crushing the bones and skulls to powder beneath their feet, and entered the huge, square doorway, which looked like a rectangle of blackness against the grey-white of the wall. Even through their asbestos-woven clothing they felt a sudden shock of icy cold. In those few steps they had passed from a temperature of tenfold summer heat into one far below that of the coldest spots on earth. They turned on the electric lamps which were fitted to the breast-plates of their dresses, but they could see nothing save the glow of the lamps. All about them was darkness impenetrable, and so they reluctantly turned back to the doorway, leaving all the mysteries which the vast temple might contain to remain mysteries to the end of time. They passed down the steps again and crossed the square, and for the next half hour Zaidie, who was photographer to the expedition, was busy taking photographs of the Pyramid with its ghastly surroundings, and a few general views of this strange City of the dead.

Then they went back to the Astronef. They found Murgatroyd pacing up and down under the dome looking about him with serious eyes, but yet betraying no particular curiosity. The wonderful vessel was at once his home and his idol, and nothing but the direct orders of his master would have induced him to leave her even in a world in which there was probably not a living human being to dispute possession of her.

When they had resumed their ordinary clothing, she rose rapidly from the surface of the plain, crossed the encircling wall at the height of a few hundred feet, and made her way at a speed of about fifty miles an hour towards the regions of the South Pole. Behind them to the north-west they could see from their elevation of nearly thirty thousand feet the vast expanse of the Sea of Clouds. Dotted here and there were the shining points and ridges of light, marking the peaks and crater walls which the rays of the rising sun had already touched. Before them and to the right and left of them rose a vast maze of crater-rings and huge ramparts of mountain-walls enclosing plains so far below their summits that the light of neither sun nor earth ever reached them.

By directing the force exerted by what might now be called the propelling part of the engines against the mountain masses, which they crossed to right and left and behind, Redgrave was able to take a zigzag course which carried him over many of the walled plains which were wholly or partially lit up by the sun, and in nearly all of the deepest their telescopes revealed what they had found within the crater of Tycho. At length, pointing to a gigantic circle of white light fringing an abyss of utter darkness, he said:

"There is Newton, the greatest mystery of the moon. Those inner walls are twenty-four thousand feet high; that means that the bottom, which has never been seen by human eyes, is about five thousand feet below the surface of the moon. What do you say, dear–shall we go down and see if the searchlight will show us anything? There may be air there."

"Certainly!" replied Zaidie decisively, "haven't we come to see things that nobody else has ever seen?"

Redgrave signalled to the engine-room, and presently the Astronef changed her course, and in a few minutes was hanging, bathed in sunlight, like a star suspended over the unfathomable gulf of darkness below.

As they sank beyond the sunlight, Murgatroyd turned on both the head and stern searchlights. They dropped down ever slowly and more slowly until gradually the two long, thin streams of light began to spread themselves out, and by the time the Astronef came gently to a rest they were swinging round her in broad fans of diffused light over a dark, marshy surface, with scattered patches of moss and reeds which showed dull gleams of stagnant water between them.

"Air and water at last!" said Redgrave, as he rejoined his wife on the upper deck, "air and water and eternal darkness! Well, we shall find life on the moon here if anywhere. Shall we go?"

"Of course," replied her ladyship, "what else have we come for? Must we put on the breathing-dresses?"

"Certainly," he replied, "because, although there's air we don't know yet whether it is breathable. It may be half carbon-dioxide for all we know; but a few matches will soon tell us that."

Within a quarter of an hour they were again standing on the surface. Murgatroyd had orders to follow them as far as possible with the head searchlight, which, in the comparatively rarefied atmosphere, appeared to have a range of several miles. Redgrave struck a match, and held it up level with his head. It burnt with a clear, steady, yellow flame.

"Where a match will burn a man can breathe," he said. "I'm going to see what lunar air is like."

"For Heaven's sake be careful, dear," came the reply in pleading tones across the wire.

"All right, but don't open your helmet till I tell you."

He then raised the hermetically-closed slide of glass, which formed the front of the helmets half an inch or so. Instantly he felt a sensation like the drawing of a red-hot iron across his skin. He snapped the visor down and clasped it in its place. For a moment or two he gasped for breath and then he said rather faintly:

"It's no good, it's too cold, it would freeze the blood in our veins. I think we'd better go back and explore this valley under cover. We can't do anything in the dark, and we can see just as well from the upper deck with the searchlights. Besides, as there's air and water here, there's no telling but there may be inhabitants of sorts such as we shouldn't care to meet."

He took her hand, and, to Murgatroyd's intense relief, they went back to the vessel.

Redgrave then raised the Astronef a couple of hundred feet and, by directing the repulsive force against the mountain walls, developed just sufficient energy to keep them moving at about twelve miles an hour.

They began to cross the plain with their searchlights flashing out in all directions. They had scarcely gone a mile before the headlight fell upon a moving form half walking, half crawling among some stunted brown-leaved bushes by the side of a broad, stagnant stream.

"Look!" said Zaidie, clasping her husband's arm, "is that a gorilla, or—no, it can't be a man."

The light was turned full upon the object. If it had been covered with hair it might have passed for some strange type of the ape tribe, but its skin was smooth and of a livid grey. Its lower limbs were evidently more powerful than its upper; its chest was enormously developed, but the stomach was small. The head was big and round and smooth. As they came nearer they saw that in place of finger-nails it had long white feelers which it kept extended and constantly waving about as it groped its way towards the water. As the intense light flashed full on it, it turned its head towards them. It had a nose and a mouth. The nose was long and thick, with huge mobile nostrils, and the mouth formed an angle something like a fish's lips, and of teeth there seemed none. At either side of the upper part of the nose there were two little sunken holes, in which this thing's ancestors of countless thousand years ago had possessed eyes.

As she looked upon this awful parody of what had once perhaps been a human face, Zaidie covered hers with her hands and uttered a little moan of horror.

"Horrible, isn't it?" said Redgrave. "I suppose that's what the last remnants of the lunarians have come to, evidently once men and women something like ourselves. I daresay the ancestors of that thing have lived here in coldness and darkness for hundreds of generations. It shows how tremendously tenacious nature is of life.

"Ages ago that awful thing's ancestors lived up yonder when there were seas and rivers, fields and forests just as we have them on earth; men and women who could see and breathe and enjoy everything in life and had built up civilizations like ours. Look, it's going to fish or something. Now we shall see what it feeds on. I wonder why that water isn't frozen. I suppose there must be some internal heat left still, split up into patches, I daresay, and lakes of lava. Perhaps this valley is just over one of them, and that's why these creatures have managed to survive. Ah, there's another of them, smaller not so strongly formed. That thing's mate, I suppose, female of the species. Ugh, I wonder how many hundreds of thousands of years it will take for our descendants to come to that."

"I hope our dear old earth will hit something else and be smashed to atoms before that happens!" exclaimed Zaidie, whose curiosity had now partly overcome her horror. "Look, it's trying to catch something."

The larger of the two creatures had groped its way to the edge of the sluggish, foetid water and dropped or rather rolled quietly into it. It was evidently cold-blooded or nearly so, for no warm-blooded animal could have withstood that more than glacial cold. Presently the other dropped in, too, and both disappeared for some minutes. Then suddenly there was a violent commotion in the water a few yards away; and the two creatures rose to the surface of the water, one with a wriggling eel-like fish between its jaws.

They both groped their way towards the edge, and had just reached it and were pulling themselves out when a hideous shape rose out of the water behind them. It was like the head of an octopus joined to the body of a boa-constrictor, but head and neck were both of the same ghastly, livid grey as the other two bodies. It was evidently blind, too, for it took no notice of the brilliant glare of the search-light. Still it moved rapidly towards the two scrambling forms, its long white feelers trembling out in all directions. Then one of them touched the smaller of the two creatures. Instantly the rest shot out and closed round it, and with scarcely a struggle it was dragged beneath the water and vanished.

Zaidie uttered a little low scream and covered her face again, and Redgrave said: "The same old brutal law again. Life preying upon life even on a dying world, a world that is more than half dead itself. Well, I think we've seen enough of this place. I suppose those are about the only types of life we should meet anywhere, and one acquaintance with them satisfies me completely. I vote we go and see what the invisible hemisphere is like."

"I have had all I want of this side," said Zaidie, looking away from the scene of the hideous conflict, "so the sooner the better."

A few minutes later the Astronef was again rising towards the stars with her searchlights still flashing down into the Valley of Expiring Life, which seemed worse than the Valley of Death. As he followed the rays with a pair of powerful field glasses, Redgrave fancied that he saw huge, dim shapes moving about the stunted shrubbery and through the slimy pools of the stagnant rivers, and once or twice he got a glimpse of what might well have been the ruins of towns and cities; but the gloom soon became too deep and dense for the search-lights to pierce and he was glad when the Astronef soared up into the brilliant sunlight once more. Even the ghastly wilderness of the lunar landscape was welcome after the nameless horrors of that hideous abyss.

After a couple of hours' rapid travelling, Redgrave pointed down to a comparatively small, deep crater, and said:

"There, that is Malapert. It is almost exactly at the south pole of the moon, and there," he went on pointing ahead, "is the horizon of the hemisphere which no earthborn eyes but ours and Murgatroyd's have ever seen."

Contrary to certain ingenious speculations which have been indulged in, they found that the hemisphere, which for countless ages has never been turned towards the earth, was almost an exact replica of the visible one. Fully three-fourths of it was brilliantly illuminated by the sun, and the scene which presented itself to their eyes was practically the same which they had beheld on the earth-ward side; huge groups of enormous craters and ringed mountains, long, irregular chains crowned with sharp, splintery peaks, and between these vast, deeply depressed areas, ranging in colour from dazzling white to a grey-brown, marking the beds of the vanished lunar seas.

As they crossed one of these, Redgrave allowed the Astronef to sink to within a few thousand feet of the surface, and then he and Zaidie swept it with their telescopes. Their chance search was rewarded by what they had not seen in the sea-beds of the other hemisphere. These depressions were far deeper than the others, evidently many thousands of feet deep, but the sun's rays were blazing full into this one, and, dotted round its slopes at varying elevations, they made out little patches which seemed to differ from the general surface.

"I wonder if those are the remains of cities," said Zaidie. "Isn't it possible that the populations might have built their cities along the seas, and that their descendants may have followed the waters as they retreated, I mean as they either dried up or disappeared into the centre?"

"Very probable indeed, dear," he said, "we'll go down and see."

He diminished the vertically repulsive force a little, and the Astronef dropped slantingly towards the bed of what might once have been the Pacific of the Moon. When they were within about a couple of thousand feet of the surface it became quite plain that

Zaidie was correct in her hypothesis. The vast sea-floor was literally strewn with the ruins of countless cities and towns, which had been inhabited by an equally countless series of generations of men and women, who had, perhaps, lived in the days when our own world was a glowing mass of molten rock, surrounded by the envelope of vapours which has since condensed to form its oceans.

The nearer they approached to the central and deepest depression the more perfect the buildings became until, down in the lowest depth, they found a collection of low-built square edifices, scarcely better than huts which had clustered round the little lake into which ages before the ocean had dwindled. But where the lake had been there was now only a depression covered with grey sand and brown rock.

Into this they descended and touched the lunar soil for the last time. A couple of hours' excursion among the houses proved that they had been the last refuge of the last descendants of a dying race, a race which had steadily degenerated just as the successions of cities had done, as the bitter fight for mere existence had become keener and keener until the two last essentials air and water, had failed and then the end had come.

The streets, like the square of the great temple of Tycho, were strewn with myriads and myriads of bones, and there were myriads more scattered round what had once been the shores of the dwindling lake. Here, as elsewhere, there was not a sign or a record of any kind—carving or sculpture.

Inside the great Pyramid of the City of Tycho they might, perhaps, have found something–some stone or tablet which bore the mark of the artist's hand; elsewhere, perhaps, they might have found cities reared by older races, which might have rivalled the creations of Egypt and Babylon, but there was no time to look for these. All that they had seen of the dead World had only sickened and saddened them. The untravelled regions of Space peopled by living worlds more akin to their own were before them, and the red disc of Mars was glowing in the zenith among the diamond-white clusters which gemmed the black sky behind him.

More than a hundred millions of miles had to be traversed before they would he able to set foot on his surface, and so, after one last look round the Valley of Death about them Redgrave turned on the full energy of the repulsive force in a vertical direction, and the Astronef leapt upwards in a straight line for her new destination. The unknown hemisphere spread out in a vast plain beneath them, the blazing sun rose on their left, and the brilliant silver orb of the Earth on their right, and so, full of wonder, and yet without regret, they bade farewell to the World that Was The Moon.

# Moxon's Master

by Ambrose Bierce

"Are you serious?—do you really believe that a machine thinks?"

I got no immediate reply; Moxon was apparently intent upon the coals in the grate, touching them deftly here and there with the fire-poker till they signified a sense of his attention by a brighter glow. For several weeks I had been observing in him a growing habit of delay in answering even the most trivial of commonplace questions. His air, however, was that of preoccupation rather than deliberation: one might have said that he had "something on his mind."

Presently he said:

"What is a 'machine'? The word has been variously defined. Here is one definition from a popular dictionary: 'Any instrument or organization by which power is applied and made effective, or a desired effect produced.' Well, then, is not a man a machine? And you will admit that he thinks—or thinks he thinks."

"If you do not wish to answer my question," I said, rather testily, "why not say so?—all that you say is mere evasion. You know well enough that when I say 'machine' I do not mean a man, but something that man has made and controls."

"When it does not control him," he said, rising abruptly and looking out of a window, whence nothing was visible in the blackness of a stormy night. A moment later he turned about and with a smile said: "I beg your pardon; I had no thought of evasion. I considered the dictionary man's unconscious testimony suggestive and worth something in the discussion. I can give your question a direct answer easily enough: I do believe that a machine thinks about the work that it is doing."

That was direct enough, certainly. It was not altogether pleasing, for it tended to confirm a sad suspicion that Moxon's devotion to study and work in his machine-shop had not been good for him. I knew, for one thing, that he suffered from insomnia, and that is no light affliction. Had it affected his mind? His reply to my question seemed to me then evidence that it had; perhaps I should think differently about it now. I was younger then, and among the blessings that are not denied to youth is ignorance. Incited by that great stimulant to controversy, I said:

"And what, pray, does it think with—in the absence of a brain?"

The reply, coming with less than his customary delay, took his favorite form of counter-interrogation:

"With what does a plant think—in the absence of a brain?"

"Ah, plants also belong to the philosopher class! I should be pleased to know some of their conclusions; you may omit the premises."

"Perhaps," he replied, apparently unaffected by my foolish irony, "you may be able to infer their convictions from their acts. I will spare you the familiar examples of the sensitive mimosa, the several insectivorous flowers and those whose stamens bend down and shake their pollen upon the entering bee in order that he may fertilize their distant mates. But observe this. In an open spot in my garden I planted a climbing vine. When it was barely above the surface I set a stake into the soil a yard away. The vine at once made for it, but as it was about to reach it after several days I removed it a few feet. The vine at once altered its course, making an acute angle, and again made for the stake. This manœuvre was repeated several times, but finally, as if discouraged, the vine abandoned the pursuit and ignoring further attempts to divert it traveled to a small tree, further away, which it climbed.

"Roots of the eucalyptus will prolong themselves incredibly in search of moisture. A well-known horticulturist relates that one entered an old drain pipe and followed it until it came to a break, where a section of the pipe had been removed to make way for a stone wall that had been built across its course. The root left the drain and followed the wall until it found an opening where a stone had fallen out. It crept through and following the other side of the wall back to the drain, entered the unexplored part and resumed its journey."

"And all this?"

"Can you miss the significance of it? It shows the consciousness of plants. It proves that they think."

"Even if it did—what then? We were speaking, not of plants, but of machines. They may be composed partly of wood—wood that has no longer vitality—or wholly of metal. Is thought an attribute also of the mineral kingdom?"

"How else do you explain the phenomena, for example, of crystallization?"

"I do not explain them."

"Because you cannot without affirming what you wish to deny, namely, intelligent cooperation among the constituent elements of the crystals. When soldiers form lines, or hollow squares, you call it reason. When wild geese in flight take the form of a letter V you say instinct. When the homogeneous atoms of a mineral, moving freely in solution, arrange themselves into shapes mathematically perfect, or particles of frozen moisture into the symmetrical and beautiful forms of snowflakes, you have nothing to say. You have not even invented a name to conceal your heroic unreason."

Moxon was speaking with unusual animation and earnestness. As he paused I heard in an adjoining room known to me as his "machine-shop," which no one but himself was permitted to enter, a singular thumping sound, as of somebody pounding upon a table with an open hand. Moxon heard it at the same moment and, visibly agitated, rose and hurriedly passed into the room whence it came. I thought it odd that any one else should be in there, and my interest in my friend—with doubtless a touch of unwarrantable curiosity—led me to listen intently, though, I am happy to say, not at the keyhole. There were confused sounds, as of a struggle or scuffle; the floor shook. I distinctly heard hard breathing and a hoarse whisper which said "Damn you!" Then all was silent, and presently Moxon reappeared and said, with a rather sorry smile:

"Pardon me for leaving you so abruptly. I have a machine in there that lost its temper and cut up rough."

Fixing my eyes steadily upon his left cheek, which was traversed by four parallel excoriations showing blood, I said:

"How would it do to trim its nails?"

I could have spared myself the jest; he gave it no attention, but seated himself in the chair that he had left and resumed the interrupted monologue as if nothing had occurred:

"Doubtless you do not hold with those (I need not name them to a man of your reading) who have taught that all matter is sentient, that every atom is a living, feeling, conscious being. *I* do. There is no such thing as dead, inert matter: it is all alive; all instinct with force, actual and potential; all sensitive to the same forces in its environment and susceptible to the contagion of higher and subtler ones residing in such superior organisms as it may be brought into relation with, as those of man when he is fashioning it into an instrument of his will. It absorbs something of his intelligence and purpose—more of them in proportion to the complexity of the resulting machine and that of its work.

"Do you happen to recall Herbert Spencer's definition of 'Life'? I read it thirty years ago. He may have altered it afterward, for anything I know, but in all that time I have been unable to think of a single word that could profitably be changed or added or removed. It seems to me not only the best definition, but the only possible one.

"'Life,' he says, 'is a definite combination of heterogeneous changes, both simultaneous and successive, in correspondence with external coexistences and sequences.'"

"That defines the phenomenon," I said, "but gives no hint of its cause."

"That," he replied, "is all that any definition can do. As Mill points out, we know nothing of cause except as an antecedent—nothing of effect except as a consequent. Of certain phenomena, one never occurs without another, which is dissimilar: the first in point of time we call cause, the second, effect. One who had many times seen a rabbit pursued by a dog, and had never seen rabbits and dogs otherwise, would think the rabbit the cause of the dog.

"But I fear," he added, laughing naturally enough, "that my rabbit is leading me a long way from the track of my legitimate quarry: I'm indulging in the pleasure of the chase for its own sake. What I want you to observe is that in Herbert Spencer's definition of 'life' the activity of a machine is included—there is nothing in the definition that is not applicable to it. According to this sharpest of observers and deepest of thinkers, if a man during his period of activity is alive, so is a machine when in operation. As an inventor and constructor of machines I know that to be true."

Moxon was silent for a long time, gazing absently into the fire. It was growing late and I thought it time to be going, but somehow I did not like the notion of leaving him in that isolated house, all alone except for the presence of some person of whose nature my conjectures could go no further than that it was unfriendly, perhaps malign. Leaning toward him and looking earnestly into his eyes while making a motion with my hand through the door of his workshop, I said:

"Moxon, whom have you in there?"

Somewhat to my surprise he laughed lightly and answered without hesitation:

"Nobody; the incident that you have in mind was caused by my folly in leaving a machine in action with nothing to act upon, while I undertook the interminable task of enlightening your understanding. Do you happen to know that Consciousness is the creature of Rhythm?"

"O bother them both!" I replied, rising and laying hold of my overcoat. "I'm going to wish you good night; and I'll add the hope that the machine which you inadvertently left in action will have her gloves on the next time you think it needful to stop her."

Without waiting to observe the effect of my shot I left the house.

Rain was falling, and the darkness was intense. In the sky beyond the crest of a hill toward which I groped my way along precarious plank sidewalks and across miry, unpaved streets I could see the faint glow of the city's lights, but behind me nothing was visible but a single window of Moxon's house. It glowed with what seemed to me a mysterious and fateful meaning. I knew it was an uncurtained aperture in my friend's "machine-shop," and I had little doubt that he had resumed the studies interrupted by his duties as my instructor in mechanical consciousness and the fatherhood of Rhythm. Odd, and in some degree humorous, as his convictions seemed to me at that time, I could not wholly divest myself of the feeling that they had some tragic relation to his life and character—perhaps to his destiny—although I no longer entertained the notion that they were the vagaries of a disordered mind. Whatever might be thought of his views, his exposition of them was too logical for that. Over and over, his last words came back to me: "Consciousness is the creature of Rhythm." Bald and terse as the statement was, I now found it infinitely alluring. At each recurrence it broadened in meaning and deepened in suggestion. Why, here, (I thought) is something upon which to found a philosophy. If consciousness is the product of rhythm all things *are* conscious, for all have motion, and all motion is rhythmic. I wondered if Moxon knew the significance and breadth of his thought—the scope of this momentous generalization; or had he arrived at his philosophic faith by the tortuous and uncertain road of observation?

That faith was then new to me, and all Moxon's expounding had failed to make me a convert; but now it seemed as if a great light shone about me, like that which fell upon Saul of Tarsus; and out there in the storm and darkness and solitude I experienced what Lewes calls "The endless variety and excitement of philosophic thought." I exulted in a new sense of knowledge, a new pride of reason. My feet seemed hardly to touch the earth; it was as if I were uplifted and borne through the air by invisible wings.

Yielding to an impulse to seek further light from him whom I now recognized as my master and guide, I had unconsciously turned about, and almost before I was aware of having done so found myself again at Moxon's door. I was drenched with rain, but felt no discomfort. Unable in my excitement to find the doorbell I instinctively tried the knob. It turned and, entering, I mounted the stairs to the room that I had so recently left. All was dark and silent; Moxon, as I had supposed, was in the adjoining room—the "machine-shop." Groping along the wall until I found the communicating door I knocked loudly several times, but got no response, which I attributed to the uproar outside, for the wind was blowing a gale and dashing the rain against the thin walls in sheets. The drumming upon the shingle roof spanning the unceiled room was loud and incessant.

I had never been invited into the machine-shop—had, indeed, been denied admittance, as had all others, with one exception, a skilled metal worker, of whom no one knew anything except that his name was Haley and his habit silence. But in my spiritual exaltation, discretion and civility were alike forgotten and I opened the door. What I saw took all philosophical speculation out of me in short order.

Moxon sat facing me at the farther side of a small table upon which a single candle made all the light that was in the room. Opposite him, his back toward me, sat another person. On the table between the two was a chessboard; the men were playing. I knew little of chess, but as only a few pieces were on the board it was obvious that the game was near its close. Moxon was intensely interested—not so much, it seemed to me, in the game as in his antagonist, upon whom he had fixed so intent a look that, standing though I did directly in the line of his vision, I was altogether unobserved. His face was ghastly white, and his eyes glittered like diamonds. Of his antagonist I had only a back view, but that was sufficient; I should not have cared to see his face.

He was apparently not more than five feet in height, with proportions suggesting those of a gorilla—a tremendous breadth of shoulders, thick, short neck and broad, squat head, which had a tangled growth of black hair and was topped with a crimson fez. A tunic of the same color, belted tightly to the waist, reached the seat—apparently a box—upon which he sat; his legs and feet were not seen. His left forearm appeared to rest in his lap; he moved his pieces with his right hand, which seemed disproportionately long.

I had shrunk back and now stood a little to one side of the doorway and in shadow. If Moxon had looked farther than the face of his opponent he could have observed nothing now, except that the door was open. Something forbade me either to enter or to retire, a feeling—I know not how it came—that I was in the presence of an imminent tragedy and might serve my friend by remaining. With a scarcely conscious rebellion against the indelicacy of the act I remained.

The play was rapid. Moxon hardly glanced at the board before making his moves, and to my unskilled eye seemed to move the piece most convenient to his hand, his motions in doing so being quick, nervous and lacking in precision. The response of his antagonist, while equally prompt in the inception, was made with a slow, uniform, mechanical and, I thought, somewhat theatrical movement of the arm, that was a sore trial to my patience. There was something unearthly about it all, and I caught myself shuddering. But I was wet and cold.

Two or three times after moving a piece the stranger slightly inclined his head, and each time I observed that Moxon shifted his king. All at once the thought came to me that the man was dumb. And then that he was a machine—an automaton chess-player! Then I remembered that Moxon had once spoken to me of having invented such a piece of mechanism, though I did not understand that it had actually been constructed. Was all his talk about the consciousness and intelligence of machines merely a prelude to eventual exhibition of this device—only a trick to intensify the effect of its mechanical action upon me in my ignorance of its secret?

A fine end, this, of all my intellectual transports—my "endless variety and excitement of philosophic thought!" I was about to retire in disgust when something occurred to hold my curiosity. I observed a shrug of the thing's great shoulders, as if it were irritated: and so natural was this—so entirely human—that in my new view of the matter it startled me. Nor was that all, for a moment later it struck the table sharply with its clenched hand. At that gesture Moxon seemed even more startled than I: he pushed his chair a little backward, as in alarm.

Presently Moxon, whose play it was, raised his hand high above the board, pounced upon one of his pieces like a sparrow-hawk and with the exclamation "checkmate!" rose quickly to his feet and stepped behind his chair. The automaton sat motionless.

The wind had now gone down, but I heard, at lessening intervals and progressively louder, the rumble and roll of thunder. In the pauses between I now became conscious of a low humming or buzzing which, like the thunder, grew momentarily louder and more distinct. It seemed to come from the body of the automaton, and was unmistakably a whirring of wheels. It gave me the impression of a disordered mechanism which had escaped the repressive and regulating action of some controlling part—an effect such as might be expected if a pawl should be jostled from the teeth of a ratchet-wheel. But before I had time for much conjecture as to its nature my attention was taken by the strange motions of the automaton itself. A slight but continuous convulsion appeared to have possession of it. In body and head it shook like a man with palsy or an ague chill, and the motion augmented every moment until the entire figure was in violent agitation. Suddenly it sprang to its feet and with a movement almost too quick for the eye to follow shot forward across table and chair, with both arms thrust forth to their full length—the posture and lunge of a diver. Moxon tried to throw himself backward out of reach, but he was too late: I saw the horrible thing's hands close upon his throat, his own clutch its wrists. Then the table was overturned, the candle thrown to the floor and extinguished, and all was black dark. But the noise of the struggle was dreadfully distinct, and most terrible of all were the raucous, squawking sounds made by the strangled man's efforts to breathe. Guided by the infernal hubbub, I sprang to the rescue of my friend, but had hardly taken a stride in the darkness when the whole room blazed with a blinding white light that burned into my brain and heart and memory a vivid picture of the combatants on the floor, Moxon underneath, his throat still in the clutch of those iron hands, his head forced backward, his eyes protruding, his mouth wide open and his tongue thrust out; and—horrible contrast!—upon the painted face of his assassin an expression of tranquil and profound thought, as in the solution of a problem in chess! This I observed, then all was blackness and silence.

Three days later I recovered consciousness in a hospital. As the memory of that tragic night slowly evolved in my ailing brain I recognized in my attendant Moxon's confidential workman, Haley. Responding to a look he approached, smiling.

"Tell me about it," I managed to say, faintly—"all about it."

"Certainly," he said; "you were carried unconscious from a burning house—Moxon's. Nobody knows how you came to be there. You may have to do a little explaining. The origin of the fire is a bit mysterious, too. My own notion is that the house was struck by lightning."

"And Moxon?"

"Buried yesterday—what was left of him."

Apparently this reticent person could unfold himself on occasion. When imparting shocking intelligence to the sick he was affable enough. After some moments of the keenest mental suffering I ventured to ask another question:

"Who rescued me?"

"Well, if that interests you—I did."

"Thank you, Mr. Haley, and may God bless you for it. Did you rescue, also, that charming product of your skill, the automaton chess-player that murdered its inventor?"

The man was silent a long time, looking away from me. Presently he turned and gravely said:

"Do you know that?"

"I do," I replied; "I saw it done."

That was many years ago. If asked today I should answer less confidently.

# Rats in the Belfry

by John York Cabot

This little guy Stoddard was one of the toughest customers I'd ever done business with. To look at him you'd think he was typical of the mild pleasant little sort of suburban home owner who caught the eight-oh-two six days a week and watered the lawn on the seventh. Physically, his appearance was completely that of the inconspicuous average citizen. Baldish, fortiesh, bespectacled, with the usual behind-the-desk bay window that most office workers get at his age, he looked like nothing more than the amiable citizen you see in comic cartoons on suburban life.

Yet, what I'm getting at is that this Stoddard's appearance was distinctly deceptive. He was the sort of customer that we in the contracting business would label as a combination grouser and eccentric.

When he and his wife came to me with plans for the home they wanted built in Mayfair's second subdivision, they were already full of ideas on exactly what they wanted.

This Stoddard—his name was George B. Stoddard in full—had painstakingly outlined about two dozen sheets of drafting paper with some of the craziest ideas you have ever seen.

"These specifications aren't quite down to the exact inchage, Mr. Kermit," Stoddard had admitted, "for I don't pretend to be a first class architectural draftsman. But my wife and I have had ideas on what sort of a house we want for years, and these plans are the result of our years of decision."

I'd looked at the "plans" a little sickly. The house they'd decided on was a combination of every architectural nightmare known to man. It was the sort of thing a respectable contractor would envision if he ever happened to be dying of malaria fever.

I could feel them watching me as I went over their dream charts. Watching me for the first faint sign of disapproval or amusement or disgust on my face. Watching to snatch the "plans" away from me and walk out of my office if I showed any of those symptoms.

"Ummmhumm," I muttered noncommittally.

"What do you think of them, Kermit?" Stoddard demanded.

I had a hunch that they'd been to contractors other than me. Contractors who'd been tactless enough to offend them into taking their business elsewhere.

"You have something distinctly different in mind here, Mr. Stoddard," I answered evasively.

George B. Stoddard beamed at his wife, then back to me.

"Exactly, sir," he said. "It is our dream castle."

I shuddered at the expression. If you'd mix ice cream with pickles and beer and herring and lie down for a nap, it might result in a dream castle.

"It will be a difficult job, Mr. Stoddard," I said. "This is no ordinary job you've outlined here."

"I know that," said Stoddard proudly. "And I am prepared to pay for the extra special work it will probably require."

That was different. I perked up a little.

"I'll have to turn over these plans to my own draftsman," I told him, "before I can give you an estimate on the construction."

George B. Stoddard turned to his wife.

"I told you, Laura," he said, "that sooner or later we'd find a contractor with brains and imagination."

It took fully two months haggling over the plans with Stoddard and my own draftsmen before we were able to start work on the nightmare my clients called their dream castle. Two months haggling in an effort to make Stoddard relinquish some of his more outlandish ideas on his proposed dwelling. But he didn't budge an inch, and by the time we'd laid the foundation for the dream shack, every last building quirk he'd had originally on those "plans" still held.

I took a lot of ribbing from contractors in that vicinity once the word got round that I was building Stoddard's house for him. It seems that he'd been to them all before he got around to me.

But I didn't mind the ribbing much at first. Even though Stoddard was a barrel full of trouble hanging around the building lot with an eagle eye to see that nothing was omitted, I had already cashed his first few payment checks on the construction.

He'd meant what he said about his willingness to pay more for the extra trouble entailed in the mad construction pattern we had to follow, and I couldn't call him stingy with his extra compensation by a long shot.

Financially, I was doing nicely, thank you. Mentally, I was having the devil's own time with Stoddard.

He didn't know a damned thing about architecture or construction, of course. But he did know what he wanted. Good Lord, how he knew what he wanted!

"The basement boiler layout isn't what I had on my plans!" he'd call me up to squawk indignantly.

"But it isn't greatly different the way we have it," I'd plead. "Besides, it's far safer than what you originally planned."

"Is it humanly possible to put it where I planned it?" my troublesome client would demand.

"Yes," I'd admit. "But saf—"

"Then put it where I planned it!" he would snap, hanging up. And, of course, I'd have to put it where he'd planned it.

The workmen on the job also presented a problem. They were getting fed up with Stoddard's snooping, and going crazy laying out patterns which were in absolute contradiction to sanity and good taste.

But in spite of all this, the monstrosity progressed.

If you can picture a gigantic igloo fronted by southern mansion pillars and dotted with eighteenth century gables, and having each wing done in a combination early Mexican and eastern Mosque style, you'll have just the roughest idea of what it was beginning to look like. For miles around, people were driving out to see that house in the evenings after construction men had left.

But the Stoddards were pleased. They were as happy about the whole mess as a pair of kids erecting a Tarzan dwelling in a tree. And the extra compensations I was getting for the additional trouble wasn't hurting me any.

I'll never forget the day when we completed the tiny belfry which topped off the monstrosity. Yes, a belfry. Just the kind you still see on little country churches and schoolhouses, only, of course a trifle different.

The Stoddards had come out to the lot to witness this momentous event; the completion, practically, of their dream child.

I was almost as happy as they were, for it stood as the symbol of the ending of almost all the grief for me.

My foreman came over to where I was standing with the Stoddards.

"You gonna put a bell in that belfry?" he asked.

George Stoddard looked at him as if he'd gone mad.

"What for?" he demanded.

"So you can *use* the belfry," the foreman said.

"Don't be so ridiculous, my good man," Stoddard snorted. "It will be of pleasurable use enough to us, just *looking* at it."

When the foreman had marched off, scratching his head, I turned to the Stoddards.

"Well, it's almost done," I said. "Pleased with it?"

Stoddard beamed. "You have no idea, Mr. Kermit," he said solemnly, "what a tremendous moment this is for my wife and me."

I looked at the plain, drab, smiling Laura Stoddard. From the shine in her eyes, I guess Stoddard meant what he said. Then I looked up at the belfry, and shuddered.

As I remarked before, even the belfry wasn't quite like any belfry human eyes had ever seen before. It angled in all the way around in as confusing a maze of geometrical madness you have ever seen. It was a patterned craziness, of course, having some rhyme to it, but no reason.

Looking at it, serenely topping that crazy-quilt house, I had the impression of its being an outrageously squashed cherry topping, the whipped cream of as madly a concocted sundae that a soda jerk ever made. A pleasant impression.

Stoddard's voice broke in on my somewhat sickish contemplation.

"When will we be able to start moving in?" he asked eagerly.

"The latter part of next week," I told him. "We should have it set by then."

"Good," said Stoddard. "Splendid." He put his arm around his wife, and the two of them stared starry eyed at their home. It made a lump come to your throat, seeing the bliss in their eyes as they stood there together. It made a lump come into your throat, until you realized what they were staring at.

"Incidentally," I said casually, figuring now was as good a time as any to get them used to the idea. "The startlingly different construction pattern you've had us follow will result in, ah, minor repairs in the house being necessary from time to time. Remember my telling you that at the start?"

Stoddard nodded, brushing the information away casually.

"Yes, certainly I remember your saying something about that. But don't worry. I won't hold you responsible for any minor repairs which the unique construction causes."

"Thanks," I told him dryly. "I just wanted to make certain we had that point clear."

The Stoddards moved in just as soon as the last inch of work on their dream monster was finished. I paid off my men, banked a nice profit on the job, and went back to building actual houses again. I thought my troubles with the Stoddards at an end.

But of course I was wrong.

It was fully a month after the Stoddards had been in their madhouse that I got my first indignant telephone call from George B. Stoddard himself.

"Mr. Kermit," said the angry voice on the phone, "this is George B. Stoddard."

I winced at the name and the all too familiar voice, but managed to sound cheerfully friendly.

"Yes, indeed, Mr. Stoddard," I oozed. "How are you and the Missus getting along in your dream castle?"

"That," said George B. Stoddard, "is what I called about. We have been having considerable difficulty for which I consider your construction men to be responsible."

"Now just a minute," I began. "I thought we agreed—"

"We agreed that I was to expect certain occasional minor repairs to be necessary due to the construction of the house," Stoddard broke in. "I know that."

"Then what's the trouble?" I demanded.

"This house is plagued with rats," said Stoddard angrily.

"Rats?" I echoed.

"Exactly!" my client snapped.

"But how could that be possible?" I demanded. "It's a brand new house, and rats don't—"

Stoddard broke in again. "The devil they don't. We have them, and it can't be due to any fault but those construction men of yours."

"How could it be their fault?" I was getting a little sore.

"Because it isn't my fault, nor my wife's. And the building, as you observed a minute ago, is practically new."

"Now listen," I began.

"I wish you'd come out here and see for yourself," Stoddard demanded.

"Have you caught any?"

"No," he answered.

"Have you seen any?" I demanded.

"No," Stoddard admitted, "but—"

This time I did the cutting in.

"Then how do you know you have rats?" I demanded triumphantly.

"Because," Stoddard almost shouted, "as I was going to tell you, I can hear them, and my wife can hear them."

I hadn't thought of that. "Oh," I said. Then: "Are you sure?"

"Yes, I am very sure. Now, will you please come out here and see what this is all about?" he demanded.

"Okay," I said. "Okay." And then I hung up and looked around for my hat. My visit wasn't going to be any fun, I knew. But what the hell. I had to admit that if Stoddard and his wife were hearing noises that sounded like rats, they had a legitimate squawk. For I built the house, and no amount of crazy ideas in its design by Stoddard could explain the presence of vermin.

Both the Stoddards met me at the door when I arrived out in the Mayfair subdivision where I'd built their monstrosity. As they led me into the living room, I caught a pretty good idea of their new home furnishings. They hadn't changed ideas, even to the mixing of a wild mess of various nations and periods in the junk they'd placed all around the house.

They led me past an early American library table to a deep Moroccan style couch, and both pulled up chairs of French and Dutch design before me.

Feeling thus surrounded by a small little circle of indignation, I began turning my hat around in my hands, staring uncomfortably at my surroundings.

"Nice place you've got here," I said.

"We know that," Stoddard declared, dismissing banalities. "But we'd best get immediately to the point."

"About the rats?" I asked.

"About the rats," said Stoddard. His wife nodded emphatically.

There was a silence. Maybe a minute passed. I cleared my throat.

"I thought you—" I began.

"Shhhh!" Stoddard hissed. "I want you to sit here and hear the noises, just as we have. Then you can draw your own conclusions. Silence, please."

So I didn't say a word, and neither did mine hosts. We sat there like delegates to a convention of mutes who were too tired to use their hands. This time the silence seemed even more ominous.

Several minutes must have passed before I began to hear the sounds. That was because I'd been listening for rat scrapings, and not prepared for the noises I actually began to hear.

Mr. and Mrs. Stoddard had their heads cocked to one side, and were staring hard at me, waiting for a sign that I was catching the sounds.

At first the noises seemed faint, blurred perhaps, like an almost inaudible spattering of radio static. Then, as I adjusted my ear to them, I began to get faint squeaks, and small, sharp noises that were like far distant poppings of small firecrackers.

I looked up at the Stoddards.

"Okay," I admitted. "I hear the noises. They seem to be coming from behind the walls, if anywhere."

Stoddard looked smugly triumphant.

"I told you so," he smirked.

"But they aren't rat scrapings," I said. "I know the sounds rats make, and those aren't rat sounds."

Stoddard sat bolt upright. "What?" he demanded indignantly. "Do you mean to sit there and tell me—"

"I do," I cut in. "Ever heard rat noises?"

Stoddard looked at his wife. Both of them frowned. He looked back at me.

"No-o," he admitted slowly. "That is, not until we got these rats. Never had rats before."

"So you jumped to conclusions and thought they were rat noises," I said, "even though you wouldn't recognize a rat noise if you heard one."

Stoddard suddenly stood up. "But dagnabit, man!" he exploded. "If those aren't rat noises, what are they?"

I shrugged. "I don't know," I admitted. "They sound as if they might be coming through the pipes. Perhaps we ought to take a look around the house, beginning with the basement, eh?"

Stoddard considered this a minute. Then he nodded.

"That seems reasonable enough," he admitted.

I followed the amateur designer-owner of this madhouse down into the basement. There we began our prowl for the source of the noise. He snapped on the light switch, and I had a look around. The boiler and everything else in the basement was exactly as I remembered it—in the wrong place.

There was an array of sealed tin cans, each holding about five gallons, banked around the boiler. I tapped on the sides of these and asked Stoddard what they were.

"Naphtha," he explained, "for my wife's cleaning."

"Hell of a place to put them," I commented.

A familiar light came into Stoddard's stubborn eyes.

"That's where I want to put them," he said.

I shrugged. "Okay," I told him. "But don't let the insurance people find out about it."

We poked around the basement some more, and finally, on finding nothing that seemed to indicate a source of the sound, we went back up to the first floor.

Our investigation of pipes and other possible sound carriers on the first floor was also fruitless, although the sounds grew slightly stronger than they'd been in the basement.

I looked at Stoddard, shrugging. "We'd better try the second floor," I said.

I followed him upstairs to the second floor. Aside from the crazy belfry just above the attic, it was the top floor of the wildly constructed domicile.

The sounds were distinctly more audible up there, especially in the center bedroom. We covered the second floor twice and ended back up in that center bedroom again before I realized that we were directly beneath the attic.

I mentioned this to Stoddard.

"We might as well look through the attic, then," Stoddard said.

I led the way this time as we clambered up into the attic.

"Ever looked for your so-called rats up here?" I called over my shoulder.

Stoddard joined me, snapping on a flashlight, spraying the beam around the attic rafters. "No," he said. "Of course not."

I was opening my mouth to answer, when I suddenly became

aware that the noises were now definitely louder. Noises faint, but not blurred any longer. Noises which weren't really noises, but were actually voices!

I grabbed Stoddard by the arm.

"Listen!" I ordered.

We stood there silently for perhaps half a minute. Yes, there wasn't any question about it now. I knew that the faint sounds were those of human voices.

"Good heavens!" Stoddard exclaimed.

"Rats, eh?" I said sarcastically.

"But, but—" Stoddard began. He was obviously bewildered.

"There's a sort of central pipe and wiring maze up here," I told him, "due to the plans we were forced to follow in building this house of yours. Those faint voices are carried through the pipes and wires for some reason of sound vibration, and hurled up here. Just tell me where you keep your radio, and we'll solve your problem."

Stoddard looked at me a minute.

"But we don't own a radio," he said quietly.

I was suddenly very much deflated.

"Are you sure?" I demanded.

"Don't be silly," Stoddard told me.

I stood there scratching my head and feeling foolish. Then I got another idea.

"Have you been up in that, ah, ornamental belfry since you moved in?" I asked.

"Of course not," Stoddard said. "It's to look at. Not to peek out of."

"I have a hunch the sounds might be even more audible up there," I said.

"Why?"

I scratched my head. "Just a hunch."

"Well it's a dammed fool one," Stoddard said. He turned around and started out of the attic. I followed behind him.

"You have to admit you haven't rats," I said.

Stoddard muttered something I couldn't catch. When we got down to the first floor again, Mrs. Stoddard was waiting expectantly for our arrival.

"Did you discover where the rats are?" she demanded.

Stoddard shot me a glance. "They aren't rats," he said with some reluctance. "The noises, we'd swear, are faint voices and sounds of human beings moving around. Were you talking to yourself while we were upstairs, Laura?"

Mrs. Stoddard gave her husband a surprised look. "Who was there to talk with, George?" she asked.

I had had about enough of this. I was damned tired of trotting around the weirdly laid out floors of the Stoddard home trying to track down rats which weren't rats but voices.

"If there are inexplicable echoes in this building," I said, "it is due to the construction. And don't forget, you wanted it this way. Now that I have proved to your satisfaction that you don't have rats, I might as well go. Good day."

I got my hat, and neither Stoddard nor his wife had much to say as they saw me to the door. Their accusing attitudes had vanished, however, and they both seemed even a trifle sheepish.

It was two o'clock when I left them. I'd killed better than an hour and a half prowling around the place, and another half hour driving out. I was damned disgusted by the time I got back to my office.

You can imagine my state of mind, consequently, some twenty-five minutes after I'd been back in my office, when I answered the telephone to hear Stoddard's voice coming over it.

"Mr. Kermit," he babbled excitedly, "this is George B. Stoddard again, Mr. Kermit!"

"What've you got now?" I demanded. "And don't tell me termites!"

"Mr. Kermit," Stoddard gasped, "you have to come back right away, Mr. Kermit!"

"I will like hell," I told him flatly, hanging up.

The telephone rang again in another half minute. It was Stoddard again.

"Mr. Kermit, pleeeease listen to me! I beg of you, come out here at once. It's terribly important!"

I didn't say a word this time. I just hung right up.

In another half minute the telephone was jangling again. I was purple when I picked it up this time.

"Listen," I bellowed. "I don't care what noises you're hearing now—"

Stoddard cut in desperately, shouting at the top of his lungs to do so.

"I'm not only hearing the noises, Kermit," he yelled, "I'm *seeing* the people who cause them!"

This caught me off balance.

"Huh?" I gulped.

"The belfry," he yelled, "I went up in the belfry, and you can see the people who's voices we heard!" There was a pause, while he found breath, then he shouted, "You have to come over. You're the only one I can think of to show this to!"

Stoddard was an eccentric, but only so far as his tastes in architecture were concerned. I realized this, as I sat there gaping foolishly at the still vibrating telephone in my hand.

"Okay," I said, for no earthly reason that I could think of, "okay, hang on. I'll be there in twenty minutes."

Mrs. Stoddard met me at the door this time. She was worried, almost frightened, and very bewildered.

"George is upstairs, Mr. Kermit. He won't let me come up there. He told me to send you up the minute you arrived. He's up in the attic."

"What on earth," I began.

"I don't know," his wife said. "I was down in the basement drying some clothes, when I heard this terrible yelling from George. Then he was calling you on the telephone. I don't know what it's all about."

I raced up to the attic in nothing flat, almost knocking my teeth out on the bottom step of the attic stairs.

Then I stumbled into the darkness of the attic, and saw Stoddard's flashlight bobbing around in a corner.

"Kermit?"

It was Stoddard's voice.

"Yes," I answered. "What in the hell is up? It had better be goo—"

"Hurry," Stoddard said. "Over here, quickly!"

I stumbled across the board spacings until I was standing beside Stoddard and peering up at what the beam of his flashlight revealed on the ceiling—a ragged, open hole, which he'd made by tearing several coatings of insulation from the spot.

For a minute, I couldn't make out anything in that flash beam glare. Stoddard had hold of my arm, and was saying one word over and over, urgently.

"Look. Look. Look!"

Then my eyes got adjusted to the light change, and I was aware that I was gazing up into the interior of the crazy belfry atop the monstrous house. Gazing up into the interior, while voices, quite loud and clearly distinguishable, were talking in a language which I didn't recognize immediately. As far as my vision was concerned, I might as well have been looking at a sort of grayish vaporish screen of some sort, that was all I saw.

"Shhhh!" Stoddard hissed now. "Don't say a word. Just listen to them!"

I held my breath, although it wasn't necessary. As I said, the voices coming down from that belfry were audible enough to have been a scant ten or twelve feet away. But I held my breath anyway, meanwhile straining my eyes to pierce that gray screen of vapor on which the light was focused.

And then I got it. The voices were talking in German, two of them, both harsh, masculine.

"What in the hell," I began. "Is there a short wave set up there or—"

Stoddard cut me off. "Can't you see it yet?" he hissed.

The voices went on talking, while I strained my eyes even more in an effort to pierce that gray fog covering the rent in the ceiling. And then I saw. Saw at first, as if through a thin gray screen of gauze.

I was looking up into a room of some sort. A big room. An incredibly big room. A room so big that two dozen belfry rooms would have fit into it!

And then it got even clearer. There was a desk at the end of the room. A tremendously ornate desk. A desk behind which was sitting a small, gray uniformed, moustached man.

There was another uniformed person of porcine girth standing beside that desk and pointing to a map on the wall in front of him. He was jabbering excitedly to the little man at the desk, and he wore a uniform that was so plushily gaudy it was almost ridiculous.

The two kept chattering back and forth to each other in German, obviously talking about the map at which the fat, plush-clad one was pointing.

I turned incredulously to Stoddard.

"Wh-wh-what in the hell goes?" I demanded.

Stoddard seemed suddenly vastly relieved. "So you see it and hear it, too!" he exclaimed. "Thank God for that! I thought I'd lost my mind!"

I grabbed hard on his arm. "But listen," I began.

"Listen, nothing," he hissed. "We *both* can't be crazy. Those are the voices we kept hearing before. And those two people are the talkers. Those two German (five words censored) louses. Hitler and Goering!"

There, he'd said it. I hadn't dared to. It sounded too mad, too wildly, babblingly insane to utter. But now I looked back through that thin gray cheesecloth of fog, back into the room.

The two occupants couldn't be anyone other than Hitler and Goering. And I was suddenly aware that the map Goering pointed to so frequently was a map of Austria.

"But what," I started again.

Stoddard looked me in the eye. "I can understand a little German," he said. "They're talking about an invasion of Austria, and if you will look hard at the corner of that map, you'll see a date marked—1938!"

I did look hard, and of course I saw that date. I turned back to Stoddard.

"We're both crazy," I said a little wildly, "we're both stark, raving nuts. Let's get out of here."

"We are looking back almost five years into the past," Stoddard hissed. "We are looking back five years into Germany, into a room in which Hitler and Goering are talking over an approaching invasion of a country called Austria. I might have believed I was crazy when I first found this alone, but not now!"

Maybe we were both crazy. Maybe he was wrong. But then and there I believed him, and I knew that somehow, in some wild, impossible fashion, that belfry on Stoddard's asinine house had become a door leading through space and time, back five years into Germany, into the same room where Adolf Hitler and Hermann Goering planned the conquest of Austria!

Stoddard was taking something out of his pocket.

"Now that you're here I can try it," he said. "I didn't dare do so before, since I felt I couldn't trust my own mind alone in the thing."

I looked at what he held in his hands. A stone, tied to a long piece of string.

"What's that for?" I demanded.

"I want to see if that veil, that gray fog door, can be penetrated," he hissed.

Stoddard was swinging the stone on a string in a sharp arc now. And suddenly he released it, sending it sailing through the grayish aperture in the ceiling, straight into the belfry, or rather, the big room.

I saw and heard the stone on the string hit the marble floor of that room. Then, just as sharply, Stoddard jerked it back, yanking it into the attic again.

The result in the room beyond the fog sheet was instantaneous. Goering wheeled from the map on the wall, glaring wildly around the room. A pistol was in his hand.

Hitler had half risen behind that ornate desk, and was searching the vast, otherwise unoccupied room wildly with his eyes.

Of course neither saw anything. Stoddard, breathing excitedly at my side, had pulled the stone back into our section of time and space. But his eyes were gleaming.

"It can be done," he whispered fiercely. "It can be crossed!"

"But what on—" I started. He cut me off with a wave of his hand, pointing back to the gray screen covering the hole in the ceiling.

Goering had put the pistol back in the holster at his side, and was grinning sheepishly at der Fuehrer, who was resuming his seat behind the desk in confused and angry embarrassment.

The voices picked up again.

"They're saying how silly, to be startled by a sound," Stoddard hissed in my ear.

Then he grabbed my arm. "But come, we can't wait any longer. Something has to be done immediately."

He was pulling me away from the rent in the ceiling, away from the door that had joined our time and space to the time and space of a world and scene five years ago.

As we emerged from the attic and started blinkingly down the steps, Stoddard almost ran ahead of me.

"We must hurry," he said again and again.

"To where?" I demanded bewilderedly. "Hadn't we better do something about th—"

"Exactly," Stoddard panted. "We're really going to do something about that phenomenon in the belfry. We're going to the first place in two where we can buy two rifles, quick!"

"Rifles?" I gasped, still not getting it.

"For that little moustached swine up there," Stoddard said, pointing toward the attic. "If a stone can cross that gray barrier, so can bullets. We are both going to draw bead on Adolf Hitler in the year of 1938, and thus avert this hell he's spread since then. With two of us firing, we can't miss."

And then, of course, I got it. It was incredible, impossible. But that gray screen covering the rent in the attic ceiling upstairs wasn't impossible. I'd seen it. Neither was the room behind it, the room where the belfry was supposed to be, but where Adolf Hitler's inner sanctum was instead. I'd seen that, too. So was it impossible that we'd be able to eliminate the chief cause of the world's trouble by shooting accurately back across time and space?

At that moment I didn't think so!

Our mad clattering dash down the attic steps, and then down to the first floor brought Mrs. Stoddard up from the basement. She looked frightenedly from her husband to me, then back to him again.

"What's wrong?" she quavered.

"Nothing," Stoddard said, pushing her gently but quickly aside as we dashed for the door.

"But, George!" Mrs. Stoddard shrilled behind us. We heard her footsteps hurrying toward the door, even as we were out of it.

"My car," I yelled. "It's right in front. I know the closest place where we can get the guns!"

Stoddard and I piled into the car like a pair of high school kids when the last bell rings. Then I was gunning the motor, while out of the corner of my eye I could see Stoddard's wife running down the front steps shouting shrilly after us.

We jumped from the curb like a plane from a catapult, doing fifty by my quick shift to second gear. Then we were tearing the quiet streets of Mayfair's second subdivision apart with the noise of a blasting horn and a snarling motor.

It was ten minutes later when I screeched to a stop in front of the sports and gun store I'd remembered existed in Mayfair's first subdivision. The clerk was amazed at the wild speed with which we raced in, grabbed the guns, threw the money on the counter, and dashed out.

We must have looked like something out of a gangster movie as we raced back to Stoddard's place.

I was doing the driving, and Stoddard had clambered in beside me, both rifles, and several cartridge packages in his hands. He was rocking back and forth in mad impatience, as if by rocking he could increase our speed. The expression on his face was positively bloodthirsty.

And then we heard the sirens behind us. Shrill, coming up like comet wails in spite of our own speed.

"Oh, God!" Stoddard groaned. "Police!"

I squinted up into my rear vision mirror. We were less than two blocks from the Stoddard house, now, and the thought of being overhauled by police at the juncture was sickening, unbearable even to contemplate.

And then I saw the reason for the sirens. Saw them in the rear vision mirror. Two fire engines, one a hook and ladder outfit, the other a hose truck!

"It's all right," I yelped. "It's only two fire trucks!"

"Thank God!" Stoddard gasped.

We were a block from his place now, with only one corner left to turn before we'd see the mad architectural monstrosity he called his home; before we'd see the crazy belfry which held the salvation of the world in its screwballish, queer-angled lines.

And then the fire trucks and the sirens were nearer and louder, less than a block behind us. At that instant we turned the corner and came into full view of the Stoddard place.

It was a mass of flames, utterly, roaringly ablaze!

I almost drove us off the street and into a tree. And by the time I'd gotten a grip on myself, we were just a few houses away from the blazing inferno of Stoddard's crazy quilt dwelling.

I stopped by the curb, and clambered out of the car onto knees which would scarcely support me. My stomach was turning over and over in an apparently endless series of nauseating somersaults.

Stoddard, white-faced, frozen, stood there beside me, clutching the guns and the cartridge boxes foolishly in his hands.

Then someone was running up to us. Running and crying sobbingly, breathlessly. It was Stoddard's wife.

The fire trucks screeched to a stop before the blazing building at that instant, and her first words were drowned in the noise they made.

"... just drying out some clothes, George," she sobbed. "Just drying them out and turned on the furnace to help dry them. You left like that, and I got frightened. I ran to a neighbor's. The explosion and fire started not five minutes later."

Sickly, I thought of the naphtha Stoddard had piled near his boiler. I didn't say anything, though, for I knew he was thinking of it also.

He dropped the guns and cartridge boxes, and in a tight, strained voice, while putting his arms comfortingly around his wife, said:

"That's all right, Laura. It wasn't your fault. We'll have another house like this. So help me God, *just like this*!"

It has been six months now since Stoddard's architectural eyesight burned to the ground. He started rebuilding immediately after that. I turned over all the drafts my company made from his first crude "plans," and he handed them to the supervisor of the construction company he bought out. You see, he took every dime he owned, sold out his insurance business, and has gone into the building game in dead earnest.

He explained it to me this way.

"I couldn't go on having house after house built and torn down on the same spot, Kermit. It would break me in no time. This way, with my own company to construct the house every time, I'll save about half each time."

"Then you're going to build precisely the same house?" I demanded.

His jaw went hard, and he peered from behind his spectacles with the intense glare of a fanatic. For once he didn't look like Mr. Suburbanite.

"You know damned well I am," he said. "And until it is *precisely* the same as the first, I'll keep tearing 'em down and putting 'em up again. I don't care if I have to build a thousand to do it, right on this spot!"

Of course I knew what he meant by precisely the same. And I wondered what on earth the odds were he was bucking. Through chance and a mad combination of angles, that time and space door had appeared the first time. But it might have been hanging on the tiniest atom of a fractional difference.

Stoddard has already finished his second house, and although it *looks* exactly like the monstrosity I first built for him, it can't be *precisely* like it. For he didn't get the gray shrouded door when he poked a hole in the attic ceiling and looked up into the second crazy belfry. All he saw was the belfry.

Tomorrow he starts tearing down to build another, and pretty soon people are going to be certain he's crazy.

As a matter of fact, they'll soon be pretty sure I'm loony also. For of course I can't help going over there now and then to sort of lend a hand....

# On the Martian Way

by Harry Gore Bishop

The New York office force of the R.D. Jones Co. caught its breath in a gasp of astonishment when it was announced that Captain Goff was to take out the *Columbia* with passengers only. Even the superintendent seemed ashamed of the directors' decision, for he had sent the word out to old Williams, the veteran chief clerk, scribbled on a slip of paper, and had then promptly gone out by way of his private entrance.

Williams read the note with rapidly rising indignation and broke up the office routine for a full thirty minutes, while he raged about the room, alternately denouncing the superintendent, the president and the board of directors, and assailing luckless clerks for stopping work to listen to him.

"Why," he cried, "old R. D. would turn over in his grave if he knew how these boys are running the company into the ground. It was bad enough when they commenced fillin' up empty cargo space with furniture, vegetables and dry goods, but now turnin' the *Columbia* into a passenger boat! A man-hauler! And not ordinary, healthy passengers with sound legs and good digestions, but a lot of consumptives, anaemics, and sick babies, raked up from the East Side, on account of"—here referring to the superintendent's note—"on account of the New York *Eagle's* Fresh Air Fund. Wish old R. D. was here for about five minutes." And then he added most prophetically, "It's bad business this haulin' of passengers and the company'll regret it."

The R. D. Jones Co. was a fast freight line making weekly sailings to Mars from their Westchester station. The older Jones, long since gathered to his forefathers, had begun life as a clerk on a Lunar tramp and graduated from that to purser on a Martian oil boat. Being naturally a keen observer he soon discovered that while the people of Mars were particularly partial to mutton, the genus sheep failed to thrive on that husky planet. Those were the days when concessions were being granted right and left, and upon his second return to the earth, after this important discovery, young Jones brought back such valuable iron-clad rights to certain trade privileges that a fast freight line carrying outward-bound refrigerated meat and returning either in ballast or fruit-laden, was put into being by New York capitalists. From the two old tramp tubs originally leased the "Mutton Run" had grown to a corporation, owning outright thirty boats and leasing a score more.

But hard times come, even to corporations as wealthy and powerful as the R. D. Jones Co. Some of the concessions were now expiring and the profits had been horribly mutilated. Martians, too, seemed to be losing their appetites for American meat and the R. D. Jones Co. was now bidding for other classes of freight at ridiculous margins. Then, to cap the climax, the *Montezuma* and the *Princess Irene*, two immense, brand new boats, carrying valuable cargoes and running neck and neck, outward bound, had dashed, head on, into an unpredicted meteoric shower and had gone to join the vast congregation of inter-stellar derelicts.

So, although it was a mighty departure from a policy now well-nigh a century old, the directors had decided that instead of putting the *Columbia* out of commission, they would charter her to the *Eagle* for at least one passenger run, and notwithstanding old Williams, busy workmen were soon transferring her cargo compartments into dormitories and hospital wards.

The chief dispatcher of the R. D. Jones Co. was one Winston, a clean-cut, steady-going man, just turned thirty, for whom great things were predicted by his friends, for nature had endowed him with a reasoning ability and a genius for mathematics far above the ordinary. Furthermore, he was a direct descendant of the great Sir Francis Winston who had first expounded and proved that the gravitational attraction of any mass had characteristics peculiarly its own; and that just as certain substances arrest certain colors of the spectrum and permit others to pass through, certain magnetic fields could be created which were impermeable to the attraction of certain masses, though uninfluencing that of others; thus first rendering interplanetary passage possible.

On the fifteenth of October the *Columbia* was reported ready, and on the eighteenth Winston received his instruction from the traffic manager.

> Prepare sailing data for the Columbia to be launched about noon on the 20th inst., for through run to Nekhoboh, planet Mars. Full speed from atmosphere to atmosphere. No cargo. Passengers only.

He was too busy that day to attend to the matter, for the *Chryse*, an ancient Jones tub, inward bound with a heavy cargo, was having trouble with Venus, and some rapid calculations and appropriate orders for her anxious skipper, who was keeping the receivers hot with appeals for help, were needed, to keep that planet from adding another satellite to her train.

At last Winston slammed down the covers on the two computing machines and was reaching for his coat when the messenger handed him two envelopes. One was official, a radiogram addressed to the chief dispatcher of the R. D. Jones Co. He tore it open and read:

October 19th.

National Observatory, Himalaya Peaks.

To all Interplanetary Dispatchers:
Nebulous matter first observed and reported by Captain Clarke of the *Juno*, U. S. Mail and Express Line, on October 7th, when fourteen days out of Jupiter, is supposed to be Biela's comet reunited. Exact data as to orbit will be sent out at ten o'clock tonight. First trial calculations show that this body will strongly affect Martian routes from November 15th to 20th.

De Saussure.

"The devil!" Winston gasped. "It means calculating over again the whole of the second leg. However, that can be done tomorrow forenoon." He thrust the radiogram into his pocket and started for the door opening the other envelope, which was addressed to him personally in a woman's bold, black handwriting.

There wasn't much in the note. Winston read it almost at a glance, but the light suddenly died out of his eyes and in its place came a frightened, hunted look; his face turned an ashy white; things seemed to whirl about him and then grow black. Someone gave him water, and he stumbled out into the light of the setting sun with unseeing eyes.

It was the old story of those who love and are loved by woman. A high-spirited girl, brooding over a fancied inattention; a sleepless night; a hastily penned note ending all for ever.

Just what he did that night Winston never knew. At the trial they testified that he had come into the club about ten o'clock. Somebody had won on the aerial races that afternoon and was buying champagne, and Winston drank, drank, drank, until friends, knowing his usual temperate habits had put him to bed. They testified also that he had written a receipt for a radiogram about eleven o'clock, giving the details of the comet's orbit.

All that night an army of workmen swarmed in and over the hull of the *Columbia*, giving her the finishing touches for her flight, and at daybreak their places were taken by another shift.

At ten o'clock Winston came in and mechanically sat down at his desk, pale, heavy-eyed, his mind a blank. His first assistant handed him the sailing orders and together they rechecked the calculations. The computations balanced; and the instructions for laying the different courses were concise and clear.

"We haven't missed anything, have we?" he asked, passing a trembling hand across his hot, dry forehead. "Something seems to tell me that there is an error somewhere."

"Errors!" sniffed the assistant. "We don't make errors here."

Winston took the neatly typed sheets and walked out into the main office where old Captain Goff was talking earnestly with the second vice president, a smug-faced German Jew, who was in charge of the company's communication system.

"Don't you vorry, gapting," he was saying, "dose radio receivers will vork like all get oudt shust as soon as you glear der earth's atmosvere. Don't vorry, de vill be O. K."

"But remember, Mr. Oldstein," the captain added, gently stroking his long white beard and fixing his deep blue eyes anxiously on the Jew's shifting gaze—"remember I carry passengers on this trip, and I would feel greatly relieved if you would have De Muth & Co. send up one of their experts to have a look at them."

"Vot! Und delay der sailing!" exclaimed the second vice president. "Und vot you t'ink dem eggsperts cost? Vun t'ousand dollars! Ach! But here is Meester Vinston mit der orders. Good-by, gapting."

The old man smiled sadly at the departing official and turned to Winston, grasping his hand and glancing benignantly at him over the gold rims of his spectacles as he took the orders and read them through aloud, as required by law, and affixed his signature to the retained copy in token of understanding.

"It has always been my desire," said the captain in his deep, solemn voice—a voice that seemed to have acquired some peculiar magnetic quality from the unfathomable depths of the ever-mysterious voids between the worlds in which he had spent almost half of his three score years—"to some day command a passenger boat; and it has pleased the good Lord to gratify at last my worldly wishes in a manner far surpassing my fondest dreams, for what could be greater or grander than to command a boat filled with these poor unfortunates? God grant us a safe and speedy voyage."

The grand old man bade an affectionate farewell to the office force from old Williams down to the office boys and messengers; and with Winston walked over to the launching cradles.

A few belated passengers were hurrying aboard, and the decks of the *Columbia* still open to the sunshine were teeming with life.

Hunchbacks and dwarfs, their little beady eyes glistening with excitement, gazed eagerly about; consumptives and asthmatics lined the rails, their faces reflecting the hope of a speedy cure in the rarified Martian atmosphere; babies of all colors and nationalities, some sitting quietly content or speechlessly frightened, others loudly wailing, and a few clapping diminutive hands and kicking tiny feet to the time of the big band up forward on the observation deck. Two little Martian orphans, going back to relatives, a boy and a girl, each clasping a hand of their special nurse, were dancing boisterously around her, their big pear-shaped heads, stocky chests and pipestem legs contrasting strangely with the other children. Off to one side, a group of bored doctors were trying to retort amiably to the raillery of friends in the yards below.

The old man bade a cheery good-by, and mounting to the pilot bridge, stood for a moment looking backward over his boat, his long white hair waving in the gentle spring breeze. Then he gave a signal and the lights flared up over the vessel, hull shutters slid suddenly into place, and the craft was sealed up for her long flight through the heavens.

Winston never forgot that morning, brain-clouded though he was. The great black hull of the *Columbia*, with her white-haired captain up forward at his post; and the pitiful unfortunates swarming her decks; the sudden obliteration of the scene as the shutters closed over it was indelibly imprinted on his imagination. There was a turning and grinding of the great motors at the rear of the cradle as they worked the gravitation screens under the vessel, one from the front and one from the rear; then, as the earth's attraction reluctantly gave up its grip on the mighty mass of iron and steel gouged from her own vitals, it slowly rose, level keeled, until its stern butted against the top girders of the cradle. He remembered the loose ends of several cables, knocked over on the screens, suddenly rose uncannily and stood straight up, serpent-like in the air. A careless workman had left a pipe-wrench lying on the framework, and it had suddenly leaped upward, banged against the hull, danced around a moment like a thing possessed, then sliding swiftly up along the sloping side had shot off into space. Winston remembered he had laughed, when the wrench started on its journey. But the laugh had died on his lips. There was something queer about this launching. He had felt it vaguely all morning and it recurred then with added intensity.

As the yard master, high up on the launching deck of the cradle, shouted his directions to the operators at the motors, in response to the captain's signals, Winston closed his eyes, and his brilliant mind, drink-clouded though it was, went far out into space, going over again, step by step, the calculations for the flight. There was no mistake in the figures, but something was wrong. He started toward the yard master's station to stop the launching. He even cried out. But he was too late.

Twelve minutes later the Westchester station radiograph receivers picked up Captain Goff's message, saying that he had safely cleared the earth's atmosphere, had rigged all his earth screens and thanks to the greedy attraction of the sun and two handy planets, her nose was set to the proper point on the celestial sphere and she was bowling along the first leg at seventy miles a second.

At three o'clock that afternoon the first assistant in the dispatcher's department found the De Saussure radiograms lying on Winston's desk, read them, hastily recalculated the second leg and rushed white-faced into the traffic manager's office.

"What's that you are saying?" demanded the traffic manager whirling about in his swivel chair and facing the breathless computer.

"Simply this," returned the man, controlling himself with difficulty, "I just found these radiograms on Mr. Winston's desk, reporting the re-appearance of Biela's comet, with an orbit intersecting the Martian routes about November 15th. For some reason Winston had forgotten them and the *Columbia* is off with sailing orders that will run her plump into the comet's mass if she isn't held back."

"Hell!" exclaimed the traffic manager, springing to his feet. "Where's Winston?"

"Don't know," replied the computer. "Haven't seen him since the sailing. He got a letter last night that seemed to upset him and he acted dippy all morning."

It is unnecessary to recite in detail all that occurred during the next three weeks. Old and middle aged persons will recall that the papers talked of little else, and that the civilized worlds of three planets followed day by day the course of the white-haired skipper and his boat of 1,800 happy, excited women, children and the earth's unfortunates, speeding through the black night of the imponderable ether to their sure destruction. Nor is it necessary to again tell how sweating, heat-blistered engineers at every interplanetary radiograph station on three planets, stood by their generators until they were carried out unconscious, speeding up their machines, to the calls of set-faced operators for higher voltage, as they hurled radiogram after radiogram out into space, under a pressure that damaged receivers on boats as far away as Jupiter but which failed to excite the wornout and leaky induction coils of the *Columbia's* instruments. Day after day, regularly at the twelfth hour, came the punctilious, diurnal "report of progress" from Captain Goff, for his sending apparatus was working beautifully, and day after day as he reported another six million miles put astern of the *Columbia's* flaming tail lights, the worlds shuddered with renewed horror.

Winston had been found early on the morning after the sailing, wandering the streets, still dazed and unknowing, and had been taken to the Tombs, where two companies of federal troops were guarding him from an East Side mob. Here also, soon came Oldstein, for with the *Eagle* in the lead, the press and populace were frantic for the blood of those persons held responsible.

On the 4th of November Captain Goff reported successfully that he had turned the "angles."

On the 6th he reported by heliocentric co-ordinates the appearance of a strange, luminous mass, which—so he had calculated, was moving in a path likely to carry it across his own. On the 8th he was evidently ill at ease, for he apologetically referred to the inability of his subordinates to get the receiving apparatus in order, and again referred to the unknown mass coming up on him. His "progress report" showed that he had diminished speed.

On the 9th he reported that the *Columbia* was "wobbling," apparently under the influence of the comet, as he had now determined that body to be; that he had reversed and rigged screens to hold her steady. Two hours later he sent another message that the *Columbia* was drifting from her course. Another hour and he "regretted to report that he could no longer keep her head up." Short, sharp messages they were, indicating that the old man was using every resource to avoid the danger and was wasting little time over the radiograph.

At twenty minutes past two on the morning of the 10th of November Captain Robert Goff's last message began to spark from the induction coils at the Westchester station.

> "I regret to report that at two minutes past midnight I lost control of the Columbia, notwithstanding gallant efforts on part of the crew, and that she is now falling into the comet at a frightful velocity. The celestial sphere ahead of us is a mass of flame. Temperature in pilot bridge compartment 107 degrees F. and increasing rapidly. Outer skin of hull is fusing. Crew standing by their posts nobly, though all realize case is hopeless. Passengers informed of danger. Doctors and nurses doing nobly allaying panic. *** Regret report many weaker adults and children suffocating. * * * Gregg taking observation on comet reports brilliant sodium and magnesium markings. * * * Potassium visible. * * * Temperature 125. * * * May God have mercy on our souls and comfort * * * leave behind us. * * * Gregg says platin—"

Here the receiver gave a final gasp and the spark died away.

The trial came soon and was pushed to a speedy finish, but all too slow for an insistent press and an almost riotous populace. Without leaving their seats, the jury found Winston guilty of criminal carelessness, and the judge said: "Fifteen years." The second vice president was given ten years.

Every night when the turnkey closed his cell door, Winston's spirit went out and rode hour after hour along the Milky Way in the blistered, heat-warped hull of the *Columbia*. Sometimes he rode in the pilot bridge compartment with a gentle, silent old man, who was forever straining ahead with a sextant to his eyes; sometimes below, where a phantom crew was eternally struggling with gravitation screens.

* * *

Winston shook hands silently with the warden and walked dumbly out of the penitentiary. He had two years yet to serve and the pardon was a total surprise to him. They had not taken him out to work that morning, but had almost immediately given him a suit of civilian's clothes, told him to dress, and opened the gates to him. He was free. Free to work or idle as he chose; to come and go at his will; to eat and drink the things he liked. How often in the long thirteen years of his confinement he had pictured this moment!

But now that the time had actually come he felt old and oppressed, infinitely old; his steps were heavy and slow, like those of a man carrying a weight.

For a month Winston wandered about lower New York, glutting himself with all manner of excesses and wonderingly surveying the changes that had occurred during his thirteen years' absence; but his money was running low, and clearly he must go to work. But where? There was only one business of which he knew anything and his soul revolted at the thought of ever again seeing an interplanetary vessel. Yet in the end he found himself up at the Three Hundred and Fortieth street yards of the Mercantile Company sharing the subdued excitement that always existed about such places.

The vast concourse sheltered a busy crowd, for not only was the *Trenton* sailing for Mars that forenoon, but a Jupiter liner was due at any moment. Winston worked his way through the throng to the dispatcher's office and gazed longingly in at the scene of activity. From the flashes of the radiograph receiver he made out that the Hamburg firm was asking permission for one of their liners, which had met with some mishap, to drop back into the Mercantile Company's cradles for repairs. He saw her in a few minutes, a gradually growing blur in the heavens, that soon resolved itself into one of the big, fat, snub-nosed boats so indicative of German construction, her cautious Teutonic skipper dropping her gently, a hundred feet at a time, between pauses.

Winston saw two persons within the dispatcher's office whom he took to be the chief dispatcher and the traffic manager in serious conversation.

"And you've got only two radiograph operators aboard the Trenton?" the traffic manager was asking.

"Yes," answered the chief dispatcher, "not another operator in New York to be had for love or money."

"It won't do, it won't do," snarled the manager. "The Trenton must sail at noon and you've got to get another man. You know the law requires three." And he stalked out of the office.

Winston waited for no more, but bolted inside and over to the dispatcher's desk.

"I can operate a radiograph, and I want a job," he said, when the dispatcher looked up at him.

"Who're you?" he demanded.

"I'll tell you in your private office," Winston answered.

Thirty minutes later he was aboard the *Trenton*, and had scarce time to stow away a few articles of clothing he had picked up from nearby shops, when a sudden lightness in his legs and a lack of weight in the suitcase he held in his hand told him that the boat was sealed, and that the gravitation screens were in place, while the sudden succeeding rise in temperature gave evidence that the craft was under way and scudding through the thin layer of the earth's atmosphere at a rate that was warming her hull to a bright red.

The radiographs were located in a little compartment just aft the pilot bridge room, and Winston soon picked up all the details of the course. The work was not heavy, and hour after hour, during his tours of duty, he stood in the doorway of the instrument room, watching the deck officers taking the angles of the various celestial bodies noted in their sailing orders as markers. He heard the low spoken orders to the quartermasters at the controllers to shift the screens this way and that way until the thirty thousand tons of steel had been steadied to its course after some far-off mass had caught her in the relentless grip of its gravitation and sucked her a hundred thousand miles from her computed path before their watchful eyes could detect the diversion. And thus day by day with ever increasing velocity the *Trenton* put the earth behind her; and Mars stood out bright and clear, with a rapidly growing parallax amid the multitude of heavenly bodies.

They were routed for the passage in twenty-eight days, but on the twentieth day Winston, sitting moodily over his instruments, heard voices on the bridge pitched a little higher than usual. He went to the door and looked up. The captain and most of the officers were there and appeared to be making simultaneous observations on some of the fixed stars. For an hour they worked, shifting the screens, taking observations, making computations. Then the captain spoke:

"Gentlemen, we are hung up on the neutral. But not one word of this anywhere in the boat but here on the bridge."

Winston understood and smiled grimly. Faulty calculations had routed the *Trenton* closer to the sun than the power of her sun screens warranted, and that great incandescent mass had seized her in a relentless grip and was holding her powerless and immovable against the pull of the planet, like a fly in a spider web, but so nicely balanced that the feeble strength of a little child against her big hulk would again put her in the friendly grasp of the planet.

But what did he care. He felt that he might as well die now as live the life of a pariah. He found himself wishing that the generators would fail for one brief instant and the full power of the sun come tearing through the frail network of wires, whose magnetic vitality was holding him at bay, and suck them down into his fiery abyss.

For forty-eight hours the *Trenton's* engineers struggled manfully in an effort to cut off even an ounce of the back pull; then they gave it up, staring hopelessly at the whirring dynamos that alone were keeping them from a swift and fiery death.

Things were getting serious. No word of the predicament had as yet reached the passengers, but some Yale students aboard had been amusing themselves and improving their astronomy by taking observations with an old sextant and they suddenly announced that the boat was standing still so far as Mars was concerned, notwithstanding the bogus daily runs, hung out as usual in the saloon, and people were holding up the officers and asking embarrassing questions.

Then a wild idea came into Winston's head as he hammered out a despairing message for the captain. The more he thought of it the more he liked it. When his "relief" came he walked down one of the gangways and out on the balcony above the passenger's dining room. It was the dinner hour and the passengers were at the tables. Men in evening clothes and women in all the splendor of the modiste's art were talking and laughing, all unconscious that death in its most horrible form was lurking only a few inches beyond the upholstered walls. Dark-skinned waiters in the liner's gorgeous livery darted here and there in well-ordered precision.

On the platform, at the forward end of the room, half concealed by swaying silken portieres and mammoth palms, the orchestra was discoursing some weird Martian melody. Over all, the hundreds of incandescent lamps shed a soft pale light, reflected in a thousand scintillating brilliant points from napery, silver, glass and wonderful jeweled ornaments.

He passed on and out over the saloon. In one corner a fair-haired girl and a youth sat in silent happiness watching the amusing gesticulations of a big Martian professor expounding his theory of the fourth dimensions to a group of the Yale men. Winston turned back into the gangway and peered out through one of the heavily glazed ports into the inky blackness of space. He shuddered as he thought of the awful cold, but as he looked he seemed to see flitting by a long black craft, a white-haired old man peering through the forward conning port, and he turned and walked rapidly to the captain's office, his jaws set and his eyes narrowed to tiny slits.

Three times he tried before he was admitted, but once within he remained an hour, and when he left the captain came out with him.

Shortly there was unusual activity below the passenger decks. All the heavy freight was slowly moved forward, and the tired engineers stood by their machines ready to speed them up for a last attempt to diminish the back pull. Even the passengers, on one pretext or another were collected in the forward end of the boat, to lighten as much as possible that part of her pointing sunwards. Then Winston, the captain and the first officer silently made their way aft until they came to the ports leading to the lifeboats secured outside on the *Trenton's* hull. The annular cover of one of these ports was unscrewed. The two officers wrung Winston's hands silently but with fervor that made words unnecessary, and he disappeared into the dark cavity and the cover was replaced.

Through the after port they saw the metal case release its grip on the hull and slide slowly along the *Trenton's* back until it hung suspended in the illimitable void, directly in prolongation of her length, glistening with reflected light like a ball of fire. There was a pause of a few minutes, then both men were conscious of a perceptible jar. The shining lifeboat silently parted from the *Trenton's* stern and floated gracefully away. They watched it as it slowly gathered headway, moving always on, on, towards where the Sun glowed, a blood-red orb, and both men stood, still, silent and thoughtful long after it was invisible to the eye. On the pilot bridge, the third officer suddenly dropped his sextant and exclaimed, "By the Lord! We are under way again."

The following is from the New York *Commercial Review*, a trade journal devoted to interplanetary traffic:

We are informed that the International Astronomical Society has determined that the infinitesimal body lately discovered revolving as another satellite of Venus is the life-boat containing the remains of John R. Winston, who sacrificed himself to rescue the Mercantile [N. Y.] Company's passenger boat *Trenton*, last June by pushing her off when she lay stranded on the "neutral" between Mars and the Sun. The society has named it Winstonius Venus [satellite fourteen]. Muller computes its sidereal period 7 h. 14 m. 11.5 s. Dist. In equatorial radii of planet, 2.841; dis. In miles, 5,463.

# Within an Ace of the End of the World

by Robert Barr

## THE SCIENTIST'S SENSATION

The beginning of the end was probably the address delivered by Sir William Crookes to the British Association at Bristol, on September 7th, 1898, although Herbert Bonsel, the young American experimenter, alleged afterward that his investigations were well on the way to their final success at the time Sir William spoke. All records being lost in the series of terrible conflagrations which took place in 1904, it is now impossible to give any accurate statement regarding Sir William Crookes' remarkable paper; but it is known that his assertions attracted much attention at the time, and were the cause of editorial comment in almost every newspaper and scientific journal in the world. The sixteen survivors out of the many millions who were alive at the beginning of 1904 were so much occupied in the preservation of their own lives, a task of almost insurmountable difficulty, that they have handed down to us, their descendants, an account of the six years beginning with 1898 which is, to say the least, extremely unsatisfactory to an exact writer. Man, in that year, seems to have been a bread-eating animal, consuming, per head, something like six bushels of wheat each year. Sir William appears to have pointed out to his associates that the limit of the earth's production of wheat had been reached, and he predicted universal starvation, did not science step in to the aid of a famine-stricken world. Science, however, was prepared. What was needed to increase the wheat production of the world to something like double its then amount was nitrate of soda; but nitrate of soda did not exist in the quantity required—*viz.*, some 12,000,000 tons annually. However, a supposedly unlimited supply of nitrogen existed in the atmosphere surrounding the earth, and from this storehouse science proposed to draw, so that the multitude might be fed. Nitrogen in its free state in the air was useless as applied to wheat-growing, but it could be brought into solid masses for practical purposes by means of electricity generated by the waterfalls which are so abundant in many mountainous lands. The cost of nitrates made from the air by water-power approached £5 a ton, as compared with £26 a ton when steam was used. Visionary people had often been accused of living in castles in the air, but now it was calmly proposed to feed future populations from granaries in the air. Naturally, as has been said, the project created much comment, although it can hardly be asserted that it was taken seriously.

It is impossible at this time, because of the absence of exact data, to pass judgment on the conflicting claims of Sir William Crookes and Mr. Herbert Bonsel; but it is perhaps not too much to say that the actual beginning of disaster was the dinner given by the Marquis of Surrey to a number of wealthy men belonging to the city of London, at which Mr. Bonsel was the guest of the evening.

## THE DINNER AT THE HOTEL CECIL

Early in April, 1899, a young man named Herbert Bonsel sailed for England from New York. He is said to have been a native of Coldwater, Michigan, and to have spent some sort of apprenticeship in the workshops of Edison, at Orange, New Jersey. It seems he did not prosper there to his satisfaction, and, after trying to interest people in New York in the furthering of his experiments, he left the metropolis in disgust and returned to Coldwater, where he worked for some time in a carriage-building establishment. Bonsel's expertness with all kinds of machinery drew forth the commendation of his chief, and resulted in a friendship springing up between the elder and the younger man which ultimately led to the latter's divulging at least part of his secret to the former. The obstacle in the way of success was chiefly scarcity of money, for the experiments were costly in their nature. Bonsel's chief, whose name is not known, seems to have got together a small syndicate, which advanced a certain amount of capital, in order to allow the young man to try his fortune once more in New York, and, failing there, to come on to London. Again his efforts to enlist capital in New York were fruitless, the impending war with France at that period absorbing public attention to the exclusion of everything else. Therefore, in April, he sailed for England.

Bonsel's evil star being in the ascendant, he made the acquaintance of the wealthy Marquis of Surrey, who became much interested in the young man and his experiments. The Marquis bought out the Coldwater syndicate, returning the members tenfold what they had invested, and took Bonsel to his estate in the country, where, with ample means now at his disposal, the youthful scientist pushed his investigations to success with marvellous rapidity. Nothing is known of him until December of that year, when the Marquis of Surrey gave a dinner in his honour at the Hotel Cecil, to which were invited twenty of the richest men in England. This festival became known as "The Millionaires' Dinner"; and although there was some curiosity excited regarding its purport, and several paragraphs appeared in the papers alluding to it, no surmise concerning it came anywhere near the truth. The Marquis of Surrey presided, with Bonsel at his right and the Lord Mayor of London at his left. Even the magnates who sat at that table, accustomed as they were to the noted dinners in the City, agreed unanimously that they had never partaken of a better meal, when, to their amazement, the chairman asked them, at the close of the feast, how they had relished it.

## A STRIKING AFTER-DINNER SPEECH

The Marquis of Surrey, before introducing the guest of the evening, said that, as they were all doubtless aware, this was not a social but a commercial dinner. It was the intention, before the company separated, to invite subscriptions to a corporation which would have a larger capitalization than any limited liability concern that had ever before been floated. The young American at his right would explain the discoveries he had made and the inventions he had patented, which this newly formed corporation would exploit. Thus introduced, Herbert Bonsel rose to his feet and said—

"Gentlemen,—I was pleased to hear you admit that you liked the dinner which was spread before us tonight. I confess that I have never tasted a better meal, but most of my life I have been poor, and therefore I am not so capable of passing an opinion on a banquet as any other here, having always been accustomed to plain fare. I have, therefore, to announce to you that all the foods you have tasted and all the liquors you have consumed were prepared by me in my laboratory. You have been dining simply on various forms of nitrogen, or on articles of which nitrogen is a constituent. The free nitrogen of the air has been changed to fixed nitrogen by means of electricity, and the other components of the food placed on the board have been extracted from various soils by the same means. The champagne and the burgundy are the product of the laboratory, and not of the wine-press, the soil used in their composition having been exported from the vine-bearing regions of France only just before the war which ended so disastrously for that country. More than a year ago Sir William Crookes announced what the nitrogen free in the air might do for the people of this world. At the time I read his remarks I was engaged in the experiments that have now been completed. I trembled, fearing I was about to be forestalled; but up to this moment, so far as I know, there has been made no effort to put his theories into practical use. Sir William seemed to think it would be sufficient to use the nitrates extracted from the atmosphere for the purpose of fertilizing the ground. But this always appeared to me a most round-about method. Why should we wait on slow-footed Nature? If science is capable of wringing one constituent of our food from the air, why should it shrink from extracting the others from earth or water? In other words, why leave a job half finished? I knew of no reason; and, luckily, I succeeded in convincing our noble host that all food products may be speedily compounded in the laboratory, without waiting the progress of the tardy seasons. It is proposed, therefore, that a company be formed with a capital so large that it can control practically all the water-power available in the world. We will extract from earth, air, and water whatever we need, compound the products in our factories, and thus feed the whole world. The moment our plant is at work, the occupations of agriculturist, horticulturist, and stock-breeder are gone. There is little need to dwell on the profit that must accrue to such a company as the one now projected. All commercial enterprises that have hitherto existed, or even any combination of them, cannot be compared for wealth-producing to the scheme we have now in hand. There is no man so poor but he must be our customer if he is to live, and none so rich that he can do without us."

## THE GREAT FOOD CORPORATION [LIMITED]

After numerous questions and answers the dinner party broke up, pledged to secrecy, and next day a special train took the twenty down to the Marquis of Surrey's country place, where they saw in operation the apparatus that transformed simple elements into palatable food. At the mansion of the Marquis was formed The Great Food Corporation (Limited), which was to have such an amazing effect upon the peoples of this earth. Although the company proved one of the the most lucrative investments ever undertaken in England, still it did not succeed in maintaining the monopoly it had at first attempted. In many countries the patents did not hold, some governments refusing to sanction a monopoly on which life itself depended, others deciding that, although there were certain ingenious novelties in Bonsel's processes, still the general principles had been well known for years, and so the final patents were refused. Nevertheless, these decisions did not interfere as much as might have been expected with the prosperity of The Great Food Producing Corporation (Limited). It had been first in the field, and its tremendous capitalization enabled it to crush opposition somewhat ruthlessly, aided by the advantage of having secured most of the available water-power of the world. For a time there was reckless speculation in food-manufacturing companies, and much money was lost in consequence. Agriculture was indeed killed, as Bonsel had predicted, but the farmers of Western America, in spite of the decline of soil-tilling, continued to furnish much of the world's food. They erected windmills with which electricity was generated, and, drawing on the soil and the air, they manufactured nourishment almost as cheaply as the great water-power corporation itself. This went on in every part of the world where the Bonsel patents were held invalid. In a year or two everyone became accustomed to the chemically compounded food, and even though a few old fogies kept proclaiming that they would never forsake the ancient wheaten loaf for its modern equivalent, yet nobody paid any attention to these conservatives; and presently even they could not get the wheaten loaf of bygone days, as grain was no longer grown except as a curiosity in some botanist's garden.

## REMARKABLE SCENE IN THE GUILDHALL

The first three years of the twentieth century were notable for the great increase of business confidence all over the world. A reign of universal prosperity seemed to have set in. Political questions appeared easier of solution. The anxieties that hitherto had oppressed the public mind, such as the ever-present poverty problem, provision for the old age of the labourers, and so forth, lifted like a rising cloud and disappeared. There were still the usual number of poor people; but, somehow, lack of wealth had lost its terror. It was true that the death-rate increased enormously; but nobody seemed to mind that. The episode at the Guildhall dinner in 1903 should have been sufficient to awaken the people, had an awakening been possible in the circumstances; but that amazing lesson, like others equally ominous, passed unheeded. When the Prime Minister who had succeeded Lord Salisbury was called upon to speak, he said—

"My Lord Mayor, Your Royal Highnesses, Your Excellencies, Your Graces, My Lords and Gentlemen: It has been the custom of Prime Ministers from time immemorial to give at this annual banquet some indication of the trend of mind of the Government. I propose, with your kind permission, to deviate in slight measure from that ancient custom (cheers). I think that hitherto we have all taken the functions of Government rather more seriously than their merits demand, and a festive occasion like this should not be marred by the introduction of debatable subjects (renewed cheering). If, therefore, the band will be good enough to strike up that excellent tune, 'There will be a Hot Time in the Old Town Tonight,' I shall have pleasure of exhibiting to you a quick-step I have invented to the rhythm of that lively composition (enthusiastic acclaim)."

The Prime Minister, with the aid of some of the waiters, cleared away the dishes in front of him, stepped from the floor to the chair, and from the chair to the table, where, accompanied by the energetic playing of the band, he indulged in a break-down that would have done credit to any music-hall stage. All the applauding diners rose to their feet in the wildest excitement. His Royal Highness the Crown Prince of Alluria placed his hands on the shoulders of the Lord Mayor, the German Ambassador placed his hands on the shoulders of the Crown Prince, and on down the table, until the distinguished guests formed a connected ring around the board on which the Prime Minister was dancing. Then all, imitating the quick-step, and keeping time with the music, began circling round the table, one after the other, shouting and hurrahing at the top of their voices. There were loud calls for the American Ambassador, a celebrated man, universally popular; and the Prime Minister, reaching out a hand, helped him up on the table. Amidst vociferous cheering, he said that he took the selection of the tune as a special compliment to his countrymen, the American troops having recently entered Paris to its melodious strains. His Excellency hoped that this hilarious evening would cement still further the union of the English-speaking races, which in fact it really did, though not in the manner the honourable gentleman anticipated at the time of speaking. The company, headed by the band and the Prime Minister, then made their way to the street, marched up Cheapside, past St. Paul's, and along Fleet Street and the Strand, until they came to Westminster. Everyone along the route joined the processional dance, and upward of 50,000 persons were assembled in the square next to the Abbey and in the adjoining streets. The Prime Minister, waving his hand towards the Houses of Parliament, cried, "Three cheers for the good old House of Commons!" These being given with a tiger appended, a working-man roared, "Three cheers for 'is Lordship and the old duffers what sits with him in the 'Ouse of Lords." This was also honoured in a way that made the echoes reach the Mansion House.

The *Times* next morning, in a jocular leading article, congratulated the people of England on the fact that at last politics were viewed in the correct light. There had been, as the Prime Minister truly said, too much solidity in the discussion of public affairs; but, linked with song and dance, it was now possible for the ordinary man in the street to take some interest in them, etc., etc. Foreign comment, as cabled from various countries, was entirely sympathetic to the view taken of the occurrence by all the English newspapers, which was that we had entered a new era of jollity and good will.

## A WARNING FROM OXFORD

I have now to speak of my great-grandfather, John Rule, who, at the beginning of the twentieth century, was a science student at Balliol College, Oxford, aged twenty-four. It is from the notes written by him and the newspaper clippings which he preserved that I am enabled to compile this imperfect account of the disaster of 1904 and the events leading to it. I append, without alteration or comment, his letter to the *Times*, which appeared the day after that paper's flippant references to the conduct of the Prime Minister and his colleagues:

### "*THE GUILDHALL INCIDENT.* TO THE EDITOR OF THE 'TIMES':

"Sir,—The levity of the Prime Minister's recent conduct; the levity of your own leading article thereon; the levity of foreign references to the deplorable episode, indicate but too clearly the crisis which mankind is called upon to face, and to face, alas! Under conditions which make the averting of the greatest calamity well-nigh impossible. To put it plainly, every man, woman, and child on this earth, with the exception of eight persons in the United States and eight in England, are drunk—not with wine, but with oxygen. The numerous factories all over the world which are working night and day making fixed nitrates from the air, are rapidly depleting the atmosphere of its nitrogen. When this disastrous manufacture was begun 100 parts of air, roughly speaking, contained 76•9 parts of nitrogen and 23•1 parts oxygen. At the beginning of this year the atmosphere round Oxford was composed of nitrogen 53•218, oxygen 46•782. And here we have the explanation of the largely increased death-rate. Man is simply burning up. Today the normal proportions of the two gases in the air are nearly reversed, standing – nitrogen, 27•319, oxygen 72•681, a state of things simply appalling: due in a great measure to the insane folly of Russia, Germany, and France competing with each other in raising mountain ranges of food products as a reserve in case of war, just as the same fear of a conflict brought their armies to such enormous proportions a few years ago. The nitrogen factories must be destroyed instantly, if the people of this earth are to remain alive. If this is done, the atmosphere will gradually become nitrogenized once more. I invite the editor of the *Times* to come to Oxford and live for a few days with us in our iron building, erected on Port Meadow, where a machine supplies us with nitrogen and keeps the atmosphere within the hut similar to that which once surrounded the earth. If he will direct the policy of the *Times* from this spot, he may bring an insane people to their senses. Oxford yesterday bestowed a degree of D.C.L. on a man who walked the whole length of the High on his hands; so it will be seen that it is time something was done. I am, sir, yours, etc.,

"JOHN RULE.
"Balliol College, Oxford."

The *Times* in an editorial note said that the world had always been well provided with alarmists, and that their correspondent, Mr. Rule, was a good example of the class. That newspaper, it added, had been for some time edited in Printing House Square, and it would be continued to be conducted in that quarter of London, despite the attractions of the sheet-iron house near Oxford.

## THE TWO NITROGEN COLONIES

The coterie in the iron house consisted of the Rev. Mr. Hepburn, who was a clergyman and tutor; two divinity students, two science students, and three other undergraduates, all of whom had withdrawn from colleges, awaiting with anxiety the catastrophe they were powerless to avert. Some years before, when the proposal to admit women to the Oxford colleges was defeated, the Rev. Mr. Hepburn and John Rule visited the United States to study the working of co-education in that country. There Mr. Rule became acquainted with Miss Sadie Armour, of Vassar College, on the Hudson, and the acquaintance speedily ripened into friendship, with a promise of closer relationship that was yet to come. John and Sadie kept up a regular correspondence after his return to Oxford, and naturally he wrote to her regarding his fears for the future of mankind, should the diminution of the nitrogen in the air continue. He told her of the precautions he and his seven comrades had taken, and implored her to inaugurate a similar colony near Vassar. For a long time the English Nitrogenists, as they were called, hoped to be able to awaken the world to the danger that threatened; and by the time they recognized that their efforts were futile, it was too late to attempt the journey to America which had long been in John Rule's mind. Parties of students were in the habit of coming to the iron house and jeering at the inmates. Apprehending violence one day the Rev. Mr. Hepburn went outside to expostulate with them. He began seriously, then paused, a comical smile lighting up his usually sedate face, and finally broke out into roars of laughter, inviting those he had left to come out and enjoy themselves. A moment later he began to turn somersaults round the iron house, all the students outside hilariously following his example, and screaming that he was a jolly good fellow. John Rule and one of the most stalwart of the divinity students rushed outside, captured the clergyman, and dragged him into the house by main force, the whirling students being too much occupied with their evolutions to notice the abduction. One of the students proposed that the party should return to Carfax by handsprings, and thus they all set off, progressing like jumping-jacks across the meadow, the last human beings other than themselves that those within the iron house were to see for many a day. Rule and his companions had followed the example set by Continental countries, and had, while there was yet time, accumulated a small mountain of food products inside and outside of their dwelling. The last letter Rule received from America informed him that the girls of Vassar had done likewise.

## THE GREAT CATASTROPHE

The first intimation that the Nitrogenists had of impending doom was from the passage of a Great Western train running northward from Oxford. As they watched it, the engine suddenly burst into a brilliant flame, which was followed shortly by an explosion, and a moment later the wrecked train lay along the line blazing fiercely. As evening drew on they saw that Oxford was on fire, even the stonework of the college seeming to burn as if it had been blocks of wax. Communication with the outside world ceased, and an ominous silence held the earth. They did not know then that London, New York, Paris, and many other cities had been consumed by fire; but they surmised as much. Curiously enough, the carbon dioxide evolved by these numerous and widespread conflagrations made the outside air more breathable, notwithstanding the poisonous nature of this mitigant of oxygenic energy. For days they watched for any sign of human life outside their own dwelling, but no one approached.

As a matter of fact, all the inhabitants of the world were dead except themselves and the little colony in America, although it was long after that those left alive became aware of the full extent of the calamity that had befallen their fellows. Day by day they tested the outside air, and were overjoyed to note that it was gradually resuming its former quality. This process, however, was so slow that the young men became impatient, and endeavoured to make their house movable, so that they might journey with it, like a snail, to Liverpool, for the one desire of each was to reach America and learn the fate of the Vassar girls. The moving of the house proved impracticable, and thus they were compelled to remain where they were until it became safe to venture into the outside air, which they did some time before it reached its normal condition.

It seems to have been fortunate that they did so, for the difficulties they had to face might have proved insurmountable had they not been exhilarated by the excess of oxygen in the atmosphere. The diary which John Rule wrote showed that within the iron house his state of depression was extreme when he remembered that all communication between the countries was cut off, and that the girl to whom he was betrothed was separated from him by 3,000 miles of ocean, whitened by no sail. After the eight set out, the whole tone of his notes changed, an optimism scarcely justified by the circumstances taking the place of his former dismay. It is not my purpose here to dwell on the appalling nature of the foot journey to Liverpool over a corpse-strewn land. They found, as they feared, that Liverpool also had been destroyed by fire, only a fringe of the river front escaping the general conflagration. So enthusiastic were the young men, according to my great-grandfather's notes, that on the journey to the seaport they had resolved to walk to America by way of Behring Straits, crossing the English Channel in a row-boat, should they find that the shipping at Liverpool was destroyed. This seems to indicate a state of oxygen intoxication hardly less intense than that which had caused the Prime Minister to dance on the table.

## A VOYAGE TO RUINED NEW YORK

They found the immense steamship *Teutonic* moored at the landing-stage, not apparently having had time to go to her dock when the universal catastrophe culminated. It is probable that the city was on fire when the steamer came in, and perhaps an attempt was made to board her, the ignorant people thinking to escape the fate that they felt overtaking them by putting out to sea. The landing-stage was packed with lifeless human beings, whole masses still standing up, so tightly were they wedged. Some stood transfixed, with upright arms above their heads, and death seemed to have come to many in a form like suffocation. The eight at first resolved to take the *Teutonic* across the Atlantic, but her coal bunkers proved nearly empty, and they had no way of filling them. Not one of them knew anything of navigation beyond theoretical knowledge, and Rule alone was acquainted with the rudiments of steam-engineering. They selected a small steam yacht, and loaded her with the coal that was left in the *Teutonic's* bunkers. Thus they started for the West, the Rev. Mr. Hepburn acting as captain and John Rule as engineer. It was fourteen days before they sighted the coast of Maine, having kept much too far north. They went ashore at the ruins of Portland; but embarked again, resolved to trust rather to their yacht than undertake a long land journey through an unknown and desolated country. They skirted the silent shores of America until they came to New York, and steamed down the bay. My great-grandfather describes the scene as sombre in the extreme. The Statue of Liberty seemed to be all of the handiwork of man that remained intact. Brooklyn Bridge was not entirely consumed, and the collapsed remains hung from two pillars of fused stone, the ragged ends of the structure which once formed the roadway dragging in the water. The city itself presented a remarkable appearance. It was one conglomerate mass of grey-toned, semi-opaque glass, giving some indication of the intense heat that had been evolved in its destruction. The outlines of its principal thoroughfares were still faintly indicated, although the melting buildings had flowed into the streets like lava, partly obliterating them. Here and there a dome of glass showed where an abnormally high structure once stood, and thus the contour of the city bore a weird resemblance to its former self—about such as the grim outlines of a corpse over which a sheet has been thrown bear to a living man. All along the shore lay the gaunt skeletons of half-fused steamships. The young men passed this dismal calcined graveyard in deep silence, keeping straight up the broad Hudson. No sign of life greeted them until they neared Poughkeepsie, when they saw, flying above a house situated on the top of a hill, that brilliant fluttering flag, the Stars and Stripes. Somehow its very motion in the wind gave promise that the vital spark had not been altogether extinguished in America. The great sadness which had oppressed the voyagers was lifted, and they burst forth into cheer after cheer. One of the young men rushed into the chart-room, and brought out the Union Jack, which was quickly hauled up to the mast-head, and the reverend captain pulled the cord that, for the first time during the voyage, let loose the roar of the steam whistle, rousing the echoes of the hills on either side of the noble stream. Instantly, on the verandah of the flag-covered house, was seen the glimmer of a white summer dress, then of another and another and another, until eight were counted.

## AND FINALLY

THE events that followed belong rather to the region of romances than to a staid, sober narrative of fact like the present; indeed, the theme has been a favourite one with poets and novelists, whose pens would have been more able than mine to do justice to this international idyll. America and England were indeed joined, as the American Ambassador had predicted at the Guildhall, though at the time his words were spoken he had little idea of the nature and complete accord of that union. While it cannot be denied that the unprecedented disaster which obliterated human life in 1904 seemed to be a calamity, yet it is possible to trace the design of a beneficent Providence in this wholesale destruction. The race which now inhabits the earth is one that includes no savages and no war lords. Armies are unknown and unthought of. There is no battleship on the face of the waters. It is doubtful if universal peace could have been brought to the world short of the annihilation of the jealous, cantankerous, quarrelsome peoples who inhabited it previous to 1904. Humanity was destroyed once by flood, and again by fire; but whether the race, as it enlarges, will deteriorate after its second extinguishment, as it appears to have done after its first, must remain for the future to determine.

# The Phoenix on the Sword

by Robert E. Howard

## I

*"Know, oh prince, that between the years when the oceans drank Atlantis and the gleaming cities, and the years of the rise of the Sons of Aryas, there was an Age undreamed of, when shining kingdoms lay spread across the world like blue mantles beneath the stars—Nemedia, Ophir, Brythunia, Hyperborea, Zamora with its dark-haired women and towers of spider-haunted mystery, Zingara with its chivalry, Koth that bordered on the pastoral lands of Shem, Stygia with its shadow-guarded tombs, Hyrkania whose riders wore steel and silk and gold. But the proudest kingdom of the world was Aquilonia, reigning supreme in the dreaming west. Hither came Conan, the Cimmerian, black-haired, sullen-eyed, sword in hand, a thief, a reaver, a slayer, with gigantic melancholies and gigantic mirth, to tread the jeweled thrones of the Earth under his sandalled feet."*

*—The Nemedian Chronicles*

Over shadowy spires and gleaming towers lay the ghostly darkness and silence that runs before dawn. Into a dim alley, one of a veritable labyrinth of mysterious winding ways, four masked figures came hurriedly from a door, which a dusky hand furtively opened. They spoke not but went swiftly into the gloom, cloaks wrapped closely about them; as silently as the ghosts of murdered men they disappeared in the darkness. Behind them a sardonic countenance was framed in the partly opened door; a pair of evil eyes glittered malevolently in the gloom.

"Go into the night, creatures of the night," a voice mocked. "Oh, fools, your doom hounds your heels like a blind dog, and you know it not."

The speaker closed the door and bolted it, then turned and went up the corridor, candle in hand. He was a somber giant, whose dusky skin revealed his Stygian blood. He came into an inner chamber, where a tall, lean man in worn velvet lounged like a great lazy cat on a silken couch, sipping wine from a huge golden goblet.

"Well, Ascalante," said the Stygian, setting down the candle, "your dupes have slunk into the streets like rats from their burrows. You work with strange tools."

"Tools?" replied Ascalante. "Why, they consider me that. For months now, ever since the Rebel Four summoned me from the southern desert, I have been living in the very heart of my enemies, hiding by day in this obscure house, skulking through dark alleys and darker corridors at night. And I have accomplished what those rebellious nobles could not. Working through them, and through other agents, many of whom have never seen my face, I have honeycombed the empire with sedition and unrest. In short I, working in the shadows, have paved the downfall of the king who sits throned in the sun. By Mitra, I was a statesman before I was an outlaw."

"And these dupes who deem themselves your masters?"

"They will continue to think that I serve them, until our present task is completed. Who are they to match wits with Ascalante? Volmana, the dwarfish count of Karaban; Gromel, the giant commander of the Black Legion; Dion, the fat baron of Attalus; Rinaldo, the hare-brained minstrel. I am the force which has welded together the steel in each, and by the clay in each, I will crush them when the time comes. But that lies in the future; tonight the king dies."

"Days ago I saw the imperial squadrons ride from the city," said the Stygian.

"They rode to the frontier which the heathen Picts assail—thanks to the strong liquor which I've smuggled over the borders to madden them. Dion's great wealth made that possible. And Volmana made it possible to dispose of the rest of the imperial troops which remained in the city. Through his princely kin in Nemedia, it was easy to persuade King Numa to request the presence of Count Trocero of Poitain, seneschal of Aquilonia; and of course, to do him honor, he'll be accompanied by an imperial escort, as well as his own troops, and Prospero, King Conan's righthand man. That leaves only the king's personal bodyguard in the city—beside the Black Legion. Through Gromel I've corrupted a spendthrift officer of that guard, and bribed him to lead his men away from the king's door at midnight.

"Then, with sixteen desperate rogues of mine, we enter the palace by a secret tunnel. After the deed is done, even if the people do not rise to welcome us, Gromel's Black Legion will be sufficient to hold the city and the crown."

"And Dion thinks that crown will be given to him?"

"Yes. The fat fool claims it by reason of a trace of royal blood. Conan makes a bad mistake in letting men live who still boast descent from the old dynasty, from which he tore the crown of Aquilonia.

"Volmana wishes to be reinstated in royal favor as he was under the old regime, so that he may lift his poverty-ridden estates to their former grandeur. Gromel hates Pallantides, commander of the Black Dragons, and desires the command of the whole army, with all the stubbornness of the Bossonian. Alone of us all, Rinaldo has no personal ambition. He sees in Conan a red-handed, rough-footed barbarian who came out of the north to plunder a civilized land. He idealizes the king whom Conan killed to get the crown, remembering only that he occasionally patronized the arts, and forgetting the evils of his reign, and he is making the people forget. Already they openly sing *The Lament for the King* in which Rinaldo lauds the sainted villain and denounces Conan as 'that black-hearted savage from the abyss.' Conan laughs, but the people snarl."

"Why does he hate Conan?"

"Poets always hate those in power. To them perfection is always just behind the last corner, or beyond the next. They escape the present in dreams of the past and future. Rinaldo is a flaming torch of idealism, rising, as he thinks, to overthrow a tyrant and liberate the people. As for me—well, a few months ago I had lost all ambition but to raid the caravans for the rest of my life; now old dreams stir. Conan will die; Dion will mount the throne. Then he, too, will die. One by one, all who oppose me will die—by fire, or steel, or those deadly wines you know so well how to brew. Ascalante, king of Aquilonia! How like you the sound of it?"

The Stygian shrugged his broad shoulders.

"There was a time," he said with unconcealed bitterness, "when I, too, had my ambitions, beside which yours seem tawdry and childish. To what a state I have fallen! My old-time peers and rivals would stare indeed could they see Thoth-amon of the Ring serving as the slave of an outlander, and an outlaw at that; and aiding in the petty ambitions of barons and kings!"

"You laid your trust in magic and mummery," answered Ascalante carelessly. "I trust my wits and my sword."

"Wits and swords are as straws against the wisdom of the Darkness," growled the Stygian, his dark eyes flickering with menacing lights and shadows. "Had I not lost the Ring, our positions might be reversed."

"Nevertheless," answered the outlaw impatiently, "you wear the stripes of my whip on your back, and are likely to continue to wear them."

"Be not so sure!" the fiendish hatred of the Stygian glittered for an instant redly in his eyes. "Some day, somehow, I will find the Ring again, and when I do, by the serpent-fangs of Set, you shall pay—"

The hot-tempered Aquilonian started up and struck him heavily across the mouth. Thoth reeled back, blood starting from his lips.

"You grow over-bold, dog," growled the outlaw. "Have a care; I am still your master who knows your dark secret. Go upon the housetops and shout that Ascalante is in the city plotting against the king—if you dare."

"I dare not," muttered the Stygian, wiping the blood from his lips.

"No, you do not dare," Ascalante grinned bleakly. "For if I die by your stealth or treachery, a hermit priest in the southern desert will know of it, and will break the seal of a manuscript I left in his hands. And having read, a word will be whispered in Stygia, and a wind will creep up from the south by midnight. And where will you hide your head, Thoth-amon?"

The slave shuddered and his dusky face went ashen.

"Enough!" Ascalante changed his tone peremptorily. "I have work for you. I do not trust Dion. I bade him ride to his country estate and remain there until the work tonight is done. The fat fool could never conceal his nervousness before the king today. Ride after him, and if you do not overtake him on the road, proceed to his estate and remain with him until we send for him. Don't let him out of your sight. He is mazed with fear, and might bolt—might even rush to Conan in a panic, and reveal the whole plot, hoping thus to save his own hide. Go!"

The slave bowed, hiding the hate in his eyes, and did as he was bidden. Ascalante turned again to his wine. Over the jeweled spires was rising a dawn crimson as blood.

## II

*When I was a fighting-man, the kettle-drums they beat,*
*The people scattered gold-dust before my horses' feet;*
*But now I am a great king, the people hound my track*
*With poison in my wine-cup, and daggers at my back.*

*—The Road of Kings*

The room was large and ornate, with rich tapestries on the polished, panelled walls, deep rugs on the ivory floor, and with the lofty ceiling adorned with intricate carvings and silver scrollwork. Behind an ivory, gold-inlaid writing-table sat a man whose broad shoulders and sun-browned skin seemed out of place among those luxuriant surroundings. He seemed more a part of the sun and winds and high places of the outlands. His slightest movement spoke of steel-spring muscles knit to a keen brain with the co-ordination of a born fighting-man. There was nothing deliberate or measured about his actions. Either he was perfectly at rest—still as a bronze statue—or else he was in motion, not with the jerky quickness of over-tense nerves, but with a cat-like speed that blurred the sight that tried to follow him.

His garments were of rich fabric, but simply made. He wore no ring or ornaments, and his square-cut black mane was confined merely by a cloth-of-silver band about his head.

Now he laid down the golden stylus with which he had been laboriously scrawling on waxed papyrus, rested his chin on his fist, and fixed his smoldering blue eyes enviously on the man who stood before him. This person was occupied in his own affairs at the moment, for he was taking up the laces of his gold-chased armor, and abstractedly whistling—a rather unconventional performance, considering that he was in the presence of a king.

"Prospero," said the man at the table, "these matters of statecraft weary me as all the fighting I have done never did."

"All part of the game, Conan," answered the dark-eyed Poitainian. "You are king—you must play the part."

"I wish I might ride with you to Nemedia," said Conan enviously. "It seems ages since I had a horse between my knees—but Publius says that affairs in the city require my presence. Curse him!

"When I overthrew the old dynasty," he continued, speaking with the easy familiarity which existed only between the Poitainian and himself, "it was easy enough, though it seemed bitter hard at the time. Looking back now over the wild path I followed, all those days of toil, intrigue, slaughter and tribulation seem like a dream.

"I did not dream far enough, Prospero. When King Numedides lay dead at my feet and I tore the crown from his gory head and set it on my own, I had reached the ultimate border of my dreams. I had prepared myself to take the crown, not to hold it. In the old free days all I wanted was a sharp sword and a straight path to my enemies. Now no paths are straight and my sword is useless.

"When I overthrew Numedides, then I was the Liberator—now they spit at my shadow. They have put a statue of that swine in the temple of Mitra, and people go and wail before it, hailing it as the holy effigy of a saintly monarch who was done to death by a red-handed barbarian. When I led her armies to victory as a mercenary, Aquilonia overlooked the fact that I was a foreigner, but now she cannot forgive me.

"Now in Mitra's temple there come to burn incense to Numedides' memory, men whom his hangmen maimed and blinded, men whose sons died in his dungeons, whose wives and daughters were dragged into his seraglio. The fickle fools!"

"Rinaldo is largely responsible," answered Prospero, drawing up his sword-belt another notch. "He sings songs that make men mad. Hang him in his jester's garb to the highest tower in the city. Let him make rimes for the vultures."

Conan shook his lion head. "No, Prospero, he's beyond my reach. A great poet is greater than any king. His songs are mightier than my scepter; for he has near ripped the heart from my breast when he chose to sing for me. I shall die and be forgotten, but Rinaldo's songs will live for ever.

"No, Prospero," the king continued, a somber look of doubt shadowing his eyes, "there is something hidden, some undercurrent of which we are not aware. I sense it as in my youth I sensed the tiger hidden in the tall grass. There is a nameless unrest throughout the kingdom. I am like a hunter who crouches by his small fire amid the forest, and hears stealthy feet padding in the darkness, and almost sees the glimmer of burning eyes. If I could but come to grips with something tangible, that I could cleave with my sword! I tell you, it's not by chance that the Picts have of late so fiercely assailed the frontiers, so that the Bossonians have called for aid to beat them back. I should have ridden with the troops."

"Publius feared a plot to trap and slay you beyond the frontier," replied Prospero, smoothing his silken surcoat over his shining mail, and admiring his tall lithe figure in a silver mirror. "That's why he urged you to remain in the city. These doubts are born of your barbarian instincts. Let the people snarl! The mercenaries are ours, and the Black Dragons, and every rogue in Poitain swears by you. Your only danger is assassination, and that's impossible, with men of the imperial troops guarding you day and night. What are you working at there?"

"A map," Conan answered with pride. "The maps of the court show well the countries of south, east and west, but in the north they are vague and faulty. I am adding the northern lands myself. Here is Cimmeria, where I was born. And—"

"Asgard and Vanaheim," Prospero scanned the map. "By Mitra, I had almost believed those countries to have been fabulous."

Conan grinned savagely, involuntarily touching the scars on his dark face. "You had known otherwise, had you spent your youth on the northern frontiers of Cimmeria! Asgard lies to the north, and Vanaheim to the northwest of Cimmeria, and there is continual war along the borders."

"What manner of men are these northern folk?" asked Prospero.

"Tall and fair and blue-eyed. Their god is Ymir, the frost-giant, and each tribe has its own king. They are wayward and fierce. They fight all day and drink ale and roar their wild songs all night."

"Then I think you are like them," laughed Prospero. "You laugh greatly, drink deep and bellow good songs; though I never saw another Cimmerian who drank aught but water, or who ever laughed, or ever sang save to chant dismal dirges."

"Perhaps it's the land they live in," answered the king. "A gloomier land never was—all of hills, darkly wooded, under skies nearly always gray, with winds moaning drearily down the valleys."

"Little wonder men grow moody there," quoth Prospero with a shrug of his shoulders, thinking of the smiling sun-washed plains and blue lazy rivers of Poitain, Aquilonia's southernmost province.

"They have no hope here or hereafter," answered Conan. "Their gods are Crom and his dark race, who rule over a sunless place of everlasting mist, which is the world of the dead. Mitra! The ways of the Æsir were more to my liking."

"Well," grinned Prospero, "the dark hills of Cimmeria are far behind you. And now I go. I'll quaff a goblet of white Nemedian wine for you at Numa's court."

"Good," grunted the king, "but kiss Numa's dancing-girls for yourself only, lest you involve the states!"

His gusty laughter followed Prospero out of the chamber.

## III

*Under the caverned pyramids great Set coils asleep;*
*Among the shadows of the tombs his dusky people creep.*
*I speak the Word from the hidden gulfs that never knew the sun*
*Send me a servant for my hate, oh scaled and shining One!*

The sun was setting, etching the green and hazy blue of the forest in brief gold. The waning beams glinted on the thick golden chain which Dion of Attalus twisted continually in his pudgy hand as he sat in the flaming riot of blossoms and flower-trees which was his garden. He shifted his fat body on his marble seat and glanced furtively about, as if in quest of a lurking enemy. He sat within a circular grove of slender trees, whose interlapping branches cast a thick shade over him. Near at hand a fountain tinkled silverly, and other unseen fountains in various parts of the great garden whispered an everlasting symphony.

Dion was alone except for the great dusky figure which lounged on a marble bench close at hand, watching the baron with deep somber eyes. Dion gave little thought to Thoth-amon. He vaguely knew that he was a slave in whom Ascalante reposed much trust, but like so many rich men, Dion paid scant heed to men below his own station in life.

"You need not be so nervous," said Thoth. "The plot cannot fail."

"Ascalante can make mistakes as well as another," snapped Dion, sweating at the mere thought of failure.

"Not he," grinned the Stygian savagely, "else I had not been his slave, but his master."

"What talk is this?" peevishly returned Dion, with only half a mind on the conversation.

Thoth-amon's eyes narrowed. For all his iron self-control, he was near bursting with long pent-up shame, hate and rage, ready to take any sort of a desperate chance. What he did not reckon on was the fact that Dion saw him, not as a human being with a brain and a wit, but simply a slave, and as such, a creature beneath notice.

"Listen to me," said Thoth. "You will be king. But you little know the mind of Ascalante. You can not trust him, once Conan is slain. I can help you. If you will protect me when you come to power, I will aid you.

"Listen, my lord. I was a great sorcerer in the south. Men spoke of Thoth-amon as they spoke of Rammon. King Ctesphon of Stygia gave me great honor, casting down the magicians from the high places to exalt me above them. They hated me, but they feared me, for I controlled beings from outside which came at my call and did my bidding. By Set, mine enemy knew not the hour when he might awake at midnight to feel the taloned fingers of a nameless horror at his throat! I did dark and terrible magic with the Serpent Ring of Set, which I found in a nighted tomb a league beneath the earth, forgotten before the first man crawled out of the slimy sea.

"But a thief stole the Ring and my power was broken. The magicians rose up to slay me, and I fled. Disguised as a camel-driver, I was traveling in a caravan in the land of Koth, when Ascalante's reavers fell upon us. All in the caravan were slain except myself; I saved my life by revealing my identity to Ascalante and swearing to serve him. Bitter has been that bondage!

"To hold me fast, he wrote of me in a manuscript, and sealed it and gave it into the hands of a hermit who dwells on the southern borders of Koth. I dare not strike a dagger into him while he sleeps, or betray him to his enemies, for then the hermit would open the manuscript and read—thus Ascalante instructed him. And he would speak a word in Stygia—"

Again Thoth shuddered and an ashen hue tinged his dusky skin.

"Men knew me not in Aquilonia," he said. "But should my enemies in Stygia learn my whereabouts, not the width of half a world between us would suffice to save me from such a doom as would blast the soul of a bronze statue. Only a king with castles and hosts of swordsmen could protect me. So I have told you my secret, and urge that you make a pact with me. I can aid you with my wisdom, and you can protect me. And some day I will find the Ring—"

"Ring? Ring?" Thoth had underestimated the man's utter egoism. Dion had not even been listening to the slave's words, so completely engrossed was he in his own thoughts, but the final word stirred a ripple in his self-centeredness.

"Ring?" he repeated. "That makes me remember—my ring of good fortune. I had it from a Shemitish thief who swore he stole it from a wizard far to the south, and that it would bring me luck. I paid him enough, Mitra knows. By the gods, I need all the luck I can have, what with Volmana and Ascalante dragging me into their bloody plots—I'll see to the ring."

Thoth sprang up, blood mounting darkly to his face, while his eyes flamed with the stunned fury of a man who suddenly realizes the full depths of a fool's swinish stupidity. Dion never heeded him. Lifting a secret lid in the marble seat, he fumbled for a moment among a heap of gewgaws of various kinds—barbaric charms, bits of bones, pieces of tawdry jewelry—luck-pieces and conjures which the man's superstitious nature had prompted him to collect.

"Ah, here it is!" He triumphantly lifted a ring of curious make. It was of a metal like copper, and was made in the form of a scaled serpent, coiled in three loops, with its tail in its mouth. Its eyes were yellow gems which glittered balefully. Thoth-amon cried out as if he had been struck, and Dion wheeled and gaped, his face suddenly bloodless. The slave's eyes were blazing, his mouth wide, his huge dusky hands outstretched like talons.

"The Ring! By Set! The Ring!" he shrieked. "My Ring—stolen from me—" Steel glittered in the Stygian's hand and with a heave of his great dusky shoulders he drove the dagger into the baron's fat body. Dion's high thin squeal broke in a strangled gurgle and his whole flabby frame collapsed like melted butter. A fool to the end, he died in mad terror, not knowing why. Flinging aside the crumpled corpse, already forgetful of it, Thoth grasped the ring in both hands, his dark eyes blazing with a fearful avidness.

"My Ring!" he whispered in terrible exultation. "My power!"

How long he crouched over the baleful thing, motionless as a statue, drinking the evil aura of it into his dark soul, not even the Stygian knew. When he shook himself from his reverie and drew back his mind from the nighted abysses where it had been questing, the moon was rising, casting long shadows across the smooth marble back of the garden-seat, at the foot of which sprawled the darker shadow which had been the lord of Attalus.

"No more, Ascalante, no more!" whispered the Stygian, and his eyes burned red as a vampire's in the gloom. Stooping, he cupped a handful of congealing blood from the sluggish pool in which his victim sprawled, and rubbed it in the copper serpent's eyes until the yellow sparks were covered by a crimson mask.

"Blind your eyes, mystic serpent," he chanted in a blood-freezing whisper. "Blind your eyes to the moonlight and open them on darker gulfs! What do you see, oh serpent of Set? Whom do you call from the gulfs of the Night? Whose shadow falls on the waning Light? Call him to me, oh serpent of Set!"

Stroking the scales with a peculiar circular motion of his fingers, a motion which always carried the fingers back to their starting place, his voice sank still lower as he whispered dark names and grisly incantations forgotten the world over save in the grim hinterlands of dark Stygia, where monstrous shapes move in the dusk of the tombs.

There was a movement in the air about him, such a swirl as is made in water when some creature rises to the surface. A nameless, freezing wind blew on him briefly, as if from an opened door. Thoth felt a presence at his back, but he did not look about. He kept his eyes fixed on the moonlit space of marble, on which a tenuous shadow hovered. As he continued his whispered incantations, this shadow grew in size and clarity, until it stood out distinct and horrific. Its outline was not unlike that of a gigantic baboon, but no such baboon ever walked the earth, not even in Stygia. Still Thoth did not look, but drawing from his girdle a sandal of his master—always carried in the dim hope that he might be able to put it to such use—he cast it behind him.

"Know it well, slave of the Ring!" he exclaimed. "Find him who wore it and destroy him! Look into his eyes and blast his soul, before you tear out his throat! Kill him! Aye," in a blind burst of passion, "and all with him!"

Etched on the moonlit wall Thoth saw the horror lower its misshapen head and take the scent like some hideous hound. Then the grisly head was thrown back and the thing wheeled and was gone like a wind through the trees. The Stygian flung up his arms in maddened exultation, and his teeth and eyes gleamed in the moonlight.

A soldier on guard without the walls yelled in startled horror as a great loping black shadow with flaming eyes cleared the wall and swept by him with a swirling rush of wind. But it was gone so swiftly that the bewildered warrior was left wondering whether it had been a dream or a hallucination.

## IV

*When the world was young and men were weak, and the fiends of the night walked free,*
*I strove with Set by fire and steel and the juice of the upas tree;*
*Now that I sleep in the mount's black heart, and the ages take their toll,*
*Forget ye him who fought with the Snake to save the human soul?*

Alone in the great sleeping-chamber with its high golden dome King Conan slumbered and dreamed. Through swirling gray mists he heard a curious call, faint and far, and though he did not understand it, it seemed not within his power to ignore it. Sword in hand he went through the gray mist, as a man might walk through clouds, and the voice grew more distinct as he proceeded until he understood the word it spoke—it was his own name that was being called across the gulfs of Space or Time.

Now the mists grew lighter and he saw that he was in a great dark corridor that seemed to be cut in solid black stone. It was unlighted, but by some magic he could see plainly. The floor, ceiling and walls were highly polished and gleamed dull, and they were carved with the figures of ancient heroes and half-forgotten gods. He shuddered to see the vast shadowy outlines of the Nameless Old Ones, and he knew somehow that mortal feet had not traversed the corridor for centuries.

He came upon a wide stair carved in the solid rock, and the sides of the shaft were adorned with esoteric symbols so ancient and horrific that King Conan's skin crawled. The steps were carven each with the abhorrent figure of the Old Serpent, Set, so that at each step he planted his heel on the head of the Snake, as it was intended from old times. But he was none the less at ease for all that.

But the voice called him on, and at last, in darkness that would have been impenetrable to his material eyes, he came into a strange crypt, and saw a vague white-bearded figure sitting on a tomb. Conan's hair rose up and he grasped his sword, but the figure spoke in sepulchral tones.

"Oh man, do you know me?"

"Not I, by Crom!" swore the king.

"Man," said the ancient, "I am Epemitreus."

"But Epemitreus the Sage has been dead for fifteen hundred years!" stammered Conan.

"Harken!" spoke the other commandingly. "As a pebble cast into a dark lake sends ripples to the further shores, happenings in the Unseen world have broken like waves on my slumber. I have marked you well, Conan of Cimmeria, and the stamp of mighty happenings and great deeds is upon you. But dooms are loose in the land, against which your sword cannot aid you."

"You speak in riddles," said Conan uneasily. "Let me see my foe and I'll cleave his skull to the teeth."

"Loose your barbarian fury against your foes of flesh and blood," answered the ancient. "It is not against men I must shield you. There are dark worlds barely guessed by man, wherein formless monsters stalk—fiends which may be drawn from the Outer Voids to take material shape and rend and devour at the bidding of evil magicians. There is a serpent in your house, oh king—an adder in your kingdom, come up from Stygia, with the dark wisdom of the shadows in his murky soul. As a sleeping man dreams of the serpent which crawls near him, I have felt the foul presence of Set's neophyte. He is drunk with terrible power, and the blows he strikes at his enemy may well bring down the kingdom. I have called you to me, to give you a weapon against him and his hell-hound pack."

"But why?" bewilderedly asked Conan. "Men say you sleep in the black heart of Golamira, whence you send forth your ghost on unseen wings to aid Aquilonia in times of need, but I—I am an outlander and a barbarian."

"Peace!" the ghostly tones reverberated through the great shadowy cavern. "Your destiny is one with Aquilonia. Gigantic happenings are forming in the web and the womb of Fate, and a blood-mad sorcerer shall not stand in the path of imperial destiny. Ages ago Set coiled about the world like a python about its prey. All my life, which was as the lives of three common men, I fought him. I drove him into the shadows of the mysterious south, but in dark Stygia men still worship him who to us is the arch-demon. As I fought Set, I fight his worshipers and his votaries and his acolytes. Hold out your sword."

Wondering, Conan did so, and on the great blade, close to the heavy silver guard, the ancient traced with a bony finger a strange symbol that glowed like white fire in the shadows. And on the instant crypt, tomb and ancient vanished, and Conan, bewildered, sprang from his couch in the great golden-domed chamber. And as he stood, bewildered at the strangeness of his dream, he realized that he was gripping his sword in his hand. And his hair prickled at the nape of his neck, for on the broad blade was carven a symbol—the outline of a phoenix. And he remembered that on the tomb in the crypt he had seen what he had thought to be a similar figure, carven of stone. Now he wondered if it had been but a stone figure, and his skin crawled at the strangeness of it all.

Then as he stood, a stealthy sound in the corridor outside brought him to life, and without stopping to investigate, he began to don his armor; again he was the barbarian, suspicious and alert as a gray wolf at bay.

## V

*What do I know of cultured ways, the gilt, the craft and the lie?*
*I, who was born in a naked land and bred in the open sky.*
*The subtle tongue, the sophist guile, they fail when the broadswords sing;*
*Rush in and die, dogs—I was a man before I was a king.*

*—The Road of Kings*

Through the silence which shrouded the corridor of the royal palace stole twenty furtive figures. Their stealthy feet, bare or cased in soft leather, made no sound either on thick carpet or bare marble tile. The torches which stood in niches along the halls gleamed red on dagger, sword and keen-edged ax.

"Easy all!" hissed Ascalante. "Stop that cursed loud breathing, whoever it is! The officer of the night-guard has removed most of the sentries from these halls and made the rest drunk, but we must be careful, just the same. Back! Here come the guard!"

They crowded back behind a cluster of carven pillars, and almost immediately ten giants in black armor swung by at a measured pace. Their faces showed doubt as they glanced at the officer who was leading them away from their post of duty. This officer was rather pale; as the guard passed the hiding-places of the conspirators, he was seen to wipe the sweat from his brow with a shaky hand. He was young, and this betrayal of a king did not come easy to him.

He mentally cursed the vainglorious extravagance which had put him in debt to the money-lenders and made him a pawn of scheming politicians.

The guardsmen clanked by and disappeared up the corridor.

"Good!" grinned Ascalante. "Conan sleeps unguarded. Haste! If they catch us killing him, we're undone—but few men will espouse the cause of a dead king."

"Aye, haste!" cried Rinaldo, his blue eyes matching the gleam of the sword he swung above his head. "My blade is thirsty! I hear the gathering of the vultures! On!"

They hurried down the corridor with reckless speed and stopped before a gilded door which bore the royal dragon symbol of Aquilonia.

"Gromel!" snapped Ascalante. "Break me this door open!"

The giant drew a deep breath and launched his mighty frame against the panels, which groaned and bent at the impact. Again he crouched and plunged. With a snapping of bolts and a rending crash of wood, the door splintered and burst inward.

"In!" roared Ascalante, on fire with the spirit of the deed.

"In!" yelled Rinaldo. "Death to the tyrant!"

They stopped short. Conan faced them, not a naked man roused mazed and unarmed out of deep sleep to be butchered like a sheep, but a barbarian wide-awake and at bay, partly armored, and with his long sword in his hand.

For an instant the tableau held—the four rebel noblemen in the broken door, and the horde of wild hairy faces crowding behind them—all held momentarily frozen by the sight of the blazing-eyed giant standing sword in hand in the middle of the candle-lighted chamber. In that instant Ascalante beheld, on a small table near the royal couch, the silver scepter and the slender gold circlet which was the crown of Aquilonia, and the sight maddened him with desire.

"In, rogues!" yelled the outlaw. "He is one to twenty and he has no helmet!"

True; there had been lack of time to don the heavy plumed casque, or to lace in place the side-plates of the cuirass, nor was there now time to snatch the great shield from the wall. Still, Conan was better protected than any of his foes except Volmana and Gromel, who were in full armor.

The king glared, puzzled as to their identity. Ascalante he did not know; he could not see through the closed vizors of the armored conspirators, and Rinaldo had pulled his slouch cap down above his eyes. But there was no time for surmise. With a yell that rang to the roof, the killers flooded into the room, Gromel first. He came like a charging bull, head down, sword low for the disembowelling thrust. Conan sprang to meet him, and all his tigerish strength went into the arm that swung the sword. In a whistling arc the great blade flashed through the air and crashed on the Bossonian's helmet. Blade and casque shivered together and Gromel rolled lifeless on the floor. Conan bounded back, still gripping the broken hilt.

"Gromel!" he spat, his eyes blazing in amazement, as the shattered helmet disclosed the shattered head; then the rest of the pack were upon him. A dagger point raked along his ribs between breastplate and backplate, a sword-edge flashed before his eyes. He flung aside the dagger-wielder with his left arm, and smashed his broken hilt like a cestus into the swordsman's temple. The man's brains spattered in his face.

"Watch the door, five of you!" screamed Ascalante, dancing about the edge of the singing steel whirlpool, for he feared that Conan might smash through their midst and escape. The rogues drew back momentarily, as their leader seized several and thrust them toward the single door, and in that brief respite Conan leaped to the wall and tore therefrom an ancient battle-ax which, untouched by time, had hung there for half a century.

With his back to the wall he faced the closing ring for a flashing instant, then leaped into the thick of them. He was no defensive fighter; even in the teeth of overwhelming odds he always carried the war to the enemy. Any other man would have already died there, and Conan himself did not hope to survive, but he did ferociously wish to inflict as much damage as he could before he fell. His barbaric soul was ablaze, and the chants of old heroes were singing in his ears.

As he sprang from the wall his ax dropped an outlaw with a severed shoulder, and the terrible back-hand return crushed the skull of another. Swords whined venomously about him, but death passed him by breathless margins. The Cimmerian moved in, a blur of blinding speed. He was like a tiger among baboons as he leaped, side-stepped and spun, offering an ever-moving target, while his ax wove a shining wheel of death about him.

For a brief space the assassins crowded him fiercely, raining blows blindly and hampered by their own numbers; then they gave back suddenly—two corpses on the floor gave mute evidence of the king's fury, though Conan himself was bleeding from wounds on arm, neck and legs.

"Knaves!" screamed Rinaldo, dashing off his feathered cap, his wild eyes glaring. "Do ye shrink from the combat? Shall the despot live? Out on it!"

He rushed in, hacking madly, but Conan, recognizing him, shattered his sword with a short terrific chop and with a powerful push of his open hand sent him reeling to the floor. The king took Ascalante's point in his left arm, and the outlaw barely saved his life by ducking and springing backward from the swinging ax. Again the wolves swirled in and Conan's ax sang and crushed. A hairy rascal stooped beneath its stroke and dived at the king's legs, but after wrestling for a brief instant at what seemed a solid iron tower, glanced up in time to see the ax falling, but not in time to avoid it. In the interim, one of his comrades lifted a broadsword with both hands and hewed through the king's left shoulder-plate, wounding the shoulder beneath. In an instant Conan's cuirass was full of blood.

Volmana, flinging the attackers right and left in his savage impatience, came plowing through and hacked murderously at Conan's unprotected head. The king ducked deeply and the sword shaved off a lock of his black hair as it whistled above him. Conan pivoted on his heel and struck in from the side. The ax crunched through the steel cuirass and Volmana crumpled with his whole left side caved in.

"Volmana!" gasped Conan breathlessly. "I'll know that dwarf in Hell—" He straightened to meet the maddened rush of Rinaldo, who charged in wild and wide open, armed only with a dagger. Conan leaped back, lifting his ax.

"Rinaldo!" his voice was strident with desperate urgency. "Back! I would not slay you—"

"Die, tyrant!" screamed the mad minstrel, hurling himself headlong on the king. Conan delayed the blow he was loth to deliver, until it was too late. Only when he felt the bite of the steel in his unprotected side did he strike, in a frenzy of blind desperation.

Rinaldo dropped with his skull shattered, and Conan reeled back against the wall, blood spurting from between the fingers which gripped his wound.

"In, now, and slay him!" yelled Ascalante.

Conan put his back against the wall and lifted his ax. He stood like an image of the unconquerable primordial—legs braced far apart, head thrust forward, one hand clutching the wall for support, the other gripping the ax on high, with the great corded muscles standing out in iron ridges, and his features frozen in a death snarl of fury—his eyes blazing terribly through the mist of blood which veiled them. The men faltered—wild, criminal and dissolute though they were, yet they came of a breed men called civilized, with a civilized background; here was the barbarian—the natural killer. They shrank back—the dying tiger could still deal death.

Conan sensed their uncertainty and grinned mirthlessly and ferociously. "Who dies first?" he mumbled through smashed and bloody lips.

Ascalante leaped like a wolf, halted almost in midair with incredible quickness and fell prostrate to avoid the death which was hissing toward him. He frantically whirled his feet out of the way and rolled clear as Conan recovered from his missed blow and struck again. This time the ax sank inches deep into the polished floor close to Ascalante's revolving legs.

Another misguided desperado chose this instant to charge, followed half-heartedly by his fellows. He intended killing Conan before the Cimmerian could wrench his ax from the floor, but his judgment was faulty. The red ax lurched up and crashed down and a crimson caricature of a man catapulted back against the legs of the attackers.

At that instant a fearful scream burst from the rogues at the door as a black misshapen shadow fell across the wall. All but Ascalante wheeled at that cry, and then, howling like dogs, they burst blindly through the door in a raving, blaspheming mob, and scattered through the corridors in screaming flight.

Ascalante did not look toward the door; he had eyes only for the wounded king. He supposed that the noise of the fray had at last roused the palace, and that the loyal guards were upon him, though even in that moment it seemed strange that his hardened rogues should scream so terribly in their flight. Conan did not look toward the door because he was watching the outlaw with the burning eyes of a dying wolf. In this extremity Ascalante's cynical philosophy did not desert him.

"All seems to be lost, particularly honor," he murmured. "However, the king is dying on his feet—and—" Whatever other cogitation might have passed through his mind is not to be known; for, leaving the sentence uncompleted, he ran lightly at Conan just as the Cimmerian was perforce employing his ax-arm to wipe the blood from his blinded eyes.

But even as he began his charge, there was a strange rushing in the air and a heavy weight struck terrifically between his shoulders. He was dashed headlong and great talons sank agonizingly in his flesh. Writhing desperately beneath his attacker, he twisted his head about and stared into the face of Nightmare and lunacy. Upon him crouched a great black thing which he knew was born in no sane or human world. Its slavering black fangs were near his throat and the glare of its yellow eyes shrivelled his limbs as a killing wind shrivels young corn.

The hideousness of its face transcended mere bestiality. It might have been the face of an ancient, evil mummy, quickened with demoniac life. In those abhorrent features the outlaw's dilated eyes seemed to see, like a shadow in the madness that enveloped him, a faint and terrible resemblance to the slave Thoth-amon. Then Ascalante's cynical and all-sufficient philosophy deserted him, and with a ghastly cry he gave up the ghost before those slavering fangs touched him.

Conan, shaking the blood-drops from his eyes, stared frozen. At first he thought it was a great black hound which stood above Ascalante's distorted body; then as his sight cleared he saw that it was neither a hound nor a baboon.

With a cry that was like an echo of Ascalante's death-shriek, he reeled away from the wall and met the leaping horror with a cast of his ax that had behind it all the desperate power of his electrified nerves. The flying weapon glanced singing from the slanting skull it should have crushed, and the king was hurled half-way across the chamber by the impact of the giant body.

The slavering jaws closed on the arm Conan flung up to guard his throat, but the monster made no effort to secure a death-grip. Over his mangled arm it glared fiendishly into the king's eyes, in which there began to be mirrored a likeness of the horror which stared from the dead eyes of Ascalante. Conan felt his soul shrivel and begin to be drawn out of his body, to drown in the yellow wells of cosmic horror which glimmered spectrally in the formless chaos that was growing about him and engulfing all life and sanity. Those eyes grew and became gigantic, and in them the Cimmerian glimpsed the reality of all the abysmal and blasphemous horrors that lurk in the outer darkness of formless voids and nighted gulfs. He opened his bloody lips to shriek his hate and loathing, but only a dry rattle burst from his throat.

But the horror that paralyzed and destroyed Ascalante roused in the Cimmerian a frenzied fury akin to madness. With a volcanic wrench of his whole body he plunged backward, heedless of the agony of his torn arm, dragging the monster bodily with him. And his outflung hand struck something his dazed fighting-brain recognized as the hilt of his broken sword. Instinctively he gripped it and struck with all the power of nerve and thew, as a man stabs with a dagger. The broken blade sank deep and Conan's arm was released as the abhorrent mouth gaped as in agony. The king was hurled violently aside, and lifting himself on one hand he saw, as one mazed, the terrible convulsions of the monster from which thick blood was gushing through the great wound his broken blade had torn. And as he watched, its struggles ceased and it lay jerking spasmodically, staring upward with its grisly dead eyes. Conan blinked and shook the blood from his own eyes; it seemed to him that the thing was melting and disintegrating into a slimy unstable mass.

Then a medley of voices reached his ears, and the room was thronged with the finally roused people of the court—knights, peers, ladies, men-at-arms, councillors—all babbling and shouting and getting in one another's way. The Black Dragons were on hand, wild with rage, swearing and ruffling, with their hands on their hilts and foreign oaths in their teeth. Of the young officer of the door-guard nothing was seen, nor was he found then or later, though earnestly sought after.

"Gromel! Volmana! Rinaldo!" exclaimed Publius, the high councillor, wringing his fat hands among the corpses. "Black treachery! Someone shall dance for this! Call the guard."

"The guard is here, you old fool!" cavalierly snapped Pallantides, commander of the Black Dragons, forgetting Publius' rank in the stress of the moment. "Best stop your caterwauling and aid us to bind the king's wounds. He's likely to bleed to death."

"Yes, yes!" cried Publius, who was a man of plans rather than action. "We must bind his wounds. Send for every leech of the court! Oh, my lord, what a black shame on the city! Are you entirely slain?"

"Wine!" gasped the king from the couch where they had laid him. They put a goblet to his bloody lips and he drank like a man half dead of thirst.

"Good!" he grunted, falling back. "Slaying is cursed dry work."

They had stanched the flow of blood, and the innate vitality of the barbarian was asserting itself.

"See first to the dagger-wound in my side," he bade the court physicians.

"Rinaldo wrote me a deathly song there, and keen was the stylus."

"We should have hanged him long ago," gibbered Publius. "No good can come of poets—who is this?"

He nervously touched Ascalante's body with his sandaled toe.

"By Mitra!" ejaculated the commander. "It is Ascalante, once count of Thune! What devil's work brought him up from his desert haunts?"

"But why does he stare so?" whispered Publius, drawing away, his own eyes wide and a peculiar prickling among the short hairs at the back of his fat neck. The others fell silent as they gazed at the dead outlaw.

"Had you seen what he and I saw," growled the king, sitting up despite the protests of the leeches, "you had not wondered. Blast your own gaze by looking at—" He stopped short, his mouth gaping, his finger pointing fruitlessly. Where the monster had died, only the bare floor met his eyes.

"Crom!" he swore. "The thing's melted back into the foulness which bore it!"

"The king is delirious," whispered a noble. Conan heard and swore with barbaric oaths.

"By Badb, Morrigan, Macha and Nemain!" he concluded wrathfully. "I am sane! It was like a cross between a Stygian mummy and a baboon. It came through the door, and Ascalante's rogues fled before it. It slew Ascalante, who was about to run me through. Then it came upon me and I slew it—how I know not, for my ax glanced from it as from a rack. But I think that the Sage Epemitreus had a hand in it—"

"Hark how he names Epemitreus, dead for fifteen hundred years!" they whispered to each other.

"By Ymir!" thundered the king. "This night I talked with Epemitreus! He called to me in my dreams, and I walked down a black stone corridor carved with old gods, to a stone stair on the steps of which were the outlines of Set, until I came to a crypt, and a tomb with a phœnix carved on it—"

"In Mitra's name, lord king, be silent!" It was the high-priest of Mitra who cried out, and his countenance was ashen.

Conan threw up his head like a lion tossing back its mane, and his voice was thick with the growl of the angry lion.

"Am I a slave, to shut my mouth at your command?"

"Nay, nay, my lord!" The high-priest was trembling, but not through fear of the royal wrath. "I meant no offense." He bent his head close to the king and spoke in a whisper that carried only to Conan's ears.

"My lord, this is a matter beyond human understanding. Only the inner circle of the priestcraft know of the black stone corridor carved in the black heart of Mount Golamira, by unknown hands, or of the phoenix-guarded tomb where Epemitreus was laid to rest fifteen hundred years ago. And since that time no living man has entered it, for his chosen priests, after placing the Sage in the crypt, blocked up the outer entrance of the corridor so that no man could find it, and today not even the high-priests know where it is. Only by word of mouth, handed down by the high-priests to the chosen few, and jealously guarded, does the inner circle of Mitra's acolytes know of the resting-place of Epemitreus in the black heart of Golamira. It is one of the Mysteries, on which Mitra's cult stands."

"I cannot say by what magic Epemitreus brought me to him," answered Conan. "But I talked with him, and he made a mark on my sword. Why that mark made it deadly to demons, or what magic lay behind the mark, I know not; but though the blade broke on Gromel's helmet, yet the fragment was long enough to kill the horror."

"Let me see your sword," whispered the high-priest from a throat gone suddenly dry.

Conan held out the broken weapon and the high-priest cried out and fell to his knees.

"Mitra guard us against the powers of darkness!" he gasped. "The king has indeed talked with Epemitreus this night! There on the sword—it is the secret sign none might make but him—the emblem of the immortal phoenix which broods forever over his tomb! A candle, quick! Look again at the spot where the king said the goblin died!"

It lay in the shade of a broken screen. They threw the screen aside and bathed the floor in a flood of candlelight. And a shuddering silence fell over the people as they looked. Then some fell on their knees calling on Mitra, and some fled screaming from the chamber.

There on the floor where the monster had died, there lay, like a tangible shadow, a broad dark stain that could not be washed out;

the thing had left its outline clearly etched in its blood, and that outline was of no being of a sane and normal world. Grim and horrific it brooded there, like the shadow cast by one of the apish gods that squat on the shadowy altars of dim temples in the dark land of Stygia.

# The Tower of the Elephant

by Robert E. Howard

## I

Torches flared murkily on the revels in the Maul, where the thieves of the east held carnival by night. In the Maul they could carouse and roar as they liked, for honest people shunned the quarters, and watchmen, well paid with stained coins, did not interfere with their sport. Along the crooked, unpaved streets with their heaps of refuse and sloppy puddles, drunken roisterers staggered, roaring. Steel glinted in the shadows where wolf preyed on wolf, and from the darkness rose the shrill laughter of women and the sounds of scufflings and strugglings. Torchlight licked luridly from broken windows and wide-thrown doors, and out of those doors, stale smells of wine and rank, sweaty bodies, clamor of drinking-jacks and fists hammered on rough tables, snatches of obscene songs, rushed like a blow in the face.

In one of these dens merriment thundered to the low smoke-stained roof, where rascals gathered in every stage of rags and tatters—furtive cut-purses, leering kidnappers, quick-fingered thieves, swaggering bravoes with their wenches, strident-voiced women clad in tawdry finery. Native rogues were the dominant element—dark-skinned, dark-eyed Zamorians, with daggers at their girdles and guile in their hearts. But there were wolves of half a dozen outland nations there as well. There was a giant Hyperborean renegade, taciturn, dangerous, with a broadsword strapped to his great gaunt frame—for men wore steel openly in the Maul. There was a Shemitish counterfeiter, with his hook nose and curled blueblack beard. There was a bold-eyed Brythunian wench, sitting on the knee of a tawny-haired Gunderman—a wandering mercenary soldier, a deserter from some defeated army. And the fat, gross rogue whose bawdy jests were causing all the shouts of mirth was a professional kidnapper come up from distant Koth to teach woman-stealing to Zamorians who were born with more knowledge of the art than he could ever attain.

This man halted in his description of an intended victim's charms, and thrust his muzzle into a huge tankard of frothing ale. Then, blowing the foam from his fat lips, he said, "By Bel, god of all thieves, I'll show them how to steal wenches: I'll have her over the Zamorian border before dawn, and there'll be a caravan waiting to receive her. Three hundred pieces of silver, a count of Ophir promised me for a sleek young Brythunian of the better class. It took me weeks, wandering among the border cities as a beggar, to find one I knew would suit. And is she a pretty baggage!"

He blew a slobbery kiss in the air.

"I know lords in Shem who would trade the secret of the Elephant Tower for her," he said, returning to his ale.

A touch on his tunic sleeve made him turn his head, scowling at the interruption. He saw a tall, strongly made youth standing beside him. This person was as much out of place in that den as a gray wolf among mangy rats of the gutters. His cheap tunic could not conceal the hard, rangy lines of his powerful frame, the broad, heavy shoulders, the massive chest, lean waist, and heavy arms. His skin was brown from outland suns, his eyes blue and smoldering; a shock of tousled black hair crowned his broad forehead. From his girdle hung a sword in a worn leather scabbard.

The Kothian involuntarily drew back; for the man was not one of any civilized race he knew.

"You spoke of the Elephant Tower," said the stranger, speaking Zamorian with an alien accent. "I've heard much of this tower; what is its secret?"

The fellow's attitude did not seem threatening, and the Kothian's courage was bolstered up by the ale, and the evident approval of his audience. He swelled with self-importance.

"The secret of the Elephant Tower?" he exclaimed. "Why, any fool knows that Yara the priest dwells there with the great jewel men call the Elephant's Heart, that is the secret of his magic."

The barbarian digested this for a space.

"I have seen this tower," he said. "It is set in a great garden above the level of the city, surrounded by high walls. I have seen no guards. The walls would be easy to climb. Why has not somebody stolen this secret gem?"

The Kothian stared wide-mouthed at the other's simplicity, then burst into a roar of derisive mirth, in which the others joined.

"Harken to this heathen!" he bellowed. "He would steal the jewel of Yara! Harken, fellow," he said, turning portentously to the other, "I suppose you are some sort of a northern barbarian—"

"I am a Cimmerian," the outlander answered, in no friendly tone. The reply and the manner of it meant little to the Kothian; of a kingdom that lay far to the south, on the borders of Shem, he knew only vaguely of the northern races.

"Then give ear and learn wisdom, fellow," said he, pointing his drinking jack at the discomfited youth. "Know that in Zamora, and more especially in this city, there are more bold thieves than anywhere else in the world, even Koth. If mortal man could have stolen the gem, be sure it would have been filched long ago. You speak of climbing the walls, but once having climbed, you would quickly wish yourself back again. There are no guards in the gardens at night for a very good reason—that is, no human guards. But in the watch-chamber, in the lower part of the tower, are armed men, and even if you passed those who roam the gardens by night, you must still pass through the soldiers, for the gem is kept somewhere in the tower above."

"But if a man could pass through the gardens," argued the Cimmerian, "why could he not come at the gem through the upper part of the tower and thus avoid the soldiers?"

Again the Kothian gaped at him.

"Listen to him!" he shouted jeeringly. "The barbarian is an eagle who would fly to the jeweled rim of the tower, which is only a hundred and fifty feet above the earth, with rounded sides slicker than polished glass!"

The Cimmerian glared about, embarrassed at the roar of mocking laughter that greeted this remark. He saw no particular humor in it, and was too new to civilization to understand its discourtesies. Civilized men are more discourteous than savages because they know they can be impolite without having their skulls split, as a general thing. He was bewildered and chagrined, and doubtless would have slunk away, abashed, but the Kothian chose to goad him further.

"Come, come!" he shouted. "Tell these poor fellows, who have only been thieves since before you were spawned, tell them how you would steal the gem!"

"There is always a way, if the desire be coupled with courage," answered the Cimmerian shortly, nettled.

The Kothian chose to take this as a personal slur. His face grew purple with anger.

"What!" he roared. "You dare tell us our business, and intimate that we are cowards? Get along; get out of my sight!" And he pushed the Cimmerian violently.

"Will you mock me and then lay hands on me?" grated the barbarian, his quick rage leaping up; and he returned the push with an open-handed blow that knocked his tormenter back against the rude-hewn table. Ale splashed over the jack's lip, and the Kothian roared in fury, dragging at his sword.

"Heathen dog!" he bellowed. "I'll have your heart for that!"

Steel flashed and the throng surged wildly back out of the way. In their flight they knocked over the single candle and the den was plunged into darkness, broken by the crash of upset benches, drum of flying feet, shouts, oaths of people tumbling over one another and a single strident yell of agony that cut the din like a knife. When a candle was relighted, most of the guests had gone out by doors and broken windows, and the rest huddled behind stacks of wine kegs and under tables. The barbarian was gone; the center of the room was deserted except for the gashed body of the Kothian. The Cimmerian, with the unerring instinct of the barbarian, had killed his man in the darkness and confusion.

## II

The lurid lights and drunken revelry fell away behind the Cimmerian. He had discarded his torn tunic, and walked through the night naked except for a loincloth and his high-strapped sandals. He moved with the supple ease of a great tiger, his steely muscles rippling under his brown skin.

He had entered the part of the city reserved for the temples. On all sides of him they glittered white in the starlight—snowy marble pillars and golden domes and silver arches, shrines of Zamora's myriad strange gods. He did not trouble his head about them; he knew that Zamora's religion, like all things of a civilized, long-settled people, was intricate and complex, and had lost most of the pristine essence in a maze of formulas and rituals. He had squatted for hours in the courtyards of the philosophers, listening to the arguments of theologians and teachers, and come away in a haze of bewilderment, sure of only one thing, and that, that they were all touched in the head.

His gods were simple and understandable; Crom was their chief, and he lived on a great mountain, whence he sent forth dooms and death. It was useless to call on Crom, because he was a gloomy, savage god and he hated weaklings. But he gave a man courage at birth, and the will and might to kill his enemies, which, in the Cimmerian's mind, was all any god should be expected to do.

His sandaled feet made no sound on the gleaming pave. No watchmen passed, for even the thieves of the Maul shunned the temples, where strange dooms had been known to fall on violators. Ahead of him he saw, looming against the sky, the Tower of the Elephant. He mused, wondering why it was so named. No one seemed to know. He had never seen an elephant, but he vaguely understood that it was a monstrous animal, with a tail in front as well as behind. This a wandering Shemite had told him, swearing that he had seen such beasts by the thousands in the country of the Hyrkanians; but all men knew what liars were the men of Shem. At any rate, there were no elephants in Zamora.

The shimmering shaft of the tower rose frostily in the stars. In the sunlight it shone so dazzlingly that few could bear its glare, and men said it was built of silver. It was round, a slim perfect cylinder, a hundred and fifty feet in height, and its rim glittered in the starlight with the great jewels which crusted it. The tower stood among the waving exotic trees of a garden raised high above the general level of the city. A high wall enclosed this garden, and outside the wall was a lower level, likewise enclosed by a wall. No lights shone forth; there seemed to be no windows in the tower—at least not above the level of the inner wall. Only the gems high above sparkled frostily in the starlight.

Shrubbery grew thick outside the lower or outer wall. The Cimmerian crept close and stood beside the barrier, measuring it with his eye. It was high, but he could leap and catch the coping with his fingers. Then it would be child's play to swing himself up and over, and he did not doubt that he could pass the inner wall in the same manner. But he hesitated at the thought of the strange perils which were said to await within. These people were strange and mysterious to him; they were not of his kind—not even of the same blood as the more westerly Brythunians, Nemedians, Kothians and Aquilonians, whose civilized mysteries had awed him in times past. The people of Zamora were very ancient and, from what he had seen of them, very evil.

He thought of Yara, the high priest, who worked strange dooms from this jeweled tower, and the Cimmerian's hair prickled as he remembered a tale told by a drunken page of the court—how Yara had laughed in the face of a hostile prince, and held up a glowing, evil gem before him, and how rays shot blindingly from that unholy jewel to envelop the prince, who screamed and fell down and shrank to a withered blackened lump that changed to a black spider which scampered wildly about the chamber until Yara set his heel upon it.

Yara came not often from his tower of magic, and always to work evil on some man or some nation. The king of Zamora feared him more than he feared death, and kept himself drunk all the time because that fear was more than he could endure sober. Yara was very old—centuries old, men said, and added that he would live forever because of the magic of his gem, which men called the Heart of the Elephant, for no better reason than they named his hold the Elephant's Tower.

The Cimmerian, engrossed in these thoughts, shrank quickly against the wall. Within the garden someone was passing, who walked with a measured stride. The listener heard the clink of steel. So after all a guard did pace those gardens. The Cimmerian waited, expected to hear him pass again on the next round, but silence rested over the mysterious gardens.

At last curiosity overcame him. Leaping lightly he grasped the wall and swung himself up to the top with one arm. Lying flat on the broad coping, he looked down into the wide space between the walls. No shrubbery grew near him, though he saw some carefully trimmed bushes near the inner wall. The starlight fell on the even sward and somewhere a fountain tinkled.

The Cimmerian cautiously lowered himself down on the inside and drew his sword, staring about him. He was shaken by the nervousness of the wild at standing thus unprotected in the naked starlight, and he moved lightly around the curve of the wall, hugging its shadow, until he was even with the shrubbery he had noticed. Then he ran quickly toward it, crouching low, and almost tripped over a form that lay crumpled near the edges of the bushes.

A quick look to right and left showed him no enemy in sight at least, and he bent close to investigate. His keen eyes, even in the dim starlight, showed him a strongly built man in the silvered armor and crested helmet of the Zamorian royal guard. A shield and a spear lay near him and it took but an instant's examination to show that he had been strangled. The barbarian glanced about uneasily. He knew that this man must be the guard he had heard pass his hiding place by the wall. Only a short time had passed, yet in that interval nameless hands had reached out of the dark and choked out the soldier's life.

Straining his eyes in the gloom, he saw a hint of motion through the shrubs near the wall. Thither he glided, gripping his sword. He made no more noise than a panther stealing through the night, yet the man he was stalking heard. The Cimmerian had a dim glimpse of a huge bulk close to the wall, felt relief that it was at least human; then the fellow wheeled quickly with a gasp that sounded like panic, made the first motion of a forward plunge, hands clutching, then recoiled as the Cimmerian's blade caught the starlight. For a tense instant neither spoke, standing ready for anything.

"You are no soldier," hissed the stranger at last. "You are a thief like myself."

"And who are you?" asked the Cimmerian in a suspicious whisper.

"Taurus of Nemedia."

The Cimmerian lowered his sword.

"I've heard of you. Men call you a prince of thieves."

A low laugh answered him. Taurus was tall as the Cimmerian, and heavier; he was big-bellied and fat, but his every movement betokened a subtle dynamic magnetism, which was reflected in the keen eyes that glinted vitally, even in the starlight. He was barefooted and carried a coil of what looked like a thin, strong rope, knotted at regular intervals.

"Who are you?" he whispered.

"Conan, a Cimmerian," answered the other. "I came seeking a way to steal Yara's jewel, that men call the Elephant's Heart."

Conan sensed the man's great belly shaking in laughter, but it was not derisive. "By Bel, god of thieves!" hissed Taurus. "I had thought only myself had courage to attempt that poaching. These Zamorians call themselves thieves—bah! Conan, I like your grit. I never shared an adventure with anyone but, by Bel, we'll attempt this together if you're willing."

"Then you are after the gem, too?"

"What else? I've had my plans laid for months, but you, I think, have acted on sudden impulse, my friend."

"You killed the soldier?"

"Of course. I slid over the wall when he was on the other side of the garden. I hid in the bushes; he heard me, or thought he heard something. When he came blundering over, it was no trick at all to get behind him and suddenly grip his neck and choke out his fool's life. He was like most men, half-blind in the dark. A good thief should have eyes like a cat."

"You made one mistake," said Conan.

Taurus' eyes flashed angrily.

"I? I, a mistake? Impossible!"

"You should have dragged the body into the bushes."

"Said the novice to the master of the art. They will not change the guard until past midnight. Should any come searching for him now and find his body, they would flee at once to Yara, bellowing the news, and give us time to escape. Were they not to find it, they'd go beating up the bushes and catch us like rats in a trap."

"You are right," agreed Conan.

"So. Now attend. We waste time in this cursed discussion. There are no guards in the inner garden—human guards, I mean, though there are sentinels even more deadly. It was their presence which baffled me for so long, but I finally discovered a way to circumvent them."

"What of the soldiers in the lower part of the tower?"

"Old Yara dwells in the chambers above. By that route we will come—and go, I hope. Never mind asking me how. I have arranged a way. We'll steal down through the top of the tower and strangle old Yara before he can cast any of his accursed spells on us. At least we'll try; it's the chance of being turned into a spider or a toad, against the wealth and power of the world. All good thieves must know how to take risks."

"I'll go as far as any man," said Conan, slipping off his sandals.

"Then follow me." And turning, Taurus leaped up, caught the wall and drew himself up. The man's suppleness was amazing, considering his bulk; he seemed almost to glide up over the edge of the coping. Conan followed him, and lying flat on the broad top, they spoke in wary whispers.

"I see no light," Conan muttered. The lower part of the tower seemed much like that portion visible from outside the garden—a perfect, gleaming cylinder, with no apparent openings.

"There are cleverly constructed doors and windows," answered Taurus, "but they are closed. The soldiers breathe air that comes from above."

The garden was a vague pool of shadows, where feathery bushes and low-spreading trees waved darkly in the starlight. Conan's wary soul felt the aura of waiting menace that brooded over it. He felt the burning glare of unseen eyes, and he caught a subtle scent that made the short hairs on his neck instinctively bristle as a hunting dog bristles at the scent of an ancient enemy.

"Follow me," whispered Taurus, "keep behind me, as you value your life."

Taking what looked like a copper tube from his girdle, the Nemedian dropped lightly to the sward inside the wall. Conan was close behind him, sword ready, but Taurus pushed him back, close to the wall, and showed no inclination to advance himself. His whole attitude was of tense expectancy, and his gaze, like Conan's, was fixed on the shadowy mass of shrubbery a few yards away. This shrubbery was shaken, although the breeze had died down. Then two great eyes blazed from the waving shadows and behind them other sparks of fire glinted in the darkness.

"Lions!" muttered Conan.

"Aye. By day they are kept in subterranean caverns below the tower. That's why there are no guards in this garden."

Conan counted the eyes rapidly.

"Five in sight; maybe more back in the bushes. They'll charge in a moment—"

"Be silent!" hissed Taurus, and he moved out from the wall cautiously, as if treading on razors, lifting the slender tube. Low rumblings rose from the shadows and the blazing eyes moved forward. Conan could sense the great slavering jaws, the tufted tails lashing tawny sides. The air grew tense—the Cimmerian gripped his sword, expecting the charge and the irresistible hurtling of giant bodies. Then Taurus brought the mouth of the tube to his lips and blew powerfully. A long jet of yellowish powder shot from the other end of the tube and billowed out instantly in a thick green-yellow cloud that settled over the shrubbery, blotting out the glaring eyes.

Taurus ran back hastily to the wall. Conan glared without understanding. The thick cloud hid the shrubbery, and from it no sound came.

"What is that mist?" the Cimmerian asked uneasily.

"Death!" hissed the Nemedian. "If a wind springs up and blows it back upon us, we must flee over the wall. But no, the wind is still, and now it is dissipating. Wait until it vanishes entirely. To breathe it is death."

Presently only yellowish shreds hung ghostily in the air; then they were gone, and Taurus motioned his companion forward. They stole toward the bushes, and Conan gasped. Stretched out in the shadows lay five great tawny shapes, the fire of their grim eyes dimmed forever. A sweetish cloying scent lingered in the atmosphere.

"They died without a sound!" muttered the Cimmerian. "Taurus, what was that powder?"

"It was made from the black lotus, whose blossoms wave in the lost jungles of Khitai, where only the yellow-skulled priests of Yun dwell. Those blossoms strike dead any who smell of them."

Conan knelt beside the great forms, assuring himself that they were indeed beyond power of harm. He shook his head; the magic of the exotic lands was mysterious and terrible to the barbarians of the north.

"Why can you not slay the soldiers in the tower in the same way?" he asked.

"Because that was all the powder I possessed. The obtaining of it was a feat which in itself was enough to make me famous among the thieves of the world. I stole it out of a caravan bound for Stygia, and I lifted it, in its cloth-of-gold bag, out of the coils of the great serpent which guarded it, without awaking him. But come, in Bel's name! Are we to waste the night in discussion?"

They glided through the shrubbery to the gleaming foot of the tower, and there, with a motion enjoining silence, Taurus unwound his knotted cord, on one end of which was a strong steel hook. Conan saw his plan, and asked no questions as the Nemedian gripped the line a short distance below the hook, and began to swing it about his head. Conan laid his ear to the smooth wall and listened, but could hear nothing. Evidently the soldiers within did not suspect the presence of intruders, who had made no more sound than the night wind blowing through the trees. But a strange nervousness was on the barbarian; perhaps it was the lion-smell which was over everything.

Taurus threw the line with a smooth, ripping motion of his mighty arm. The hook curved upward and inward in a peculiar manner, hard to describe, and vanished over the jeweled rim. It apparently caught firmly, for cautious jerking and then hard pulling did not result in any slipping or giving.

"Luck the first cast," murmured Taurus. "I—"

It was Conan's savage instinct which made him wheel suddenly; for the death that was upon them made no sound. A fleeting glimpse showed the Cimmerian the giant tawny shape, rearing upright against the stars, towering over him for the death-stroke. No civilized man could have moved half so quickly as the barbarian moved. His sword flashed frostily in the starlight with every ounce of desperate nerve and thew behind it, and man and beast went down together.

Cursing incoherently beneath his breath, Taurus bent above the mass, and saw his companion's limbs move as he strove to drag himself from under the great weight that lay limply upon him. A glance showed the startled Nemedian that the lion was dead, its slanting skull split in half. He laid hold of the carcass and, by his aid, Conan thrust it aside and clambered up, still gripping his dripping sword.

"Are you hurt, man?" gasped Taurus, still bewildered by the stunning swiftness of that touch-and-go episode.

"No, by Crom!" answered the barbarian. "But that was as close a call as I've had in a life no-ways tame. Why did not the cursed beast roar as he charged?"

"All things are strange in this garden," said Taurus. "The lions strike silently—and so do other deaths. But come—little sound was made in that slaying, but the soldiers might have heard, if they are not asleep or drunk. That beast was in some other part of the garden and escaped the death of the flowers, but surely there are no more. We must climb this cord—little need to ask a Cimmerian if he can."

"If it will bear my weight," grunted Conan, cleansing his sword on the grass. "It will bear thrice my own," answered Taurus. "It was woven from the tresses of dead women, which I took from their tombs at midnight, and steeped in the deadly wine of the upas tree, to give it strength. I will go first—then follow me closely."

The Nemedian gripped the rope and crooking a knee about it, began the ascent; he went up like a cat, belying the apparent clumsiness of his bulk. The Cimmerian followed. The cord swayed and turned on itself, but the climbers were not hindered; both had made more difficult climbs before. The jeweled rim glittered high above them, jutting out from the perpendicular of the wall, so that the cord hung perhaps a foot from the side of the tower—a fact which added greatly to the ease of the ascent.

Up and up they went, silently, the lights of the city spreading out further and further to their sight as they climbed, the stars above them more and more dimmed by the glitter of the jewels along the rim. Now Taurus reached up a hand and gripped the rim itself, pulling himself up and over. Conan paused a moment on the very edge, fascinated by the great frosty jewels whose gleams dazzled his eyes—diamonds, rubies, emeralds, sapphires, turquoises, moonstones, set thick as stars in the shimmering silver. At a distance their different gleams had seemed to merge into a pulsing white glare;

but now, at close range, they shimmered with a million rainbow tints and lights, hypnotizing him with their scintillations.

"There is a fabulous fortune here, Taurus," he whispered; but the Nemedian answered impatiently, "Come on! If we secure the Heart, these and all other things shall be ours."

Conan climbed over the sparkling rim. The level of the tower's top was some feet below the gemmed ledge. It was flat, composed of some dark blue substance, set with gold that caught the starlight, so that the whole looked like a wide sapphire flecked with shining gold dust. Across from the point where they had entered there seemed to be a sort of chamber, built upon the roof. It was of the same silvery material as the walls of the tower, adorned with designs worked in smaller gems; its single door was of gold, its surface cut in scales, and crusted with jewels that gleamed like ice.

Conan cast a glance at the pulsing ocean of lights which spread far below them, then glanced at Taurus. The Nemedian was drawing up his cord and coiling it. He showed Conan where the hook had caught—a fraction of an inch of the point had sunk under a great blazing jewel on the inner side of the rim.

"Luck was with us again," he muttered. "One would think that our combined weight would have torn that stone out. Follow me; the real risks of the venture begin now. We are in the serpent's lair, and we know not where he lies hidden."

Like stalking tigers they crept across the darkly gleaming floor and halted outside the sparkling door. With a deft and cautious hand Taurus tried it. It gave without resistance, and the companions looked in, tensed for anything. Over the Nemedian's shoulder Conan had a glimpse of a glittering chamber, the walls, ceiling and floor of which were crusted with great white jewels which lighted it brightly, and which seemed its only illumination. It seemed empty of life.

"Before we cut off our last retreat," hissed Taurus, "go you to the rim and look over on all sides; if you see any soldiers moving in the gardens, or anything suspicious, return and tell me. I will await you within this chamber."

Conan saw scant reason in this, and a faint suspicion of his companion touched his wary soul, but he did as Taurus requested. As he turned away, the Nemedian slipped inside the door and drew it shut behind him. Conan crept about the rim of the tower, returning to his starting-point without having seen any suspicious movement in the vaguely waving sea of leaves below. He turned toward the door—suddenly from within the chamber there sounded a strangled cry.

The Cimmerian leaped forward, electrified—the gleaming door swung open and Taurus stood framed in the cold blaze behind him. He swayed and his lips parted, but only a dry rattle burst from his throat. Catching at the golden door for support, he lurched out upon the roof, then fell headlong, clutching at his throat. The door swung to behind him.

Conan, crouching like a panther at bay, saw nothing in the room behind the stricken Nemedian, in the brief instant the door was partly open—unless it was not a trick of the light which made it seem as if a shadow darted across the gleaming floor. Nothing followed Taurus out on the roof, and Conan bent above the man.

The Nemedian stared up with dilated, glazing eyes, that somehow held a terrible bewilderment. His hands clawed at his throat, his lips slobbered and gurgled; then suddenly he stiffened, and the astounded Cimmerian knew that he was dead. And he felt that Taurus had died without knowing what manner of death had stricken him. Conan glared bewilderedly at the cryptic golden door. In that empty room, with its glittering jeweled walls, death had come to the prince of thieves as swiftly and mysteriously as he had dealt doom to the lions in the gardens below.

Gingerly the barbarian ran his hands over the man's half-naked body, seeking a wound. But the only marks of violence were between his shoulders, high up near the base of his bull-neck—three small wounds, which looked as if three nails had been driven deep in the flesh and withdrawn. The edges of these wounds were black, and a faint smell as of putrefaction was evident. "Poisoned darts?" thought Conan—but in that case the missiles should be still in the wounds.

Cautiously he stole toward the golden door, pushed it open, and looked inside. The chamber lay empty, bathed in the cold, pulsing glow of the myriad jewels. In the very center of the ceiling he idly noted a curious design—a black eight-sided pattern, in the center of which four gems glittered with a red flame unlike the white blaze of the other jewels. Across the room there was another door, like the one in which he stood, except that it was not carved in the scale pattern. Was it from that door that death had come?—And having struck down its victim, had it retreated by the same way?

Closing the door behind him, the Cimmerian advanced into the chamber. His bare feet made no sound on the crystal floor. There were no chairs or tables in the chamber, only three or four silken couches, embroidered with gold and worked in strange serpentine designs, and several silver-bound mahogany chests. Some were sealed with heavy golden locks; others lay open, their carven lids thrown back, revealing heaps of jewels in a careless riot of splendor to the Cimmerian's astounded eyes. Conan swore beneath his breath; already he had looked upon more wealth that night than he had ever dreamed existed in all the world, and he grew dizzy thinking of what must be the value of the jewel he sought.

He was in the center of the room now, going stooped forward, head thrust out warily, sword advanced, when again death struck at him soundlessly. A flying shadow that swept across the gleaming floor was his only warning, and his instinctive sidelong leap all that saved his life. He had a flashing glimpse of a hairy black horror that swung past him with a clashing of frothing fangs, and something splashed on his bare shoulder that burned like drops of liquid hell-fire. Springing back, sword high, he saw the horror strike the floor, wheel and scuttle toward him with appalling speed—a gigantic black spider, such as men see only in nightmare dreams.

It was as large as a pig, and its eight thick hairy legs drove its ogreish body over the floor at headlong pace; its four evilly gleaming eyes shone with a horrible intelligence, and its fangs dripped venom that Conan knew, from the burning of his shoulder where only a few drops had splashed as the thing struck and missed, was laden with swift death. This was the killer that had dropped from its perch in the middle of the ceiling on a strand of its web, on the neck of the Nemedian. Fools that they were not to have suspected that the upper chambers would be guarded as well as the lower!

These thoughts flashed briefly through Conan's mind as the monster rushed. He leaped high, and it passed beneath him, wheeled and charged back. This time he evaded its rush with a sideways leap, and struck back like a cat. His sword severed one of the hairy legs, and again he barely saved himself as the monstrosity swerved at him, fangs clicking fiendishly. But the creature did not press the pursuit; turning, it scuttled across the crystal floor and ran up the wall to the ceiling, where it crouched for an instant, glaring down at him with its fiendish red eyes. Then without warning it launched itself through space, trailing a strand of slimy grayish stuff.

Conan stepped back to avoid the hurtling body—then ducked frantically, just in time to escape being snared by the flying web-rope. He saw the monster's intent and sprang toward the door, but it was quicker, and a sticky strand cast across the door made him a prisoner. He dared not try to cut it with his sword; he knew the stuff would cling to the blade, and before he could shake it loose, the fiend would be sinking its fangs into his back.

Then began a desperate game, the wits and quickness of the man matched against the fiendish craft and speed of the giant spider. It no longer scuttled across the floor in a direct charge, or swung its body through the air at him. It raced about the ceiling and the walls, seeking to snare him in the long loops of sticky gray web-strands, which it flung with a devilish accuracy. These strands were thick as ropes, and Conan knew that once they were coiled about him, his desperate strength would not be enough to tear him free before the monster struck.

All over the chamber went on that devil's dance, in utter silence except for the quick breathing of the man, the low scuff of his bare feet on the shining floor, the castanet rattle of the monstrosity's fangs. The gray strands lay in coils on the floor; they were looped along the walls; they overlaid the jewel chests and silken couches, and hung in dusky festoons from the jeweled ceiling. Conan's steel-trap quickness of eye and muscle had kept him untouched, though the sticky loops had passed him so close they rasped his naked hide. He knew he could not always avoid them; he not only had to watch the strands swinging from the ceiling, but to keep his eye on the floor, lest he trip in the coils that lay there. Sooner or later a gummy loop would writhe about him, python-like, and then, wrapped like a cocoon, he would lie at the monster's mercy.

The spider raced across the chamber floor, the gray rope waving out behind it. Conan leaped high, clearing a couch—with a quick wheel the fiend ran up the wall, and the strand, leaping off the floor like a live thing, whipped about the Cimmerian's ankle. He caught himself on his hands as he fell, jerking frantically at the web which held him like a pliant vise, or the coil of a python. The hairy devil was racing down the wall to complete its capture. Stung to frenzy, Conan caught up a jewel chest and hurled it with all his strength. It was a move the monster was not expecting. Full in the midst of the branching black legs the massive missile struck, smashing against the wall with a muffled sickening crunch. Blood and greenish slime spattered, and the shattered mass fell with the burst gem-chest to the floor. The crushed black body lay among the flaming riot of jewels that spilled over it; the hairy legs moved aimlessly, the dying eyes glittered redly among the twinkling gems.

Conan glared about, but no other horror appeared, and he set himself to working free of the web. The substance clung tenaciously to his ankle and his hands, but at last he was free and, taking up his sword, he picked his way among the gray coils and loops to the inner door. What horrors lay within he did not know. The Cimmerian's blood was up, and since he had come so far, and overcome so much peril, he was determined to go through to the grim finish of the adventure, whatever that might be. And he felt that the jewel he sought was not among the many so carelessly strewn about the gleaming chamber.

Stripping off the loops that fouled the inner door, he found that it, like the other, was not locked. He wondered if the soldiers below were still unaware of his presence. Well, he was high above their heads, and if tales were to be believed, they were used to strange noises in the tower above them—sinister sounds, and screams of agony and horror.

Yara was on his mind, and he was not altogether comfortable as he opened the golden door. But he saw only a flight of silver steps leading down, dimly lighted by what means he could not ascertain. Down these he went silently, gripping his sword. He heard no sound, and came presently to an ivory door, set with blood stones. He listened, but no sound came from within; only thin wisps of smoke drifted lazily from beneath the door, bearing a curious exotic odor unfamiliar to the Cimmerian. Below him the silver stair wound down to vanish in the dimness, and up that shadowy well no sound floated; he had an eery feeling that he was alone in a tower occupied only by ghosts and phantoms.

# III

Cautiously he pressed against the ivory door and it swung silently inward. On the shimmering threshold Conan stared like a wolf in strange surroundings, ready to fight or flee on the instant. He was looking into a large chamber with a domed golden ceiling; the walls were of green jade, the floor of ivory, partly covered by thick rugs. Smoke and exotic scent of incense floated up from a brazier on a golden tripod, and behind it sat an idol on a sort of marble couch. Conan stared aghast; the image had the body of a man, naked and green in color; but the head was one of nightmare and madness. Too large for the human body, it had no attributes of humanity. Conan stared at the wide flaring ears, the curling proboscis, on either side of which stood white tusks tipped with round golden balls. The eyes were closed, as if in sleep.

This then, was the reason for the name, the Tower of the Elephant, for the head of the thing was much like that of the beasts described by the Shemitish wanderer. This was Yara's god; where then should the gem be, but concealed in the idol, since the stone was called the Elephant's Heart?

As Conan came forward, his eyes fixed on the motionless idol, the eyes of the thing opened suddenly! The Cimmerian froze in his tracks. It was no image—it was a living thing, and he was trapped in its chamber!

That he did not instantly explode in a burst of murderous frenzy is a fact that measures his horror, which paralyzed him where he stood. A civilized man in his position would have sought doubtful refuge in the conclusion that he was insane; it did not occur to the Cimmerian to doubt his senses. He knew he was face to face with a demon of the Elder World, and the realization robbed him of all his faculties except sight.

The trunk of the horror was lifted and quested about, the topaz

eyes stared unseeingly, and Conan knew the monster was blind. With the thought came a thawing of his frozen nerves, and he began to back silently toward the door. But the creature heard. The sensitive trunk stretched toward him, and Conan's horror froze him again when the being spoke, in a strange, stammering voice that never changed its key or timbre. The Cimmerian knew that those jaws were never built or intended for human speech.

"Who is here? Have you come to torture me again, Yara? Will you never be done? Oh, Yag-kosha, is there no end to agony?"

Tears rolled from the sightless eyes, and Conan's gaze strayed to the limbs stretched on the marble couch. And he knew the monster would not rise to attack him. He knew the marks of the rack, and the searing brand of the flame, and tough-souled as he was, he stood aghast at the ruined deformities which his reason told him had once been limbs as comely as his own. And suddenly all fear and repulsion went from him, to be replaced by a great pity. What this monster was, Conan could not know, but the evidence of its sufferings was so terrible and pathetic that a strange aching sadness came over the Cimmerian, he knew not why. He only felt that he was looking upon a cosmic tragedy, and he shrank with shame, as if the guilt of a whole race were laid upon him.

"I am not Yara," he said. "I am only a thief. I will not harm you."

"Come near that I may touch you," the creature faltered, and Conan came near unfearingly, his sword hanging forgotten in his hand. The sensitive trunk came out and groped over his face and shoulders, as a blind man gropes, and its touch was light as a girl's hand.

"You are not of Yara's race of devils," sighed the creature. "The clean, lean fierceness of the wastelands marks you. I know your people from of old, whom I knew by another name in the long, long ago when another world lifted its jeweled spires to the stars. There is blood on your fingers."

"A spider in the chamber above and a lion in the garden," muttered Conan.

"You have slain a man too, this night," answered the other. "And there is death in the tower above. I feel; I know."

"Aye," muttered Conan. "The prince of all thieves lies there dead from the bite of a vermin."

"So—and so!" the strange inhuman voice rose in a sort of low chant. "A slaying in the tavern and a slaying on the roof—I know; I feel. And the third will make the magic of which not even Yara dreams—oh, magic of deliverance, green gods of Yag!"

Again tears fell as the tortured body was rocked to and fro in the grip of varied emotions. Conan looked on, bewildered.

Then the convulsions ceased; the soft, sightless eyes were turned toward the Cimmerian, the trunk beckoned.

"Oh man, listen," said the strange being. "I am foul and monstrous to you, am I not? Nay, do not answer; I know. But you would seem as strange to me, could I see you. There are many worlds besides this earth, and life takes many shapes. I am neither god nor demon, but flesh and blood like yourself, though the substance differ in part, and the form be cast in different mold.

"I am very old, oh man of the waste countries; long and long ago I came to this planet with others of my world, from the green planet Yag, which circles forever in the outer fringe of this universe. We swept through Space on mighty wings that drove us through the cosmos quicker than light, because we had warred with the kings of Yag and were defeated and outcast. But we could never return, for on earth our wings withered from our shoulders. Here we abode apart from earthly life. We fought the strange and terrible forms of life which then walked the earth, so that we became feared, and were not molested in the dim jungles of the east, where we had our abode.

"We saw men grow from the ape and build the shining cities of

Valusia, Kamelia, Commoria, and their sisters. We saw them reel before the thrusts of the heathen Atlanteans and Picts and Lemurians. We saw the oceans rise and engulf Atlantis and Lemuria, and the isles of the Picts and the shining cities of civilization. We saw the survivors of Pictdom and Atlantis build their stone-age empires, and go down to ruin, locked in bloody wars. We saw the Picts sink into abysmal savagery, the Atlanteans into apedom again. We saw new savages drift southward in conquering waves from the Arctic Circle to build a new civilization, with new kingdoms called Nemedia, and Koth, and Aquilonia and their sisters. We saw your people rise under a new name from the jungles of the apes that had been Atlanteans. We saw the descendants of the Lemurians who had survived the cataclysm, rise again through savagery and ride westward, as Hyrkanians. And we saw this race of devils, survivors of the ancient civilization that was before Atlantis sank, come once more into culture and power—this accursed kingdom of Zamora.

"All this we saw, neither aiding nor hindering the immutable cosmic law, and one by one we died; for we of Yag are not immortal, though our lives are as the lives of planets and constellations. At last I alone was left, dreaming of old times among the ruined temples of jungle-lost Khitai, worshiped as a god by an ancient yellow-skinned race. Then came Yara, versed in dark knowledge handed down through the days of barbarism, since before Atlantis sank.

"First he sat at my feet and learned wisdom. But he was not satisfied with what I taught him, for it was white magic, and he wished evil lore, to enslave kings and glut a fiendish ambition. I would teach him none of the black secrets I had gained, through no wish of mine, through the eons.

"But his wisdom was deeper than I had guessed; with guile gotten among the dusky tombs of dark Stygia, he trapped me into divulging a secret I had not intended to bare; and turning my own power upon me, he enslaved me. Ah, gods of Yag, my cup has been bitter since that hour!

"He brought me up from the lost jungles of Khitai where the gray apes danced to the pipes of the yellow priests, and offerings of fruit and wine heaped my broken altars. No more was I a god to kindly jungle-folk—I was slave to a devil in human form."

Again tears stole from the unseeing eyes.

"He pent me in this tower, which at his command I built for him in a single night. By fire and rack he mastered me, and by strange unearthly tortures you would not understand. In agony I would long ago have taken my own life, if I could. But he kept me alive—mangled, blinded, and broken—to do his foul bidding. And for three hundred years I have done his bidding, from this marble couch, blackening my soul with cosmic sins, and staining my wisdom with crimes, because I had no other choice. Yet not all my ancient secrets has he wrested from me, and my last gift shall be the sorcery of the Blood and the Jewel.

"For I feel the end of time draw near. You are the hand of Fate. I beg of you, take the gem you will find on yonder altar."

Conan turned to the gold and ivory altar indicated, and took up a great round jewel, clear as crimson crystal; and he knew that this was the Heart of the Elephant.

"Now for the great magic, the mighty magic, such as earth has not seen before and shall not see again, through a million million of millenniums. By my life-blood I conjure it, by blood born on the green breast of Yag, dreaming far-poised in the great blue vastness of Space.

"Take your sword, man, and cut out my heart; then squeeze it so that the blood will flow over the red stone. Then go you down these stairs and enter the ebony chamber where Yara sits wrapped in lotus-dreams of evil. Speak his name and he will awaken. Then lay this gem before him, and say, 'Yag-kosha gives you a last gift and a last enchantment.' Then get you from the tower quickly; fear not, your way shall be made clear. The life of man is not the life of Yag, nor is human death the death of Yag. Let me be free of this cage of broken, blind flesh, and I will once more be Yogah of Yag, morning-crowned and shining, with wings to fly, and feet to dance, and eyes to see, and hands to break."

Uncertainly Conan approached, and Yag-kosha, or Yogah, as if sensing his uncertainty, indicated where he should strike. Conan set his teeth and drove the sword deep. Blood streamed over the blade and his hand, and the monster started convulsively, then lay back quite still. Sure that life had fled, at least life as he understood it, Conan set to work on his grisly task and quickly brought forth something that he felt must be the strange being's heart, though it differed curiously from any he had ever seen. Holding the still pulsing organ over the blazing jewel, he pressed it with both hands, and a rain of blood fell on the stone. To his surprise, it did not run off, but soaked into the gem, as water is absorbed by a sponge.

Holding the jewel gingerly, he went out of the fantastic chamber and came upon the silver steps. He did not look back; he instinctively felt that some sort of transmutation was taking place in the body on the marble couch, and he further felt that it was of a sort not to be witnessed by human eyes.

He closed the ivory door behind him, and without hesitation descended the silver steps. It did not occur to him to ignore the instructions given him. He halted at an ebony door, in the center of which was a grinning silver skull, and pushed it open. He looked into a chamber of ebony and jet, and saw, on a black silken couch, a tall, spare form reclining. Yara the priest and sorcerer lay before him, his eyes open and dilated with the fumes of the yellow lotus, far-staring, as if fixed on gulfs and nighted abysses beyond human ken.

"Yara!" said Conan, like a judge pronouncing doom. "Awaken!"

The eyes cleared instantly and became cold and cruel as a vulture's.

The tall, silken-clad form lifted erect, and towered gauntly above the Cimmerian.

"Dog!" His hiss was like the voice of a cobra. "What do you here?"

Conan laid the jewel on the great ebony table.

"He who sent this gem bade me say, 'Yag-kosha gives a last gift and a last enchantment.'"

Yara recoiled, his dark face ashy. The jewel was no longer crystal-clear; its murky depths pulsed and throbbed, and curious smoky waves of changing color passed over its smooth surface. As if drawn hypnotically, Yara bent over the table and gripped the gem in his hands, staring into its shadowed depths, as if it were a magnet to draw the shuddering soul from his body. And as Conan looked, he thought that his eyes must be playing him tricks. For when Yara had risen up from his couch, the priest had seemed gigantically tall; yet now he saw that Yara's head would scarcely come to his shoulder. He blinked, puzzled, and for the first time that night, doubted his own senses. Then with a shock he realized that the priest was shrinking in stature—was growing smaller before his very gaze.

With a detached feeling he watched, as a man might watch a play; immersed in a feeling of overpowering unreality, the Cimmerian was no longer sure of his own identity; he only knew that he was looking upon the external evidence of the unseen play of vast Outer forces, beyond his understanding.

Now Yara was no bigger than a child; now like an infant he sprawled on the table, still grasping the jewel. And now the sorcerer suddenly realized his fate, and he sprang up, releasing the gem. But still he dwindled, and Conan saw a tiny, pigmy figure rushing wildly about the ebony table-top, waving tiny arms and shrieking in a voice that was like the squeak of an insect.

Now he had shrunk until the great jewel towered above him like a hill, and Conan saw him cover his eyes with his hands, as if to shield them from the glare, as he staggered about like a madman.

Conan sensed that some unseen magnetic force was pulling Yara to the gem. Thrice he raced wildly about it in a narrowing circle, thrice he strove to turn and run out across the table; then with a scream that echoed faintly in the ears of the watcher, the priest threw up his arms and ran straight toward the blazing globe.

Bending close, Conan saw Yara clamber up the smooth, curving surface, impossibly, like a man climbing a glass mountain. Now the priest stood on the top, still with tossing arms, invoking what grisly names only the gods know. And suddenly he sank into the very heart of the jewel, as a man sinks into a sea, and Conan saw the smoky waves close over his head. Now he saw him in the crimson heart of the jewel, once more crystal-clear, as a man sees a scene far away, tiny with great distance. And into the heart came a green, shining winged figure with the body of a man and the head of an elephant—no longer blind or crippled. Yara threw up his arms and fled as a madman flees, and on his heels came the avenger. Then, like the bursting of a bubble, the great jewel vanished in a rainbow burst of iridescent gleams, and the ebony table-top lay bare and deserted—as bare, Conan somehow knew, as the marble couch in the chamber above, where the body of that strange transcosmic being called Yag-kosha and Yogah had lain.

The Cimmerian turned and fled from the chamber, down the silver stairs. So amazed was he that it did not occur to him to escape from the tower by the way he had entered it. Down that winding, shadowy silver well he ran, and came into a large chamber at the foot of the gleaming stairs. There he halted for an instant; he had come into the room of the soldiers. He saw the glitter of their silver corselets, the sheen of their jeweled sword-hilts. They sat slumped at the banquet board, their dusky plumes waving somberly above their drooping helmeted heads; they lay among their dice and fallen goblets on the wine-stained lapis-lazuli floor. And he knew that they were dead. The promise had been made, the word kept; whether

sorcery or magic or the falling shadow of great green wings had stilled the revelry, Conan could not know, but his way had been made clear. And a silver door stood open, framed in the whiteness of dawn.

Into the waving green gardens came the Cimmerian, and as the dawn wind blew upon him with the cool fragrance of luxuriant growths, he started like a man waking from a dream. He turned back uncertainly, to stare at the cryptic tower he had just left. Was he bewitched and enchanted? Had he dreamed all that had seemed to have passed? As he looked he saw the gleaming tower sway against the crimson dawn, its jewel-crusted rim sparkling in the growing light, and crash into shining shards.

# The Shadow Kingdom

by Robert E. Howard

## I. A KING COMES RIDING

The blare of the trumpets grew louder, like a deep golden tide surge, like the soft booming of the evening tides against the silver beaches of Valusia. The throng shouted, women flung roses from the roofs as the rhythmic chiming of silver hosts came clearer and the first of the mighty array swung into view in the broad white street that curved round the golden-spired Tower of Splendor.

First came the trumpeters, slim youths, clad in scarlet, riding with a flourish of long, slender golden trumpets; next the bowmen, tall men from the mountains; and behind these the heavily armed footmen, their broad shields clashing in unison, their long spears swaying in perfect rhythm to their stride. Behind them came the mightiest soldiery in all the world, the Red Slayers, horsemen, splendidly mounted, armed in red from helmet to spur. Proudly they sat upon their steeds, looking neither to right nor to left, but aware of the shouting for all that. Like bronze statues they were, and there was never a waver in the forest of spears that reared above them.

Behind those proud and terrible ranks came the motley files of the mercenaries, fierce, wild-looking warriors, men of Mu and of Kaa-u and of the hills of the east and the isles of the west. They bore spears and heavy swords, and a compact group that marched somewhat apart were the bowmen of Lemuria. Then came the light foot of the nation, and more trumpeters brought up the rear.

A brave sight, and a sight which aroused a fierce thrill in the soul of Kull, king of Valusia. Not on the Topaz Throne at the front of the regal Tower of Splendor sat Kull, but in the saddle, mounted on a great stallion, a true warrior king. His mighty arm swung up in reply to the salutes as the hosts passed. His fierce eyes passed the gorgeous trumpeters with a casual glance, rested longer on the following soldiery; they blazed with a ferocious light as the Red Slayers halted in front of him with a clang of arms and a rearing of steeds, and tendered him the crown salute. They narrowed slightly as the mercenaries strode by. They saluted no one, the mercenaries. They walked with shoulders flung back, eyeing Kull boldly and straightly, albeit with a certain appreciation; fierce eyes, unblinking; savage eyes, staring from beneath shaggy manes and heavy brows.

And Kull gave back a like stare. He granted much to brave men, and there were no braver in all the world, not even among the wild tribesmen who now disowned him. But Kull was too much the savage to have any great love for these. There were too many feuds. Many were age-old enemies of Kull's nation, and though the name of Kull was now a word accursed among the mountains and valleys of his people, and though Kull had put them from his mind, yet the old hates, the ancient passions still lingered. For Kull was no Valusian but an Atlantean.

The armies swung out of sight around the gem-blazing shoulders of the Tower of Splendor and Kull reined his stallion about and started toward the palace at an easy gait, discussing the review with the commanders that rode with him, using not many words, but saying much.

"The army is like a sword," said Kull, "and must not be allowed to rust." So down the street they rode, and Kull gave no heed to any of the whispers that reached his hearing from the throngs that still swarmed the streets.

"That is Kull, see! Valka! But what a king! And what a man! Look at his arms! His shoulders!"

And an undertone of more sinister whispering:

"Kull! Ha, accursed usurper from the pagan isles."

"Aye, shame to Valusia that a barbarian sits on the Throne of Kings."

Little did Kull heed. Heavy-handed had he seized the decaying throne of ancient Valusia and with a heavier hand did he hold it, a man against a nation.

After the council chamber, the social palace where Kull replied to the formal and laudatory phrases of the lords and ladies, with carefully hidden grim amusement at such frivolities; then the lords and ladies took their formal departure and Kull leaned back upon the ermine throne and contemplated matters of state until an attendant requested permission from the great king to speak, and announced an emissary from the Pictish embassy.

Kull brought his mind back from the dim mazes of Valusian statecraft where it had been wandering, and gazed upon the Pict with little favor. The man gave back the gaze of the king without flinching. He was a lean-hipped, massive-chested warrior of middle height, dark, like all his race, and strongly built. From strong, immobile features gazed dauntless and inscrutable eyes.

"The chief of the Councilors, Ka-nu of the tribe right hand of the king of Pictdom, sends greetings and says: 'There is a throne at the feast of the rising moon for Kull, king of kings, lord of lords, emperor of Valusia.'"

"Good," answered Kull. "Say to Ka-nu the Ancient, ambassador of the western isles, that the king of Valusia will quaff wine with him when the moon floats over the hills of Zalgara." Still the Pict lingered.

"I have a word for the king, not"—with a contemptuous flirt of his hand—"for these slaves."

Kull dismissed the attendants with a word, watching the Pict warily.

The man stepped nearer, and lowered his voice:

"Come alone to feast tonight, lord king. Such was the word of my chief."

The king's eyes narrowed, gleaming like gray sword steel, coldly.

"Alone?"

"Aye."

They eyed each other silently, their mutual tribal enmity seething beneath their cloak of formality. Their mouths spoke the cultured speech, the conventional court phrases of a highly polished race, a race not their own, but from their eyes gleamed the primal traditions of the elemental savage. Kull might be the king of Valusia and the Pict might be an emissary to her courts, but there in the throne hall of kings, two tribesmen glowered at each other, fierce and wary, while ghosts of wild wars and world-ancient feuds whispered to each.

To the king was the advantage and he enjoyed it to its fullest extent. Jaw resting on hand, he eyed the Pict, who stood like an image of bronze, head flung back, eyes unflinching.

Across Kull's lips stole a smile that was more a sneer.

"And so I am to come—alone?" Civilization had taught him to speak by innuendo and the Pict's dark eyes glittered, though he made no reply. "How am I to know that you come from Ka-nu?"

"I have spoken," was the sullen response.

"And when did a Pict speak truth?" sneered Kull, fully aware that the Picts never lied, but using this means to enrage the man.

"I see your plan, king," the Pict answered imperturbably. "You wish to anger me. By Valka, you need go no further! I am angry enough. And I challenge you to meet me in single battle, spear, sword or dagger, mounted or afoot. Are you king or man?"

Kull's eyes glinted with the grudging admiration a warrior must needs give a bold foeman, but he did not fail to use the chance of further annoying his antagonist.

"A king does not accept the challenge of a nameless savage," he sneered, "nor does the emperor of Valusia break the Truce of Ambassadors. You have leave to go. Say to Ka-nu I will come alone."

The Pict's eyes flashed murderously. He fairly shook in the grasp of the primitive blood-lust; then, turning his back squarely upon the king of Valusia, he strode across the Hall of Society and vanished through the great door.

Again Kull leaned back upon the ermine throne and meditated.

So the chief of the Council of Picts wished him to come alone? But for what reason? Treachery? Grimly Kull touched the hilt of his great sword. But scarcely. The Picts valued too greatly the alliance with Valusia to break it for any feudal reason. Kull might be a warrior of Atlantis and hereditary enemy of all Picts, but too, he was king of Valusia, the most potent ally of the Men of the West.

Kull reflected long upon the strange state of affairs that made him ally of ancient foes and foe of ancient friends. He rose and paced restlessly across the hall, with the quick, noiseless tread of a lion. Chains of friendship, tribe and tradition had he broken to satisfy his ambition. And, by Valka, god of the sea and the land, he had realized that ambition! He was king of Valusia—a fading, degenerate Valusia, a Valusia living mostly in dreams of bygone glory, but still a mighty land and the greatest of the Seven Empires. Valusia—Land of Dreams, the tribesmen named it, and sometimes it seemed to Kull that he moved in a dream. Strange to him were the intrigues of court and palace, army and people. All was like a masquerade, where men and women hid their real thoughts with a smooth mask. Yet the seizing of the throne had been easy—a bold snatching of opportunity, the swift whirl of swords, the slaying of a tyrant of whom men had wearied unto death, short, crafty plotting with ambitious statesmen out of favor at court—and Kull, wandering adventurer, Atlantean exile, had swept up to the dizzy heights of his dreams: he was lord of Valusia, king of kings. Yet now it seemed that the seizing was far easier than the keeping.

The sight of the Pict had brought back youthful associations to his mind, the free, wild savagery of his boyhood. And now a strange feeling of dim unrest, of unreality, stole over him as of late it had been doing. Who was he, a straightforward man of the seas and the mountain, to rule a race strangely and terribly wise with the mysticisms of antiquity? An ancient race—

"I am Kull!" said he, flinging back his head as a lion flings back his mane. "I am Kull!"

His falcon gaze swept the ancient hall. His self-confidence flowed back… And in a dim nook of the hall a tapestry moved—slightly.

## II. THUS SPAKE THE SILENT HALLS OF VALUSIA

The moon had not risen, and the garden was lighted with torches aglow in silver cressets when Kull sat down on the throne before the table of Ka-nu, ambassador of the western isles. At his right hand sat the ancient Pict, as much unlike an emissary of that fierce race as a man could be. Ancient was Ka-nu and wise in statecraft, grown old in the game. There was no elemental hatred in the eyes that looked at Kull appraisingly; no Tribal traditions hindered his judgments. Long associations with the statesmen of the civilized nations had swept away such cobwebs. Not: who and what is this man? was the question ever foremost in Ka-nu's mind, but: can I use this man, and how? Tribal prejudices he used only to further his own schemes.

And Kull watched Ka-nu, answering his conversation briefly, wondering if civilization would make of him a thing like the Pict. For Ka-nu was soft and paunchy. Many years had stridden across the sky-rim since Ka-nu had wielded a sword. True, he was old, but Kull had seen men older than he in the forefront of battle. The Picts were a long-lived race. A beautiful girl stood at Ka-nu's elbow, refilling his goblet, and she was kept busy. Meanwhile Ka-nu kept up a running fire of jests and comments, and Kull, secretly contemptuous of his garrulity, nevertheless missed none of his shrewd humor.

At the banquet were Pictish chiefs and statesmen, the latter jovial and easy in their manner, the warriors formally courteous, but plainly hampered by their tribal affinities. Yet Kull, with a tinge of envy, was cognizant of the freedom and ease of the affair as contrasted with like affairs of the Valusian court. Such freedom prevailed in the rude camps of Atlantis—Kull shrugged his shoulders. After all, doubtless Ka-nu, who had seemed to have forgotten he was a Pict as far as time-hoary custom and prejudice went, was right and he, Kull, would better become a Valusian in mind as in name.

At last when the moon had reached her zenith, Ka-nu, having eaten and drunk as much as any three men there, leaned back upon his divan with a comfortable sigh and said, "Now, get you gone, friends, for the king and I would converse on such matters as concern not children. Yes, you too, my pretty; yet first let me kiss those ruby lips—so; now, dance away, my rose-bloom."

Ka-nu's eyes twinkled above his white beard as he surveyed Kull, who sat erect, grim and uncompromising.

"You are thinking, Kull," said the old statesman, suddenly, "that Ka-nu is a useless old reprobate, fit for nothing except to guzzle wine and kiss wenches!"

In fact, this remark was so much in line with his actual thoughts, and so plainly put, that Kull was rather startled, though he gave no sign.

Ka-nu gurgled and his paunch shook with his mirth. "Wine is red and women are soft," he remarked tolerantly. "But—ha! Ha!—think not old Ka-nu allows either to interfere with business."

Again he laughed, and Kull moved restlessly. This seemed much like being made sport of, and the king's scintillating eyes began to glow with a feline light.

Ka-nu reached for the wine-pitcher, filled his beaker and glanced questioningly at Kull, who shook his head irritably.

"Aye," said Ka-nu equably, "it takes an old head to stand strong drink. I am growing old, Kull, so why should you young men begrudge me such pleasures as we oldsters must find? Ah me, I grow ancient and withered, friendless and cheerless."

But his looks and expressions failed far of bearing out his words. His rubicund countenance fairly glowed, and his eyes sparkled, so that his white beard seemed incongruous. Indeed, he looked remarkably elfin, reflected Kull, who felt vaguely resentful. The old scoundrel had lost all of the primitive virtues of his race and of Kull's race, yet he seemed more pleased in his aged days than otherwise.

"Hark ye, Kull," said Ka-nu, raising an admonitory finger, "'tis a chancy thing to laud a young man, yet I must speak my true thoughts to gain your confidence."

"If you think to gain it by flattery—"

"Tush. Who spake of flattery? I flatter only to disguard."

There was a keen sparkle in Ka-nu's eyes, a cold glimmer that did not match his lazy smile. He knew men, and he knew that to gain his end he must smite straight with this tigerish barbarian, who, like a wolf scenting a snare, would scent out unerringly any falseness in the skein of his wordweb.

"You have power, Kull," said he, choosing his words with more care than he did in the council rooms of the nation, "to make yourself mightiest of all kings, and restore some of the lost glories of Valusia. So. I care little for Valusia—though the women and wine be excellent—save for the fact that the stronger Valusia is, the stronger is the Pict nation. More, with an Atlantean on the throne, eventually Atlantis will become united—"

Kull laughed in harsh mockery. Ka-nu had touched an old wound.

"Atlantis made my name accursed when I went to seek fame and fortune among the cities of the world. We—they—are age-old foes of the Seven Empires, greater foes of the allies of the Empires, as you should know."

Ka-nu tugged his beard and smiled enigmatically.

"Nay, nay. Let it pass. But I know whereof I speak. And then warfare will cease, wherein there is no gain; I see a world of peace and prosperity—man loving his fellow man—the good supreme. All this can you accomplish—if you live!"

"Ha!" Kull's lean hand closed on his hilt and he half rose, with a sudden movement of such dynamic speed that Ka-nu, who fancied men as some men fancy blooded horses, felt his old blood leap with a sudden thrill. Valka, what a warrior! Nerves and sinews of steel and fire, bound together with the perfect co-ordination, the fighting instinct, that makes the terrible warrior.

But none of Ka-nu's enthusiasm showed in his mildly sarcastic tone.

"Tush. Be seated. Look about you. The gardens are deserted, the seats empty, save for ourselves. You fear not me?"

Kull sank back, gazing about him warily.

"There speaks the savage," mused Ka-nu. "Think you if I planned treachery I would enact it here where suspicion would be sure to fall upon me? Tut. You young tribesmen have much to learn. There were my chiefs who were not at ease because you were born among the hills of Atlantis, and you despise me in your secret mind because I am a Pict. Tush. I see you as Kull, king of Valusia, not as Kull, the reckless Atlantean, leader of the raiders who harried the western isles. So you should see in me, not a Pict but an international man, a figure of the world. Now to that figure, hark! If you were slain tomorrow who would be king?"

"Kaanuub, baron of Blaal."

"Even so. I object to Kaanuub for many reasons, yet most of all for the fact that he is but a figure-head."

"How so? He was my greatest opponent, but I did not know that he championed any cause but his own."

"The night can hear," answered Ka-nu obliquely. "There are worlds within worlds. But you may trust me and you may trust Brule, the

Spear-slayer. Look!" He drew from his robes a bracelet of gold representing a winged dragon coiled thrice, with three horns of ruby on the head.

"Examine it closely. Brule will wear it on his arm when he comes to you tomorrow night so that you may know him. Trust Brule as you trust yourself, and do what he tells you to. And in proof of trust, look ye!"

And with the speed of a striking hawk, the ancient snatched something from his robes, something that flung a weird green light over them, and which he replaced in an instant.

"The stolen gem!" exclaimed Kull recoiling. "The green jewel from the Temple of the Serpent! Valka! You! And why do you show it to me?"

"To save your life. To prove my trust. If I betray your trust, deal with me likewise. You hold my life in your hand. Now I could not be false to you if I would, for a word from you would be my doom."

Yet for all his words the old scoundrel beamed merrily and seemed vastly pleased with himself.

"But why do you give me this hold over you?" asked Kull, becoming more bewildered each second.

"As I told you. Now, you see that I do not intend to deal you false, and tomorrow night when Brule comes to you, you will follow his advice without fear of treachery. Enough. An escort waits outside to ride to the palace with you, lord."

Kull rose. "But you have told me nothing."

"Tush. How impatient are youths!" Ka-nu looked more like a mischievous elf than ever. "Go you and dream of thrones and power and kingdoms, while I dream of wine and soft women and roses. And fortune ride with you, King Kull."

As he left the garden, Kull glanced back to see Ka-nu still reclining lazily in his seat, a merry ancient, beaming on all the world with jovial fellowship.

A mounted warrior waited for the king just without the garden and Kull was slightly surprised to see that it was the same that had brought Ka-nu's invitation. No word was spoken as Kull swung into the saddle nor as they clattered along the empty streets.

The color and the gayety of the day had given way to the eerie stillness of night. The city's antiquity was more than ever apparent beneath the bent, silver moon. The huge pillars of the mansions and palaces towered up into the stars. The broad stairways, silent and deserted, seemed to climb endlessly until they vanished in the shadowy darkness of the upper realms. Stairs to the stars, thought Kull, his imaginative mind inspired by the weird grandeur of the scene.

Clang! Clang! Clang! sounded the silver hoofs on the broad, moon-flooded streets, but otherwise there was no sound. The age of the city, its incredible antiquity, was almost oppressive to the king; it was as if the great silent buildings laughed at him, noiselessly, with unguessable mockery. And what secrets did they hold?

"You are young," said the palaces and the temples and the shrines, "but we are old. The world was wild with youth when we were reared. You and your tribe shall pass, but we are invincible, indestructible. We towered above a strange world, ere Atlantis and Lemuria rose from the sea; we still shall reign when the green waters sigh for many a restless fathom above the spires of Lemuria and the hills of Atlantis and when the isles of the Western Men are the mountains of a strange land."

"How many kings have we watched ride down these streets before Kull of Atlantis was even a dream in the mind of Ka, bird of Creation? Ride on, Kull of Atlantis; greater shall follow you; greater came before you. They are dust; they are forgotten; we stand; we know; we are. Ride, ride on, Kull of Atlantis; Kull the king, Kull the fool!"

And it seemed to Kull that the clashing hoofs took up the silent refrain to beat it into the night with hollow re-echoing mockery; "Kull-the-king! Kull-the-fool!"

Glow, moon; you light a king's way! Gleam, stars; you are torches in the train of an emperor! And clang, silver-shod hoofs; you herald that Kull rides through Valusia.

Ho! Awake, Valusia! It is Kull that rides, Kull the king!

"We have known many kings," said the silent halls of Valusia.

And so in a brooding mood Kull came to the palace, where his bodyguard, men of the Red Slayers, came to take the rein of the great stallion and escort Kull to his rest. There the Pict, still sullenly speechless, wheeled his steed with a savage wrench of the rein and fled away in the dark like a phantom; Kull's heightened imagination pictured him speeding through the silent streets like a goblin out of the Elder World.

There was no sleep for Kull that night, for it was nearly dawn and he spent the rest of the night hours pacing the throne-room, and pondering over what had passed. Ka-nu had told him nothing, yet he had put himself in Kull's complete power. At what had he hinted when he had said the baron of Blaal was naught but a figurehead? And who was this Brule who was to come to him by night, wearing the mystic armlet of the dragon? And why? Above all, why had Ka-nu shown him the green gem of terror, stolen long ago from the temple of the Serpent, for which the world would rock in wars were it known to the weird and terrible keepers of that temple, and from whose vengeance not even Ka-nu's ferocious tribesmen might be able to save him? But Ka-nu knew he was safe, reflected Kull, for the statesman was too shrewd to expose himself to risk without profit. But was it to throw the king off his guard and pave the way to treachery? Would Ka-nu dare let him live now? Kull shrugged his shoulders.

## III. THEY THAT WALK THE NIGHT

The moon had not risen when Kull, hand to hilt, stepped to a window. The windows opened upon the great inner gardens of the royal palace, and the breezes of the night, bearing the scents of spice trees, blew the filmy curtains about. The king looked out. The walks and groves were deserted; carefully trimmed trees were bulky shadows; fountains near by flung their slender sheen of silver in the starlight and distant fountains rippled steadily. No guards walked those gardens, for so closely were the outer walls guarded that it seemed impossible for any invader to gain access to them.

Vines curled up the walls of the palace, and even as Kull mused upon the ease with which they might be climbed, a segment of shadow detached itself from the darkness below the window and a bare, brown arm curved up over the sill. Kull's great sword hissed halfway from the sheath; then the King halted. Upon the muscular forearm gleamed the dragon armlet shown him by Ka-nu the night before.

The possessor of the arm pulled himself up over the sill and into the room with the swift, easy motion of a climbing leopard.

"You are Brule?" asked Kull, and then stopped in surprise not unmingled with annoyance and suspicion; for the man was he whom Kull had taunted in the Hall of Society; the same who had escorted him from the Pictish embassy.

"I am Brule, the Spear-slayer," answered the Pict in a guarded voice; then swiftly, gazing closely in Kull's face, he said, barely above a whisper:

"Ka nama kaa lajerama!"

Kull started. "Ha! What mean you?"

"Know you not?"

"Nay, the words are unfamiliar; they are of no language I ever heard—and yet, by Valka!—somewhere—I have heard—"

"Aye," was the Pict's only comment. His eyes swept the room, the study room of the palace. Except for a few tables, a divan or two and great shelves of books of parchment, the room was barren compared to the grandeur of the rest of the palace.

"Tell me, king, who guards the door?"

"Eighteen of the Red Slayers. But how come you, stealing through the gardens by night and scaling the walls of the palace?"

Brule sneered. "The guards of Valusia are blind buffaloes. I could steal their girls from under their noses. I stole amid them and they saw me not nor heard me. And the walls—I could scale them without the aid of vines. I have hunted tigers on the foggy beaches when the sharp east breezes blew the mist in from seaward and I have climbed the steppes of the western sea mountain. But come—nay, touch this armlet."

He held out his arm and, as Kull complied wonderingly, gave an apparent sigh of relief.

"So. Now throw off those kingly robes; for there are ahead of you this night such deeds as no Atlantean ever dreamed of."

Brule himself was clad only in a scanty loin-cloth through which was thrust a short, curved sword.

"And who are you to give me orders?" asked Kull, slightly resentful.

"Did not Ka-nu bid you follow me in all things?" asked the Pict irritably, his eyes flashing momentarily. "I have no love for you, lord, but for the moment I have put the thought of feuds from my mind. Do you likewise. But come."

Walking noiselessly, he led the way across the room to the door. A slide in the door allowed a view of the outer corridor, unseen from without, and the Pict bade Kull look.

"What see you?"

"Naught but the eighteen guardsmen."

The Pict nodded, motioned Kull to follow him across the room. At a panel in the opposite wall Brule stopped and fumbled there a moment. Then with a light movement he stepped back, drawing his sword as he did so. Kull gave an exclamation as the panel swung silently open, revealing a dimly lighted passageway.

"A secret passage!" swore Kull softly. "And I knew nothing of it! By Valka, someone shall dance for this!"

"Silence!" hissed the Pict.

Brule was standing like a bronze statue as if straining every nerve for the slightest sound; something about his attitude made Kull's hair prickle slightly, not from fear but from some eery anticipation. Then beckoning, Brule stepped through the secret doorway which stood open behind them. The passage was bare, but not dust-covered as should have been the case with an unused secret corridor. A vague, gray light filtered through somewhere, but the source of it was not apparent. Every few feet Kull saw doors, invisible, as he knew, from the outside, but easily apparent from within.

"The palace is a very honeycomb," he muttered. "Aye. Night and day you are watched, king, by many eyes."

The king was impressed by Brule's manner. The Pict went forward slowly, warily, half crouching, blade held low and thrust forward. When he spoke it was in a whisper and he continually flung glances from side to side.

The corridor turned sharply and Brule warily gazed past the turn.

"Look!" he whispered. "But remember! No word! No sound—on your life!"

Kull cautiously gazed past him. The corridor changed just at the bend to a flight of steps. And then Kull recoiled. At the foot of those stairs lay the eighteen Red Slayers who were that night stationed to watch the king's study room. Brule's grip upon his mighty arm and Brule's fierce whisper at his shoulder alone kept Kull from leaping down those stairs.

"Silent, Kull! Silent, in Valka's name!" hissed the Pict. "These corridors are empty now, but I risked much in showing you, that you might then believe what I had to say. Back now to the room of study." And he retraced his steps, Kull following; his mind in a turmoil of bewilderment.

"This is treachery," muttered the king, his steel-gray eyes a-smolder, "foul and swift! Mere minutes have passed since those men stood at guard."

Again in the room of study Brule carefully closed the secret panel and motioned Kull to look again through the slit of the outer door. Kull gasped audibly. For without stood the eighteen guardsmen!

"This is sorcery!" he whispered, half-drawing his sword. "Do dead men guard the king?"

"Aye!" came Brule's scarcely audible reply; there was a strange expression in the Pict's scintillant eyes. They looked squarely into each other's eyes for an instant, Kull's brow wrinkled in a puzzled scowl as he strove to read the Pict's inscrutable face. Then Brule's lips, barely moving, formed the words: "The—snake—that—speaks!"

"Silent!" whispered Kull, laying his hand over Brule's mouth. "That is death to speak! That is a name accursed!"

The Pict's fearless eyes regarded him steadily.

"Look, again, King Kull. Perchance the guard was changed."

"Nay, those are the same men. In Valka's name, this is sorcery—this is insanity! I saw with my own eyes the bodies of those men, not eight minutes agone. Yet there they stand."

Brule stepped back, away from the door, Kull mechanically following.

"Kull, what know ye of the traditions of this race ye rule?"

"Much—and yet, little. Valusia is so old—"

"Aye," Brule's eyes lighted strangely, "we are but barbarians—infants compared to the Seven Empires. Not even they themselves know how old they are. Neither the memory of man nor the annals of the historians reach back far enough to tell us when the first men came up from the sea and built cities on the shore. But Kull, men were not always ruled by men!"

The king started. Their eyes met.

"Aye, there is a legend of my people—"

"And mine!" broke in Brule. "That was before we of the isles were allied with Valusia. Aye, in the reign of Lion-fang, seventh war chief of the Picts, so many years ago no man remembers how many. Across the sea we came, from the isles of the sunset, skirting the shores of Atlantis, and falling upon the beaches of Valusia with fire and sword. Aye, the long white beaches resounded with the clash of spears, and the night was like day from the flame of the burning castles. And the king, the king of Valusia, who died on the red sea sands that dim day—" His voice trailed off; the two stared at each other, neither speaking; then each nodded.

"Ancient is Valusia!" whispered Kull. "The hills of Atlantis and Mu were isles of the sea when Valusia was young."

The night breeze whispered through the open window. Not the free, crisp sea air such as Brule and Kull knew and reveled in, in their land, but a breath like a whisper from the past, laden with musk, scents of forgotten things, breathing secrets that were hoary when the world was young.

The tapestries rustled, and suddenly Kull felt like a naked child before the inscrutable wisdom of the mystic past. Again the sense of unreality swept upon him. At the back of his soul stole dim, gigantic phantoms, whispering monstrous things. He sensed that Brule experienced similar thoughts. The Pict's eyes were fixed upon his face with a fierce intensity. Their glances met. Kull felt warmly a sense of comradeship with this member of an enemy tribe. Like rival leopards turning at bay against hunters, these two savages made common cause against the inhuman powers of antiquity. Brule again led the way back to the secret door. Silently they entered and silently they proceeded down the dim corridor, taking the opposite direction from that in which they previously traversed it. After a while the Pict stopped and pressed close to one of the secret doors, bidding Kull look with him through the hidden slot.

"This opens upon a little-used stair which leads to a corridor running past the study-room door."

They gazed, and presently, mounting the stair silently, came a silent shape.

"Tu! Chief councilor!" exclaimed Kull. "By night and with bared dagger! How, what means this, Brule?"

"Murder! And foulest treachery!" hissed Brule. "Nay"—as Kull would have flung the door aside and leaped forth—"we are lost if you meet him here, for more lurk at the foot of those stairs. Come!"

Half running, they darted back along the passage. Back through the secret door Brule led, shutting it carefully behind them, then across the chamber to an opening into a room seldom used. There he swept aside some tapestries in a dim corner nook and, drawing Kull with him, stepped behind them. Minutes dragged. Kull could hear the breeze in the other room blowing the window curtains about, and it seemed to him like the murmur of ghosts. Then through the door, stealthily, came Tu, chief councilor of the king. Evidently he had come through the study room and, finding it empty, sought his victim where he was most likely to be.

He came with upraised dagger, walking silently. A moment he halted, gazing about the apparently empty room, which was lighted dimly by a single candle. Then he advanced cautiously, apparently at a loss to understand the absence of the king. He stood before the hiding place—and "Slay!" hissed the Pict.

Kull with a single mighty leap hurled himself into the room. Tu spun, but the blinding, tigerish speed of the attack gave him no chance for defense or counterattack. Sword steel flashed in the dim light and grated on bone as Tu toppled backward, Kull's sword standing out between his shoulders.

Kull leaned above him, teeth bared in the killer's snarl, heavy brows ascowl above eyes that were like the gray ice of the cold sea. Then he released the hilt and recoiled, shaken, dizzy, the hand of death at his spine.

For as he watched, Tu's face became strangely dim and unreal;

the features mingled and merged in a seemingly impossible manner. Then, like a fading mask of fog, the face suddenly vanished and in its stead gaped and leered a monstrous serpent's head! "Valka!" gasped Kull, sweat beading his forehead, and again; "Valka!"

Brule leaned forward, face immobile. Yet his glittering eyes mirrored something of Kull's horror.

"Regain your sword, lord king," said he. "There are yet deeds to be done."

Hesitantly Kull set his hand to the hilt. His flesh crawled as he set his foot upon the terror which lay at their feet, and as some jerk of muscular reaction caused the frightful mouth to gape suddenly, he recoiled, weak with nausea. Then, wrathful at himself, he plucked forth his sword and gazed more closely at the nameless thing that had been known as Tu, chief councilor. Save for the reptilian head, the thing was the exact counterpart of a man.

"A man with the head of a snake!" Kull murmured. "This, then, is a priest of the serpent god?"

"Aye. Tu sleeps unknowing. These fiends can take any form they will. That is, they can, by a magic charm or the like, fling a web of sorcery about their faces, as an actor dons a mask, so that they resemble anyone they wish to."

"Then the old legends were true," mused the king; "the grim old tales few dare even whisper, lest they die as blasphemers, are no fantasies. By Valka, I had thought—I had guessed—but it seems beyond the bounds of reality. Ha! The guardsmen outside the door—"

"They too are snake-men. Hold! What would you do?"

"Slay them!" said Kull between his teeth.

"Strike at the skull if at all," said Brule. "Eighteen wait without the door and perhaps a score more in the corridors. Hark ye, king, Ka-nu learned of this plot. His spies have pierced the inmost fastnesses of the snake priests and they brought hints of a plot. Long ago he discovered the secret passageways of the palace, and at his command I studied the map thereof and came here by night to aid you, lest you die as other kings of Valusia have died. I came alone for the reason that to send more would have roused suspicion. Many could not steal into the palace as I did. Some of the foul conspiracy you have seen. Snake-men guard your door, and that one, as Tu, could pass anywhere else in the palace; in the morning, if the priests failed, the real guards would be holding their places again, nothing knowing, nothing remembering; there to take the blame if the priests succeeded. But stay you here while I dispose of this carrion."

So saying, the Pict shouldered the frightful thing stolidly and vanished with it through another secret panel. Kull stood alone, his mind a-whirl. Neophytes of the mighty serpent, how many lurked among his cities? How might he tell the false from the true? Aye, how many of his trusted councilors, his generals, were men? He could be certain—of whom?

The secret panel swung inward and Brule entered.

"You were swift."

"Aye!" The warrior stepped forward, eyeing the floor. "There is gore upon the rug. See?"

Kull bent forward; from the corner of his eye he saw a blur of movement, a glint of steel. Like a loosened bow he whipped erect, thrusting upward. The warrior sagged upon the sword, his own clattering to the floor. Even at that instant Kull reflected grimly that it was appropriate that the traitor should meet his death upon the sliding, upward thrust used so much by his race. Then, as Brule slid from the sword to sprawl motionless on the floor, the face began to merge and fade, and as Kull caught his breath, his hair a-prickle, the human features vanished and there the jaws of a great snake gaped hideously, the terrible beady eyes venomous even in death.

"He was a snake priest all the time!" gasped the king. "Valka! What an elaborate plan to throw me off my guard! Ka-nu there, is he a man? Was it Ka-nu to whom I talked in the gardens? Almighty

Valka!" as his flesh crawled with a horrid thought; "are the people of Valusia men or are they all serpents?"

Undecided he stood, idly seeing that the thing named Brule no longer wore the dragon armlet. A sound made him wheel.

Brule was coming through the secret door.

"Hold!" Upon the arm upthrown to halt the king's hovering sword gleamed the dragon armlet. "Valka!" The Pict stopped short. Then a grim smile curled his lips.

"By the gods of the seas! These demons are crafty past reckoning. For it must be that one lurked in the corridors, and seeing me go carrying the carcass of that other, took my appearance. So. I have another to do away with."

"Hold!" there was the menace of death in Kull's voice; "I have seen two men turn to serpents before my eyes. How may I know if you are a true man?"

Brule laughed. "For two reasons. King Kull. No snake-man wears this"—he indicated the dragon armlet—"nor can any say these words," and again Kull heard the strange phrase; "Ka nama kaa lajerama."

"Ka nama kaa lajerama" Kull repeated mechanically. "Now, where, in Valka's name, have I heard that? I have not! And yet—and yet—"

"Aye, you remember, Kull," said Brule. "Through the dim corridors of memory those words lurk; though you never heard them in this life, yet in the bygone ages they were so terribly impressed upon the soul mind that never dies, that they will always strike dim chords in your memory, though you be reincarnated for a million years to come. For that phrase has come secretly down the grim and bloody eons, since when, uncounted centuries ago, those words were watch-words for the race of men who battled with the grisly beings of the Elder Universe. For none but a real man of men may speak them, whose jaws and mouth are shaped different from any other creature. Their meaning has been forgotten but not the words themselves."

"True," said Kull. "I remember the legends—Valka!" He stopped short, staring, for suddenly, like the silent swinging wide of a mystic door, misty, unfathomed reaches opened in the recesses of his consciousness and for an instant he seemed to gaze back through the vastness that spanned life and life; seeing through the vague and ghostly fogs dim shapes reliving dead centuries — men in combat with hideous monsters, vanquishing a planet of frightful terrors. Against a gray, ever-shifting background moved strange nightmare forms, fantasies of lunacy and fear; and man, the jest of the gods, the blind, wisdom-less striver from dust to dust, following the long bloody trail of his destiny, knowing not why, bestial, blundering, like a great murderous child, yet feeling somewhere a spark of divine fire... Kull drew a hand across his brow, shaken; these sudden glimpses into the abysses of memory always startled him.

"They are gone," said Brule, as if scanning his secret mind; "the bird-women, the harpies, the bat-men, the flying fiends, the wolf-people, the demons, the goblins—all save such as this being that lies at our feet, and a few of the wolf-men. Long and terrible was the war, lasting through the bloody centuries, since first the first men, risen from the mire of apedom, turned upon those who then ruled the world."

"And at last mankind conquered, so long ago that naught but dim legends come to us through the ages. The snake-people were the last to go, yet at last men conquered even them and drove them forth into the waste lands of the world, there to mate with true snakes until some day, say the sages, the horrid breed shall vanish utterly. Yet the Things returned in crafty guise as men grew soft and degenerate, forgetting ancient wars. Ah, that was a grim and secret war! Among the men of the Younger Earth stole the frightful monsters of the Elder Planet, safeguarded by their horrid wisdom and mysticisms, taking all forms and shapes, doing deeds of horror secretly. No man knew who was true man and who false. No man could trust any man. Yet by means of their own craft they formed ways by which the false might be known from the true. Men took for a sign and a standard the figure of the flying dragon, the winged dinosaur, a monster of past ages, which was the greatest foe of the serpent. And men used those words which I spoke to you as a sign and symbol, for as I said, none but a true man can repeat them. So mankind triumphed. Yet again the fiends came after the years of forgetfulness had gone by — for man is still an ape in that he forgets what is not ever before his eyes. As priests they came; and for that men in their luxury and might had by then lost faith in the old religions and worships, the snake-men, in the guise of teachers of a new and truer cult, built a monstrous religion about the worship of the serpent god. Such is their power that it is now death to repeat the old legends of the snake-people, and people bow again to the serpent god in new form; and blind fools that they are, the great hosts of men see no connection between this power and the power men overthrew eons ago. As priests the snake-men are content to rule —and yet—" He stopped.

"Go on." Kull felt an unaccountable stirring of the short hair at the base of his scalp.

"Kings have reigned as true men in Valusia," the Pict whispered, "and yet, slain in battle, have died serpents—as died he who fell beneath the spear of Lion-fang on the red beaches when we of the isles harried the Seven Empires. And how can this be, Lord Kull? These kings were born of women and lived as men! Thus—the true kings died in secret—as you would have died tonight—and priests of the Serpent reigned in their stead, no man knowing."

Kull cursed between his teeth. "Aye, it must be. No one has ever seen a priest of the Serpent and lived, that is known. They live in utmost secrecy."

"The statecraft of the Seven Empires is a mazy, monstrous thing," said Brule. "There the true men know that among them glide the spies of the Serpent, and the men who are the Serpent's allies—such as Kaanuub, baron of Blaal—yet no man dares seek to unmask a suspect lest vengeance befall him. No man trusts his fellow and the true statesmen dare not speak to each other what is in the minds of all. Could they be sure, could a snake-man or plot be unmasked before them all, then would the power of the Serpent be more than half broken; for all would then ally and make common cause, sifting out the traitors. Ka-nu alone is of sufficient shrewdness and courage to cope with them, and even Ka-nu learned only enough of their plot to tell me what would happen—what has happened up to this time. Thus far I was prepared; from now on we must trust to our luck and our craft. Here and now I think we are safe; those snake-men without the door dare not leave their post lest true men come here unexpectedly. But tomorrow they will try something else, you may be sure. Just what they will do, none can say, not even Ka-nu; but we must stay at each other's sides. King Kull, until we conquer or both be dead. Now come with me while I take this carcass to the hiding-place where I took the other being."

Kull followed the Pict with his grisly burden through the secret panel and down the dim corridor. Their feet, trained to the silence of the wilderness, made no noise. Like phantoms they glided through the ghostly light, Kull wondering that the corridors should be deserted; at every turn he expected to run full upon some frightful apparition. Suspicion surged back upon him; was this Pict leading him into ambush? He fell back a pace or two behind Brule, his ready sword hovering at the Pict's unheeding back. Brule should die first if he meant treachery. But if the Pict was aware of the king's suspicion, he showed no sign. Stolidly he tramped along, until they came to a room, dusty and long unused, where moldy tapestries hung heavy. Brule drew aside some of these and concealed the corpse behind them.

Then they turned to retrace their steps, when suddenly Brule

halted with such abruptness that he was closer to death than he knew; for Kull's nerves were on edge.

"Something moving in the corridor," hissed the Pict. "Ka-nu said these ways would be empty, yet—"

He drew his sword and stole into the corridor, Kull following warily.

A short way down the corridor a strange, vague glow appeared that came toward them. Nerves a-leap, they waited, backs to the corridor wall; for what they knew not, but Kull heard Brule's breath hiss through his teeth and was reassured as to Brule's loyalty.

The glow merged into a shadowy form. A shape vaguely like a man it was, but misty and illusive, like a wisp of fog, that grew more tangible as it approached, but never fully material. A face looked at them, a pair of luminous great eyes, that seemed to hold all the tortures of a million centuries. There was no menace in that face, with its dim, worn features, but only a great pity—and that face—that face—

"Almighty gods!" breathed Kull, an icy hand at his soul; "Eallal, king of Valusia, who died a thousand years ago!"

Brule shrank back as far as he could, his narrow eyes widened in a blaze of pure horror, the sword shaking in his grip, unnerved for the first time that weird night. Erect and defiant stood Kull, instinctively holding his useless sword at the ready; flesh a-crawl, hair a-prickle, yet still a king of kings, as ready to challenge the powers of the unknown dead as the powers of the living.

The phantom came straight on, giving them no heed; Kull shrank back as it passed them, feeling an icy breath like a breeze from the arctic snow. Straight on went the shape with slow, silent footsteps, as if the chains of all the ages were upon those vague feet; vanishing about a bend of the corridor.

"Valka!" muttered the Pict, wiping the cold beads from his brow; "that was no man! That was a ghost!"

"Aye!" Kull shook his head wonderingly. "Did you not recognize the face? That was Eallal, who reigned in Valusia a thousand years ago and who was found hideously murdered in his throne-room—the room now known as the Accursed Room. Have you not seen his statue in the Fame Room of Kings?"

"Yes, I remember the tale now. Gods, Kull! That is another sign of the frightful and foul power of the snake priests—that king was slain by snake-people and thus his soul became their slave, to do their bidding throughout eternity! For the sages have ever maintained that if a man is slain by a snake-man his ghost becomes their slave."

A shudder shook Kull's gigantic frame. "Valka! But what a fate! Hark ye"—his fingers closed upon Brule's sinewy arm like steel—"hark ye! If I am wounded unto death by these foul monsters, swear that ye will smite your sword through my breast lest my soul be enslaved."

"I swear," answered Brule, his fierce eyes lighting. "And do ye the same by me, Kull."

Their strong right hands met in a silent sealing of their bloody bargain.

## IV. MASKS

Kull sat upon his throne and gazed broodily out upon the sea of faces turned toward him. A courtier was speaking in evenly modulated tones, but the king scarcely heard him. Close by, Tu, chief councilor, stood ready at Kull's command, and each time the king looked at him, Kull shuddered inwardly. The surface of court life was as the unrippled surface of the sea between tide and tide. To the musing king the affairs of the night before seemed as a dream, until his eyes dropped to the arm of his throne. A brown, sinewy hand rested there, upon the wrist of which gleamed a dragon armlet; Brule stood beside his throne and ever the Pict's fierce secret whisper brought him back from the realm of unreality in which he moved.

No, that was no dream, that monstrous interlude. As he sat upon his throne in the Hall of Society and gazed upon the courtiers, the ladies, the lords, the statesmen, he seemed to see their faces as things of illusion, things unreal, existent only as shadows and mockeries of substance. Always he had seen their faces as masks, but before he had looked on them with contemptuous tolerance, thinking to see beneath the masks shallow, puny souls, avaricious, lustful, deceitful; now there was a grim undertone, a sinister meaning, a vague horror that lurked beneath the smooth masks. While he exchanged courtesies with some nobleman or councilor he seemed to see the smiling face fade like smoke and the frightful jaws of a serpent gaping there. How many of those he looked upon were horrid, inhuman monsters, plotting his death, beneath the smooth mesmeric illusion of a human face?

Valusia—land of dreams and nightmares—a kingdom of the shadows, ruled by phantoms who glided back and forth behind the painted curtains, mocking the futile king who sat upon the throne—himself a shadow.

And like a comrade shadow Brule stood by his side, dark eyes glittering from immobile face. A real man, Brule! And Kull felt his friendship for the savage become a thing of reality and sensed that Brule felt a friendship for him beyond the mere necessity of statecraft.

And what, mused Kull, were the realities of life? Ambition, power, pride? The friendship of man, the love of women—which Kull had never known—battle, plunder, what? Was it the real Kull who sat upon the throne or was it the real Kull who had scaled the hills of Atlantis, harried the far isles of the sunset, and laughed upon the green roaring tides of the Atlantean sea? How could a man be so many different men in a lifetime? For Kull knew that there were many Kulls and he wondered which was the real Kull. After all, the priests of the Serpent went a step further in their magic, for all men wore masks, and many a different mask with each different man or woman; and Kull wondered if a serpent did not lurk under every mask. So he sat and brooded in strange, mazy thought-ways, and the courtiers came and went and the minor affairs of the day were completed, until at last the king and Brule sat alone in the Hall of Society save for the drowsy attendants.

Kull felt a weariness. Neither he nor Brule had slept the night before, nor had Kull slept the night before that, when in the gardens of Ka-nu he had had his first hint of the weird things to be. Last night nothing further had occurred after they had returned to the study room from the secret corridors, but they had neither dared nor cared to sleep. Kull, with the incredible vitality of a wolf, had aforetime gone for days upon days without sleep, in his wild savage days but now his mind was edged from constant thinking and from the nerve-breaking eeriness of the past night. He needed sleep, but sleep was furthest from his mind.

And he would not have dared sleep if he had thought of it. Another thing that had shaken him was the fact that though he and Brule had kept a close watch to see if, or when, the study-room guard was changed, yet it was changed without their knowledge; for the next morning those who stood on guard were able to repeat the magic words of Brule, but they remembered nothing out of the ordinary. They thought that they had stood at guard all night, as usual, and Kull said nothing to the contrary. He believed them true men, but Brule had advised absolute secrecy, and Kull also thought it best.

Now Brule leaned over the throne, lowering his voice so not even a lazy attendant could hear: "They will strike soon, I think, Kull. A while ago Ka-nu gave me a secret sign. The priests know that we know of their plot, of course, but they know not, how much we know. We must be ready for any sort of action. Ka-nu and the Pictish chiefs will remain within hailing distance now until this is settled one way or another. Ha, Kull, if it comes to a pitched battle, the streets and the castles of Valusia will run red!"

Kull smiled grimly. He would greet any sort of action with a ferocious joy. This wandering in a labyrinth of illusion and magic was extremely irksome to his nature. He longed for the leap and clang of swords, for the joyous freedom of battle.

Then into the Hall of Society came Tu again, and the rest of the councilors.

"Lord king, the hour of the council is at hand and we stand ready to escort you to the council room."

Kull rose, and the councilors bent the knee as he passed through the way opened by them for his passage, rising behind him, and following. Eyebrows were raised as the Pict strode defiantly behind the king, but no one dissented. Brule's challenging gaze swept the smooth faces of the councilors with the defiance of an intruding savage.

The group passed through the halls and came at last to the council chamber. The door was closed, as usual, and the councilors arranged themselves in the order of their rank before the dais upon which stood the king. Like a bronze statue Brule took up his stand behind Kull.

Kull swept the room with a swift stare. Surely no chance of treachery here. Seventeen councilors there were, all known to him; all of them had espoused his cause when he ascended the throne.

"Men of Valusia—" he began in the conventional manner, then halted, perplexed. The councilors had risen as a man and were moving toward him. There was no hostility in their looks, but their actions were strange for a council room. The foremost was close to him when Brule sprang forward, crouched like a leopard.

"Ka nama kaa lajerama!" his voice crackled through the sinister silence of the room and the foremost councilor recoiled, hand flashing to his robes; and like a spring released, Brule moved and the man pitched headlong and lay still while his face faded and became the head of a mighty snake.

"Slay, Kull!" rasped the Pict's voice. "They be all serpent men!"

The rest was a scarlet maze. Kull saw the familiar faces dim like fading fog and in their places gaped horrid reptilian visages as the whole band rushed forward. His mind was dazed but his giant body faltered not.

The singing of his sword filled the room, and the onrushing flood broke in a red wave. But they surged forward again, seemingly willing to fling their lives away in order to drag down the king. Hideous jaws gaped at him; terrible eyes blazed into his unblinkingly; a frightful fetid scent pervaded the atmosphere—the serpent scent that Kull had known in southern jungles. Swords and daggers leaped at him and he was dimly aware that they wounded him. But Kull was in his element; never before had he faced such grim foes but it mattered little; they lived, their veins held blood that could be spilt and they died when his great sword cleft their skulls or drove through their bodies. Slash, thrust, thrust and swing. Yet had Kull died there but for the man who crouched at his side, parrying and thrusting. For the king was clear berserk, fighting in the terrible Atlantean way, that seeks death to deal death; he made no effort to avoid thrusts and slashes, standing straight up and ever plunging forward, no thought in his frenzied mind but to slay. Not often did Kull forget his fighting craft in his primitive fury, but now some chain had broken in his soul, flooding his mind with a red wave of slaughter-lust. He slew a foe at each blow, but they surged about him, and time and again Brule turned a thrust that would have slain, as he crouched beside Kull, parrying and warding with cold skill, slaying not as Kull slew with long slashes and plunges, but with short overhand blows and upward thrusts.

Kull laughed, a laugh of insanity. The frightful faces swirled about him in a scarlet blaze. He felt steel sink into his arm and dropped his sword in a flashing arc that cleft his foe to the breast-bone.

Then the mists faded and the king saw that he and Brule stood alone above a sprawl of hideous crimson figures who lay still upon the floor.

"Valka! What a killing!" said Brule, shaking the blood from his eyes. "Kull, had these been warriors who knew how to use the steel, we had died here. These serpent priests know naught of swordcraft and die easier than any men I ever slew. Yet had there been a few more, I think the matter had ended otherwise."

Kull nodded. The wild berserker blaze had passed, leaving a mazed feeling of great weariness. Blood seeped from wounds on breast, shoulder, arm and leg. Brule, himself bleeding from a score of flesh wounds, glanced at him in some concern.

"Lord Kull, let us hasten to have your wounds dressed by the women."

Kull thrust him aside with a drunken sweep of his mighty arm.

"Nay, we'll see this through ere we cease. Go you, though, and have your wounds seen to—I command it."

The Pict laughed grimly. "Your wounds are more than mine, lord king—" he began, then stopped as a sudden thought struck him. "By Valka, Kull, this is not the council room!"

Kull looked about and suddenly other fogs seemed to fade. "Nay, this is the room where Eallal died a thousand years ago—since unused and named 'Accursed.'"

"Then by the gods, they tricked us after all!" exclaimed Brule in a fury, kicking the corpses at their feet. "They caused us to walk like fools into their ambush! By their magic they changed the appearance of all—"

"Then there is further deviltry afoot," said Kull, "for if there be true men in the councils of Valusia they should be in the real council room now. Come swiftly."

And leaving the room with its ghastly keepers they hastened council halls that seemed deserted until they came to the real council room.

Then Kull halted with a ghastly shudder. From the council room sounded a voice speaking, and—the voice was his!

With a hand that shook he parted the tapestries and gazed into the room. There sat the councilors, counterparts of the men he and Brule had just slain, and upon the dais stood Kull, king of Valusia.

He stepped back, his mind reeling.

"This is insanity!" he whispered. "Am I Kull? Do I stand here or is that Kull yonder in very truth, and am I but a shadow, a figment of thought?"

Brule's hand clutching his shoulder, shaking him fiercely, brought him to his senses.

"Valka's name, be not a fool! Can you yet be astounded after all we have seen? See you not that those are true men bewitched by a snake-man who has taken your form, as those others took their forms? By now you should have been slain, and yon monster reigning in your stead, unknown by those who bowed to you. Leap and slay swiftly or else we are undone. The Red Slayers, true men, stand close on each hand and none but you can reach and slay him. Be swift!"

Kull shook off the onrushing dizziness, flung back his head in the old, defiant gesture. He took a long, deep breath as does a strong swimmer before diving into the sea; then, sweeping back the tapestries, made the dais in a single lion-like bound. Brule had spoken truly. There stood men of the Red Slayers, guardsmen trained to move quick as the striking leopard; any but Kull had died ere he could reach the usurper. But the sight of Kull, identical with the man upon the dais, held them in their tracks, their minds stunned for an instant, and that was long enough. He upon the dais snatched for his sword. But even as his fingers closed upon the hilt, Kull's sword stood out behind his shoulders and the thing that men had thought the king pitched forward from the dais to lie silent upon the floor.

"Hold!" Kull's lifted hand and kingly voice stopped the rush that had started, and while they stood astounded he pointed to the thing which lay before them—whose face was fading into that of a snake. They recoiled, and from one door came Brule and from another came Ka-nu.

These grasped the king's bloody hand and Ka-nu spoke: "Men of Valusia, you have seen with your own eyes. This is the true Kull, the mightiest king to whom Valusia has ever bowed. The power of the Serpent is broken and ye be all true men. King Kull, have you commands?"

"Lift that carrion," said Kull, and men of the guard took up the thing.

"Now follow me," said the king, and he made his way to the Accursed Room. Brule, with a look of concern, offered the support of his arm but Kull shook him off.

The distance seemed endless to the bleeding king, but at last he stood at the door and laughed fiercely and grimly when he heard the horrified ejaculations of the councilors.

At his orders the guardsmen flung the corpse they carried beside the others, and motioning all from the room Kull stepped out last and closed the door.

A wave of dizziness left him shaken. The faces turned to him, pallid and wonderingly, swirled and mingled in a ghostly fog. He felt the blood from his wound trickling down his limbs and he knew that what he was to do, he must do quickly or not at all.

His sword rasped from its sheath.

"Brule, are you there?"

"Aye!" Brule's face looked at him through the mist, close to his shoulder, but Brule's voice sounded leagues and eons away.

"Remember our vow, Brule. And now, bid them stand back."

His left arm cleared a space as he flung up his sword. Then with all his waning power he drove it through the door into the jamb, driving the great sword to the hilt and sealing the room forever.

Legs braced wide, he swayed drunkenly, facing the horrified councilors. "Let this room be doubly accursed. And let those rotting skeletons lie there forever as a sign of the dying might of the Serpent. Here I swear that I shall hunt the serpent-men from land to land, from sea to sea, giving no rest until all be slain, that good triumph and the power of Hell be broken. This thing I swear—I—Kull—king—of—Valusia."

His knees buckled as the faces swayed and swirled. The councilors leaped forward, but ere they could reach him, Kull slumped to the floor, and lay still, face upward.

The councilors surged about the fallen king, chattering and shrieking. Ka-nu beat them back with his clenched fists, cursing savagely.

"Back, you fools! Would you stifle the little life that is yet in him? How, Brule, is he dead or will he live?"—to the warrior who bent above the prostrate Kull.

"Dead?" sneered Brule irritably. "Such a man as this is not so easily killed. Lack of sleep and loss of blood have weakened him—by Valka, he has a score of deep wounds, but none of them mortal. Yet have those gibbering fools bring the court women here at once."

Brule's eyes lighted with a fierce, proud light.

"Valka, Ka-nu, but here is such a man as I knew not existed in these degenerate days. He will be in the saddle in a few scant days and then may the serpentmen of the world beware of Kull of Valusia. Valka! But that will be a rare hunt! Ah, I see long years of prosperity for the world with such a king upon the throne of Valusia."

# The Sea-Witch

by Nictzin Dyalhis

**"By the power I hold, I call you forth from your hiding-place of flesh—come ye out."**

Heldra Helstrom entered my life in a manner peculiarly her own. And while she was the most utterly damnable woman in all the world, at the same time, in my opinion, she was the sweetest and the most superbly lovely woman who ever lived. A three-day northeast gale was hammering at the coast. It was late in the fall of the year, and cold as only our North Atlantic coast can very well be, but in the very midst of the tempest I became afflicted with a mild form of claustrophobia. So I donned sea-boots, oilskins and sou'wester hat, and sallied forth for a walk along the shore. My little cottage stood at the top of a high cliff. There was a broad, safe path running down to the beach, and down it I hurried. The short winter day was even then drawing to a close, and after I'd trudged a quarter of a mile along the shore, I decided I'd best return to my comfortable fireside. The walk had at least given me a good appetite. There was none of the usual lingering twilight of a clear winter evening. Darkness fell so abruptly I was glad I'd brought along a powerful flashlight. I'd almost reached the foot of my path up the cliff when I halted, incredulous, yet desiring to make sure.

I turned the ray of the flashlight on the great comber just curling to break on the shore, and held the light steady, my breath gasping in my throat. Such a thing as I thought I'd seen couldn't be—yet it was!

I started to run to the rescue, and could not move a foot. A power stronger than my own will held me immovable. I could only watch, spellbound. And even as I stared, that gigantic comber gently subsided, depositing its precious living burden on the sands as softly as any nurse laying a babe into a cradle.

Waist-deep in a smother of foam she stood for a brief second, then calmly waded ashore and walked with free swinging stride straight up the beam of my flashlight to where I stood. Regardless of the hellish din and turmoil of the tempest, I thrilled, old as I am, at the superb loveliness of this most amazing specimen of flotsam ever a raging sea cast ashore within memory of man. Never a shred of clothing masked her matchless body, yet her flesh glowed rosy-white, when by all natural laws it should have been blue-white from the icy chill of wintry seas. "Well!" I exclaimed. "Where did you come from? Are you real—or am I seeing that which is not?"

"I am real," replied a clear, silvery voice. "And I came from out there." An exquisitely molded arm flung a gesture toward the raging ocean. "The ship I was on was sinking, so I stripped off my garb, flung myself on Ran's bosom, and Ran's horses gave me a most magnificent ride! But well for you that you stood still as I bade you, while I walked ashore. Ran is an angry god, and seldom well-disposed toward mortals."

"Ran?" The sea-god of the old Norse vikings! What strange woman was this, who talked of "Ran" and his "horses," the white-maned waves of old ocean? But then I bethought me of her naked state in that unholy tempest. "Surely you must be Ran's daughter," I said. "That reef is ten miles off land! Come—I have a house near by, and comforts—you cannot stand here."

"Lead, and I will follow," she replied simply.

She went up that path with greater ease than I, and walked companionably beside me from path-top to house, although she made no talk. Oddly, I felt that she was reading me, and that what she read gave her comfort.

When I opened the door, it seemed as if she held back for a merest moment.

"Enter," I bade her, a bit testily. "I should think you'd had enough of this weather by now!"

She bowed her head with a natural stateliness which convinced me that she was no common person, and murmured something too low for me to catch, but the accents had a distinct Scandinavian trend. "What did you say?" I queried, for I supposed she'd spoken to me.

"I invoked the favor of the old gods on the hospitable of heart, and on the sheltering rooftree," she replied. Then she crossed my threshold, but she reached out her arm and rested her shapely white hand lightly yet firmly on my left forearm as she stepped within.

She went direct to the big stove, which was glowing dull-red, and stood there, smiling slightly, calm, serene, wholly ignoring her nakedness, obviously enjoying the warmth, and not by a single shiver betraying that she had any chill as result of exposure.

"I think you need this," I said, proffering a glass of brandy. "There's time enough for exchanging names and giving explanations, later," I added. "But right now, I'll try and find something for you to put on. I have no women's things in the house, as I live alone, but will do the best I can."

I passed into my bedroom, laid out a suit of pajamas and a heavily quilted bathrobe, and returned to the living-room where she stood.

"You are a most disconcertingly beautiful young woman," I stated bluntly; "which you know quite well without being told. But doubtless you will feel more at ease if you go in there and don some things I've laid out for you. When you come out, I'll get some supper ready."

She was back instantly, still unclad. I stared, wonderingly.

"Those things did not fit," she shrugged. "And that heavy robe—in this warm house?"

"But—" I began.

"But—this," she smiled, catching up a crimson silk spread embroidered in gold, which covered a sandalwood table I'd brought from the orient many years before. A couple of swift motions and the gorgeous thing became a wondrous robe adorning her lovely figure, clinging, and in some subtle manner hinting at the flawless splendor of her incomparable body. A long narrow scarf of black silk whereon twisted a silver dragon was whipped from its place on a shelf and transposed into a sash from her swelling breasts to her sloping hips, bringing out more fully every exquisite curve of her slender waist and torso—and she smiled again.

"Now," she laughed softly, "am I still a picture for your eyes? I hope so, for you have befriended me this night—I who sorely need a friend; and it is such a little thing I can do—making myself pleasing in your sight.

"And because you have holpen me"—I stared at the archaic form she used—" and will continue to aid and befriend (for so my spirit tells me), I will love you always, love you as Ragnar Wave-Flame loved Jarl Wulf Red-Brand, as a younger sister, or a dutiful niece."

"Yet of her it is told," I interrupted, deliberately speaking Swedish and watching keenly to see the effect, "that the love given by the foam-born Sea-Witch brought old Earl Wulf of the Red-Sword but little luck, and that not of a sort desired by most men!"

"That is ill said," she retorted. "His fate was from the Norns, as is the fate of all. Not hers the fault of his doom, and when his carles within the hour captured his three slayers, she took red vengeance. With her own foam-white hands she flayed them alive, and covered their twitching bodies with salt ere she placed the old Jarl in his long-ship and set it afire. And she sailed with that old man on his last seafaring, steering his blazing dragon-ship out of the stead, singing of his great deeds in life, that the heroes in Valhalla might know who honored them by his coming."

She paused, her superb bosom heaving tumultuously. Then with a visible effort she calmed herself.

"But you speak my tongue, and know the old tales of the Skalds. Are you, then, a Swede?"

"I speak the tongue, and the old tales of the Skalds, the ancient minstrels, I learned from my grandmother, who was of your race."

"Of my race?" her tone held a curious inflection. "Ah, yes! All women are of one race . . . perhaps."

"But I spoke of supper," I said, moving toward the kitchen.

"But—no!" She barred my progress with one of her lovely hands laid flat against my chest. "It is not meet and fitting, Jarl Wulf, that you should cook for me, like any common house-carle! Rather, let your niece, Heldra, prepare for you a repast."

"'Heldra'? That, then, is your name?"

"Heldra Helstrom, and your loving niece," she nodded.

"But why call me Jarl Wulf?" I demanded, curious to understand. She had bestowed the name seriously, rather than in playful banter.

"Jarl Wulf you were, in a former life," she asserted flatly. "I knew you on the shore, even before Ran's horse stood me on my feet!"

"Surely, then, you must be Ragnar Wave-Flame born again," I countered.

"How may that be?" she retorted. "Ragnar Wave-Flame never died; and surely I do not look that old! The sea-born witch returned to the sea-caves whence she came, when the dragon-ship burned out. . . . But ask me not of myself, now.

"Yet one thing more I will say: The warp and woof of this strange pattern wherein we both are depicted was woven of the Norns ere the world began. We have met before—we meet again, here and now—we shall meet yet again; but how, and when, and where, I may not say."

"Of a truth, you are 'fey'," I muttered.

"At times—I am," she assented. Then her wondrous sapphire eyes gleamed softly into my own hard gray eyes, her smile was tender, wistful, womanly, and my doubts were dissipated like wisps of smoke. Yet I shook an admonitory forefinger at her:

"Witch at least I know you to be," I said in mock harshness. "Casting glamyr on an old man."

"No need for witchery," she laughed. "All women possess that power!"

During the "repast" she spread before me, I told her that regardless of who I might have been in a dim and remote past of which I had no memory, in this present life I was plain John Craig, retired professor of anthropology, ethnology and archeology, and living on a very modest income. I explained that while I personally admired her, and she was welcome to remain in my home for ever, yet in the village near by were curious minds, and gossiping tongues, and evil thoughts a-plenty, and if I were to tell the truth of her arrival—

"But I have nowhere to go, and none save you to befriend me; all I loved or owned is out there." Again she indicated the general direction of the reef. "And you say that I may remain here, indefinitely? I will be known as your niece, Heldra, no? Surely, considering the differences in our age and appearance, there can be no slander."

Her eyes said a thousand things no words could convey. There was eagerness, sadness, and a strange tenderness ... I came to an abrupt decision. After all, whose business was it? ... "I am alone in the world, as you are," I said gravely. "As my niece, Heldra, you shall remain. If you will write out a list of a woman's total requirements in wearing-apparel, I will send away as soon as possible and have them shipped here in haste. I am old, as all can see, and I do not think any sensible persons will suspect aught untoward in your making your home with me. And I will think up a plausible story which will satisfy the minds of fools without telling, in reality, anything."

Our repast ended, we arose from the table and returned to the living-room. I filled and lighted a nargilyeh, a three-stemmed water-pipe, and settled myself in my armchair. She helped herself to a cigarette from a box on the table, then stretched her long, slender body at full length on my divan, in full relaxation of comfort.

I told her enough of myself and my forebears to insure her being able to carry out the fiction of being my niece. And in return I learned mighty little about her. But what she did tell me was sufficient. I never was unduly curious about other people's business.

Unexpectedly, and most impolitely, I yawned. Yet it was natural enough, and it struck me that she needed a rest, if anyone ever did. But before I could speak, she forestalled me. With a single graceful movement she rose from her reclining posture and came and stood before me within easy arm's-reach. Two swift motions, and her superb body flashed rosy-white, as nude as when she waded ashore.

The crimson silken spread she'd worn as regally as any robe was laid at my feet with a single gesture, the black scarf went across my knees, and the glorious creature was kneeling before me in attitude of absolute humility. Before I could remonstrate or bid her arise, her silvery voice rang softly, solemnly, like a muted trumpet:

"Thus, naked and with empty hands, out of the wintry seas in a twilight gray and cold, on a night of storm I came. And you lighted a beacon for my tired eyes, that I might see my way ashore. You led me up the cliff and to your hospitable hearth, and in your kindly heart you had already given the homeless a home.

"And now, kneeling naked before you, as I came, I place my hands between your hands—thus—and all that I am, and such service as I can render, are yours, hand-fasted."

I stared, well-nigh incredulous. In effect, in the old Norse manner, she was declaring herself to all intents and purposes my slave! But her silvery voice went on: "And now, I rise and cover myself again with the mantle of your bounty, that you may know me, indeed your niece, as Jarl Wulf knew Ragnar Wave-Flame!"

"Truly," I gasped in amazement when I could catch my breath, "you are a strange mixture of the ancient days and this modern period. I have known you but for a few hours, yet I feel toward you as that old Jarl must have felt toward that other sea-witch, unless indeed you and she are one!"

"Almost," she replied a trifle somberly. "At least, she was my ancestress!" Then she added swiftly: "Do not misunderstand. Leman to the old Jarl she never was. But later, after he went to Valhalla, in the sea-girt isle where she dwelt she mated with a young viking whom Ran had cast ashore sorely wounded and insensible. She nursed him back to life for sake of his beauty, and he made love to her. "But he soon tired of her and her witch ways; wherefore, in wrath she gave him back to Ran—and he was seen no more. Of that mating was born a daughter, also given to Ran, who pitied her and bore her to an old man and his wife whose steading was nigh to the mouth of a fjord; and they, being childless, called her Ranhild, and reared her as their daughter. In course of time, she wed, and bore three tall sons and a daughter. . . .

"That was long and long ago—yet I have dived into Ragnar's hidden sea-cave and talked with Ragnar Wave-Flame face to face. All one night I lay in her arms, and in the dawning she breathed her breath on my brow, lips, and bosom; and all that following day she talked and I listened, and much I learned of the wisdom that an elder world termed witchcraft."

For a moment she lapsed into silence. Then she leaned forward, laid her shapely, cool hands on my temples and kissed me on my furrowed old forehead, very solemnly, yet with ineffable gentleness. "And now," she murmured, "ask me never again aught concerning myself, I pray you; for I have told all I may, and further questioning will drive me back to the sea. And I would not have that happen—yet!" Without another word she turned, flung herself at full length again on the divan, and, like any tired child, went instantly to sleep. Decidedly, I thought, this "niece" of mine was not as are other women; and later I found that she possessed certain abilities it is well for the world that few indeed can wield.

She gave me another proof of that belief, by demonstrating her unholy powers, on the night of the next full moon after her arrival.

It was her custom of an evening to array herself as she had done on her first night—in crimson robe and black sash and naught else, despite the fact that her wardrobe which I had ordered from the great city forty miles away contained all any woman's heart could wish for. But I admit I enjoyed seeing her in that semi-barbaric attire. At times she would sit on the arm of my chair, often with her smooth cool cheek laid against my rough old face, and her exquisitely modeled arm curved about my leathery old neck. The first time she had done that, I had demanded ironically:

"Witch, are you making love to me?"

But her sighing, wistful reply had disarmed me, and likewise had brought a lump into my throat.

"Nay! Not that, O Jarl from of old! But—I never knew a father."

"Nor I a fair daughter," I choked. And thereafter, when that mood was upon her I indulged in no more ironies, and we'd sit for hours, neither speaking, engrossed in thoughts for which there are no words. But on the night whereof I write, she pressed her scarlet lips to my cheek, and I asked jestingly:

"Is there something you want, Heldra?"

"There is," she replied gravely. "Will you get a boat—one with oars and a sail, but no engine? Ran hates those."

"But surely you do not want it now, tonight, do you?"

"Yes, if you will be so kind to me."

"You must have a very good reason, or you'd not ask," I said. "I'll go and get a centerboard dory and bring it to the beach at the foot of the cliff path. It's clear weather, and the sea is calm, with but a moderate breeze blowing; yet it is colder on the water than you imagine, so you'd best bundle up warmly."

"You will hasten," she implored anxiously.

"Surely," I nodded.

I went out and down to the wharves in the village, where I kept the boat I said I'd get. But when I beached the dory at foot of the path I stared, swearing softly under my breath. Not one stitch of apparel did that witch have on, save the crimson silk robe and black sash she'd worn when I left the cottage!

"Do you want to freeze?" I was provoked, I admit. "The very sight of you dressed like that gives me the shivers!"

"Neither you nor I will be cold this night," she laughed. "Isn't it glorious? And this is a good boat you brought. Please, let me sail it, and ask me no questions."

She took the tiller, hauled in on the sheet; the sail filled, and she began singing, with a queer, wild strain running through her song. That dory fairly flew—and I swear there was not enough wind to drive us at such speed.

Finally I saw something I didn't admire. No one does, who dwells on that part of the coast.

"Are you crazy, girl?" I demanded sharply. "That reef is dead ahead! Can't you see the breakers?"

"Why, so it is—the reef! And am I to be affrighted by a few puny breakers? Nay, it is in the heart of those breakers that I wish to be! But you—have you fear, O Jarl Wulf?"

I suspected from her tone that the witch was laughing at me; so I subsided, but fervently wished that I'd not been so indulgent of her whim for a moonlight sail on a cold winter's night. Then we hit those breakers—or rather, we didn't! For they seemed to part as the racing dory sped into them, making a smooth clear lane of silvery glinting water over which we glided as easily as if on a calm inland mill-pond!

"Drop the sail and unstep the mast," she called suddenly.

I was beyond argument, and obeyed dumbly, like any boat-carle of the olden days.

"Now, take to the oars," she directed, "and hold the boat just hereabouts for a while," and even as I slid the oars into the oarlocks she made that swift movement of hers and stood nude, the loveliest sight that grim, ship-shattering, life-destroying reef had ever beheld.

Suddenly she flung up both shapely white arms with a shrill, piercing cry, thrice repeated. Then without a word she went overside in a long clean dive, with never a splash to show where she'd hit the water. "Hold the boat about here for a while," she'd bidden me! All I'd ever loved in this world was somewhere down below, in the hellish cross-currents of that icy water! I'd hold that boat there, if need were, in the teeth of a worse tempest than raged the night she came to me. She'd find me waiting. And if she never came up, I'd hold that boat there till its planks rotted and I joined her in the frigid depths. It seemed an eternity, and I know that it was an hour ere a glimmer of white appeared beneath the surface. Then her shapely arm emerged and her hand grasped the gunwale, her regal head broke water, she blew like a porpoise; then she laughed in clear ringing triumph.

"You old dearling!" she cried in her archaic Norse. "Did I seem long gone? The boat has not moved a foot from where I dove. Come, bear a hand and lift my burden; it is heavy, and I am near spent. There are handles by which to grasp it."

The burden proved to be a greenish metal coffer—bronze, I judged—which I estimated to measure some twenty inches long by twelve wide and nine inches deep. And how she rose to the surface weighted with that, passes my understanding. But how she knew it was down there passes my comprehension, too. But then, Heldra Helstrom herself was an enigma.

She re-wrapped herself in her flimsy silken robe of crimson and smiled happily, when she should have been shivering almost to pieces.

"If you'll ship the mast and spread the sail again, Uncle John," she said, surprisingly matter-of-fact now that her errand was successfully accomplished, "we'll go home. I'd like a glass of brandy and a smoke, myself; and I read in your mind that such is your chief desire, at present."

Back at the cottage again, and comfortable once more, Heldra requested me to bear the coffer into her room, which I did. For over an hour she remained in there, then returned to the living-room where I sat, and I stared at the picture she presented. If she had always been beautiful, now she was surpassingly glorious.

Instead of the usual crimson robe, her lovely body was sheathed in a sleeveless, sheer, tightly fitting silken slip, cut at the throat in a long sloping V reaching nearly to her waist. The garment was palest sea-green, so flimsy in texture that it might as well have been compounded of mingled moon-mist and cobwebs. Her rosy-pearl flesh gleamed through the fabric with an alluring shimmer which thrilled a-new my jaded old senses at the artistic wonder of her.

A gold collar, gem-studded, unmistakably of ancient Egyptian workmanship, was resting on her superb shoulders—loot of some viking foray into the far South-lands, doubtless. A broad girdle of gold plates, squared, and also gem-studded, was about her sloping hips, and was clasped in front by a broader plate with a sun-emblem in jeweled sets; from which plate or buckle it fell in two broad bands nearly to her white slender feet.

Broad torques of gold on upper arms and about her wrists, and an intricately wrought golden tiara with disks of engraved gold pendent by chains and hanging over her ears, set off her loveliness as never before. Even her red-gold hair, braided in two thick ropes, falling over her breasts to below her waist, were clasped by gem-set brooches of gold. "Ragnar Wave-Flame's gift to me, O Jarl Wulf," she breathed softly. "Do you like your niece thus arrayed?"

Norse princess out of an elder day, or Norse witch from an even older and wickeder period of the world—whichever this Heldra Helstrom was, of one thing I was certain, no lovelier woman ever lived than this superb being who styled herself my "niece." And so I told her, and was amply rewarded by the radiance of her smile, and the ecstatic kiss she implanted on my cheek. Despite her splendid array, she perched on the arm of my chair, and began toying with my left hand. Presently she lifted it to the level of my eyes, laughing softly. I'd felt nothing, yet she'd slipped a broad tarnished silver ring of antique design on my third finger.

"It was yours in the ancient days, O Jarl Wulf," she whispered in her favorite tongue—the archaic form of the Norsk language. "Yours again is the ancient ring, now! Ragnar herself carved the mystic runes upon it. Shall I read them, O Jarl, or will you?"

"They are beyond my skill," I confessed. "The words are in the 'secret' language that only the Rime-Kanaars' understood. Nor was it well for others than witches and warlocks to seek to understand them."

"Ragnar took that ring from Jarl Wulf's finger ere she set fire to the dragon-ship," Heldra murmured. "Had those runes been on the ring when your foes set upon you—they, not you, would have perished in the sword-play, Jarl Red-Sword!

"But the sea-born witch knew that you would weary of Valhalla in a day to come, and would return to this world of strife and slaying, of loss and grief, of hate and the glutting of vengeance—and, knowing, she carved the runes, that in time the charmed ring would return to its proper owner.

"It is her express command that I read them to you, for knowing the runes, never shall water drown or fire burn; nor sword or spear or ax ever wound you, so be it that in time of danger you speak the weird words!

"And for my sake—you who are my 'Uncle John' to all the rest of the world, but to me are dearer than old Jarl Wulf was to Ragnar the sea-witch—I implore you to learn the runic charm, and use it if ever danger menaces. Promise me! Promise me, I say!"

Her silvery voice was vibrant with fierce intensity. She caught my right hand and pressed it against her palpitant body, just beneath her proudly swelling left breast. "Promise!" she reiterated. "I beg your promise! With your right hand on my heart I adjure you to learn the rune."

"No fool like an old fool," I grumbled, adding a trifle maliciously, "particularly when in the hands of a lovely woman. But such a fuss you make over a few words of outlandish gibberish! Read me the rune, then, witch-maid! I'd learn words worse than those can be to please you and set your mind at rest."

With her scarlet lips close to my ear, with bated breath, and in a tone so low I could barely catch her carefully enunciated syllables, she whispered the words. And although her whisper was softer than the sighing of gentlest summer breeze, the tones rang on my inner hearing like strokes of a great war-hammer smiting on a shield of bronze. There was no need to repeat them—either on her part or mine. There was no likelihood of my ever forgetting that runic charm. I could not, even if I would.

"Surely," I muttered, "you are an adept in the ancient magic. Well for me that you love me, else your witcheries might."

Most amazingly she laughed, a clear, ringing merriment with no trace of the mystic about it.

"Let me show you something—a game, a play; one that will amuse me and entertain you."

She fairly danced across the room and into her own room, emerging with an antique mirror of some burnished, silver-like metal. This she held out to me. I grasped it by its handle obediently enough, humoring this new whim.

"Look into it and say if it is a good mirror," she bade, her sapphire eyes a-dance with elfin mirth.

I looked. All I could see was my same old face, tanned and wrinkled, which I daily saw whenever I shaved or combed my hair, and I told her so. She perched again on the arm of my chair, laid her cheek against mine, and curved her cool arm about my neck.

"Now look again!"

Again the mirror told truth. I saw my face the same as ever, and hers as well, "Like a rose beside a granite boulder," as I assured her.

"You do but see yourself as you think of yourself," she murmured softly, "and me you behold as you believe me to be."

She brought her lips close to the mirror and breathed upon its surface with her warm breath. It clouded over, then cleared. Her voice came, more murmurous than before, but with a definite note of sadness: "Once more, look! Behold yourself as I see you always; and behold me as I know myself to be! And when I am gone beyond your ken, remember the witch-maid, Heldra, as one woman who loved you so truly that she showed you herself as she actually was!"

The man's face was still my own, but mine as it was in the days of early manhood, ere life's thunders had graven their scars on brow and cheeks and lips, and before the snows of many winters had whitened my hair.

Her features were no less beautiful, but in her reflected eyes I saw ages and ages of life, and bitter experience, and terrible wisdom that was far more wicked than holy; and it came to me with conviction irrefutable that beside this young-appearing girl, maid, or woman, all my years were but as the span of a puling babe compared to the ageless age of an immortal.

"That, at least, is no glamyr," her voice sighed drearily, heavy with the burden of her own knowledge of herself.

I laid my thick, heavy old arm across her smooth satiny white shoulders, and I turned her head until her sapphire eyes met mine fairly. Very gently I kissed her on her brow.

"Heldra Helstrom," I said, and my voice sounded husky with emotion, "you may be all you have just shown me, or worse! You may be Ragnar Wave-Flame herself, the sea-witch who never dies. You may be even what I sometimes suspect, the empress of Hell, come amongst mortals for no good purpose! But be you what you may, old or young, maid or woman, good or evil, witch, spirit, angel or she-devil, such as you are, you are you and I am I, and for some weird reason we seem to love each other in our own way; so let there be an end to what you are or have been, or who I was in other lives, and content ourselves with what is!"

Were those bright glitters in her sapphire eyes tear-drops ready to fall? If so, I was not sure, for with a cry like that of a lost soul who has found sanctuary, she buried her face on my shoulder.... After a long silence, she slipped from the arm of my chair, and wordlessly, her face averted, she passed into her room. After an hour or so, I went to my own room—but I could not sleep.... Time passed, and I dwelt in a "fool's paradise," dreaming that it would last for ever. The summer colony began to arrive. There were cottages all along the shore, but there were likewise big estates, whose owners were rated as "somebodies," to put it mildly.

A governor of a great and sovereign state; an ex-president of our nation; several foreign diplomats and some of their legation attachés—but why enumerate, when one man only concerns this narrative? Michael Commnenus, tall, slight, dapper, inclined to swarthiness, with black eyes under crescent-curved black eyebrows; with supercilious smiling lips, a trifle too red for a man; with suave Old World manners, and a most amazingly conceited opinion of himself as a "Lady-charmer."

It was not his first summer in our midst; and although when he was in Washington at his legation I never gave him a thought, when

I saw his too handsome face on the beach, I felt a trifle sick! I knew, positively, that the minute he set eyes on Heldra. . . . Of course I knew, too, that my witch-niece could take care of herself; but just the same, I sensed annoyance, and perhaps, tragedy. Well, I was in nowise mistaken.

Heldra and I were just about to shove off in my dory for a sail. It was her chief delight, and mine too, for that matter.

Casually, along strolled Michael Commnenus, twirling a slender stick, caressing a slender black thread he styled a mustache, smiling his approbation of himself. I'd seen that variety of casual approach before. As our flippant young moderns say: It was "old stuff."

Out of the corner of my eye I watched. The Don Juan smirk faded when his calculating, appraising eyes met her sapphire orbs, now shining like the never-melting polar ice. An expression of bewilderment spread over his features. His swarthy skin went a sickly greenish-bronze. Involuntarily he crossed himself and passed on. The man was afraid, actually fear-struck!

"Ever see him before, Heldra?" I queried. "He looked at you as if the devil would be a pleasanter sight. That's one man who failed to fall for your vivid beauty, you sea-witch!"

"Who is he?" she asked in a peculiar tone. "I liked his looks even less than he liked mine."

"Michael Commnenus," I informed her, and was about to give her his pedigree as we local people knew him, but was interrupted by her violently explosive:

"Who?"

"Michael Commnenus," I stated again, a trifle testily. "And you needn't shout! What's he done?" but again she interrupted, speaking her archaic Norsk:

"Ho! Varang Chiefs of the Guard Imperial! Thorfinn! Arvid! Sven! And ye who followed them—Gudrun! Randvar! Haakon! Smid! And all ye Varangs in Valhalla, give ear! And ye, O fiends, witches, warlocks, trolls, vampyrs, and all the dark gods who dwell in Hel's halls where the eternal frozen fires blaze without heat, give ear to my voice, and cherish my words, for I give ye all joyous tidings.

"He lives! After all these long centuries Michael Commnenus dwells again on the bosom of fair Earth! In a body of flesh and blood and bone, of nerve and tissue and muscle he lives! He lives, I say! And I have found him!

"Oh, now I know why the Norns who rule all fate sent me to this place. And I shall not fail ye, heroes! Content ye, one and all, I shall not fail!"

Was this the gorgeous beauty I'd learned to love for her gentleness? Hers was the face of a furious female demon for a moment; but then her normal expression returned and she sighed heavily.

"Heed me not, Uncle John," she said drearily. "I did but recall an ancient talc of foul treachery perpetrated on sundry Norsemen in the Varangian Guard of a Byzantine emperor ages agone.

"The niddering—worse than 'coward'—who wrought the bane of some thirty-odd vikings, was a Commnenus, nephew to the Emperor Alexander Commnenus.... I live too much in memories of the past, I fear, and for the moment somewhat forgot myself in the hate all good Norse maids should hold toward any who bear the accursed name of the Commneni.

"Still, even as I know you to be old Jarl Wulf Red-Brand returned to this world through the gateway of birth—it would be nothing surprising if this spawn of the Commneni were in truth that same Michael Commnenus of whom the tale is told."

"The belief in reincarnation is age-old," I said reflectively. "And in several parts of the world it is a fundamental tenet of religion. If there be truth in the idea, there is, as you say, nothing surprising if anybody now living should have been anybody else in some former life. . . . And that sample of the Commneni appears quite capable of any treachery that might serve a purpose at the moment! But,

Heldra," I implored her, struck by a sudden intuition, "I beg of you not to indulge in any of your devilries, witcheries, or Norse magic. If this Michael is that other Michael, yet that was long ago; and if he has not already atoned for his sin, you may be very sure that somewhere, sometime, somehow he will atone; so do not worry your regal head about him."

"Spoken like a right Saga-man," she smiled as I finished my brief homily. "I thank you for your words of wisdom. And now, Jarl Wulf Red-Brand, I know you to be fey as well as I am. 'Surely he will atone for his sin' . . . oh! a most comforting thought! So let us think no more about the matter."

I glanced sharply at her. Her too instant acquiescence was suspicious. But her sapphire eyes met mine fairly, smilingly, sending as always a warm glow of contentment through me. So I accepted her assurance as it sounded, and gave myself up to the enjoyment of the sail and the sound of her silvery voice as she sang an old English love ballad I'd known as a young man. And under the spell of her magnetic personality gradually the episode of Michael Commnenus faded into nothingness—for a while.

A couple of days later, just about dark, Heldra came down the stairs from the attic, where she'd been rummaging. In her hand she carried an old violin-case. I looked and grinned ruefully. "You are a bad old Uncle John," she scolded. "Why did you not tell me you played the 'fidel,' even as Jarl Wulf played one in his time? Think of all the sweet music you might have made in the past winter nights, and think of the dances I might have danced for your delight while you played—even as Ragnar danced for her old Jarl."

"But I did not tell you that I played a fiddle—because I don't," I stated flatly. "That is a memento of an absurd ambition I once cherished, but which died a-borning. I tried to learn the thing, but the noises I extracted were so abominable that I quit before I'd fairly got started."

"You are teasing," she retorted, her eyes sparkling with mischief. "But I am not to be put off thus easily. Tonight you will play, and I will dance—such a dance as you have never beheld even when you were Jarl Wulf."

"If I try to play that thing," I assured her seriously, "you'll have a time dancing to my discords, you gorgeous tease!"

"We'll see," she nodded. "But even as my magic revealed to me the whereabouts of the 'fidel,' so my spirit tells me that you play splendidly."

"Your 'magic' may be all right, but your 'spirit' has certainly misinformed you," I growled.

"My spirit has never yet lied to me—nor has it done so this time." Her tone was grave, yet therein was a lurking mockery; and I became a trifle provoked.

"All right," I assented grouchily. "Whenever you feel like hearing me 'play,' I'll do it. And you'll never want to listen to such noises again."

She went into her room laughing sweetly, and took the fiddle with her. After supper she said nothing about me playing that old fiddle, and I fatuously thought she'd let the matter drop. But about ten o'clock she went to her room without a word. She emerged after a bit, wearing naught but a sheer loose palest blue silk robe, held at the waist only by a tiny jeweled gold filigree clasp. Loose as the robe was, it clung lovingly to her every curve as if caressing the beauteous, statuesque body it could not and would not conceal.

She was totally devoid of all ornament save that tiny brooch, and her wondrous fiery-gold hair was wholly unconfined, falling below her waist in a cascade of shimmering sunset hues, against which her rose-pearl body gleamed through the filmy gossamer-like robe.

Again she sat and talked for a while. But along toward midnight she broke a short silence with:

"I'll be back in a minute. I wish to prepare for my dancing."

From her room she brought four antique bronze lamps and a strangely shaped urn of oil. She filled the lamps and placed one at each corner of the living-room, on the floor.

Back into her room she went, and out again with an octagonal-shaped stone, flat on both sides, about an inch thick, and some four inches across. This she placed on the low taboret whereon I usually kept my nargilyeh. She propped up that slab of stone as if placing a mirror—which I decided it couldn't very well be, as it did not even reflect light but seemed as dull as a slab of slate.

As a final touch, she brought out that confounded old fiddle! And on her scarlet lips was a smile that a seraph might have envied, so innocent and devoid of guile it seemed.

"What's this?" I demanded—as if I didn't know!

"Your little 'fidel' with which you will make for your Heldra such rapturous music," she smiled caressingly.

"Um-m-m-m!" I grunted. "And what are those lamps for—and that ugly slab of black rock?"

"That black slab is a 'Hel-stone,' having the property of reflecting whatever is directly before it, if illumined by those four lamps placed at certain angles; and later it will give off those same reflections—even as the stuff called luminous calcium sulfide absorbs light-rays until surcharged, and then emits them, when properly exposed. So, you see, we can preserve the picture of my dance."

"Heldra," I demanded sharply, "are you up to some devilishness? All this looks amazingly like the stage-setting for witch-working!"

"I have sung for you, on different nights," she replied in gentlest reproach, "and have told old tales, and have attired myself again and again for your pleasure in beholding me. Have all these things ever bewitched you, or harmed anyone? How, then, can the fact of my dancing for my own satisfaction, before the mystic Hel-stone, do any harm?"

As ever, she won. Her sapphire orbs did queer things to me whenever they looked into my own gray, faded old eyes—trusting me to understand and approve whatever she did, simply because she was she and I was I.

"All right," I said. "But you're making a fool of me—insisting that I play this old fiddle. Well—I'll teach you a lesson!" And I drew the bow over the strings with a most appalling wail.

And with the unexpected swiftness of a steel trap closing on its victim, icy fingers locked about my wrist, and I knew very definitely that another and alien personality was guiding my arm and fingers! But there came likewise a swift certitude that if I behaved, no harm would ensue—to me, at least. So I let the thing have its way—and listened to such music as I had not believed could be played on any instrument devised by a mortal.

I wish that I could describe that music, but I do not know the right words. I doubt if they have been invented. It was wild, barbaric, savage, but likewise it was alluring, seductive, stealing away all inhibitions—too much of it would have corrupted the angels in heaven. I was almost in a stupor, intoxicated, like a hasheesh-eater in a drugged dream, spellbound, unable to break from the thralldom holding my will, drowning in rapture well-nigh unbearable.

Heldra suddenly blew out the big kerosene lamp standing on the table, leaving as sole illumination the rays from those four bronze lights standing in the corners.

Her superb body moved gracefully, slowly at first, then faster, into the intricate figure and pattern of a dance that was old when the world was young. . . .

With inward horror I knew the why and wherefore of that entire ceremonial; knew I'd been be-cozened and be-japed; yet knew, likewise, that it was too late for interference. I could not even speak. I could but watch, while some personality alien to my body played maddeningly on my fiddle, and the 'niece' I loved danced a dance deliberately planned to seduce a man who hated and feared the dancer—and for what devilish purpose I could well guess!

I saw the light-rays converge on her alluring, statuesque body, saw them apparently pass through her and impinge on the surface of that black, sullen, octagonal Hel-stone, and be greedily swallowed up, until the dull, black surface glowed like a rare black Australian opal; and ever the dancing of the witch-girl grew more alluring, more seductive, more abandoned. And I knew why Heldra was thus shamefully—shamelessly, rather—conducting! She had read Michael Commnenus and his character very accurately; knew that his soul had recognized her hatred for him, and feared her—and that her one chance to get him in her clutches lay in inflaming his senses . . . and she'd even told me the properties of that most damnable Hel-stone!

Wilder and faster came the music, and swifter and still more alluring grew the rhythmic response as Heldra's lovely body swayed and spun and swooped and postured; until ultimately her waving arms brought her fluttering hands, in the briefest of touches, into contact with the tiny brooch at her waist and the filmy robe was swept away in a single gesture that was faithfully recorded on the sullen surface of the Hel-stone.

Instantly the dancer stopped as if petrified, her arms outstretched as in invitation, her regal head thrown back, showing the long smooth white column of her throat, her clear, half-closed, sapphire-blue eyes a-gleam with subtle challenge. . . .

The uncanny music died in a single sighing, sobbing whisper, poison-sweet . . . the clutching, icy fingers were gone from my wrist . . . my first coherent thought was: Had that spell been directed at me, the old adage anent "old fools" would have been swiftly justified!

And I knew that to all intents and purposes, Michael Commnenus was sunk!

Just the same, I was furious. Heldra had gone too far, and I told her so, flatly. I pointed out in terms unmistakable that what she planned was murder, or worse; and that this was modern America wherein witchcraft had neither place nor sanction, and that I'd be no accessory to any such devilishness as she was contriving. Oh, I made myself and my meaning plain.

And she stood and looked at me with a most injured expression. She made me feel as if I'd wantonly struck a child across the face in the midst of its innocent diversions!

"I don't actually care if the devil flies off with Michael Commnenus," I concluded wrathfully, "but I won't have him murdered by you while you're living here, posing as my niece! No doubt it's quite possible for you to evade any legal consequences by disappearing, but what of me? As accessory, I'd be liable to life imprisonment, at the least!"

Her face lightened as by magic, and her voice was genuinely regretful, and in her eyes was a light of sincere love. She came to me and wrapped her white arms about my neck, murmuring terms of affectionate consolation.

"Poor dear Uncle John! Heldra was thoughtless—wicked me! And I might have involved you in serious trouble? I am ashamed! But the fate laid upon me by the Norns is heavy, and I may not evade it, even for you, whom I love. Tell me," she demanded suddenly, "if I should destroy the vile earthworm without any suspicion attaching to you, or to me, would you love me as before, even knowing what I had done?"

"No!" I fairly snarled the denial. I wanted it to be emphatic.

She smiled serenely, and kissed me full on my lips.

"I never thought to thank a mortal for lying to me, but now I do! Deep in your heart I can read your true feeling, and I am glad! But now"—and her tone took on a sadness most desolate—"I regret to say that on the morrow I leave you. The lovely garments you gave me, and the trunks containing them, I take with me, as you would not wish that I go empty-handed. Nor will I insult you, O Jarl Wulf, by talk of payment.

"When I am gone, you will just casually mention that I have returned to my home, and the local gossips will not suspect aught untoward. And soon I shall be forgotten, and no one will suspect, or possibly connect you, or me, with what inevitably must happen to that spawn of the Commneni.

"But of this be very sure: Somewhere, sometime, you and I shall be together again . . ." Her voice broke, she kissed me fiercely on the lips, then tenderly on both cheeks, then lastly, with a queer reverence, on my furrowed old brow. Then she turned, went straight to her room, shut the door, and I heard the click of the key as she locked herself in, for the first time during her stay in my house . . . Next morning, as she'd planned, she departed on the first train cityward. I'd given her money enough for all her requirements—more, indeed, than she was willing to take at first, declaring that she intended selling some few of her jewels.

And with her departure went all which made life worth living. . . .

Heavily I dragged my reluctant feet back to the empty shell of a cottage which until then had been an earthly paradise to an old man—and the very first thing I laid eyes on was that accursed Hel-stone, lying on the living-room table.

I picked it up, half minded to shatter it to fragments, but an idea seized me. I bore it down-cellar, where semi-darkness prevailed, and the Hel-stone glowed softly with its witch-light, showing me the loveliness of her who had departed from me. And I pressed the cold octagon to my lips, thankful that she'd left me the thing as a feeble substitute for her presence. Then I turned and went back upstairs, found an old ivory box of Chinese workmanship, and placed the Hel-stone therein, very carefully, as a thing priceless.

I went to bed early that night. There was no reason to sit up.

But I could not sleep. I lay there in my bed, cursing the entire line of Commneni, root, trunk and branch, from the first of that ilk whom history records to this latest scion, or "spawn," as Heldra had termed him.

Around midnight, being still wakeful, I arose, got the Hel-stone and sat in the darkness—and gradually became aware that I was not alone! Looking up, I saw her standing in a witch-glow of phosphorescent light. I knew at once that it was not Heldra in person, but her "scin-loecca" or "shining double," a "sending," and that it was another of her witcheries.

"But even this is welcome," I thought. Then I felt her thought expressed through that phantasmal semblance of her own gorgeous self—and promptly strove, angrily, to resist her command. Much good it did me! Utterly helpless, yet fully cognizant of my actions, but oddly assured that about me was a cloak of invisibility—the "glamyr" of the ancient Alrunas—I dresssed, took the Hel-stone, and passed out into the night.

Straight to the cottage of Commnenus I went, pawed about under the door-step, and planted there the Hel-stone; then, still secure in the mystic glamor, I returned to my own abode. And no sooner had I seated myself in my chair for a smoke, than I realized fully the utter devilishness of that witch from out the wintry seas whom I had taken into my home and had sponsored as my "niece" in the eyes of the world.

Right then I decided to go back and get that Hel-stone, and smash it—and couldn't do it! I got sleepy so suddenly that I awoke to find that it was broad daylight, and nine-thirty a. m. And from then on, as regularly as twilight came, I could only stay awake so long as I kept my thoughts away from that accursed Hel-stone; wherefore I determined that the thing could stay where it was until it rotted, for all me! Then Commnenus came along the beach late one afternoon. He raised his hat in his Old World, courtly fashion, and tried to make some small talk. I grunted churlishly and ignored him. But finally he came out bluntly with:

“Professor Craig, I know your opinion of me, and admit it is to some extent justifiable. I seem to have acquired the reputation of being a Don Juan. But I ask you to believe that I bitterly regret that—now! Yet, despite that reputation, I’d like to ask you a most natural question, if I may.”

I nodded assent, unprepared for what was coming, yet somehow assured it would concern Heldra. Nor was I at all disappointed, for he fairly blurted out:

“When do you expect Miss Helstrom to return, if at all?”

I was flabbergasted! That is the only word adequate. I glared at him in a black fury. When I could catch my breath I demanded:

“How did even you summon up the infernal gall to ask me that?”

His reply finished flattening me out.

“Because I love her! Wait”—he begged—“and hear me out, please! Even a criminal is allowed that courtesy.” Then as I nodded grudgingly, he resumed:

“The first time I saw her, something deep within me shrank away from her with repulsion. Still, I admired her matchless beauty. But of late, since her departure, there is not a night I do not see her in my mind’s eye, and I know that I love her, and hope that she will return; hence my query.

“I will be frank—I even hope that she noticed me and read my admiration without dislike. Perhaps two minds can reach each other—sometimes. For invariably I see her with head thrown back, her eyes half closed, and her arms held out as if calling me to come to her. And if I knew her whereabouts I’d most certainly go, nor would I be ‘trifling,’ where she is concerned. I want to win her, if possible, as my wife; and an emperor should be proud to call her that.”

“Very romantic,” I sneered. “But, Mr. Woman-Chaser, I cut my eye-teeth a long while before you were born, and I’m not so easily taken in. The whereabouts of my niece are no concern of yours. So get away from me before I lose my temper, or I'll not be answerable for my actions. Get!"

He went! The expression of my face and the rage in my eyes must have warned him that I was in a killing humor. Well, I was. But likewise, I was sick with fear. What he'd just told me was sufficient to sicken me—the Hel-stone had gotten in its damnable work. My very soul was aghast as it envisioned the inevitable consequences. . . .

An idea obsessed me, and I needed the shades of night to cloak my purpose. Aimlessly I wandered from room to room in my cottage, and finally drifted into the room which had been Heldra's. Still aimlessly I pulled open drawer after drawer in the dresser, and in the lowest one I heard a faint metallic clink.

The four antique bronze lamps were there. I shrewdly suspected she had left them there as means of establishing contact with her, should need arise. I examined them, and found, as I'd hoped, that they were filled.

Around ten o'clock I placed those lamps in the four corners of the living-room, and lighted them, precisely as I'd seen Heldra do. Then I tried my talents at making an invocation.

"Heldra! Heldra! Heldra!" I called. "I, John Craig, who gave you shelter at your need, call to you now, wheresoever you be, to come to me at my need!"

The four lights went out, yet not a breath of air stirred in the room. A faintly luminous glow, the witch-light, ensued; and there she stood, or rather, the scin-loecca, her shining double! But I knew that anything I might say to it would be the same as if she were there in the flesh.

"Heldra," I beseeched that witch-lighted simulacrum, "by the love you gave me, as Ragnar loved Jarl Wulf Red-Sword, I ask that you again enshroud me with the mantle of invisibility, the 'glamyr,' and allow me to lift that accursed Hel-stone from where you compelled me to conceal it. Let me return it to you, at any place you may appoint, so that it can do no more harm.

"Already that poor bewitched fool is madly in love with you, because the radiations of that enchanted stone have saturated him every time he put foot on the door-step beneath which I buried it!

"Heldra, grant me this one kindness, and I will condone all sins you ever did in all your witch-life."

The shining wraith nodded slowly, unmistakably assenting to my request. As from a far distance I heard a faint whisper:

"Since it is your desire, get the Hel-stone, and bear it yourself to the sea-cave at the foot of the great cliff guarding the north passage into the harbor. Once you have borne it there, its work, and yours, are done.

"And I thank you for saying that you will condone all I have ever done, for the burden of the past is heavy, and your words have made it easier to bear."

The shining wraith vanished, and I went forth into the darkness. Straight to the house where I'd hidden the Hel-stone I betook myself, felt under the step, found what I sought, took it with an inward prayer of gratitude that because of Heldra's "glamyr" I had not been caught at something questionable in appearance, and started up the beach.

The tide was nearly out; so I walked rapidly, as I had some distance to go, and the sea-cave Heldra had designated could not be entered at high tide, although once within, one was safe enough and could leave when the entrance was once more exposed.

I entered the cave believing that I'd promptly be rid of the entire mess, once and for all. But there was no one there, and the interior of the cave was as dark as Erebus. I lit a match, and saw nothing. The match burned out. I fumbled for another—a dazzling ray from a flashlight blinded me for a moment, then left my face and swept

the cave. A hated voice, suave yet menacing, said:

"Well, Professor Craig, you may now hand me whatever it was that you purloined from under my door-step!"

An extremely business-like automatic pistol was aimed in the exact direction of my solar plexus—and the speaker was none other than Michael Commnenus!

Very evidently the mystic "glamyr" had failed to work that time. And I was in a rather nasty predicament.

Then, abruptly, Heldra came! She looked like an avenging fury, emerging out of nowhere, apparently, and the tables were turned. She wore a dark cloak or long mantle draped over her head and falling to her feet.

Her right hand was outstretched, and with her left hand she seized the Hel-stone from my grasp. She pointed one finger at Commnenus, and did not even touch him; yet had she smote with an ancient war-hammer the effect would have been the same.

"You dog, and son of a long line of dogs!" her icy voice rang with excoriating virulence. "Drop that silly pistol! Drop it, I say!"

A faint blue flicker snapped from her extended finger—the pistol fell from a flaccid hand. Commnenus seemed totally paralyzed. Heldra's magic held him completely in thralldom . . . I snapped into activity and scooped up the gun.

"Followed me, did you?" I snarled.

"Wait, Jarl Wulf!" Heldra's tone was frankly amused. "No need for you to do aught! Mine is the blood-feud, mine the blood-right! And ere I finish with yon Michael Commnenus, an ancient hate will be surfeited, and an ancient vengeance, too long delayed, will be consummated."

"Heldra," I began, for dread seized me at the ominous quality of her words, "I will not stand for this affair going any farther! I—"

"Be silent! Seat yourself over there against the wall and watch and hear, but move not nor speak again, lest I silence you for ever!"

A force irresistible hurled me across the cave and set me down, hard, on a flat rock. I realized fully that I was obeying her mandate—I couldn't speak, couldn't even move my eyelids, so thoroughly had she inhibited any further interference on my part.

Paying no further attention to Commnenus for the moment, she crossed over to me, bent and kissed me on my lips, her sapphire eyes laughing into my own blazing, wrathful eyes. "Poor dear! It is too bad, but you made me do it. I wanted you to help me all the way through this tangled coil—but you have been so difficult to manage! Yet in some ways you have played into my hands splendidly. Yes, even to bringing the Hel-stone back to me—and I would not care to lose that for a king's ransom. And I put it into yon fool's head to be wakeful tonight, and see you regain the Hel-stone, and follow you—and thus walk into my nice little trap.

"And now!"

She whirled and faced Commnenus. And for all that he was spell-bound, in his eyes I read fear and a ghastly foreknowledge of some dreadful fate about to be meted out to him at her hands. She picked up the flashlight he had dropped and extinguished it with the dry comment:

"We need a different light here—the Hel-light from Hela's halls!" And at her word, a most peculiar light pervaded the cave, and there was that about its luminance that actually affrighted. Again she spoke: "Michael Commnenus, you utterly vile worm of the earth! You know that your doom is upon you—but as yet you know not why. O beast lower than the swine! Harken and remember my words even after eternity is swallowed up in the Twilight of the Gods! You are a modern, and know not that the self, the soul, is eternal, undying, changing its body and name in every clime and period, yet ever the same soul, responsible for the deeds of its bodies. You have even prated of your soul—when in fact, you are the property of the soul!

"Watch, now!" She pointed to the cave entrance. "Behold there the wisps of sea-fog gathering; and gradually will come the rising tide. And on the curtain of that cold, swirling mist, behold the pictures of the past—a past centuries old; a past wherein your craven, treacherous soul sinned beyond all pardon!

"Look you, too, Jarl Wulf Red-Brand, so that in all the days remaining to you upon Earth, you may know that his doom was just, and that Heldra is but executing a merited penalty!

"And while the shuttles of the Norns weave the tapestry of the sin of this Cornmnenus, I will tell all the tale of his crimes.

"In Byzantium reigned the emperor, Alexander Commnenus. Secure his throne, guarded by the ponderous axes and the long swords of the Varangians, the splendid sons of the Norse-lands, who had gone a-viking. Trusted and loved were the Varangs by the emperor, and oft he boasted of their fidelity, swearing on the cross of Constantine that to the last man would his Varangs perish ere one would flinch a step from over-whelming foes, citing in proof their battle-cry:

"'Valhalla! Valhalla! Victory or Valhalla!'

"Into the harbor of the Golden Horn sailed the viking long-ship, the *Grettir*. Three noble brothers owned her—Thorfinn, Arvid, Sven. With them sailed their sister . . . her fame as an Alruna-maid, prophetess and priestess, was sung throughout the Norse-lands. No man so low but bore her reverence. Sin it was to cast eyes of desire on any Alruna, and the sister of the three brothers was held especially holy. Between the hands of the Emperor Alexander Commnenus, the three brethren placed their hands, swearing fealty for a year and a day. Thirty fighting-men, their crew, followed wherever the three brothers led. And the great emperor, hearing of their war-fame from others of the Varangian guard, gave the brothers high place in his esteem, and held them nigh his own person.

"Their sister, the Alruna-maid, was treated as became her rank and holy repute. Aye! Even in Christian Byzantium respect and honor were shown her by the priests of an alien belief. But one man in Byzantium aspired more greatly than any other, Norseman or Byzantine, had ever dared.

"A Commnenus he, grand admiral of Byzantium's war fleet, nephew to the emperor, enjoying to the full the confidence and love of his imperial uncle. Notorious for his profligacy, he cast his libertine eyes on the Norse Alruna-maid, but with no thought of making her his wife. Nay! 'Twas only as his Leman he desired her.

". . . So, he plotted. . . .

"The three brothers, Thorfinn, Arvid, Sven, with their full crew, in the long-ship *Grettir* were ordered to sea to cruise against certain pirates harrying a portion of the emperor's coasts.

"Every man of the *Grettir's* crew died the deaths of rats—poison in the water-casks! . . . They died as no Norseman should die, brutes' deaths, unfit for Valhalla and the company of heroes who had passed in battle! And their splendid bodies, warped and distorted by pangs of the poison, were cast overside as prey for sharks, by two creatures of this grand admiral, whom he had sent with the three brothers as pilots knowing the coast. They placed the drug in the casks, they flung over the dead and dying, they ran the *Grettir* aground and set fire to her—but his was the command—and his the crime!"

And as Heldra told the tale, in a voice whose dreary tones made the recital seem even worse—the watching Commnenus and I saw clearly depicted on the curtain of the mist, each separate incident. . . . Heldra turned to the wildly glaring Michael.

"There was but one person in all Byzantium who knew the truth," she screamed in sudden frenzy. "I give back for a moment your power of speech. Say, O fool! Coward! Niddering! Who am I?" Abruptly she tore off the somber cloak and stood in all her loveliness, enhanced by every ornament she once had worn for my pleasure in beholding her thus arrayed.

A cry of unearthly terror broke from the staring Commnenus. His voice was a strangled croak as he gasped:

"The Alruna-maid, Heldra! The red-haired sea-witch—sister to the three brothers, Thorfinn, Arvid, Sven!"

"Aye, you foul dog! And me you took at night, after they sailed away, and me you shut up where my cries for aid could not be heard; and me you would have despoiled—me, the Alruna-maid, sworn to chastity! Me you jeered at and reviled, boasting of your recent crimes against all that the Norse-folk hold most sacred!

"Yet I escaped from that last dreadful dungeon wherein you immured me—how?

"By that magic known to such as I, I called upon the empress of the Underworld, Hela herself, and pledged her my service in return for indefinitely continued life, until I could repay you and avenge the heroes denied the joys of Valhalla—by you!

"And now—comes swiftly the doom I have planned for you . . . you who now remember!"

Heldra spoke truly. Swiftly it came! Sitting where I was, I saw it plainly, a great dragon-ship with round shields displayed along her gunwales, with a big square sail of crimson embroidered in gold, with long oars dipping and lifting in unison—in faint ghostly tones I could hear the deep-sea rowers chanting, "Duch! Hey! Sa-sa-sa! Hey-sa, Hey-sa, Hey-sa, Hey-sa!" and knew it for the time-beat rowing-song of the ancient vikings!

The whole picture was limned in the cold sea-fires from whence that terrible viking ghost-ship had risen with its crew of long-dead Norsemen who were not dead—the men too good for Hel, and denied Valhalla. . . .

Straight to the mouth of the cave came the ghost-ship, and its crew disembarked and entered. Heldra cried out in joyous welcome:

"Even from out of the deeps, ye heroes, one and all, have ye heard my silent summons, and obeyed the voice of your Alruna from old time! Now your waiting is at an end!

"Yonder stands the Commnenus. That other concerns ye not—but mark him well, for in a former life he was Jarl Wulf Red-Brand! See, on his left hand is still the old silver ring with its runes of Ragnar Wave-Flame!"

The ghost-vikings turned their dead eyes on me with a curious fixity. One and all, they saluted. Evidently, Jarl Wulf must have been somebody, in his time. Then ignoring me, they turned to Heldra, awaiting her further commands. Commnenus they looked at, fiercely, avidly.

Heldra's voice came, heavily, solemnly, with a curious bell-like tone sounding the knell of doom incarnate:

"Michael Commnenus! This your present body has never wrought me harm, nor has it harmed any of these. It is not with your body that we hold our feud. Wherefore, your body shall go forth from this cave as it entered—as handsome as ever, bearing no mark of scathe.

"But your niddering soul, O most accursed, shall be drawn from out its earthly tenement this night and given over to these souls you wronged, who now await their victim and their vengeance! And I tell you, Michael Commnenus, that what they have in store for you will make the Hades of your religion seem as a devoutly-to-be-desired paradise!" Heldra stepped directly before Commnenus. Her shapely white arms were outstretched, palms down, fingers stiffly extended. A queer, violet-tinged radiance streamed from her fingers, gradually enveloping Commnenus—he began to glow, as if he had been immersed and had absorbed all his body could take up. . . .

Heldra's voice took on the tone of finality:

"Michael Commnenus! Thou accursed soul, by the power I hold, given me by Hela's self, I call you forth from your hiding-place of flesh—come ye out!"

The living body never moved, but from out its mouth emerged a faint silvery-tinted vapor flowing toward the Alruna-maid, and as it came, the violet glow diminished. The accumulating silvery mist swirled and writhed, perceptibly taking on the semblance of the body from whence it was being extracted. There remained finally but a merest thread of silvery shimmer connecting soul and body. Heldra spoke beneath her breath:

"One of you hew that cord asunder!"

A double-bladed Norse battle-ax whirled and a ghostly voice croaked: "Thor Hulf!"

Thor, the old Norse war-god, must have helped, for the great ghost-ax evidently encountered a solid cable well-nigh as strong as tempered steel. Thrice the ax rose and fell, driven by the swelling thews of the towering giant wielding it, ere the silver cord was broken by the blade.

A tittering giggle burst from the lips of the present-day Michael Commnenus.

I realized with a sudden sickness at the pit of my stomach that an utterly mindless imbecile stood there, grinning vacuously!

"That Thing," Heldra said, coldly scornful as she pointed to the silvery shining soul, "is yours, heroes! Do with it as ye will!"

Two of the gigantic wraiths clamped their great hands on its shoulders. It turned a dull leaden-gray, the color of abject fear. Cringing and squirming, it was hustled aboard the ghostly dragon-ship. The other ghost-vikings went aboard, taking their places at the oars yet they waited. Heldra turned to me.

"Be free of the spell I laid upon you!" Her tone was as gentle as it had been in her sweetest moments while she dwelt in my home as my niece.

I gasped, rose and stretched. I wanted to be angry—and dared not. I'd seen too much of her hellish powers to risk incurring her displeasure. And reading my mind, she laughed merrily.

Then her cool, soft, white arms went about my neck, her wondrous sapphire eyes looked long and tenderly into mine—and I will not write the message I read in those softly shining orbs. Once again her silvery voice spoke:

"Jarl Wulf Red-Brand! John Craig! I am the grand-daughter of Ragnar Wave-Flame! And once I went a-viking with my three brothers, to far Byzantium. You know that tale. Now, once I said that Ragnar Wave-Flame never died. Also, I said that I had dived into her sea-cave and lain in her arms—and now I tell you the rest of that mystery: with her breath she entered this my body where ever since we have dwelt as one soul. I needed aid in seeking my vengeance, for it was after I'd escaped the clutches of the Commnenus, and had passed through adventures incredible while making my way back to the Norse-lands—and my spirit was very bitter. And when I sought her council, Ragnar helped.

"This now do I ask of you: Do you, as I have sometimes thought, love me as a man loves a maid? Reflect well, ere you answer, and recall what I once showed you in a mirror—I am older than you! So, knowing that, despite my witcheries of the long, bitter past, and those of tonight, would you take me, were you and I young once more?"

"By all the gods in Valhalla, and by all the devils in Hela's halls: yes!" My reply was given without need of reflecting, or counting cost.

"Then, in a day to come, you shall take me—I swear it!"

Full upon my mouth she pressed her scarlet lips, and a surging flame suffused my entire body. Yet it was life—not death. Against my chest I felt the pressure of her swelling breasts, and fires undreamable streamed from her heart to mine. Time itself stood still. After an eon or so she unwound her clinging arms from about my neck and turned away, and with never a backward glance she entered that waiting, ghostly dragon-ship. The oars dipped. . . .

"Juch! Hey! Sa-sa-sa! Hey-sa! Hey-sa! Hey-sa! Hey-sa!" and repeated . . . and again . . . until the faint, ghostly chant was swallowed by distance. . . .

I left the cave.

The driveling idiot who had been Michael Commnenus was already gone. Later, the gossip ran that he'd "lost his mind," and that his embassy had returned him to his own land. None ever suspected, or coupled me or my "niece" with his affliction. And he himself had absolutely no memory—had lost even his own name when his soul departed! But within a month, I sold my cottage, packed and stored all my belongings until I could find a new location, where I'd be totally unknown; and then I went away from where I had dwelt for years—and with urgent reason.

The fire with which Heldra had imbued me from her breath and breast was renewing my youth! My hair was shades darker, my wrinkles almost gone; my step was brisker, I looked to be nearer forty than almost sixty. So marked was the change that the villagers stared openly at what seemed at least a miracle . . . tongues were wagging . . . old superstitions were being revived and dark hints were being bandied about . . . So I finally decided to leave, and go where my altered appearance would cause no comment.

I wonder if—

# The Dancer in the Crystal

by Francis Flagg

## I

They who lived during that terrible time will never forget it—twenty-five years ago, when the lights went out.

It was in 1956.

All over the world, in the same hour, and practically at the same minute, electrical machinery ceased to function.

The youth of today can hardly realize what a terrible disaster that was for the people of the middle Twentieth Century. England and America, as well as the major nations of Europe, had just finished electrifying their railroads and scrapping the ponderous steam engines which did duty on some lines up until as late as the summer of 1954. A practical method of harnessing the tides and using their energy to develop electricity, coupled with the building of dams and the generating of cheap power through the labor of rushing rivers and giant waterfalls, and the invention of a device for broadcasting it by wireless as cheaply as it was generated, had hastened this electrification. The perfection of a new vacuum tube by the General Electric Company at Schenectady, in the United States, had made gas economically undesirable. The new method, by which it was possible to relay heat for all purposes at one-third the cost of illuminating gas, swept the various gas companies into oblivion. Even the steamers which plied the seven seas, and the giant planes that soared the air, received the power that turned their propellers, warmed their cabins and cooked their foods, in much the same fashion as did the factories, the railroads, and the private homes and the hotels ashore. Therefore when electricity ceased to drive the machines, the world stopped. Telegraph, telephone, and wireless communication ceased. Country was cut off from country, city from city, and neighborhood from neighborhood. Automobiles broke down; streetcars and electric trains refused to run; powerhouses were put out of commission; and at night, save for the flickering light of what lanterns, candles, and oil lamps could be resurrected, cities, towns, and hamlets were smothered in darkness.

I have before me the records of that time. It was ten and eleven o'clock in London, Paris, Berlin, and other continental cities when it happened. Restaurants, theaters, hospitals and private homes were plunged into darkness. Mighty thoroughfares that a moment before had glittered and glowed with thousands of lights and wheeling signs became gloomy canyons where people at first paused, questioned, and later plunged through in terrified clamor. Various men who later wrote their impressions for newspapers and magazines say that the thing which shook their nerves the most was the sudden silence which prevailed when all traffic ceased—that, and five minutes later the maddened cries and groans and curses of men and women fighting like wild beasts to escape from crowded restaurants and theaters.

People coursed through the streets shouting to one another that the power-houses had been blown up, that an earthquake had shaken them down. The most absurd statements were made, tossed from mouth to mouth, and added to the general bewilderment and panic. On the street corners religious fanatics suddenly sprang up, proclaiming that the end of the world had come, and that the sinners had better repent of their sins before it was too late. In the hospitals, nurses and doctors found themselves working under a frightful handicap. Gruesome tales are told of doctors caught in the midst of emergency operations. Because of the darkness it was impossible properly to attend the sick. Whenever available, candles, oil lamps and lanterns were pressed into service; but there were pitifully few of these to be had, and nowhere to turn for more. Telephone wires were dead, and automobiles, cars and buses stalled. To add to the horror, fire broke out in various places. There was no way of ringing in an alarm about them, and the fire apparatus could not have responded if there had been. So the fires spread. And the people of those neighborhoods where the flames leapt to heaven, at last had light—the light of their burning homes.

And then in the midst of all this horror and tumult the denizens of the dark, festering spots of the city crept forth. They swarmed from the filthy alleys and from the dives of the professional criminal, furtive-eyed, predatory; and houses were robbed, men killed, and women assaulted. The police were powerless to act; their mobility was gone; burglar alarms did not warn; and the city lay like a giant Samson shorn of its strength.

So that night passed, not for one city alone, but for hundreds of cities!

## II

While all this was happening in the old world, chaos gripped the new.

Across the Atlantic, in the eastern cities of the United States and Canada, and as far west as Montreal and Chicago, the wheels stopped going at that hour when the workers began to pour forth from the factories and shops, and when the late shopping crowds were thronging the trains and the subways. On the surface cars and on the streets there was, of course, no immediate alarm. Moving-picture and vaudeville houses opened wide their doors, raised the blinds on their windows, and evacuated their patrons in good order. But underground in the various tubes and subways it was a different matter. Hundreds of cars bearing thousands of passengers were stalled in stifling blackness. Guards labored heroically to still the rising hysteria and panic. For perhaps fifteen or twenty minutes—in some cases as long as half an hour—they managed to maintain a species of order. But the great pumps and fans that usually circulated fresh air through the tunnels were no longer functioning. When the foul air fogged the lungs, the passengers went mad. Sobbing and cursing and praying, they fought to escape from the cars, as at the same moment the people of Berlin, Paris and London were fighting to escape from restaurants and theaters. They smashed the windows of the coaches, and in wriggling through them impaled the flesh of their bodies, their hands and faces, on jagged slivers of glass. They trampled each other under foot and flowed in terrified mobs along the right of way, searching madly for exits. In New York alone ten thousand of them perished. They bled to death, were crushed, or died of heart-failure and suffocation.

Above ground, the streets and avenues were thronged with millions of human beings trying to get home on foot. For hours dense crowds of workers, shoppers and businessmen filled the highways and byways. Here again panic was caused by the crashing planes. In Montreal the Royal Dominion air liner, *Edward VII*, on route on a non-stop flight from Halifax to Vancouver with four hundred passengers, fell from a height of three thousand feet onto Windsor Station, killing her own passengers and crew, and blotting out the lives of hundreds of people who were in the station at the time. In New York, Boston and Chicago, where the then new magnetic runabouts were making their initial appearance, hundreds of airplanes plunged to the ground, killing and maiming not only their passengers, but the men, women and children on whom they fell. "It was," states an eye-witness in a book he later wrote, called *The Great Debacle*, "a sight fit to appal the stoutest heart. Subway exits were disgorging ghastly mobs of clawing people; a crashing plane had turned a nearby

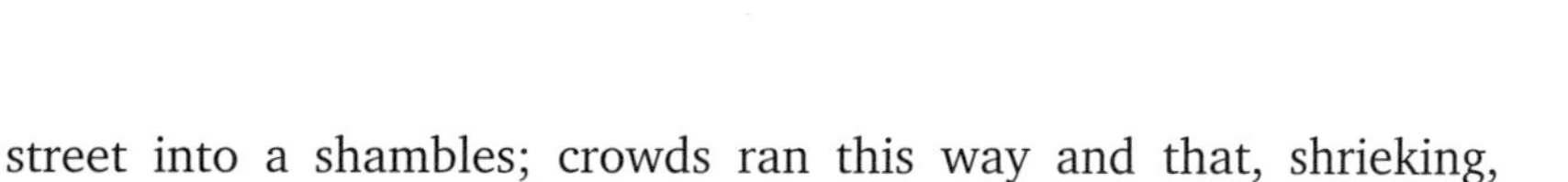


street into a shambles; crowds ran this way and that, shrieking, praying. Everywhere was panic."

Panic indeed! Yet the records show that what they could do, the police and fire departments did. Mounted policemen were utilized to carry candles and oil lamps to hospitals, to scour the countryside for every available horse, and to ride through the city in an effort to calm the people. Firemen were marched to various points of vantage with axes and chemical containers, to combat any fire that might break out. But in the aggregate these precautions amounted to nothing. Whole hospitals passed the night in darkness; patients died by the hundreds; the flames of myriad fires lit up the sky; and rumors ran from mouth to mouth adding to the terror and chaos.

America, screamed the mobs, was being attacked by a foreign power. The power-houses had been rendered useless by a powerful magnet. There had been a terrible storm down south; all South America was sinking; North America would go next. No one knew anything; everyone knew something. Nothing was too wild or absurd for millions to believe. Deprived of their accustomed sources of information, the inhabitants became a prey to their own fancies and the disordered fancies of others. Religious fanatics by the light of huge bonfires preached the second coming of Christ and the destruction of the world. Thousands of hysterical people prostrated themselves on the hard street pavements, babbling, weeping, praying. Thousands of others looted wine and strong drinks from the cellars of hotels and cafés and reeled drunken through the streets, adding to the din and the panic. Nor did daylight bring much relief. For some obscure reason, all over Europe, Asia, and America, during the hours of daylight, the sky was strangely dulled. Seemingly the sun shone with all its usual splendor, but the air was perceptibly darkened. Why this should be so, not even the scientists could tell. Yet even under the light of what millions of people on earth believed to be their last day, human wolves came out of their dens and prowled through the cities, sacking stores and private homes, blowing open safes, and killing and robbing with impunity. The day that succeeded the night was more horrible than the night that preceded the day, because hundreds of thousands of people who had slept through the hours of darkness awoke and joined their fellows on the streets, and because there is something terrible about a big city in which no cars run and no factory whistles blow, in which the machine has died.

And while the cities and the inhabitants thereof were given over to madness and destruction, tragedy took its toll of the skies and stalked the seas. The aircraft of the world were virtually wiped out. Only those escaped which were at rest in their hangars, or which by some miracle of navigation glided safely to earth. Hardly a year passes now but that on some wild mountain peak, or in a gloomy canyon or the heart of the Sahara, fragments of those airships are found. Nor did ocean-going vessels suffer less. In the space of twenty hours, two thousand ships of all classes and tonnage met with disaster—disaster that ultimately wiped out the great firm of Lloyds, in London, and a host of lesser insurance companies. Fifteen hundred steamers vanished, never to be heard of more, thirty-five of these being giant passenger boats carrying upward of twenty thousand passengers. Of the other five hundred ships, some were dashed to pieces on inhospitable coasts, others drifted ashore and broke up, and the remainder were abandoned at sea. The fate of the missing steamers may be partly inferred from what happened to the *Olympia* and the *Oranta*. This is taken from the account of the second officer of the former ship:

"The night was clear and starry, a heavy sea running. We were forging full speed ahead about two hundred miles off the Irish coast. Because of our electrically controlled gyroscope, however, the ship was as steady as a rock. A dance was being given in both the first and second class ballrooms, the music for them being supplied by the Metropolitan dance orchestra of London. In the third class theater a television moving-picture was being shown. Couples were walking or sitting on the promenade decks as, though a stiff breeze was blowing, the night was warm. From the bridge I could see the *Orania* coming toward us. She made a wonderful sight, her portholes gleaming tier on tier, and her deck lights glowing and winking, for all the world looking like a giant glowworm or a fabulous trireme. Doubtless, to watchers on her bridge and decks, we presented the same glorious sight, because we were sister ships, belonging to the same line, and of the same build and tonnage. All the time she was coming up I conversed with the first officer on her bridge by means of our wireless phone; and it was while in the midst of this conversation, and while we were still a mile apart and he was preparing (so he said) to have the wheel put over so as to take the *Orania* to starboard of us that, without warning, her lights went out.

"Hardly crediting my eyes, I stared at the spot where a moment before she had been. 'What is the matter with you?' I called through my phone, but there was no answer; and even as I realized that the phone had gone dead, I was overcome with the knowledge that my own ship was plunged in darkness. The decks beneath me were black. I could hear the voices of passengers calling out, some in jest and others in rising alarm, questioning what had happened. 'I can't get the engine room; the ship doesn't answer her helm,' I said, facing the captain, who had clambered to the bridge. 'Quick, Mr. Crowley!' he cried. 'Down with you and turn out the crew. Put men at every cabin door and stairway and keep the passengers off the decks.' His voice thundered into the microphone, which repeated his words through loud-speaking devices in every saloon, cabin, and on every deck of the ship—or should have so repeated them if the instruments had been functioning. 'There is no need for alarm. A little trouble to the engines, and incidentally to the dynamos, has caused the lights to go out. I beg of you to be calm. In a half-hour everything will be fixed.' But even as I rushed to obey his orders, even as his crisp voice rang out on the night-air, I saw the enormous dark bulk bearing down on us, and the heart leapt in my throat. It was the *Orania*, helpless, without guidance, as were we ourselves, rushing ahead under the momentum acquired by her now stilled engines.

"She struck us, bow on, to one side, shearing through steel plates as if they were so much cheese. At that terrific impact, in the dark and the gloom, all order and discipline were swept away. Something had happened to the gyroscopes, and the ships were pitching and tossing, grinding and crashing against each other, our own ship settling by the head, the stern rising.

"Then ensued a terrible time. The night became hideous with the clamor of terrified voices. Maddened passengers fought their ways to the decks, and to the boats. Crowded boats went down into the surging waves bow on or stern first, spilling their human freight into the sea. Hundreds of passengers, believing that the steamers would at any moment sink, leapt overboard with life-preservers, and in nearly all cases were drowned. All this in the first thirty minutes. After that the panic ebbed; it turned into dull despair. The crews of both steamers, what could be rallied of them, began to control the situation.

"Morning found the *Orania* practically intact, only making water in her No. 1 compartment. The *Olympia* forward compartments were all flooded, taking her down at the head, but the rear eight still held intact, and as long as they did so she could not sink. If the passengers had, from the beginning, remained calm and tractable, hardly a life need have been lost."

The second officer of the *Olympia* goes on to point out that both the giant liners had been thoroughly equipped with the most modern of electromechanical devices for use in emergencies; that they carried twin power-receiving engines; that they were electrically steered; and that from the pilot-house and the bridge communication could be had and orders and instructions given, to crew and passengers in every part of the ships. It was, he points out, the sudden and startling going out of the lights, and the totally unexpected breakdown of all machinery, which precipitated the tragedy, and not any negligence on the part of the officers and the crews.

Such is the story of one marine disaster; but the records are full of similar accounts, hundreds of them, which it is needless to set down here.

## III

On the Pacific coast, especially in the cities of Los Angeles and San Francisco, better order was maintained than in the big cities of the Middle West and the East. Panic there was loss of life and damage to property both from fire and theft, but not on so colossal a scale. This was due to the fact that the authorities had several hours of daylight in which to prepare for darkness, and because in the two cities mentioned there were no subways to speak of. In the downtown districts clerks and businessmen were advised to stick to their offices and stores. Policemen, mounted and afoot, were sent to the residential districts and to the factories. Instead of allowing the workers to scatter, they formed them into groups of twenty, deputized, armed, and as nearly as possible set to patrolling the streets of the neighborhoods in which they lived. These prompt measures did much to avert the worst features of the horrors which swept New York and Chicago and the cities of Europe and Asia. But in spite of them the hospitals knew untold suffering, whole city blocks were destroyed by flames, religious frenzy ran high, and millions of people passed the hours of darkness in fear and trembling.

I was twenty-two at that time, living in Altadena, which is a suburb of Pasadena, about twenty miles from Los Angeles, and trying to write. That morning I had taken a book and a lunch and climbed

up the Old Pole Road to the top of Mount Echo, intending to return by the cable car which for years has operated from the purple depths of Rubio Canyon to the towering peak. I reached the top of the mountain after a steep climb, ate my lunch on the site of the old Lowe Observatory, and then became absorbed in my book.

The first inkling I had that something was wrong was when the light darkened. "It's clouding over," I thought, looking up, but the sky overhead was perfectly clear, the sun particularly bright.

Not a little disturbed in mind, and thinking, I must admit, of earthquakes, I strolled over to where a group of Mexican section workers, under the supervision of a white boss, had been doing some track repairing. The Mexicans were gesticulating and pointing to the cities and the countryside rolling away far beneath us. Now usually on a clear, sunny day there is a haze in the valley and one can not see for very many miles in any direction. But on this day there was an unwonted clarity in the air. Everything on which we gazed was sharply etched—no blurring, no fogging of lines. The houses stood out starkly; so did the spires of churches and the domes of public buildings. Though it was miles away to the westward, the mighty tower of the Los Angeles City Hall could be plainly seen. The light had darkened, yes; but the effect was that of gazing through slightly tinted glasses.

"What do you think it means?" I asked the track boss. But before he could make a reply, a Mexican cried out volubly, pointing one shaking hand up the steep ridge which rose behind us and crossing himself rapidly with the other.

It was an awe-inspiring sight on which we gazed. Over Mount Lowe a luminous, dancing light was growing. I did not know it then, but as far east as Denver and Omaha, and as far south as St. Louis and Galveston, men saw that light. Seen from the western cities of Calgary and Edmonton in Canada it was a pillar of blue flame growing out of the earth and, as the hours passed, mounting higher and higher into the heavens. Millions of eyes from all over the United States and the Dominion fearfully and superstitiously turned toward that glow. As night deepened upon the Pacific coast, the inhabitants of Southern California saw the sky to the north of them cloven asunder by a leaping sword. No wonder millions of people thought that the heavens had opened and Christ was coming.

But before night I had descended the steep slope of Mount Echo and walked the trackway into Altadena. Women and men called to me from doorways and wanted to know if there was a forest fire farther back in the hills. I could give them no answer. On Lake Avenue I saw the automobiles, street-cars, and motor-busses stranded.

"What is the matter?" I asked a conductor.

"I don't know," he said. "There isn't any power. They say all the power plants and machinery have stopped. A man rode through from downtown a few minutes ago and told us so."

I walked on into Pasadena. Everything was tied up. The streets were jammed with cars and people. Owing to the state ordinance which made it a penal offense for planes to fly over any California city—the air routes were so arranged, and the landing-stations and fields outside the cities, access to them being had by fast electric trains—the horror of airships falling on crowded city streets and on residences was entirely averted. People spoke, however, of having seen a huge air liner and some smaller pleasure planes plunging to earth to the west of them, turning over and over; and afterward I learned that the New York–Los Angeles special, which had just taken to the air, had crashed into an orchard with a terrible loss of life.

I went no farther than Madison Street on Colorado Boulevard and turned back. It was ominous to look from the windows and porches of the big house that night and see the city black and formless beneath us. Usually the horizon to the west and south was illuminated for thirty miles around. Now, save for the dull glare of several fires, the darkness was unbroken.

Everything that happened that night is printed indelibly on my memory. Far off, like the sound of surf beating on a rocky shore, we could hear the voice of the mob. It rose and fell, rose and fell. And once we heard the crackle of what we took to be machine-gun fire. In the Flintridge district, I heard later, houses were sacked and looted. Some men defending their homes were murdered and several women badly treated. But in Altadena, up in the foothills, no one suffered any violence. Only once were we alarmed by a procession marching up Lake Avenue, bearing torches and chanting hymns. It was a body of religious fanatics, Holy Rollers, men, women, and children, on their way to Mount Wilson, the better to wait the advent of Jesus. We could hear them shouting and singing, and in the flickering light of the torches, see them frothing at the mouth. They went by, and after that, save for a patrol from the sheriff's office, we saw no one until morning.

Dawn came, but if anything the tension and terror grew greater. All night the threatening scimitar of light over the mountains had grown taller and taller—one could see it literally growing—and the sinister brightness of it radiated like molten steel, nor did the coming of daylight dim its radiance.

None of us had slept during the night; none of us had thought of sleep. Haggard-faced we greeted the dawn, and with despair in our hearts realized that the light of day was perceptibly dimmer than it had been the day before. Could this actually be the end of the world? Were those poor fanatics who had gone by in the night right, and were the heavens opening, as they said? These, and more, were the thoughts that ran through my mind. Then—came the end!

It was 6 p. m. in London, 1 p. m. in New York, and 10 a. m. on the coast when it happened. Millions of people saw the pillar of light waver. For one pregnant moment it grew red-hot, with the crimson redness of heated iron. From its lofty summit, jagged forks of lightning leapt across the heavens and blinded the sight of those that watched. Then it vanished, was gone; and a few minutes after its going the street lights came on, the day brightened, telephone bells rang, wheels turned, and the twenty or so hours of terror and anarchy were ended!

## IV

What had been the cause of it all? No one knew. Learned men puzzled their heads over the problem. Scientists were baffled for an adequate answer. Many explanations were advanced, of course, but none of them held water. For a while there was a tendency on the part of various governments to suspect one another of having invented and utilized a fiendish machine for the undoing of rival nations. However, this suspicion was speedily dropped when it was realized how world-wide had been the nature of the disaster. Dr. LeMont of the Paris Astronomical League advanced the theory that the spots on the sun had something to do with the phenomenon; Doolittle of the Royal Academy of Science in London was of the opinion that the Cosmic Ray discovered by Millikan in 1928 was responsible; while others not so highly placed in the world of science as these two outstanding celebrities suggested anything from a dark comet, a falling meteor, to disturbances in the magnetic centers of the earth. The *Encyclopedia Britannica*, twenty-one years after the disaster which nearly wrecked civilization and perhaps the world, quotes the above theories in detail, and many more besides, but winds up with the assertion that nothing authentic as to the cause of the tragedy of 1956 has ever been forthcoming. This assertion is not true. In the fall of 1963 there was placed before the Royal Academy of Science in Canada evidence as to the origin of the great catastrophe sufficient to call forth an extended investigation on the part of that body.

Though eighteen years have passed since then, the results of that investigation have never been made public. I will not speculate as to the reason for that. In the interim a report was made of the matter to the Smithsonian Institution in Washington, to the Royal Academy of Science in London, and to the Paris Astronomical League in France—a report which these learned bodies chose to ignore. And what was the evidence the Royal Academy of Science in Canada investigated?

As I have already stated, I was in California in 1956 and lived through one phase of the great disaster. Three years later—in the summer of 1959—having broken into the pages of some of the better class magazines with my stories, I made a trip to western Canada for the purpose of writing a series of stories for a western journal. It was there, miles from any city and in the foothills of the Rockies, that I met and listened to the story of the dying recluse. He was a young man, I judged, not a whit older than myself, but in the last stages of consumption.

I came upon the ranch-house—a four-room cabin made of split logs and undressed stone—after a hard day's ride. I pitched my tent on the banks of a tumbling mountain stream about a quarter of a mile from the house, and gladly accepted the invitation of the comely young mistress of the place to take dinner with them that evening. She was, I gleaned, the sick man's sister. Her husband, now absent rounding up cattle, was proving up on an adjoining quarter section, having already done so on two others in his wife's and brother-in-law's names.

After dinner I sat on the wide veranda with the sick man, whose sleeping-porch I surmised it was, talking with him and smoking my pipe.

"Visitors are rare out this way," he said, "and an educated man a godsend."

I was surprised to find him a man of no little education himself.

"You went to college?" I hazarded.

"Yes, McGill. I took my B. A. And after that, two years of medicine."

Over the plains the sun had sunk in red splendor below the horizon and the sky was on fire with its reflected glory. Nearer in I saw a ragged black splotch on the billowing earth, burnt-looking, charred.

"A prairie fire," I not so much questioned as stated.

The invalid, propped up on his couch, followed my finger with his cavernous black eyes.

"No," he said. "No. That is where *it*—was."

"It?" I queried.

"Yes," he replied; what the papers called the pillar of fire."

Then I remembered, of course. The burnt splotch was the place where the terrible luminous glow, the cleaving sword I had seen over Mount Lowe, had had its source. I stared, fascinated.

"Nothing," said the man on the couch, "will grow there—since then. The soil has no life in it—no life. It is," he said faintly, "like ashes—black ashes."

Silence fell between us for many minutes. The shadows lengthened and the twilight deepened. It was mournful sitting there in the growing gloom, and I felt relieved when the woman turned on the light in the sitting-room and its cheerful rays flooded through the open windows and the doorway. Finally the invalid said:

"I was here at the time. My sister and her husband were absent on a visit to his folks in Calgary."

"It must have been a stupendous sight," I remarked for want of a better thing to say.

"It was hell," he said. "That's how I got this," tapping himself on the chest and bringing on a fit of coughing. "The air," he gasped; "it was hard on the lungs."

His sister came out and gave him some medicine from a black bottle.

"You mustn't talk so much, Peter; it isn't good for you," she admonished.

He waved an impatient hand, "Let be!" he said. "Let be! What difference does it make? In another day, another week—"

His voice trailed away and then picked up again on a new sentence.

"Oh, don't pity me! Don't waste your pity on the likes of me! If ever a wretch deserved his fate, I deserve mine. Three years now I've suffered the tortures of the damned. Not of flesh alone, but of mind. When I could still walk about, it wasn't so bad; but since I've been chained to this bed I've done nothing but think, think.... I think of the great disaster; of the hours of terror and despair known by millions of people. I think of the thousands and thousands of men, women and children trapped in subways and theaters, trampled to death, butchered, murdered. I visualize the hospitals full of the sick and the dying, the giant liners of the air and of the ocean crashing, colliding, going down into the sea; and I seem to hear the screams and the pitiful prayers for help of the maddened passengers. Tell me, what fate should befall the fiend who would loose such woe and misery on an unsuspecting world?"

"There, there," I said soothingly, thinking him delirious, judging his mind unhinged from too much morbid brooding. "It was frightful, of course, but no one could help what happened—no one."

But my words did not calm him. On the contrary they added to his excitement. "That isn't true," he gasped. "It isn't true. No, no, sister, I won't be still, I'm not raving! Give me a drop of brandy—so; and bring me the little cedar box from the cupboard over there."

She complied with his request.

"It's all written down and put away in here," he said, tapping the box. "Put away in here, along with the third crystal which came home in the saddle-bag of John's runaway horse."

His eyes were like two black coals fastened on my face.

"I've told no one," he said tensely "but I can't keep silent any longer. I must speak! I must!"

One of his feverish hands gripped my own. "Don't you understand?" he cried. "I'm the fiend who caused the great world disaster.

God help me! I, and one other!

"No, no," he said, correctly reading the look on my face, "I'm not crazy, I'm not raving. It is God's truth I'm telling you, and the evidence of it is in this cedar box. It began in Montreal when I was going to McGill University. The under-professor of physics there was a young French-Canadian by the name of John Cabot. He—"

A fit of coughing stopped his voice. His sister gave him a sip of water.

"Peter," she pleaded, "let it go for tonight. Tomorrow—"

But he shook his head. "I may be dead tomorrow. Let me talk now." His eyes sought mine. "Did you ever hear about the meteorite that fell back in Manitoba in 1954?"

"No."

"Nor about the seven crystals that were found in it?"

"I don't remember."

"Well, they were found," he said; "seven of them as large as grapefruit. There's nothing remarkable about finding crystals in a meteorite. That has been done before and since. But those seven crystals were not ordinary ones. They were perfectly rounded and polished, as if by hand. Nor was that all: at the core of each of them was a vibrant fluid, and in that fluid was a black spot—"

A spasm of coughing choked his utterance, and this time I joined with his sister in urging him to rest, but desisted when I saw that such advice, and any effort on my part to withdraw, only succeeded in adding to his painful excitement.

"A black spot," he gasped, "that danced and whirled and was never still. Don't try to stop me! I must tell you about it! The scientists of the world were all agog over them. Where, they asked, had the meteor come from, and what were the fluid and the spot at the center of each crystal? In the course of time the crystals were sent various places for observation and study. One went to England, another to France, two to Washington, while the remaining three stayed in Canada, finally coming to rest in the Museum of Natural Science in Montreal which is now under the jurisdiction of McGill University.

"It was during my first year at medical school that I entered the museum one afternoon, almost by accident. The sight of the crystals, newly exhibited, fascinated me. I could hardly tear myself away in time for a lecture.

"The next afternoon I came again. I watched the black spots dancing in their vibrant fluid. Sometimes they would whirl in the center of the liquid with monotonous regularity. Then suddenly they would dash at the walls which held them in and circle them with inconceivable speed. Was it my imagination, or did the specks take on shape or form? Were they prisoners forever beating their heads against the bars of a cell, seeking to be free? Engrossed in such thoughts I did not know that another had entered the museum until a voice addressed me.

"'So you have come under their spell, too, Ross.'

"I looked up with a start and recognized John Cabot. We knew each other, of course, because I had studied under him for two years.

"'They look so life-like, sir,' I replied. 'Haven't you noticed it?'

"'Perhaps,' he said quietly, 'they are life.'

"The thought stirred my imagination.

"'You know,' he went on, 'that there are scientists who claim life originally came to the earth from some other star, perhaps from outside the universe entirely. Maybe,' he said, 'it came, even as these crystals came, in a meteor.'"

The sick man paused and moistened his lips with water.

"That," he said, "was the beginning of the intimacy which sprang up between John Cabot and me. It was often possible for Cabot to take one of the crystals to his room, and then we would foregather there and ponder the mystery of it, Cabot was a sound teacher of physics, but he was more than that. He was a scientist who was also a speculative philosopher, which meant being something of a mystic. Have you ever studied mysticism? No? Then I can't tell you about that. Only from him and his speculations I struck fire. How can I describe it? Perhaps gazing in the crystal hypnotized us both. I don't know as to that. Only night and day both of us became eaten with an overwhelming curiosity.

"'What do the scientists say is inside the crystals?' I asked Cabot.

"'They don't say,' he replied. 'They don't know. A message from Mars perhaps, or from beyond the Milky Way.'

"From beyond the Milky Way," whispered the sick man. "Can't you see what that would mean to our imaginations?"

He beat the quilt that covered him with his hand.

"It meant," he said, "the forbidden. We dreamed of doing what the scientists of America and Europe said they hesitated to do for fear of the consequences—or for fear of destroying objects valuable to science. We dreamed of breaking the crystal!"

A big moth fluttered into the radius of light and the dying man followed it with his eyes. "That's what we were, Cabot and I, though we didn't know it: moths, trying to reach a searing flame."

By this time I was engrossed in his story. "What then?" I prompted.

"We stole the crystals! Perhaps you read about it at the time?"

I shook my head.

"Well, it was in all the papers."

I explained that in those days I had seldom seen a paper from one week's end to another. He nodded feebly.

"That accounts for it, then. The theft caused a sensation in university circles, and both Cabot and I were thoroughly questioned and searched. But we had been too clever!" The sick man laughed mirthlessly. "God help us! Too clever! What wouldn't I give now," cried Peter Ross bitterly, "if we had been discovered! But a malignant fate ordered otherwise. We were successful. During the holidays I took the crystal home with me, home, to these hills and plains. Later Cabot joined me."

He broke off for a moment as if exhausted.

"I wonder," he said, after a few minutes, "if I can make what we felt and thought clear to you. It wasn't just idle curiosity that was driving us. No! It was more than that. Out of the unknown itself had come a meteor with a message for mankind. Something stupendous was hidden in the cores of those crystals. Yet what had the scientists of the world done? They had contented themselves with weighing the crystals, looking at them under a microscope, photographing them, writing learned articles about them, and then putting them away on museum shelves! None of them—not one; or so it seemed to us—had had the courage to open a crystal. Their reasons—deadly germs, virulent forms of life, terrific explosions—we dismissed as cowardly vaporings. The time had come, we said, to investigate more thoroughly. God help us," whispered Peter Ross, "we blinded ourselves to what might be the consequences of our rash experiment! We eased our consciences with the reflection that we were safeguarding humanity from any danger by carrying it out in the wilderness, miles from any city or human habitation. If there were to be any martyrs, we thought egotistically, it would be us alone. We had, of course, no inkling of the terrible force we were about to loose.

"Early in the morning of the day of the disaster we rode from this place down there to the plains, down to where you saw that charred splotch. We had with us a portable outfit of chemical instruments. It was our intention to smash one of the crystals, catch the fluid in our test-tubes, isolate the black spot, and make an analysis of it and the liquid later. But we never did," he said; "we never did."

A cough rattled in his throat.

"It was Cabot who broke the crystal. Before noon, it was, but I'm not sure of the time. He knew how to do it; he had all the tools necessary. The crystal lay inside a metal container. I tell you there was something uncanny about it glimmering in the sun! The black spot was whirling madly, dashing itself with violence against the restraining walls as if it sensed that freedom was near.

"'Look at him,' said Cabot tensely. 'Look at him leaping and kicking. What a dancer! What a—in a minute now and he'll be out of that!"

"Perhaps it was the phrase; perhaps it was the masculine pronoun used in connection with the black spot; but suddenly I was afraid of the thing we would do. Fearful possibilities ran through my mind.

"'John,' I cried, stepping back several paces, 'John, don't!'

"But Cabot never heard me. His hand went up with the heavy hammer.

"Poor John! Nothing warned him—nothing stayed him!

"The blow came down. I heard the tinkling crash; then—

"'Oh my God!'

"It was Cabot's voice in a shrill scream of unutterable horror and agony. His bent figure straightened up, and from his hair and his outflung arms blue lights crackled and streamed, and all around his body a column of something shimmered and shifted and grew. So for a moment he postured; then he began to dance. I tell you he began to dance, not by any force or power that resided in his own limbs, but as if he were jerked or writhed about by an external agent. I saw what that agent was. It was the black spot! Out of the ground it rose like an evil jinnee and took on the form and shape of something monstrous, inhuman, horrible. It leapt and whirled; and yes, though I couldn't hear it, it sang and shouted. It was the nucleus of an increasing body of light. I felt searing heat scorch my cheeks and burn my throat with every breath I drew. More! I felt that streaming fingers of light were reaching out at me, clutching.

"With a sob of fear I turned and ran. Cabot's horse had broken loose and was running wildly across the plains. My own was plunging madly at the end of its picket rope. Somehow I mounted and fled, but after several miles of such flight my horse put its hoof in a prairie-dog hole and broke its leg, pitching me over its head.

"How long I lay dead to the world I don't know; but the long shadows were running eastward when I came to. The air was acrid and bitter. With fearful eyes I saw that the day was unaccountably dark and that the pillar of fire out on the plains had grown to immense proportions. Even as I gazed on it, it grew. Hour after hour it grew, adding to its circumference and height. From the four corners of the horizon, in mighty arches that dipped to a common center, flowed infinitesimal particles of what seemed golden dust. I know now that all the electricity was being sucked out of the air, darkening the day, blackening the night, and rendering all machinery useless. But then I knew only that the pillar of fire, the center to which those particles cohered, was drawing nearer and nearer to where I lay. For I could barely move, my feet seemed like lead, and there was a tight band round my chest.

"Perhaps I was delirious, out of my head; I do not know, but I got on my feet and walked and walked, and when I couldn't walk I crawled. Hours and hours I crawled, driven ahead by a growing horror of the nightmare that pursued me; yet when I stopped, exhausted, I was still far away from the foothills and the pillar of fire was nearer than ever. I could see the monstrous black thing inside of it dancing and whirling. My God! It was reaching out dark streamers of fire after me; it was calling out that it wanted me, that it would have me, that nothing this side of heaven or hell could keep it from me; and as it shot this implacable message into my senses, it grew bigger, it danced faster, and it came closer.

"Again I staggered to my feet and ran. Late night found me several miles below here, quenching my thirst at a spring of water which trickles from the side of a rock. I looked back, and the pillar of fire was now so high that it lost itself in the heavens. All around me played a livid light, a light that flung the shape of a gigantic dancing horror this way and that. Did I tell you that this light was like a pillar? Yes, it was like a pillar whose middle swelled out in a great arc; and I knew that I was doomed, that I could not escape, and swooning horror overcame me and I fell to the ground and buried my face in my hands.

"Hours passed—or was it only minutes? I cannot say. I could feel my body writhing, twisting. Every atom of my flesh was vibrating to an unnatural rhythm. I was crazy, yes, out of my head, delirious, but I swear to you that I heard John Cabot crying to me, imploring, 'For God's sake, break the crystal, break the crystal!' and I cried back into my huddled arms not speaking, yet screaming it, 'We broke the crystal! God help us! We broke the crystal!'

"Then suddenly it came to me that he meant the second crystal. Yes, yes, I understood. The fiendish thing out there on the plain was seeking, not me but its counterpart.

"The second crystal was in the knapsack still swung on my back. With insane fury I tore it out of its padded, protected housing and whirled it over my head. Filled with loathing of the terrible thing, I flung it from me as far as the strength of my arm would permit. Perhaps twenty yards away it crashed into a rock and was shattered to pieces. I saw the slivers of it glint and flash; then from the spot where it struck rose a column of light, and in the column of light was a whirling speck. Like its predecessor it grew and grew, and as it grew, receded from me in the direction of the mightier pillar whirling and calling. How can I tell you of the weird dance of the evil ones? They sang to each other, and I know the song they sang, but I cannot tell it to you because it was not sung in words.

"At what hour they came together, whether it was day or night, I do not know. Only I saw them merge. With their coming together the terrible power that was sucking in the world's electrical forces to one gigantic center became neutralized. The heavens split open as the bolts of lightning devastated the sky. Through the rent firmament I saw a black shape cleave its way. Whatever had been in the two crystals was leaving the earth, was plunging through the Milky Way, through the incalculable spaces beyond the reach of our most powerful telescopes, back back. . . ."

Two days later, in a grave beside the tumbling mountain stream, his brother-in-law and I buried all that was mortal of Peter Ross. Over his resting-place we piled a great cairn of rocks so that the spring floods might not wash his body away nor coyotes worry the tomb of the dead. When I parted with the bereaved sister, she pressed me to accept the cedar box.

"Poor Peter!" she said. "Toward the last he ran a fever all the time and was delirious; but he wanted you to have the box, and so you must take it."

I saw that she attached no importance to his story.

"He never mentioned it before," she said; "he was out of his head."

And so I was inclined to believe until I examined the contents of the box. Then I changed my mind. If what he told us had been naught but the result of morbid brooding and delirium, then he must have been morbid and delirious for years preceding his death, because the written version of his story began simply, "It is nearly a year now since," and was a bare recital of facts, written plainly and in the manner of a man with no especial gift for expressing himself in words. Nor was that all. Besides the manuscript mentioned were revealed various letters which I perused, letters from Cabot to Ross, Ross to Cabot, covering a period of years and telling of their ideas and plans and of the theft of the crystals. The whole story, save for its denouement, could be pieced together from those letters.

Incredible as Peter Ross's tale had sounded in the telling, wild and incoherent though it had been, and colored with fever and delirium none the less it was true. And as if to rout whatever disbelief might be still lurking in my mind, I saw that which finally led me to place the whole matter before the Royal Academy of Science in Canada, and before various other scientific bodies, as I have recorded; and which in this latter day, so that mankind may be warned against the menace imprisoned in the crystals, has made me put everything down here: the crowning evidence of all. For in the bottom of the box was a round object; and when I picked it up, my fascinated eyes were held by a transparent bubble the size of an orange with a black spot at its core, dancing, dancing. . . .

# The Regent of the North

by Kenneth Morris

The northern winter is altogether ghostly and elemental; there is no friendliness to man to be found in it. There, the snow has its proper habitation; there, in the gaunt valleys of Lapland, in the terrible, lonely desolations, the Frost Giants abide. They are servants of the Regent of the North: smiths, that have the awful mountains for their anvils; and, with cold for flame tempering water into hardness, fashion spears and swords of piercing ice, or raise glittering ramparts about the Pole. All for the dreadful pleasure of doing it! They go about their work silently in the gray darkness; heaven knows what dreams may be haunting them—dreams that no mind could imagine, unless death had already frozen its brain. When the wind wolves come howling down from the Pole, innumerous, unflagging, and insatiable: when the snow drives down, a horde of ghosts wandering senseless, hurrying and hurrying through the night: the giants do their work. They make no sound: they fashion terror, and illimitable terror, and terror . . . Or—is it indeed only terror that they fashion? . . .

And then spring comes, and the sun rises at last on the world of the North. The snow melts in the valleys; white wisps of cloud float over skies blue as the gentian; over a thousand lakes all turquoise and forget-me-not: waters infinitely calm and clear, infinitely lovely. Then the snow on the mountain dreams dazzling whiteness by day, defiantly glittering against the sun; dreams tenderness, all faint rose and heliotrope and amber, in the evening; blue solemn mystery in the night. Quick with this last mysterious dreaming!—for the nights are hurrying away; they grow shorter always; they slink Poleward, immersed in ghostly preoccupations; by midsummer they have vanished altogether. Then the sun peers incessantly wizard-like over the horizon; the dumb rocks and the waters are invincibly awake, alert, and radiant with some magic instilled into them by the Regent of the North . . . It is in this spring and summer-time that you shall see bloom the flowers of Lapland: great pure blossoms in blue and purple and rose and citron, such as are not found elsewhere in the world. The valleys are a dreaming, silent wonder with the myriads there are of them--silent, for the Lapps have followed the reindeer, and the reindeer have followed the snows.

Into this region it was that Halfdan the Aged came, when he was tired of the new ways and faith that had come into the south. The viking days were over forever, one could see that. Meek, crozier-bearing men had invaded the realms of Odin and Balder; laying terrible axes of soft words, of chanted prayers and hymns, to the roots of—? All the ancient virtue of the race, said Halfdan the Aged; all the mighty and mystic dreams that had been surging through the Northlands these hundreds of years; sending the brave forth to wonderful deeds and wonderful visions about the seas and coasts of the world. And Inge the king at Upsala, forgetting all things noble and generous, had foresworn Odin and battle-breaking Thor; had foresworn Balder the Beautiful; had welcomed these chanting, canting foreigners, and decreed their faith for his people. So that now nothing remained but a fat, slothful life and the straw-death at the end of it: there should be no more Viking expeditions, no more Valhalla; no more Asgard and the Gods. "Faugh!" thought Halfdan Halfdansson, old hero of a hundred raids in the west and south; "this small-souled life for them that can abide it; it is worse than death for a *Man's Son*."

Not but that his own days of action were over: had been these ten years; had passed with the age of the Vikings. Also his seven sons were in Valhalla long since, and beyond being troubled; they had fallen like men in battle before there was any talk of this Christian heaven and hell; as for his wife, she, royal-hearted woman, had died when the youngest of them was born. So that it would have been easy for him to cut himself adrift from the world and voyage down through pleasant dreams towards death, after the fashion of clean old age. He had already put by, somewhat sadly, the prospect of future expeditions, and was reconciling himself to old age and its illumination, when King Inge went besotted over the foreign faith. From his house, Bravik on the hillside, through whose door the sea-winds blew in salt and excellent, he could watch the changes of the Swan-way, and nourish peace upon the music of the sea. Below at the foot of the hill, was the harbor from which his ships used to sail; drawn up on the beach, sheer hulks, still they lay there, the *Wild Swan* and the *Dragon*, accustomed to Mediterranean voyagings of old. For his own life, he found to action to regret in it; it had all been heroic doing, clean and honorable and vigorous; and the Gods had had their proper place in it, lighting it mysteriously from within.

But what room was there for dreaming, when the cry *The glory is departed*! rang so insistent? The new order liked him so little, that in place of peace and its accompanying wisdom, the years brought him unease increasingly. With his old skalds about him, to sing to him in the hall in the evenings; with his old and pagan servants, faithful all of them to the past as to himself, he watched the change coming on Sweden with disquietude and disgust; and for the first time in his life, experienced a kind of fear. But it was a pagan and great-hearted fear, and had nought to do with his own fate or future.

He knew the kind of tales these becroziered men from the south were telling, and that were becoming increasingly a substitute for the old valiant stories of the skalds. A man had come to Bravik once, and was welcomed there, who, when the feast was over, and the poets were relating their sagas, had risen in his turn with a story to tell—of a white-faced, agonizing God, who died a felon's death amongst ignoble and unwarlike people. Halfdan had listened to it with growing anger: where was the joy, where the mighty and beautiful forms, the splendid life, of the Divine Ones in this? At the end of it he had called to the stranger:

"Thy tale is a vile one, O foreign skald! Fraught with lies it is, and unwholesome to the hearing?

"Lies it is not, but the truth of truths, O chieftain, and except thou believest, thou shalt suffer the vengeance of God throughout eternity?"

"Go!" cried the Viking; and in the one word rang all the outraged ideals that had stood him in stead for sixty years. One does not defend his standpoint, but merely states it. He saw none of the virtues of Christianity; while its crude presentation shocked his religious feelings as profoundly as the blatant negations of atheism shock those of the pious of our own day. And his aspirations had a core of real spirituality in them. The Gods, for these high-souled Pagans, were the fountain of right, the assurance and stability of virtue. Thor, probably, stood for courage, spiritual as well as physical; Odin for a secret and internal wisdom; Balder for a peace that passeth understanding. Things did not end in Berserker fury: the paths of the spirit were open, or had been of old; beyond the hero stood the God; beyond strife, a golden peace founded on the perfection of life. Wars, adventure, and strenuous living were to fashion something divinely calm and grand in the lives of men; that once established, and no possibility of evil left lurking in any human soul, Balder's reign would come, something like the glow and afterglow of sunset, or a vast and perfect music enveloping the world—there should be a love as of comrades, as of dear brothers, between all men. But that Peace of Balder and of Odin was separated by all Berserkerism from the peace that is fear or greed. It was a high, perpetual exultation: a heaven into which the meek and weak could not slide passively, but the strong man armed (spiritually) should take it by storm.—And here was negation of the doctrine of the strong man armed; here was proclaiming godhood a thing not robust, joyless, unbeautiful . . . Old Halfdan went moody and depressed for a week after the priest's visit. The serene Balder-mood, into the fulness of which now, in the evening of his life, he had the right to grow naturally had been attacked, and could not be induced to return. A God crucified! . . . his soul cried out for Gods triumphant.

Inge might launch his decrees at Upsala; at Bravik, not the least intention existed of obeying them. With dogged and defiant faith Halfdan performed the rites of the religion of Odin, having dismissed from his house all who hankered after the newly proclaimed orthodoxy. With it all, he was ill at ease; as seeing that Sweden would not long hold a man faithful to her ancient ideals. Tales were brought in, how such and such a pagan chief had suffered the king's vengeance, or had been compelled to profess and call himself Christian. Heaven knew when his own turn might come; Inge would not overlook him forever. Well, there would be no giving in for him, no lip profession--a thing not in him to understand. He could swing a battle-ax yet, at the head of his retainers; he could die in his burning house like a Viking's son. That would be something: a blow struck for olden virtue: a beacon of remembrance for Sweden, in the dark days he feared and foresaw. His religious broodings deepened; he strove incessantly to come nearer to the Gods; for although he held it a coward's creed to think They exist to help men, and a brave man's, that men exist to help Them; yet at such a time, he deemed, They might find it worth Their while to turn from vaster wars for a moment, and concern themselves with the fate of Sweden. So he prayed, but his prayer was no petition nor whining after gains; it was a silencing of the mind, a stedfast driving it upward towards heights it had not attained before: eagle altitudes, and sunlight in the windless blue, where no passion comes, and the eternal voices may be heard.

The tide of trouble drew nearer. Presently a messenger came from Inge, with a priest. Halfdan was to install the latter in his house, and learn from him the faith of the Nazarene; was to forgo the Gods, or expect the king's armies. Halfdan sent them back; to say that Inge would be welcome at Bravik: as a friend, as of old; or still more as a foe. Then he dismissed the few women there were in his house, called in his men, and prepared for a siege: thoroughly if fiercely happy at last. But there was no bottom to the king's degeneration, it seemed. After three weeks this came from Upsala: "Halfdan Halfdansson, you are senile; you will die soon, and your false religion will all but die with you. The faith of Christ commands forbearance and forgiveness. You shall die in peace, and suffer hell-flame thereafter; *I will not trouble with you*." I will not trouble with you . . . For a week the old man raged inwardly. Inge should not thus triumphantly insult him; he would not die in peace, but lead his fifty against Upsala, and go out fighting . . . Then the Balder-mood came once more; and with it, light and direction vouchsafed him. He would go a-viking.

He summoned his fifty, and proclaimed his intention in the hall. Let who would, stay behind--in a Sweden that at least would let them be. For himself, he would take the Swan-way: he would have delight again of the crisping of blue waves against his prow: he would go under purple sails into the evening, into the mystery, into the aloneness where grandeur is, and it is profitable for souls to be, and there are none to tell heart-sickening tales . . . There, what should befall him, who could say? Perhaps there would be sweet battle on the Christian coasts; perhaps he would burn and break a church or two, and silence the jangling of the bells that called ignoble races to ignoble prayer. Perhaps there would be battling only with the storm: going out into that vast unstable region the Aesir loved, perhaps they would expend their manhood nobly in war with the shrieking wind, the sweet wild tempest of heaven. At such times the Gods come near, they come very near, they buffet and slay in their love, and out of a wild and viking death, the Valkyrie ride, the Valkyrie ride!...There were fifty men in the hall that heard him; there were fifty men that rose and shouted their acclamation; fifty that would take the Swan-way with their lord.

So there came to be noise of ax and hammer in the haven under Bravik: the *Wild Swan* and the *Dragon* being refurbished and made all taut for voyaging. Within a month they set sail. But not southward, and then through Skagerack and Cattegat, out into the waters of Britain and France, as Halfdan had intended. On the first day, a sudden storm overtook them, and singing they plunged into black seas, beneath blind and battling skies. Singing they combatted the wave of the north; they went on, plunging blindly, driven for three days whither they knew nark; then, with a certain triumph in their souls, they succumbed singing, to the gale. They saw the Valkyrie ride through heaven, they gave their bodies to the foam about the rocks and rose upon the howling winds, clean and joyous of soul at the last.

Halfdan had forgotten Christianity: all thought and memory of it deserted him utterly before the storm had been beating them an hour. In the end it was all pagan, all Viking, exultant lover and fighter of the Gods, that he leaped from his sinking ship in the night, fully armed, into the driving froth and blackness; struggled as long as might be with the overwhelming waters, as befitted his manhood; then lost consciousness, and was buffeted and tossed where the grand elements listed; and thrown at last, unconscious, on the shore.

Certainly he had seen the Valkyrie riding, had heard their warsong above the winds and waves: like the lightning of heaven they had ridden, beautiful and awful beyond any of his old dreaming; why then had they not taken him? This was no Valhalla into which he had come: this dark place smokily lamp-lit; this close air, heavy, it must be said, with stench. And were these the dwarfs, these little figures that moved and chattered unintelligibly in the gloom? . . . Slowly he took in the uncouth surroundings; raising himself, rather painfully, on his elbow from the bed of dry heather on which he was lying. There, on the tent-pole, hung his armor: his helmet with the raven wings; his shield, sword, and battle-ax; these were skins with which he was covered, and of which the walls of the tent were made. He was not dead then? No; it appeared that it was still mortal flesh that he was wearing. He had been thrown on some shore by the waves, and rescued by these quaint, squat people. Ah! he had been driven into the far north, and was among Lapps in the unknown north of the world.

He lay back, exhausted by his bodily and mental effort; and the sigh that broke from him brought the Lapp woman to his side, and the Lapp man after her. They brought him hot broth, and spoke to him, their unknown and liquid tongue, in which no sound unmusical intrudes, was full of gentle kindliness; their words were almost caressing, and full of encouragement and cheer. He had no strength to sit up; the Lapp woman squatted at his head and lifted him in her arms; and while he so leaned and rested the Lapp man fed him, sup by sup; the two of them crooning and chuckling their good will the while. In three days he was on his feet; and convinced that he could not outwear the kindly hospitality of his hosts.

The weeks of the northern spring went by; the flowers of Lapland were abloom in the valley, and old Halfdan wandered daily and brooded amidst the flowers. His mood now had become very inward. He hungered no more after action, nor dwelt in pictures of the past; rather an interiority of the present haunted him: a sweetness, as of dear and near deities, in the crag-reflecting waters, in the fleet cloud-fleeces, in the heather on the hills, and in the white and yellow poppies on the valley-floor. As the summer passed this mood grew deeper: from a prevalent serene peace, it became filled with divine voices almost audibly calling. As for the Lapps, they behaved to him at all times with such tenderness as might be given to a father growing helpless in old age, but loved beyond ordinary standards.

The first frosts were withering the heather; in the valley the flowers had died; the twilight of early winter, a wan iris withering, drooped mournful petals over the world. On the hills all was ghostly whiteness: the Lapps had come south with the winter, and there was a great encampment of them in the valley; it never occurred to Halfdan to wonder why the couple that had saved him had remained during the summer so far from the snows. One day he wandered down to the shore: the sea had already frozen, and the icy leagues of it shone tinted with rose and faint violet and beryl where light from the sun, far and low in the horizon, caught them. Wonderful and beautiful seemed to him the world of the North. There was no taint in the cold, electric air; no memory to make his soul ashamed for his fellow men. The wind blew keen over the ice, blowing back his hair and his beard; it was intense and joyful for him with that Divine life of the Gods that loves and opposes us. He walked out on the ice; something at his feet caught his attention, and he stooped to examine it; it was a spar, belike from the *Wild Swan* or the *Dragon*, the ships he had loved. Then came memory in a flood. All his life had gone from him; the faces familiar of old had vanished; down there, in the south, in the Gothland, all the glory had departed; and there was nothing left for him on earth, but the queer, evil-smelling life in the Lapp tent . . . Yes, there were still the Gods . . . A strange unrest came upon him; he must away and find the Aesir . . . He had no plan; only he must find the Bright Ones: must stand in their visible presence, who had been the secret illumination of the best of his life. In mingled longing and exultation he made his way back to the camp.

He found his Lapp friends standing before their tent, and their best reindeer harnessed to an *akja*[1]; they knew, it appeared, that he was to go; and mournfully and unbidden, had made preparation.

1 The Lapp sledge of wicker and skin, capable of holding one man sitting with legs stretched out, and guiding the reindeer with a single thong of rein.

They brought out his armor, and fondled his hands as they armed him; a crowd gathered about him, all crooning and chuckling their good will, and their sorrow to lose the old man in whose shining eyes, it seemed to them, was much unearthly wisdom. On all sides, evidently, there was full understanding of his purpose, and sad acquiescence; and this did not seem to him strange at all: the Gods were near and real enough to control and arrange all things. He sat down in the *akja*, and took the rein; the Lapps heaped skins about him for warmth; then, waving farewells, amidst an outburst of sorrowful crooning and chuckling, he started. Whither the reindeer might list; whither the mighty Undying Ones might direct.

On, and on, and on. Through ghostly valleys and through the snowstorm, right into the heart of the northern night, the reindeer, never uncertain of the way, drew him. The Balder-mood came to him in the weird darkness; in the cold desolation the bright Gods seemed nearer than ever. Through ghastly passes where the north wind, driving ice particles that stung, came shrieking, boisterous and dismal, down from the Pole to oppose him, on sped the reindeer while the mind of the old Viking was gathered into dreams. Waiting for him, somewhere beyond, were Those whose presence was a growing glory on the horizon of his soul.... The snow-ghosts, wan, innumerable, and silent, came hurrying by; on sped the reindeer, a beautiful beast, heeding never the snow-ghosts over frozen rivers and frozen mountains, through ghostly cold valleys and the snow. Under vast precipices that towered up, iron and mournful into the night; or along the brink of awful cliffs, with the snowstorm howling below . . . on and on. Who was to measure time on that weird journey? There were no changes of day and night; and Halfdan, wrapped in the warmth of his dreams, hardly would have heeded them if there had been. Now and again the reindeer halted to feed, scraping in the snow for his familiar moss-diet; then on again, and on. It was the beast, or some invisible presence, not the man, who chose the way.

A valley stretched out endlessly before; and afar, afar, a mountain caught on its whiteness some light from heaven, so that amid all the ghostly darkness it shone and shot up, a little dazzling beacon of purity on the rim of the world. The snow had ceased to fall, and no longer the north wind came shrieking to oppose; there was quiet in the valley broken only by the tinkling of the reindeer bells and the scrunch of the falling hoofs on the snow. The white mountain caught the eyes, and at last the mind of the long dreaming Viking; so that he began to note the tinkling of the bells, the sound of the hoofs falling, the desolation before and around. And at last another sound also: long howling out of the mountains on this side and that; long, dreary howling behind, like the cry of ghosts in a nightmare, or the lamentation of demons driven forever through darkness beyond the margin of space. For some time he listened, before waking to knowledge that it was actual sound he listened to; and then for some time longer before it came to him to know whence the sound was. It had drawn nearer by then, much nearer; and peering forth through the glint and gloom, he saw the shadows that were wolves streaming up after him through the valley, and coming down from the mountains; singly, in twos and threes, in multitudes. The reindeer snuffed, tossed its head, and speeded on prodigiously, yet with what gathered on the hillsides, it would be a marvel if he escaped. On came the shadows, until one could see the green fire-sparks of their eyes, behind, to the right and to the left, almost before; and on sped the reindeer, and the white mountain drew nearer.

Then Halfdan the Viking scented war: he remembered his youth and its prowess; he made ready his shield and battle-ax; and thanked the Gods fervently that after all he should go out fighting. The brave reindeer should have what chance it might to escape by its own untrammeled fleetness: so he drew his sword and cut the harness. The beast was away over the snow at twice its former speed; and

Halfdan in the *akja* shot forward thirty paces, fell out, and was on his feet in a moment to wait what should come.

A black, shag shadow, the foremost of them, hurled itself howling at his throat—eyes green fire and bared teeth gleaming; the ax swept down, clave its head in midair, and the howl went out in a rattling groan and sob. No question of failing strength now; old age was a memory—forgotten. The joy of battle came to him, and as the first wolf fell he broke into song:

In the bleak of the night and the ghost-held region,
By frozen valley and frozen lake,
A son of the Vikings, breaking his battle,
Doth lovely deeds for Asgard's sake.

Odin All-Father, for thee I slew him!
For thee I slew him, bolt-wielding Thor!
Joy to ye now, ye Aesir, Brothers!
That drive the demons forevermore!

While he sang, another wolf was upon him, and then another and another; and the war-ax that had made play under Mediterranean suns of old, God, how it turned and swept and drove and clave things in the northern night! While they came up one by one, or even in twos, the fight was all in his favor, so he slew as many as a dozen at his singing; then the end began to draw near. They were in a ring about him now; rather fearful of the whirling ax, but closing in. Old age began to tell upon his limbs; he fought on wearying; and the delight of war ebbed from him; his thigh had been snapped at and torn, and he had lost much blood with the wound. Then the ax fell, and he leaned on it for support for a moment, his head bent down over his breast. The war-mood had gone altogether; his mind sped out to the Gods. Of inward time there had been enough, since the ax fell, for the change of mood, for the coming of calm wonder and exaltation; of the time we measure in minutes, enough for the leaping of a wolf. He saw it, and lifted the ax; knowing that nothing could be done. At his left it leaped up; he saw the teeth snap a hand's-breadth from his face . . . An ax that he knew not, brighter than the lightning, swung; the jaws snapped; the head and the body apart fell to the ground . . . And there was a wolf leaping on his right, and no chance in the world of his slaying it; and a spear all-glorious suddenly hurtling out of the night, and taking the wolf through the throat, and pinning it dead to the ground. And here was a man, a Viking, gray-bearded, one-eyed, glorious, fighting upon his left; and here was a man, a Viking, young and surpassing beautiful of form and face and mien, doing battle at his right. And he himself was young again, and strong; and knew that against the three of them all the wolves in the world, and all the demons in hell, would have little chance. They fled yelping into the dark; and Halfdan turned to hail those that had fought for him.

And behold, the shining mountain that had seemed so far, shone now near at hand, and for a mountain, it was a palace, exceedingly well-built, lovely with towers and pinnacles and all the fair appurtenances of a king's house. No night nor winter was near it; amidst gardens of eternal sunlight it shone; its portals flung wide, and blithe all things for his entering. And he greeted Odin All-Father, as one might who had done nothing in his life to mar the pleasant friendliness of that greeting. And in like manner he greeted Balder the Beautiful. They linked their arms in his, and in cheerful conversation he passed in with them into the Valhalla.

# The Folk of the Mountain Door

by William Morris

Of old time, in the days of the kings, there was a king of folk, a mighty man in battle, a man deemed lucky by the wise, who ruled over a folk that begrudged not his kingship, whereas they knew of his valour and wisdom and saw how by his means they prevailed over other folks, so that their land was wealthy and at peace save about its uttermost borders. And this folk was called the Folk of the Mountain Door, or more shortly, of the Door.

Strong of body was this king, tall and goodly to look on, so that the hearts of women fluttered with desire when he passed them by. In the prime and flower of his age he wedded a wife, a seemly mate, a woman of the Earl-kin, tall and white-skinned, golden haired and grey-eyed; healthy, sweet-breathed, and soft-spoken, courteous of manners, wise of heart, kind to all folk, well-beloved of little children. In early spring-tide was the wedding, and a little after Yule she was brought to bed of a man-child of whom the midwives said they had never seen a fairer. He was sprinkled with water and was named Host-lord after the name of his kindred of old.

Great was the feast of his name-day, and much people came thereto, the barons of the land, and the lords of the neighbouring folk who would fain stand well with the king; and merchants and craftsmen and sages and bards; and the king took them with both hands and gave them gifts, and hearkened to their talk and their tales, as if he were their very earthly fellow; for as fierce as he was afield with the sword in his fist, even so meek and kind he was in the hall amongst his folk and the strangers that sought to him.

Now amongst the guests that ate and drank in the hall on the even of the Name-day, the king as he walked amidst the tables beheld an old man as tall as any champion of the king's host, but far taller had he been, but that he was bowed with age. He was so clad that he had on him a kirtle of lambswool undyed and snow-white, and a white cloak, lined with ermine and welted with gold; a golden fillet set with gems was on his head, and a gold-hilted sword by his side; and the king deemed as he looked on him that he had never seen any man more like to the Kings of the Ancient World than this man. By his side sat a woman old and very old, but great of stature, and noble of visage, clad, she also, in white wool raiment embroidered about with strange signs of worms and fire-drakes, and the sun and the moon and the host of heaven.

So the king stayed his feet by them, for already he had noted that at the table whereat they sat there had been this long time at whiles greater laughter and more joyous than anywhere else in the hall, and whiles the hush of folk that hearken to what delights the inmost of their hearts. So now he greeted those ancients and said to them: "Is it well with you, neighbours?" And the old carle hailed the king, and said, "There is little lack in this house today."

"What lack at all do ye find therein?" said the king. Then there came a word into the carle's mouth and he sang in a great voice:

Erst was the earth
Fulfilled of mirth:
Our swords were sheen
In the summer green;
And we rode and ran

Through winter wan,
And long and wide
Was the feast-hall's side.
And the sun that was sunken
Long under the wold
Hung ere we were drunken
High over the gold;
And as fowl in the bushes
Of summer-tide sing
So glad as the thrushes
Sang earl-folk and king.
Though the wild wind might splinter
The oak-tree of Thor,
The hand of mid-winter
But beat on the door.

"Yea," said the king, "and dost thou say that winter hath come into my hall on the Name-day of my first-born?"

"Not so," said the carle.

"What is amiss then?" said the king. Then the carle sang again:

Were many men
In the feast-hall then,
And the worst on bench
Ne'er thought to blench
When the storm arose
In the war-god's close;
And for Tyr's high-seat,
Were the best full meet:
And who but the singer
Was leader and lord,
I steel-god, I flinger

Of adder-watched hoard?
Aloft was I sitting
Amidst of the place
And watched men a-flitting
All under my face.
And hushed for mere wonder
Were great men and small
As my voice in rhyme-thunder
Went over the hall.

"Yea," said the king, "thou hast been a mighty lord in days gone past, I thought no less when first I set eyes on thee. And now I bid thee stand up and sit on the high-seat beside me, thou and thy mate. Is she not thy very speech-friend?"

Therewith a smile lit up the ancient man's face, and the woman turned to him and he sang:

Spring came of old
In the days of gold,
In the thousandth year
Of the thousands dear,
When we twain met
And the mead was wet
With the happy tears
Of the best of the years.
But no cloud hung over
The eyes of the sun
That looked down on the lover
Ere eve was begun.
Oft, oft came the greeting
Of spring and her bliss
To the mead of our meeting,

The field of our kiss.
Is spring growing older?
Is earth on the wane
As the bold and the bolder
That come not again?

"O king of a happy land," said [the ancient man], "I will take thy bidding, and sit beside thee this night that thy wisdom may wax and the days that are to come may be better for thee than the days that are."

So he spake and rose to his feet, and the ancient woman with him, and they went with the king up to the high-seat, and all men in the feast-hall rose up and stood to behold them, and they deemed them wonderful and their coming a great thing.

But now when they were set down on the right hand and the left hand of the king, he turned to the ancient man and said to him: "O Lord of the days gone past, and of the battles that have been, wilt thou now tell me of thy name, and the name of thy mate, that I may call a health for thee first of all great healths that shall be drunk tonight."

But the old man said and sang:

King, hast thou thought
How nipped and nought
Is last year's rose
Of the snow-filled close?
Or dost thou find
Last winter's wind
Will yet avail
For thy hall-glee's tale?
E'en such and no other
If spoken tonight

Were the name of the brother
Of war-gods of might.
Yea the word that hath shaken
The walls of the house
When the warriors half waken
To battle would rouse
Ye should drowse if ye heard it
Nor turn in the chair.
O long long since they feared it
Those foemen of fear!
Unhelpful, unmeaning
Its letters are left;
For the man overweening
Of manhood is reft.

This word the king hearkened, and found no word in his mouth to answer: but he sat pondering heavy things, and sorrowful with the thought of the lapse of years, and the waning of the blossom of his youth. And all the many guests of the great feast-hall sat hushed, and the hall-glee died out amongst them.

But the old man raised his head and smiled, and he stood on his feet, and took the cup in his hand and cried out aloud: "What is this my masters, are ye drowsy with meat and drink in this first hour of the feast? Or have tidings of woe without words been borne amongst you, that ye sit like men given over to wan hope, awaiting the coming of the doom that none may gainsay, and the foe that none may overcome? Nay then, nay; but if ye be speechless I will speak; and if ye be joyless I will rejoice and bid the good wine welcome home. But first will I call a health over the cup:

"Pour, white-armed ones,
As the Rhine flood runs!

And O thanes in hall
I bid you all
Rise up, and stand
With the horn in hand,
And hearken and hear
The old name and the dear.
To HOST-LORD the health is
Who guarded of old
The House where the wealth is
The Home of the gold.
And again the Tree bloometh
Though winter it be
And no heart of man gloometh
From mountain to sea.
Come thou Lord, the rightwise,
Come Host-lord once more
To thy Hall-fellows, fightwise
The Folk of the Door!"

Huge then was the sudden clamour in the hall, and the shouts of men and clatter of horns and clashing of weapons as all folk old and young, great and little, carle and quean, stood up on the Night of the Name-day. And once again there was nought but joy in the hall of the Folk of the Door.

But amidst the clamour the inner doors of the hall were thrown open, and there came in women clad most meetly in coloured raiment, and amidst them a tall woman in scarlet, bearing in her arms the babe new born clad in fine linen and wrapped in a golden cloth, and she bore him up thus toward the high-seat, while all men shouted even more if it were possible, and set down cup and horn from their lips, and took up sword and shield and raised the shield-roar in the hall.

But the [king] rose up with a joyful countenance, and got him from out of his chair, and stood thereby: and the women stayed at the foot of the dais all but the nurse, who bore up the child to the king, and gave it into his arms; and he looked fondly on the youngling for a short space, and then raised him aloft so that all men in the hall might see him, and so laid him on the board before them and took his great spear from the wall behind him and drew the point thereof across and across the boy's face so that it well nigh grazed his flesh: at the first and at the last did verily graze it as little as might be, but so that the blood started; and while the babe wailed and cried, as was to be looked for, the king cried aloud with a great voice:

"Here mark I thee to Odin even as were all thy kin marked from of old from the time that the Gods were first upon the earth."

Then he took the child up in his arms and laid him in his own chair, and cried out: "This is Host-lord the son of Host-lord King and Duke of the Folk of the Door, who sitteth in his father's chair and shall do when I am gone to Odin, unless any of the Folk gainsay it."

When he had spoken there came a man in at the door of the hall clad in all his war-gear with a great spear in his hand, and girt with a sword, and he strode clashing through the hall up to the high-seat and stood by the chair of the king and lifted up his helm a little and cried out:

"Where are now the gainsayers, or where is the champion of the gainsayers? Here stand I Host-rock of the Falcons of the Folk of the Door, ready to meet the gainsayers?"

And he let his helm fall down again so that his face was hidden. And a man one-eyed and huge rose up from the lower benches and cried out in a loud voice: "O champion, hast thou hitherto foregone thy meat and drink to sing so idle a song over the hall-glee? Come down amongst us, man, and put off thine armour and eat and drink and be merry; for [of] thine hunger and thirst am I full certain. Here be no gainsayers, but brethren all, the sons of one Mother and one Father, though they be grown somewhat old by now."

Then was there a clamour again, joyous with laughter and many good words. And some men say, that when this man had spoken, the carle and quean ancient of days who sat beside the king's chair, were all changed and seemed to men's eyes as if they were in the flower of their days, mighty, and lovely and of merry countenance: and it is told that no man knew that big-voiced speaker, nor whence he came, and that presently when men looked for him he was gone from the hall, and they knew not how.

Be this as it may, the two ancient ones each stooped down over the chair whereas lay the little one and kissed him; and the old man took his cup and wetted the lips of the babe with red wine, and the old woman took a necklace from her neck of amber and silver and gold and did it on the youngling's neck and spake; and her voice was very sweet though she were old; and many heard the speech of her:

"O Host-lord of this even, Live long and hale! Many a woman shall look on thee and few that see thee shall forbear to love thee."

Then the nurse took up the babe again and bore him out to the bower where lay his mother, and the folk were as glad as glad might be, and no man hath told of mirth greater and better than the hall-glee of that even. And the old carle sat yet beside the king and was blithe with him and of many words, and told him tales that he had never known before; and all these were of the valiant deeds and the lives of his fathers before him, and strange stories of the Folk of the Door and what they had done, and the griefs which they had borne and the joys which they had won from the earth and the heavens and the girdling waters of the world. And the king waxed exceeding glad as he heard it all, and thought he would try to bear it in mind as long as he lived; for it seemed to him that when he had parted from those two ancient ones, that night, he should never see them again.

So wore the time and the night was so late, that had it been summer-tide, it had been no night but early day. And the king looked up from the board and those two old folk, and beheld the hall, that there were few folk therein, save those that lay along by the walls of the aisles, so swiftly had the night gone and all folk were departed or asleep. Then was he like a man newly wakened from a dream, and he turned about to the two ancients almost looking to see their places empty. But they abode there yet beside him on the right hand and on the left; so he said: "Guests, I give you all thanks for your company and the good words and noble tales wherewith ye have beguiled this night of winter, and surely tomorrow shall I rise up wiser than I was yesterday. And now me seemeth ye are old and doubtless weary with the travel and the noisy mirth of the feast-hall, nor may I ask you to abide bedless any longer, though it be great joy to me to hearken to your speech. Come then to the bower aloft and I will show you the best of beds and the soft and kind place to abide the uprising of tomorrow's sun; and late will he arise, for this is now the very midwinter, and the darkest of all days in the year."

Then answered the old man: "I thank thee, O son of the Kindred; but so it is that we have further to wend than thou mightest deem; yea, back to the land whence we came many a week of years ago and before the building of houses in the land, between the mountain and the sea. Wherefore if thou wouldest do aught to honour us, come thou a little way on the road and see us off in the open country without the walls of thy Burg: then shall we depart in such wise that we shall be dear friends as long as we live, thou and thine, and I and mine."

"This is not so great an asking," said the king, "but that I would do more for thee; yet let it be as thou wilt."

And he arose from table and they with him, and they went down the hall amidst the sleeping folk and the benches that had erst been so noisy and merry, and out a-doors they went all three and into the street of the Burg. Open were the Burg-gates and none watched there, for there was none to break the Yule-tide peace; so the king went forth clad in his feasting-raiment, and those twain went, one on either side of him. The mid-winter frost was hard upon the earth, so that few waters were running, and all the face of the world was laid under snow: high was the moon and great and round in a cloudless sky, so that the stars looked but little.

The king set his face toward the mountains and strode with great strides over the white highway betwixt the hidden fruitfulness of the acres, and he was as one wending on an errand which he may not forego; but at last he said: "Whither wend we and how far?" Then spake the old man: "Whither should we wend save to the Mountain Door, and the entrance to the land whence the folk came forth, when great were its warriors and little was the tale of them."

Then the king spake no more, but it seemed to him as if his feet sped on faster than their wont was, and as if those twain bore him up so that his feet were but light on the face of the earth.

Thuswise they passed the plain and the white-clad ridges at the mountain feet in no long while, and were come before the yawning gap and strait way into the heart of the mountains, and there was no other way thereinto save this; for otherwhere, the cliffs rose like a wall from the plain-country. Grim was that pass, and high were the sides of it beneath the snow, which lay heaped up high, so now there were smooth white slopes on either side of the narrow road of the pass; while the wind had whistled the said road in most places well nigh clear of snow, which even now went whirling and drifting about beneath the broad moon. For the wind yet blew though the night was old, and the sound of it in the clefts of the rocks and the windings of the pass was like the rolling of the summer thunder.

Up the pass they went till it widened, and there was a wide space before them, the going up whereto was as by stairs, and also the going up from it to the higher pass; and all around it the rocks were high and sheer, so that there was no way over them save for the fowl flying; and were it not winter there had been a trickling stream running round about the eastern side of the cliff wall which lost itself in the hollow places of the rocks at the lower end of that round hall of the mountain, unroofed and unpillared. Amid most the place the snow was piled up high; for there in summer was a grassy mound amidst of a little round meadow of sweet grass, treeless, bestrewn here and there with blocks that had been borne down thitherward by the waters from the upper mountain; and for ages beyond what the memory of men might tell of this had been the Holy place and Motestead of the Folk of the Door.

Now all three went up on to the snow-covered mound, and those two turned about and faced the king and he saw their faces clearly, so bright as the moon was, and now it was so that they were no more wrinkled and hollow-cheeked and sunken-eyed, though scarce might a man say that they looked young, but exceeding fair they were, and they looked on him with eyes of love, and the carle said: "Lord of the Folk of the Door, father of the son new born whom the Folk this night have taken for their father, and the image of those that have been, we have brought thee to the Holy Place that we might say a word to thee and give thee a warning of the days to come, so that if it may be thou mightest eschew the evil and ensue the good. For thou art our dear son, and thy son is yet dearer to us, since his days shall be longer if weird will so have it. Hearken to this by the token that under the grass, beneath this snow, lieth the first of the Folk of the Door of those that come on the earth and go thence; and this was my very son begotten on this woman that here standeth. For wot thou that I am Host-lord of the Ancient Days, and from me is all the blood of you come; and dear is the blood of my sons and my name even as that which I have seen spilt on field and in fold, on grass and in grange, without the walls of the watches and about the lone wells of the desert places. Hearken then, Host-lord the Father of Host-lord, for we have looked into the life of thy son; and this we say is the weird of him; childless shall he be unless he wed as his will is; for of all his kindred none is wilfuller than he. Who then shall he wed, and where is the House that is lawful to him that thou hast not heard of? For as to wedding with his will in the House whereof thou wottest, and the Line of the Sea-dwellers, look not for it. Where then is the House of his wedding, lest the Folk of the Door lose their Chieftain and become the servants of those that are worser than they? I may not tell thee; and if I did, it would help thee nought. But this I will tell thee, when thy fair son is of fifteen winters, until the time that he is twenty winters and two, evil waylayeth on him: evil of the sword, evil of the cord, evil of the shaft, evil of the draught, evil of the cave, evil of the wave. O Son and father of my son, heed my word and let him be so watched that while as none hath been watched and warded of all thy kindred who have gone before, lest when his time come and he depart from this land he wander about the further side of the bridge that goeth to the Hall of the Gods, for very fear of shaming amongst the bold warriors and begetters of kindred and fathers of the sons that I love, that shall one day sit and play at the golden tables in the Plains of Ida."

So he spake, but the king spake: "O Host-lord of the Ancients I had a deeming of what thou wert, and that thou hadst a word for me. Wilt thou now tell me one thing more? In what wise shall I ward our son from the evil till his soul is strengthened, and the Wise-wights and the Ancients are become his friends, and the life of the warrior is in his hands and the days of a chieftain of our folk?"

Then the carle smiled on him and sang:

Wide is the land
Where the houses stand,
There bale and bane
Ye scarce shall chain;
There the sword is ground
And wounds abound;
And women fair
Weave the love-nets there.

Merry hearts in the Mountain
Dales shepherd-men keep,
And about the Fair Fountain
Need more than their sheep.
Of the Dale of the Tower
Where springeth the well
In the sun-slaying hour
They talk and they tell;

And often they wonder
Whence cometh the name
And what tale lies thereunder
For honour or shame.
For beside the fount welling
No castle now is;
Yet seldom foretelling
Of weird wends amiss.

Quoth the king, "I have heard tell of the Fair Fountain and the Dale of the Tower; though I have never set eyes thereon, and I deem it will be hard to find. But dost thou mean that our son who is born the Father of the Folk shall dwell there during that while of peril?"

Again sang the carle:

Good men and true,
They deal and do
In the grassy dales
Of that land of the tales;
Where dale and down
Yet wears the crown
Of the flower and fruit
From our kinship's root.
There little man sweateth
In trouble and toil,
And in joy he forgetteth
The feud and the foil.
The weapon he wendeth
Achasing the deer,
And in peace the moon endeth
That endeth the year.
Yet there dwell our brothers,
And should they but know
They thy stem of all others
Were planted to grow
Beside the Fair Fountain,
How fain were those men
Of the God of the Mountain
So come back again.

Then the king said: "Shall I fulfill the weird and build a Tower in the Dale for our Son? And deemest thou he shall dwell there happily till the time of peril is overpast?"

But the carle cried out, "Look, look! Who is the shining one who cometh up the pass?"

And the king turned hastily and drew his sword, but beheld neither man nor mare in the mountain, and when he turned back again to